Praise for Steven Millhauser's

We Others

"One of the most inventive writers working today." —*Time Out Chicago*

"These tales teem with wild and original ideas. . . . Vivid."
—*Washington City Paper*

"Millhauser's stories lure us into dark places with promises of magic and wonder . . . some of the best contemporary gothic fiction you're likely to come across." —*Richmond Times-Dispatch*

"Fantastic and enchanting. . . . Millhauser is a master. . . . These stories will seize your attention—and your imagination—with the force of a vise grip." —*The Globe and Mail* (Toronto)

"Mesmerizing. . . . Magical. . . . Millhauser has an almost unrivaled genius." —*The Nation*

"Outstanding . . . invites the reader to enter into the strangeness of a mysterious and fascinating place." —*The Providence Journal*

"[*We Others*] is all the things a person wants a Steven Millhauser book to be: lapidary, disturbing, mandarin, brilliant, perverse, and funny. . . . Full of gorgeous writing." —*Slate*

"Executed with pinpoint accuracy. . . . [Millhauser's] fierce imagination comes with a dark temperament instead of positive humor."
—*The A.V. Club*

STEVEN MILLHAUSER

We Others

Steven Millhauser is the author of twelve works of fiction, including *Martin Dressler,* which was awarded the Pulitzer Prize in 1997, and *Dangerous Laughter*, a *New York Times Book Review* Best Book of the Year. His work has been translated into sixteen languages, and his story "Eisenheim the Illusionist" was the basis of the 2006 film *The Illusionist*. He teaches at Skidmore College and lives in Saratoga Springs, New York.

ALSO BY STEVEN MILLHAUSER

DANGEROUS LAUGHTER

THE KING IN THE TREE

ENCHANTED NIGHT

THE KNIFE THROWER

MARTIN DRESSLER

LITTLE KINGDOMS

THE BARNUM MUSEUM

FROM THE REALM OF MORPHEUS

IN THE PENNY ARCADE

PORTRAIT OF A ROMANTIC

EDWIN MULLHOUSE

WE OTHERS

NEW AND SELECTED STORIES

STEVEN MILLHAUSER

Vintage Contemporaries
VINTAGE BOOKS
A DIVISION OF RANDOM HOUSE, INC.
NEW YORK

FIRST VINTAGE CONTEMPORARIES EDITION, SEPTEMBER 2012

"Tales of Darkness and the Unknowns, Vol. XIV: The White Glove" originally appeared in *Tin House*; "Getting Closer" and "The Invasion from Outer Space" originally appeared in *The New Yorker*; and "The Next Thing" originally appeared in *Harper's*.

Selected stories in this work were previously published in the following collections: "A Protest Against the Sun" (first published in *The New Yorker*), "August Eschenburg" (first published in *Antaeus*), and "Snowman" (first published in *Grand Street*) in *In the Penny Arcade*, copyright © 1981, 1982, 1983, 1984, 1985 by Steven Millhauser (New York: Alfred A. Knopf, 1986).

"The Barnum Museum" (first published in *Grand Street*), "The Eighth Voyage of Sinbad" (first published in Grand Street), and "Eisenheim the Illusionist" (first published in *Esquire* as "The Illusionist") in *The Barnum Museum*, copyright © 1990 by Steven Millhauser (New York: Poseidon Press, 1990).

"The Knife Thrower" (first published in *Harper's*), "A Visit" (first published in *The New Yorker*), "Flying Carpets" (first published in *The Paris Review*), and "Clair de Lune" in *The Knife Thrower*, copyright © 1998 by Steven Millhauser (New York: Crown Publishers, 1998).

"Cat 'n' Mouse" (first published in *The New Yorker*), "The Disappearance of Elaine Coleman" (first published in *The New Yorker*),"History of Disturbance" (first published in *The New Yorker*), and "The Wizard of West Orange" (first published in *Harper's*) in *Dangerous Laughter* copyright © 2008 by Steven Millhauser (New York: Alfred A. Knopf, 2008).

The Library of Congress has cataloged the Knopf edition as follows:
Millhauser, Steven
p. cm.
We others : new and selected stories / Steven Millhauser.—1st ed.
New York : Alfred A. Knopf, 2011.
PS3563.I422 W42 2011
2011000078
813/.54

Vintage ISBN: 978-0-307-74342-8

www.vintagebooks.com

TO KATE

CONTENTS

Dangerous Laughter

Author's Note

The stories in this collection were written over a period of thirty years. At first I tried to choose stories that seemed to me representative, but I soon realized that the ones omitted from the collection might represent me just as well. My final method had nothing to do with being cautious or dutiful. I chose stories that seized my attention as if they'd been written by someone whose work I had never seen before. What makes a story bad, or good, or better than good, can be explained and understood up to a point, but only up to a point. What's seductive is mysterious and can never be known. I prefer to leave it at that.

NEW STORIES

The Slap

WALTER LASHER. One September evening when Walter Lasher returned from the city after a hard day's work and was walking to his car in the station parking lot, a man stepped out from between two cars, walked up to him, and slapped him hard in the face. Lasher was so startled that he did not move. The man turned and walked briskly away. Lasher was a big man, six one, with broad shoulders and a powerful neck. No one had dared to hit him since the sixth grade. He remembered it still: Jimmy Kubec had pushed him in the chest, and Lasher had swung so hard that he broke Kubec's nose. Lasher looked around. The man was gone, a few commuters were strolling to their cars. For a moment he had the sensation that he'd dreamed the whole thing: the sudden appearance of the stranger, the slap, the vanishing. His cheek stung: the man had slapped him hard. Lasher entered his car and started home. As he passed under the railroad trestle, crossed Main, and drove along streets lined with maples and sycamores, he kept summoning the little scene in the station parking lot. The man was about five ten, well built, tan trench coat, no hat. It was difficult to remember his face, though he'd made no attempt to hide it and in fact had looked directly at Lasher. What stood out was something about the eyes: a hard, determined look; not rage, exactly—more like a cold sureness. The man had hit him once, hard. Then he had walked away. Lasher pulled over to the side of the road and checked his face in the rearview mirror. He wasn't certain, but the cheek looked a little red. He pulled back onto the street. The man must have mistaken him for someone else. A crazy guy, some loony off his meds, they should keep them locked up. But he hadn't looked crazy. Maybe a client, in over his head, unhappy with the performance of his investment portfolio in a tanking market. Or maybe

Lasher had offended someone without knowing it, the man had followed him up from the city, and all because of a sharp word, an impatient look, a biting phrase, he had no time for fools, a bumped arm in the street. The man had looked directly at him. Lasher would talk it out with his wife. They'd lived here for twenty-six years and nothing like this had ever happened to him. It was why you stayed out of the city, took the long commute. A few blocks from the beach he turned onto his street, where the lights were already on. They must have come on all over town while he was driving from the station. How could he have missed it? The man had taken him by surprise. He hadn't had time to react. He didn't like the man's eyes, didn't like the thought of himself standing there doing nothing. It was probably too late to call the police—the man would already be far away. Anna would know what to do. Lasher pulled into the drive and sat motionless in the darkening car. The man had looked hard at him: there was no mistake. He should have smashed him in the mouth. Jimmy Kubec had worn a bandage on his face for two weeks. Lasher walked across the flagstones and up the steps of the front porch. In the hall he could smell roast beef and basil. He'd save his misadventure for after dinner. The man had come right up to him and slapped him: hard. As Lasher hung up his hat he understood that he would not speak of it to Anna, who was coming toward him. "Katie called—she's coming on Saturday. I said it was fine. I mean, what else could I do? Oh, and Jenkovitch left a message. He says he never can get hold of you. He wants you to call him back. Here, give me that. How was your day?"

OUR TOWN. Our town is bordered on the south by a sandy public beach that faces the waters of Long Island Sound and on the north by a stretch of pine and oak woods. To the east lies an industrial city, where streets of crumbling brick factories with smashed windows give way to neighborhoods of new ten-story apartment complexes rising above renovated two-family houses with porches on both floors. To the west lies a wealthy town of five-bedroom homes set back on rural lanes, with a private beach, a horse-riding academy with indoor and outdoor practice rings, and a harbor yacht club where powerboats and racing sailboats are moored on floating docks. We like to think of ourselves as in the middle: well off, as things go, with pockets of wealth at the shore and on Sascatuck Hill, but with plenty of modest neighborhoods where people work hard and struggle to make ends meet. In this way of thinking there's a certain amount of self-deception, of which we're perfectly aware—it pleases us to think of ourselves as in the middle, even though, as statistics show, we're well above the national average in per capita income. Although we're on the commuter line to Manhattan, many of us work right here in town or in small cities not more than half an hour away. For the most part our lawns are neat, our streets well paved, our trees trimmed once a year by men in orange hats who stand in baskets at the ends of high booms. Our school system is one of the best in the county—we believe in education and pay our teachers well. Our Main Street is lively, with cafés and restaurants and a big department store, despite the new mall out by Route 7. Because we're on the commuter line, we don't feel shut away from the center of things, as if we were stuck up in Vermont or Maine, though at the same time we're happy to be out of the city and take pride in our small-town atmosphere of tree-shaded streets, yard sales, and the annual fire department dinner. But make no mistake, there's nothing quaint about us, what with our new semiconductor headquarters and our high-end boutiques, unless it's our seventeenth-century town green, with a restored eighteenth-century inn where George Washington is supposed to have spent the night. Most of us know we're lucky to live in a town like this, where crime is low and the salt water is never more than a short drive away. We also understand that to someone from another place, to someone who is disappointed or unhappy, someone for whom life has not worked out in the way it might have, our town may seem to have a certain self-satisfaction, even a smugness. We understand that, for such a person, there may be much to dislike, in a town like ours.

AT NIGHT. In the middle of the night Walter Lasher woke beside his wife and immediately recalled the episode on the playground that had taken place forty-two years ago. He saw Jimmy Kubec with startling vividness: the thick black combed-back oily hair, the loose jaunty walk, the mocking mouth, the large long-lashed eyes. Kubec had long thin biceps, with a vein running down along each upper arm. He wore black jeans and a tight white T-shirt with the sleeves rolled up to his shoulders. He walked toward Walter, looking at him with a little taunting smile, and as he approached he held up the palm of one hand and made a pushing gesture at the air. He did not touch Walter, who nevertheless felt the mockery and the challenge. Walter had grown six inches over the summer. His shoulders were filling out, and he felt an energy in his arms that was almost like anger. The mocking little gesture cut into him like glass. He walked up to Jimmy Kubec and smashed him in the face. He could see the surprise and pain in Kubec's dark eyes, the blood streaming from the broken nose, the look that seemed to say: Why did you do that to me? Kubec had no friends. He stayed out of Walter's way after that, standing alone by a tree in a corner of the schoolyard. Lasher lay in bed and thought: Could it have been him, after all these years? The idea was absurd. The man in the trench coat had sandy hair, sharp features, grayish or bluish eyes. It must have been someone else, someone who had it in for him. He saw it again: Jimmy Kubec coming toward him, the veins in his arms, the little pushing gesture in the air. Kubec hadn't touched him. All that was in another time, another life. Anna lay with her back to him, her hair rippling over the pillow. On the street a car passed, sending a thin bar of light across one wall and up along the ceiling.

ROBERT SUTLIFF. Some sixteen hours later, Robert Sutliff arrived at the station on the 7:38. It was an hour after his usual time. The lights were on in the lot, though the sky was still gray with the last light. He had worked late—tomorrow's design presentation was a big one. He still needed a few hours after dinner to do a little fine-tuning, a little last-minute cleanup on the three logos he was planning to show them, each with six presentation pages, with and without type. That way he'd give them the illusion that they were actively involved in the decision process, that they were making a contribution to the final product, while he slowly steered them in the direction of the third mark, the one they wouldn't be able to resist: the yellow-gold ring surrounding a solid dark coffee-colored circle, as if you were looking at a cup of coffee from above, and in the center a design of classic simplicity, in five bold yellow lines: a horizon line, a half circle representing the rising sun, and three sun rays. Coffee and morning, coffee and the energy of the new day, the energy of a new beginning, all in a visually striking, distinctive, versatile design. It worked perfectly on a two-inch business card, and it would work just as well on a ten-foot billboard or the side of an eighteen-wheeler. He hurried down the platform stairs, the stone shining dully under the orange lights. He would talk up the first two designs, the tame one and the way-out one, then hit them with the winner. His car was parked toward the back of the lot, not far from a light pole. As he reached into his pocket for his key, he heard someone walking up to him. Sutliff turned. The man raised his arm and swung at Sutliff's face. Sutliff heard the sharp sound of the slap, like a gunshot. "Hey!" he shouted, but the man was striding away. His cheek burned. The man had struck him hard, but it wasn't a punch, he hadn't made a fist. Sutliff angrily began to follow him, shouted again, and stopped. That was not how he did things. He knew exactly how he did things. Sutliff looked around, rubbed his cheek, and got into his car. He drove quickly out of the lot, turned onto Main, made a left onto South Redding, and stopped at the police station. A man in a trench coat, no hat. Five ten, five eleven. Short hair, brown, darkish, hard to tell. Clean shaven, mid-thirties. A stranger. They would send a car out right away. Sutliff thanked the officer and continued on his way home. What angered him about the whole thing was that people liked him; people took to him. It was part of his success. It had been that way as far back as kindergarten. It had all come together in high school, where he'd set a new record in the hundred-meter dash, acted the part of Tom in *The Glass Menagerie*—Blow out your candles, Laura!—and nailed Sandra Harding in her living room in front of the fireplace after the spring dance. UPenn, Harvard Business. Now he was someone to watch, someone on the way up, though always with a friendly greeting, a kind word for everyone. The man had looked at him angrily. Sutliff tried to think who it could be. He had a good memory for faces; it was no one he knew. Sutliff loved his wife, his daughter, his work; there had been the one brief fling in the months before Amy's birth, but that was two years ago, no husband in the picture, no brother, she'd been good about it, disappointed but not bitter. He had nothing to reproach himself with. Who would do this? His cheek felt hot. The man had swung hard but hadn't made a fist, hadn't wanted anything from him. A crazy mistake. The police would take care of it.

AT BREAKFAST. At breakfast Walter Lasher turned over a page of the *Daily Observer* and saw a small item: Robert Sutliff, of 233 Greenfield Terrace, had been attacked by a man in the parking lot of the railroad station at 7:41 p.m. The unknown assailant had slapped his face. Police were looking for a man about five ten or eleven, with short dark hair, wearing a tan trench coat. Lasher glanced up at his wife, who was pouring herself a second cup of coffee. He was aware of a sharp, exhilarating sense of relief, almost of gratitude. The man had not singled him out from all the others, had not come after only him. Lasher knew Sutliff, though not well. Sutliff was younger, moved with a different crowd, had come up from the city a few years ago. They nodded on the morning platform, said hello in the hardware store. Lasher's sense of relief was suddenly charged with uneasiness. The man's hair had been light-colored, not dark. All the more reason for coming forward now, telling what he knew. Sutliff hadn't even mentioned the color of the eyes. Details were streaming back: the pale angry eyes, the stern mouth, the buttons on the shoulder straps, the looped belt. It would be difficult to go to the police, since he'd be forced to explain his earlier silence. Better to think it over, give it another day or so. The man had to be stopped. People had enough to worry about without this kind of crap. Lasher, reaching for his coffee, missed the handle and rattled the cup on the saucer. Anna looked up. "Nothing," he said. "I didn't say anything," she said.

CHARLES KRAUS. Charlie Kraus, marketing manager of Sportswear West, returned from the city at dusk and walked down the steps into the parking lot. He'd read the paper at breakfast that morning and had discussed the incident on the way to the city with Chip Hynes and Bob Zussman, who had said: "It's always a dame." Kraus wasn't so sure. Just like Zussman to use a word like that: dame. Kraus glanced at the rows of cars stretching from the station building to the chain-link fence at the far end. The sun had set, but the sky was still pale gray—the lights hadn't yet come on. Two feet away, the taillights of an SUV suddenly glowed red. Kraus stopped and let the car back out. He wondered, not for the first time, how many people got hit by cars in places like this each year. Parking lots were an example of efficient but flawed design: you found a way to bring as many cars as possible into a confined space, but anyone walking to or from a car was in constant danger of being struck by a vehicle backing out. All solutions were impractical. One night it came to him: a system of overhead walkways with a separate stairway leading down to each car. He could patent it and make a fortune. In the morning he'd laughed at himself. Kraus looked around. Not much place to hide: just row after row of cars. Those ailanthus trees and sumac bushes along the fence, a big trash bin over by the slope. To take you by surprise, a man would have to crouch down between two cars, where it would be a cinch to spot him—especially at this hour, with two dozen people walking to different locations, cutting across, looking around. At night it was a different story. The fluted-steel light poles were too far apart, the high-pressure sodium lights didn't give off as much illumination as the halide lights the Public Works folks had wanted, but hey, you get what you pay for. It wouldn't be all that hard to keep out of sight. The thought angered him. He'd moved to this town ten years ago because it was safe. Good schools for his kids, plenty of parks, the beach: all of it safe. That's why you moved to the suburbs. That's why you gave up delis with jars of fat pickles on the counter. If he wanted to spend his time worrying about what could happen in a parking lot after sunset he might as well go back to Brooklyn. The whole thing would probably blow over by the time he flew out to Chicago next week. The hotel had one of the best gyms in the country, with big windows high up over the lake. Just ahead, a man stepped around the back of a van. Kraus glanced over. The man strode up to him, raised his hand, and slapped him hard in the face. He looked at Kraus for a moment, then turned briskly away. The look was hostile and cold. Kraus waited for the man to disappear—he must have ducked behind a row of cars—then took out his cell phone and called the police.

COFFEE SHOPS AND RESTAURANTS. We read about it the next morning on the front page of the *Daily Observer.* We had taken note of the first incident, the one reported by Robert Sutliff, which had seemed to us a misunderstanding of some sort, a bizarre error that would soon be explained. A second attack was far more serious. It seemed to be part of a deliberate plan, though exactly what was at stake remained unclear. All over town, people were talking about it: in coffee shops and restaurants, at gas station pumps, in the post office and the CVS, in high school hallways, on slatted benches beside potted trees in the mall. We wondered who he could possibly be, this stranger who had appeared among us with his angry eyes. Some argued that the man was mentally unstable and was working out some private drama. Others insisted that he knew his victims and had lain in wait for them. Still others, a small group, claimed that the attacks were some form of social statement: it was no accident, they said, that the assailant had chosen the station parking lot during early-evening rush hour, when businessmen carrying laptops were returning from the city to their leafy suburban town. Everyone agreed that the incidents were disturbing and that the station parking lot was in need of twenty-four-hour police surveillance.

TWO DESCRIPTIONS. From the two descriptions, we learned that the assailant was a male Caucasian about five nine or ten or eleven, solid in build, clean-shaven. His hair was short, light brown or dark brown, neatly combed. He had brown or gray or blue eyes, a straight well-shaped nose, and a slightly protruding chin. He might have been thirty or thirty-five years old. Both victims agreed that the man had looked angry. He wore a beige or tan double-breasted trench coat. According to Kraus, the belt had been tied, not buckled. Sutliff, who wasn't sure about the belt, remembered the coat fairly well. It was the sort of trench coat that anyone on that train between the ages of twenty-five and sixty might have been wearing—an expensive coat, well cut, stylish in a conservative way.

RICHARD EMERICK. At 6:45 the next morning Richard Emerick parked in his space at the station, reached over to the door handle, and stopped. He glanced at his watch: too late to go back. He had made a mistake, but at least he'd caught it in time. Foolishly, without thought, he had thrown on his trench coat; the forecast was for rain in the morning, heavy at times, tapering off toward noon. But ever since the Serial Slapper had appeared, a trench coat was bound to attract suspicious attention. True, Emerick's hair was blond, and it wasn't particularly short, though who knew what "short" meant, and besides, people were careless. He slipped off his trench coat, draped it over his arm, and stepped out of the car. That was worse; the coat, on this chilly morning, drew attention to itself, as if he were trying to conceal it in some way, as in fact he was trying to do. He glanced around, folded the coat into a squarish lump, and placed it quickly under his arm. Worse still: he was ruining the coat, and it was no less conspicuous. The sky was darker than before; rain was definitely on its way. Emerick opened the door, popped the trunk, and walked to the back of the car. He shook out his trench coat, folded it twice, and laid it in the trunk on top of two eco-friendly reusable grocery bags decorated with fields of yellow wildflowers. He closed the trunk, pressed the lock button on his key, and set off toward the station as the first drops began to fall.

RAYMOND SORENSEN. That afternoon, a little before one o'clock, Ray Sorensen, a cable repairman at the end of his lunch break, walked out of the Birchwood Avenue branch of the First Puritan Savings Bank, where he had deposited his paycheck and withdrawn eighty dollars from the ATM. The money would get him through the next couple of days, with a lottery ticket thrown in. The Sunday landscaping gig ought to see him through the rest of the week, though he was a month late on his car payment and he might have to cash out his savings account to pay down his credit-card debt. The sky was overcast, a fifty-fifty chance of rain; he had to drive out of town and check a power line at a property up by the lake. As he walked toward his truck, a man stepped from the row of high bushes that grew on the concrete divider, walked between two parked cars, and turned toward the bank. As he drew near Sorensen, he swerved toward him and began to raise an arm. Only then did Sorensen remember the article he had glanced at in the paper that morning. He'd been amused; it had nothing to do with him. The slap was so sudden and so strong that for a moment he didn't understand what had happened. By the time he shouted "What the fuck!" the man in the trench coat was already walking away. Sorensen started running after him. The man stepped onto the divider and disappeared behind a high bush. Later Sorensen told the police that the stranger just seemed to vanish into thin air—though maybe he'd had time to cross to the other side of the lot and climb the fence separating the bank from the house behind it. Sorensen searched behind every bush on the divider. He walked up and down the lot, circled the bank, then returned to his truck and drove out to his job. Only when he arrived home at 5:45 did he read the paper again. He thought it over and phoned the police.

AT THE RAILROAD STATION. At the moment when Raymond Sorensen noticed a man stepping from behind the bushes on the divider outside the First Puritan Savings Bank, a patrol car was cruising slowly through the lanes of the railroad station parking lot. A few hours later a second policeman appeared on the station platform, where he walked up and down and looked out over the rows of parked cars stretching away. At 5:00, on the street overpass that looked down at the tracks, the gantries, the brick station, the taxis by the curb, and the parking lot that ran along the length of the tracks for several blocks, a third policeman stood leaning his elbows on the cast-iron railing as he surveyed the movement below. The sky was clearing. Men and women walked swiftly to their cars, looking about carefully; many of them stayed in groups, which became smaller as they came to each vehicle in turn. At 6:00 the security lights came on, an hour earlier than usual. Under the pale sky and glowing lights, the roofs and hoods of cars looked glazed, like candy. The last train arrived at 2:57 a.m. A half-moon hung in the dark blue sky, like another security light.

NEXT MORNING. We read about the attack on Raymond Sorensen the next morning in the *Daily Observer.* We were alarmed that it had taken place in broad daylight, far from the railroad station. Even more disturbing was the violation of a second pattern: this time the victim wasn't a businessman returning from his high-paying job in the city but a uniformed worker on his lunch break in town. We realized that we'd taken a kind of comfort in thinking of the attacks as confined to the station parking lot after sunset, when commuters in expensive suits were coming home for dinner; suddenly our anger, our anxiety, which had been confined to narrow bounds, burst free with a rush of energy. Where would the stranger strike next? The attack outside the bank seemed to strengthen the argument of those who believed the assaults were random. Others claimed that the opposite was clearly the case: the attacker liked to stage his event in parking lots. Those who had insisted that the assailant was seeking out suit-and-tie commuters as a form of social protest were forced to abandon or modify their argument, while those who had suggested that the attacker knew his victims saw no reason to abandon their explanation. New opinions had it that the stranger's real interest lay in disrupting order, in spreading fear, in taunting the police.

THE COAT. The coat raised a number of questions that none of us could answer. If, during the attack on Robert Sutliff and Charles Kraus, the man had been wearing steel-toe work boots, jeans, and an open-necked plaid flannel shirt over a T-shirt, then we might have subscribed to the theory of protest: the attacker, a blue-collar worker, bore a grudge against the white-collar element of our town. Since, however, the man was wearing a fashionable coat, with the belt looped in front, and was therefore dressed like a successful businessman who might easily have lived in our town and ridden our train, the theory of social or class protest was unacceptable—unless, of course, the stranger had deliberately adopted a costume that wouldn't draw attention to itself in the station parking lot. The third attack—we hadn't yet learned about Walter Lasher—complicated our already complicated sense of things. A man dressed like a businessman had attacked a cable repairman in work clothes. What could it mean? Perhaps, we thought, the stranger had lost his job; simmering with rage, he was taking out his frustration on anyone still fortunate enough to have work. It was also possible that the coat had nothing at all to do with the man and what he was after, and that we were guilty of reading into a piece of clothing a significance that was meaningless.

IN THE HARDWARE STORE. On Saturday afternoon, six hours after the *Daily Observer* reported the attack on Raymond Sorensen, Walter Lasher stood in the hardware store, examining a row of light-switch plates. As he began weighing the virtues of old-fashioned brass switch plates against a display of new steel plates in bright colors, Joan Summers, who lived three houses away from him, passed the aisle on her way to weather stripping and noticed him standing there. Joan Summers hesitated. He seemed so intent on his switch plates that she felt reluctant to disturb him, even with a greeting; at the same time, now that she had paused, she felt it would be rude to ignore him, especially if he'd happened to see her out of the corner of his eye. Instead, therefore, of entering the aisle, Joan stood at the end and called down: "Oh, hello there." What happened next surprised her. Walter Lasher glanced abruptly, as if furtively, in her direction, gave a quick nod, and turned back to his switch plates. They were not close friends, but they had been neighbors for many years and had always had pleasant exchanges. Joan Summers marched off toward the aisle of weather stripping, which she needed for the downstairs bathroom window. His behavior verged on rudeness but had not seemed rude, exactly: it had seemed peculiar. Walter Lasher was not a peculiar man. Joan Summers shook it out of her mind but was careful not to go to the cash register until she was absolutely certain that Lasher had left the store.

A RIPPLE OF DISAPPOINTMENT. As the weekend passed without incident, we wondered whether the man had been frightened away by the police presence, or whether he was lying low, waiting for another chance. It was also possible that he had settled his score, whatever it was, that he had done what he'd come to do and had left our town forever. Our sense of relief was accompanied by a ripple of disappointment. For though we were happy to be rid of him, if in fact we were rid of him, we were annoyed at our failure to catch him and troubled by our inability to understand anything whatever about who he was or what he was trying to do. Many of us, while openly expressing pleasure at his disappearance, secretly admitted that we would have been happier if something worse had happened in our town, even much worse, so long as it was something we were able to understand, like murder.

VICTIM. Even as we were growing accustomed to the word "victim" in relation to these incidents, we began to ask ourselves to what extent the word corresponded to our sense of what had actually taken place. No one doubted that something impermissible, even outrageous, had been done to all three men, but it was also true that the attacks had been carefully limited: no robbery had been committed, the stranger had inflicted no physical damage, and he had immediately walked away. Our town, it should be said, is a very safe place in which to live. We take pride in our safety and have no tolerance for crime. Nevertheless, we're part of the world and are not spared our share of serious trouble: child molestation, felony assault, rape, even two murders in the last seven years. The crime represented by a slap in the face is at most a Class A misdemeanor. To speak of a "victim" might therefore seem to exaggerate the consequences of a deed that, for all its unpleasantness, amounts to very little in the scheme of things. Even so, it seemed to most of us that the suddenness of the attack, the strength of the slap, the apparent randomness, the anger and helplessness induced in the person receiving the slap, all suggested that those who were slapped were indeed victims, though of a strange variety that kept eluding our understanding.

A MULTITUDE OF SLAPS. Although we had read about the three slaps—the ones delivered to the faces of Robert Sutliff, Charles Kraus, and Raymond Sorensen—we knew that the total number of slaps was far greater than those reported in the paper. The three slaps were the visible slaps, the public slaps, the ones that entered the police record and the pages of the *Daily Observer.* But alongside those slaps there existed a multitude of invisible slaps, of subterranean slaps, which took place solely in our minds. The other slaps struck, over and over again, the faces of Robert Sutliff, Charles Kraus, and Raymond Sorensen, and they struck our own faces as well. We imagined the hand rising, the arm swinging, the palm striking the flesh of a cheek. We heard the peculiar sound of a slap, the crisp soft-hardness of it, like that of a whip. We thought of wood snapping, of ice cracking. We thought of TV footage of distant wars, the sharp clap of gunfire in the night. As we walked along the aisles of a clothing shop in the mall, as we sat at a booth in a coffee shop in town, we heard a rustling of slaps all about us. In our beds at night we heard them, obscured by the passing cars, a distant radio, the roll of trucks on the thruway: the other slaps of our town, a whole chorus of them, rising up out of the quiet like fire crackling in the dark.

SHARON HANDS. On Monday afternoon, as police cars were pulling in and out of parking lots at banks, supermarkets, car dealerships, and medical buildings, Sharon Hands, a senior at Andrew Butler High, waved good-bye to Kelsey Donahue at the corner of Maple and Penrose and continued on her way home. Basketball practice had gone well, though she'd messed up two jump shots; tonight she had a meeting with the Thespians in the school auditorium, and she'd promised her mother that when she returned she'd help go through the pile of catalogues to find a cable-knit sweater for Aunt Debra, who was hard to please at the best of times but impossible on her birthday. There was never a minute left over in the day. She couldn't help throwing herself into things, her boyfriend had complained about it more than once, but that was who she was, at least for now, though who knew what the future held. But she loved these long walks home, the only time in the whole day, it seemed, when she was by herself. Her legs felt strong, her body was bursting with energy, even after the long school day and the two-hour basketball practice, and as she cut through the little park on the other side of the thruway overpass she looked with pleasure at the row of three swings, the climbing structure with its towers and rope ladders and slides, the slatted bench with a maroon scarf thrown across the back. People thought they knew her, but they didn't, not really. They thought all she liked was to be surrounded by friends, lots of friends, and though she loved her friends, every single one of them, even Jenny Treadwell with her endless problems and complaints, she also loved these solitary walks between school and home with her cell off, her book bag slung over her shoulder, her long hair bouncing on her back, her arms swinging, her tights showing off her legs, and why not, if you've got it flaunt it, and she had it, she knew she did, it was why she loved walking down the halls between classes, walking in town in her stretch tops and jeans, or on the beach in summer, in her pink string bikini, along the hard sand at the water's edge, the heads turning, the friends waving, the gulls skimming the water, and as she left the park and started along Woods End Road she listened with pleasure to the knock of the heels of her cognac-colored boots against the shady sidewalk. On Woods End Road the houses were large and set well back from the street. High trees rose from the lawns, and shutters spread from the windows like wings. She walked under the branches of old sycamores, their trunks such a lovely green and cream that they made you want to reach out and stroke them, as if they were big soft animals. Oh, sometimes she had strange ideas, funny ideas she shared with no one. She glanced at her watch: she'd be home in five or six minutes, just enough time to text a few friends, call Molly about Friday night, and read a chapter of *American Democracy* before dinner. As she approached Meadowbrook Lane, a squirrel scampered across a telephone line, a boy raced down a driveway on a skateboard, and in front of her, on her left, a handsome man stepped out from behind a tree. She was used to the smiles of older men. He walked up to her, stopped, and slapped her across the face. The blow hurt; she felt her head bend to one side. She felt like bursting into tears, or screaming at the sky—just screaming. Sharon raised her hand to her cheek, as if to comfort it. No one had ever hit her before: ever. By the time she thought to shout out for help, the man was no longer anywhere to be seen.

DARING. Just as we thought we had come to grips with the attack in the bank parking lot, the incident on Woods End Road shook us to the core. We had accepted, uneasily, the leap from the station parking lot at dusk to the bank parking lot in full daylight, and we had begun to absorb the change from upper-income commuter to two-job worker. Now the rules had changed again: the new victim was female, the scene of the attack a quiet residential street. The stranger, we felt, was widening his range, deliberately and with a kind of artfulness. For wasn't he announcing, by this latest move, that no one was safe anymore? Of course we condemned the attack on Sharon Hands as an act of cowardice, we were outraged by its unfairness. Still, some of us sensed in it something darker: an element of insolent daring. It was daring because it took place closer to our homes, as if the attacker were moving toward our doors and windows, and it was daring above all because the victim was no match for him in strength. It was as if he wanted us to know that he was no longer limiting himself to those who might be expected to defend themselves.

ANNA LASHER. As she tossed the salad in the cherrywood bowl on the kitchen counter, Anna Lasher realized that she was not looking forward to hearing her husband pull up in the drive. They'd had difficult patches before, but this silence, this refusal to let her know what was worrying him—well, Walter wasn't the most forthcoming of men at the best of times. Under his public manner there had always been a secretiveness. None of that was new. What was new was the averted eyes, the moody staring off, the office anecdote told coldly, without a flicker of pleasure. After dinner he cleared the table, put the dishes in the dishwasher, and retired to his study. She wondered whether this was it, the famous midlife meltdown: the craving for adventure, the affair with the blond secretary in the spike-heeled boots. She remembered a cartoon he had shown her a few months ago: he'd been tickled by the punch line, but she had noticed the violently jutting breasts of the dumb blonde sitting in the boss's lap. She carried the bowl of salad into the dining room. On the wall was a painting of Walter's mother, with two rows of pearls around her neck. Who had a painting like that in their dining room? She wondered suddenly whether she herself had brought all this on—she'd been tired lately, moody, a little short-tempered. As Anna walked into the kitchen she heard the car pull into the drive. She could feel muscles tightening all over her body, as if she were sensing danger.

HELPLESS. In an interview with a reporter from the *Daily Observer*, Sharon Hands spoke of her feeling of helplessness during the attack. "I felt like there was nothing I could do," she said. "I was completely at his mercy." She went on to say that she now knew what it must be like to be abused by a man, and that her heart went out to women everywhere. She said the stranger was a menace to society and urged everyone to cooperate fully with the police. She invited us to check out her brand-new blog; she looked forward to reading our comments. Beside the article appeared a color photograph of Sharon Hands: a pretty girl with straight blond hair, large brown eyes, and an easy smile. On her cheek was a ruddy glow that made us think of the slap. We were upset for many reasons by the attack on Sharon Hands, and we understood her feeling of terrible helplessness. At the same time we had the sense that the interview revealed a young woman who was confident, self-possessed, and not at all unhappy to have our attention.

ANALYSIS OF A SLAP. Those of us who were inclined to distance ourselves from the drama of particular instances, and to think about the slap as a phenomenon in itself, tended to see in it two opposite qualities. In one sense, it seemed to us, a slap is a form of withholding, of refusal: it presents itself as the deliberate absence of a more damaging blow. Its aim isn't to break a bone or to draw blood, but to fall short of both. The physical evidence of the slap—a redness in the cheek—conveys its meaning perfectly: it is the sign of blood, without the blood. In the same way, the pain of a slap is a sign of the greater pain not inflicted. But looked at another way, the slap doesn't merely withhold: the slap imparts. What it imparts is precisely the knowledge of greater power withheld. In that knowledge lies the genius of the slap, the deep humiliation it imposes. It invites the victim to accept a punishment that might have been worse—that will in fact be worse if the slap isn't accepted. The slap requires in the victim an unwavering submission, an utter abnegation. The victim bends in spirit before a lord. In this sense the slap is internal. It is closer to a word than to a blow. The sting passes, the redness fades, but the wound lingers, invisible. Therein lies the deepest meaning of the slap: its real work takes place secretly, out of sight, on the inside.

VALERIE KOZLOWSKI. Two days later, at 9:05 in the evening, Valerie Kozlowski sat at her kitchen table, drinking a cup of mint tea and finishing the daily crossword puzzle she had begun at breakfast. She liked coming home at 7:00 to the mail and the partly filled-in crossword; clues that had seemed vague and elusive at breakfast sometimes became transparent after a nine-hour day at the store and an hour of closing up. She put in six days a week at Now You See It, the consignment shop she co-owned with her sister; in addition, there was the sideline of estate appraisals, which sometimes had her scurrying out at night or on Sundays. They needed to hire a girl to help out, but sales were flat and her sister wanted to wait. Her sister always wanted to wait. What they really needed was a major reorganization. The vintage dresses were crowded against the back wall, pedestal tables and vanities were covered with sugar bowls and snakeskin purses and ivory netsuke warriors and fishermen, the highboy in the corner was half concealed by a rack of furs, and the sale tables along the side walls were cluttered with china teapots, antique butter dishes, and lamps with scenic shades. Items needed to be displayed clearly, without crowding, though how you did that in the cramped space of the store was another question. It was a matter of making hard choices. The Shaker rocker and the set of four nesting tables up front could be moved to the back, making room for a rack of top-of-the-line coats and jackets, but try telling that to her sister. That was why she liked coming home to her puzzle. She could sink into it and distract herself before bed, while making use of the mental energy she always brought back with her, no matter how tired she was. And she was tired at the end of the day, bone-tired, no doubt about it, especially when her sister fell into that bossy tone. She hated that tone, as though Sophia were always thirteen to Valerie's eleven. They were both pushing forty, and Sophia looked it. You could see the lines carved into her skin from her nose down to both sides of her mouth. Valerie's own skin was smooth as a girl's. Not that it did her any good. Valerie had come home in a bad mood. She'd eaten a dinner of warmed-up leftovers, gone through the mail, all worthless except for a ten-dollar coupon from a new kitchen supply store she'd been meaning to have a look at, and talked on the phone for god knows how long with her father, who complained that no one ever called even though she called every single night no matter how tired she was. Now she sat sipping her mint tea and working on her puzzle. At 9:15 she put the cup in the sink, picked up the folded newspaper, and pushed open the swinging door that led into the living room. That was where she liked to finish her puzzle, seated in the armchair with her feet up on the hassock. As she stepped into the room a figure came toward her and raised his hand, and in the instant before terror came rushing in she thought, very distinctly: It's not fair, I'm a good person, it should have been her.

THE GOOD SISTER. It was all over town the next day: the attack on Valerie Kozlowski, the invasion of her home, the crossing of some final line. We imagined him staking out the house, waiting for nightfall, making his way along the side yard, climbing the back-porch steps. The police report indicated that he had slipped in through an unlocked window. We all knew what it meant: he was coming closer. All this was upsetting enough in itself. What made it worse was that many of us knew Valerie Kozlowski, had spent time in her store. She was the one known as the Good Sister, the one you felt easy speaking to when you asked about a Chinese vase or an old record player from the 1950s. She had a good heart, you could see that. Why would anyone want to hurt her? But as soon as we began asking ourselves such questions, we understood that until this moment we had held out a kind of secret hope. With the others, there might have been some excuse, something we didn't know, which might have explained the attacks. Maybe each one of them, even Sharon Hands, had done something that deserved punishment. But the attack on the Good Sister was a simple outrage that couldn't be explained away. It was as if we'd been living with an illusion, and the attack on the Good Sister had been directed not at her but at us, at our illusion. We'd been hoping for an explanation, an easy way out—but wasn't he warning us against sentimentality? If so, it had worked. We hated him. We wanted him dead.

ANOTHER VIEW OF THE COAT. Valerie Kozlowski's description of the attacker made it clear that he was the same man, wearing the same coat. In fact it was so clear that we began to wonder why he never tried to change his appearance. Was it that he wanted us to recognize him as the one who slapped us? If, at first, he had chosen a trench coat in order to blend in with the commuters at the train station, by now the coat served the opposite purpose: it was the very symbol of danger, the sign that leaped out at us so vividly that trench coats had virtually disappeared from our town. It was, we thought, part of his daring. He was eluding the police, he was entering our homes, adorned in the very costume that allowed him the least chance of escaping detection. Out of this thought a question arose: Why this sign, rather than another? He might have chosen a windbreaker and ski mask, he might have chosen anything. The trench coat was a sign of the suburban commuter. By extension it was the sign of our town. Was he trying to say that he was one of us? Or was he not one of us, but someone who had adopted the coat contemptuously, in a spirit of parody?

WE WHO WERE NOT SLAPPED. We of course felt sympathy for those who had been slapped. It was impossible not to imagine the moment: the stranger emerging from nowhere, the flare of danger, the hand raised to strike a blow. We wondered how they must have felt, those unlucky ones, as the sound rang out, as the stranger walked away. We wondered what we ourselves would have done, as he stepped up to us with his angry eyes. We understood that our compassion for the victims had in it a touch of superiority, of condescension, which the fortunate are bound to feel for the less fortunate, and we tried not to feel too great a pleasure in having escaped their fate. We understood one other thing. Even though we were pleased to have been spared, even though we were the ones to whom nothing ugly had happened, still we wondered, at times, whether they were more fortunate than we. After all, their ordeal was over, they had been tested, they had nothing more to fear, whereas we, the innocent ones, we, the unslapped, walked in a world crackling with danger. It was as if they knew something that we didn't know. At times we even envied them a little.

WALTER LASHER AND THE FOOTSTEPS. Walter Lasher walked along the station platform, carrying his laptop in one hand and a *New York Times* folded under the other arm. It was nearly dark; he had worked late. Once again he'd drifted off at his desk in the afternoon, not a nap thank god, but close to it, sitting there with half-closed eyes and drumming temples. There was still a good crowd at this hour, though he sensed a nervous watchfulness as they approached the stairs leading down to the lot. It was lit up now by those orange lights that made everything look like a stage set awaiting the actors. He himself had no anxiety, only a dull, heavy irritation as he entered the lot and began walking toward Section B. The police were hopeless, not a clue in all this time. The town was no longer what it used to be. When he'd first moved here from the city, it still had the feeling of a small old-fashioned place tucked away at the end of the commuter line. Now you had upscale retailers fighting for prime locations, the old drugstore gone, the news store gone, corporate headquarters springing up, teardowns replaced by monster houses built out to the property line. Asians moving into the newer neighborhoods, all professionals, all very classy, even a touch of India, that woman coming out of the wine shop in a rose-colored sari carrying herself like a foreign queen. The stranger in the coat was part of it somehow, as if he'd been swept in along with everything else. It was all nonsense, he wasn't thinking straight. As Lasher walked toward his car, three rows away, he heard footsteps not far behind him. It wasn't unusual, in the station parking lot, at this hour, to hear footsteps not far behind you, but these were not usual times. Lasher felt a tension rippling through his upper back. The footsteps drew closer. As if he were moving a heavy weight, he turned his head slowly. He saw a man in a long coat coming swiftly toward him. Lasher turned his body around. He stepped forward and swung his open hand violently against the man's face. As his palm cracked against flesh, knocking the face to one side and throwing the body back against a car, he felt deeply soothed, as if he had sunk down into a warm bath after a long hard day. A moment later he saw that the coat was a double-breasted wool coat, dark, no belt, the face different, older. He understood that it was all part of a necessary pattern, and a tiredness came over him, even as he took a step forward and began talking very fast.

SILENCE. When we read in the *Daily Observer* about the assault in the station parking lot, where both men were quickly arrested, when we learned that Walter Lasher had himself been slapped but had not come forward, we didn't know whether we were more disturbed by his attack on Dr. Daniel Ettlinger, who was returning from a visit to his sister in Mamaroneck, or by the long concealment of information that might have been useful to the police. Had Walter Lasher gone immediately to the police, the man in the trench coat might have been apprehended, or at least prevented by police surveillance and public awareness from pursuing his series of attacks. It was true enough that Robert Sutliff's swift response had not stopped the stranger in any way, and in fact, when we thought more carefully about it, we didn't believe for one second that a report by Walter Lasher would have changed the course of events. Nevertheless, his silence troubled us, in a way we found difficult to define. Was it that, by his silence, he was acknowledging what many of us felt to be the dark truth of the attacks, namely, that they were a humiliation too deep to bear? We tried to imagine Walter Lasher carrying his secret with him, day after day, while police cars patrolled the streets of every neighborhood, and citizen watch committees reported the presence of any stranger, and daily editorials urged that more safety measures be taken by town authorities. We thought of Walter Lasher riding the train home from work, with his secret squatting in his chest. We imagined the secret as a small, hairy animal with sharp teeth. We wondered what it felt like, to be slapped in the face, hard, and to say nothing about it. We wondered what thoughts passed through Walter Lasher's mind, night after night, as he lay in bed, feeling his secret biting inside him.

INEVITABLE. We now lived in anticipation of the next attack, which felt inevitable. Parents drove their children to school and walked with them from the street or parking lot into the building; when the school bell rang at the end of the last class, parents were waiting grimly outside the front door. Members of neighborhood watch groups walked up and down sidewalks, displaying the yellow-and-black armbands that had become the sign of our vigilance. Police cars roamed the streets, stopping from time to time to ask us if we had noticed anything unusual, anything at all. People were urged to keep their doors and windows locked, to stay home after dark, to travel in groups whenever possible, to keep outdoor and indoor lights on throughout the night, to be watchful at all times, to report any suspicious behavior immediately. Whether our measures were effective, or whether the man was simply biding his time, we had no way of knowing, but the days passed without incident. We tried to anticipate his next step, which we imagined as a deeper violation: perhaps the invasion of a bedroom, late at night, where he would slap us in our sleep. We would wake up and see him staring down at us with his angry eyes. Or maybe, now that he'd struck a high school girl and a woman who lived alone, he would seek out a child. He would find a little girl playing alone in her yard. He would raise his hand high in the air, he would hit her so hard in the face that she'd be hurled to the ground. We ate breakfast tensely, in town we walked briskly, we turned our heads at the slightest sound.

POCKETS. It was understood that to wear a trench coat, in the present atmosphere, was foolish and even dangerous. Anyone seen in such a coat was bound to arouse suspicion. And so they hung there, the abandoned trench coats of our town, on coat racks standing by the front door, or on hangers suspended from horizontal poles in hall closets: lacquered wooden hangers with polished-steel swivel hooks, thin metal hangers, hangers of heavy-duty chrome. They hung between fleece jackets, nylon windbreakers, quilted coats with faux-fur collars, wool sweaters, leather bomber jackets, peacoats, hooded parkas, corduroy blazers. There they hung, almost but not quite forgotten. Sometimes when we thought of the abandoned trench coats, we were inspired to strange fantasies. We imagined that the trench coats had the power to leave our closets and to roam our streets at night. We saw them drifting through town like restless and unhappy ghosts. In certain moods, we imagined them swept up by a great wind. They rise swirling into the air, the abandoned trench coats of our town, and as they turn round and round, their arms wave, their tails flap, and their pockets spill, releasing, high over the night roofs, high over the dark beach with its forsaken lifeguard stands, high over the stoplights of Main Street, a great shower of quarters and dimes, half-opened rolls of cough drops, lunch receipts, house keys on flashlight chains, sticks of chewing gum, folded train schedules, small bags of cashews, halves of cider doughnuts in waxed paper, subway cards, sunglass cases, energy bars, telephone numbers on pieces of scrap paper.

MATTHEW DENNIS. Matthew Dennis, twenty-five years old, a reporter for the *Daily Observer* who had been assigned to cover the attacks after Charles Kraus had phoned the police, swung out of his seat as the train pulled into the station. He had spent the afternoon in Manhattan and was returning at the height of rush hour. It was all his boss's idea: ride the train into the city with the morning crowd, listen to the talk, get a feeling for the mood. Ride the train back, keep your ears open, give us the word on the train, the word out in the lot. Circulation was way up, everyone was following the story. Matthew had been against the whole scheme. Better to make the rounds of the neighborhoods, interview upper-management types on Sascatuck Hill, talk to the guys in the gas station next to Sal's Pizza, but who was he to turn down a free trip to the city, and besides, he'd had some good conversations down and back and had typed up most of them on his laptop. Everybody had a theory: the man would next strike at midnight, the man was an ex-cop, the man was seeking attention for a reality show. In Matthew's view the attacker was following a pattern, but one that was difficult to pin down. He'd begun with four men, then turned to women; he'd begun in the station parking lot, then changed to a parking lot in town, to a residential street, to a living room at night. It appeared that what he liked to do was raise an expectation and suddenly swerve away—he liked taking the town by surprise. Matthew walked along the platform, exchanging a few words with Charlie Kraus. Then he stood by the steps for a while, looking down at the lot: the lights were on, though the sky was still dusk-blue. People walked in careful groups, looking around, making sure. A man came up to him and asked for a light. Matthew had stopped smoking a year ago. The man was in his mid-thirties, sharp-featured, a solid build; except for the zippered jacket, he could have been the stranger. A woman laughed: a high, nervous laugh, like a laugh rehearsed for a play. "My husband picks me up," he heard someone say. "I don't park here anymore." Matthew walked down the steps. In the morning he'd first parked near the station, then changed his mind and chosen a spot farther away. He needed to walk with the crowd, listen to what people were saying, study their faces. His job on the paper was strictly temporary, until something better came along, or until he could get going on a book, but he liked it well enough, it might lead to something, you never could tell. He turned quickly when he heard what sounded like a half-stifled cry. It was only a girl who had stumbled in her heels and was clinging to her boyfriend's arm. Everyone was thinking about the stranger, looking around. Matthew had his own theory, which he sometimes believed: that everyone had a secret, a shameful thing they had done, and the reason they feared the stranger was that he made them remember that thing. He himself, for example, had done some things in college he'd rather forget. He stepped up to his car, bent over to glance through the window—one of his ideas was that the stranger concealed himself in parked cars, which he knew how to open—and placed his key in the door. He heard a step, a single crunch of gravel, and turned with a feeling of excitement and intense curiosity. The man in the trench coat had already raised a hand, and as the palm cracked against his cheek with a force that brought tears to his eyes, Matthew was aware of the look of stern anger in the stranger's eyes, as if he were delivering a judgment.

HIGHLY INTELLIGENT. We read about that judgment in next morning's *Daily Observer*, where Matthew Dennis recounted in detail his simulated commute, the overheard conversations, his thoughts on the station platform, his observations of crowd behavior, his walk to the car, the details of the attack. He did more than report the incident: he said that the stranger's return to the station parking lot was evidence of a highly intelligent plan. The attacker had led us to believe that he was intent on entering our homes, on striking our most defenseless citizens, on violating our deepest privacies. As we prepared for the next attack, as our police force and our watch committees gave their full attention to our streets and houses, he returned boldly to the original scene, which he had seemed to abandon. Not only, by this maneuver, had he eluded detection; he had also made us rethink the meaning of the attacks. Far from spreading random terror, the Slapper was making a point: his target was not particular people, but the town itself. In the attacker's mind, our town was represented largely, but not entirely, by commuters; hence four out of seven incidents had taken place in the station parking lot.

Had he wished to initiate a reign of random terror, he would have spread his attacks far more widely. Moreover, the seven victims were less different than one might suppose at first glance. Although it was impossible to condone the attacks on Sharon Hands and Valerie Kozlowski, it was important to remember that Sharon Hands, the daughter of a corporate lawyer, attended a well-funded and highly regarded public high school, a symbol of membership in the community, while Valerie Kozlowski wasn't a minimum-wage worker with no health insurance and no benefits but the co-owner of a small business. He himself, Matthew Dennis, was a reporter for the local paper, which meant that he was part of the way the town presented itself to itself. The victim who seemed to fit in least was Ray Sorensen, but that was precisely the point: Sorensen was all the others who lived in our flourishing town, all those who occupied the lower ranks of the social scale and sometimes had to work a second job in order to buy groceries and pay the bills. It was the purpose of the attacks, Matthew Dennis said, to punish all those who were guilty, not just those at the top of the heap, and what the victims were guilty of was *living in our town.* The long article ended with the hope that we would think less about our safety and more about the reasons why we might be guilty for living in a town such as ours. He himself harbored no resentment and vowed to become a better person.

NOT GUILTY. Although the details of the attack on Matthew Dennis drew our fascinated attention, our reading of the article resulted, for the most part, in impatience and resentment. Matthew Dennis, we felt, had a twisted sympathy for his attacker; we distrusted his analysis of the man's motives and, in rereading the article, we began to distrust certain details of the attack itself. Most of us would not have felt "intense curiosity" at the sight of an angry man in a parking lot at night, raising his hand to strike us in the face. We were baffled, we were exasperated, by Matthew Dennis's lack of outrage. The same absence of anger was all too evident in his analysis, which seemed less sympathetic to us than to the man who had attacked our neighbors, disrupted our peace, and frightened our children. The next morning, angry letters appeared in the *Daily Observer,* denouncing Matthew Dennis and questioning the judgment of the editors in running the story. What particularly galled us was the suggestion that all of us might be guilty and deserving of punishment. After all, we were not members of some revolutionary gang who had raided an enemy town and committed rape and murder, we were not passive citizens turning our heads away as smoke rose from the concentration camp chimneys. No, we were peaceful, law-abiding inhabitants of a suburban town, trying to raise our kids in a difficult world, while keeping our lawns mowed and our roof gutters free of leaves. The man was a criminal and needed to be put away. The next morning, an editorial acknowledged the storm of protest and stated that the opinions of the article were not necessarily those of the *Daily Observer.* The more we thought about it, the more offended we were by Matthew Dennis's report, so that we almost forgot, in our indignation, that the stranger had struck another blow.

WAITING. Again we waited, like people looking up at the sky for a storm. This time we sensed a difference. Now there was anger in our town—you could feel it like a wind. We were angry at the presence of danger in our streets, angry at the police department, angry at being put on the defensive by reporters whose job it was to give us the facts and keep their cracked ideas to themselves. You could feel a tension in public places, an uneasiness at the dinner table. On the streetcorner across from the post office in the center of town, a dozen people stood with signs that read KEEP OUR STREETS SAFE and MORE POLICE. A bearded man with a ponytail held a sign printed in large red letters: THE JUDGMENT IS COMING. Tempers were short. In the library parking lot, a fight broke out when one car backed into another. We went to bed early and lay there listening. Waking in the dark, we pushed aside the blinds and looked out our bedroom windows at houses glowing with light: the front porch lights, the living room lights, floodlights over garage doors, lanterns on lawns—as if our town were having a party all through the night.

DIVINE PUNISHMENT. One of the more bizarre developments of the lull was the emergence of certain shrill, fanatical voices, which saw the stranger as a messenger of the divine will. A letter in the opinions section of the *Daily Observer,* signed Beverly Olshan, stated that our town was being punished for its sins. We became aware of small groups, which perhaps had always been there, with names like Daughters of Jericho and Prophets of the Heavenly Host; members of the latter proclaimed that the stranger had been sent by the Lord to warn us of his wrath unless we mended our ways. Even those of us who dismissed such ideas as ignorant or childish could not escape the thought that the stranger was punishing us, like an angry father, for something we had done, or for something we had failed to do, or for something else, which we ought to have known but did not.

THE PACKAGE. Seven days after the attack on Matthew Dennis, a package addressed to the police department was deposited on the top step of the post office at some time between midnight and 5:00 a.m. At 5:00 a.m. a mail carrier starting his shift noticed it from his truck. Later that morning, post office officials met for a brief consultation and decided to summon the police. Rumors about the incident first appeared on Matthew Dennis's new website, but we had to wait for the morning paper before we could read a definitive report. The package, wrapped in brown paper, bore no return address. The police determined that the suspicious-looking parcel posed no danger. Back at the department they carefully removed the brown paper and found a plain cardboard box, tied with white string. In the box lay a tan trench coat, neatly folded. No note had been enclosed. There was little doubt, though no proof, that it was the coat of the stranger. Apparel experts had been called in, lab tests were being conducted, a thorough investigation was under way. Meanwhile we wondered what the stranger wanted us to think. Was he announcing that his attacks had come to an end, or was he warning us that we should expect a new attack in a different disguise? For a week, for two weeks, we led anxious lives, alert to the minutest signs. Toward the end of the third week, as leaves turned yellow and red and the sun shone from a cold blue sky, we began to have the sense of a burden slowly lifting.

DISSATISFACTION. Although we could feel ourselves moving toward the normal course of our lives, with all the familiar pleasures and worries, at the same time we couldn't escape a sense of incompletion. The proper ending, we felt, should have been the capture of the stranger, who would have given us the explanation we desperately needed to hear. We would have listened carefully, nodded our heads thoughtfully, and punished him to the full extent of the law. Then we would have forgotten him. Instead we'd been left with an improper ending, an ending heavy with uncertainties, which was to say, no ending at all. The police investigation had come to nothing. We asked ourselves whether the stranger had left because he found it impossible to continue his attacks without serious risk of being caught, or whether he'd left because he had completed a careful plan to attack seven people. Even if we had known the reason for his departure, we still wouldn't have known why he had come in the first place. What had he wanted from us? What had we done? In certain respects, the end of the attacks was more disturbing than the attacks themselves, since the attacks held a continual promise of capture and revelation, whereas the end of the attacks was also an end of the hope that had always accompanied them. In this sense, the end of the attacks was simply another way of continuing them—a way that could not be stopped.

THE SEVEN WHO WERE SLAPPED. It was at this time, when we were returning uneasily to our former sense of things, that meetings began to spring up all over town, for the purpose of discussing and analyzing recent events. There were large public meetings at the town hall and in the auditorium of one of our two high schools, gatherings at businessmen's associations and fraternal organizations, at the local chapter of the Daughters of the American Revolution, at the Ethical Culture Society and the Jewish Community Center, at the First Congregational Church and the Church of the Immaculate Conception, to say nothing of private get-togethers in living rooms, dens, and finished basements. Often, at these meetings, one of the seven who were slapped appeared as a special guest, with the exception of Walter Lasher, who never accepted such invitations or even acknowledged them. The guest spoke for fifteen or twenty minutes and then answered questions from the audience. What did it feel like when the stranger appeared? How much did the slap hurt? Did you fear he might kill you? What was he trying to prove? Even Valerie Kozlowski, once she overcame her reticence, took to the podium with surprising vigor. The most popular speakers proved to be Sharon Hands, whose long blond hair came sweeping down over her shoulders and lay against silky blouses of cerise, emerald, and brilliant white, and the controversial Matthew Dennis, who wore an old sport coat, a black shirt open at the neck, jeans without a belt, and white running shoes, and who liked to walk back and forth in front of us, punctuating his remarks with slashing movements of his hands and turning suddenly to face the audience. Now and then a speaker appeared even at one of the fringe groups, such as Prophets of the Heavenly Host, that had begun to attract a wider membership and now held public meetings in rented halls. As we sat in the audience and watched a speaker, we sometimes experienced an odd kind of envy, as if, by not being slapped, we had failed to be part of a profound moment, had somehow, by our caution, evaded a call to adventure. At the same time we understood that we were already forgetting the precise feel of those troubled days, which were slipping away into history and taking on the warm, soft colors of a sentimental rural painting ("Red Barn and Clouds," "Morning Sleigh Ride") suitable for the walls of banks, hospital waiting rooms, and the lobbies of office buildings.

BLOSSOMING. One morning at the station parking lot, as if by secret agreement, the trench coats returned. Tan, beige, and taupe, they emerged from car after car, like pale flowers blossoming in the early morning light. Richard Emerick had put on his trench coat in the front hall, but he had paused, thought hard, and then removed it, choosing instead the black wool coat with lambskin-trim collar that he usually saved for later in the year. As he stepped from his car in the parking lot he immediately saw his mistake. In his fingers he could feel the pressure of the belt-ends as he looped them over in front. The forecast for tomorrow was light rain in the early morning. He would be ready for it.

SUCCESS AND FAILURE. As the slaps began to recede, as even their echo in our minds was becoming fainter and fainter, we wondered whether we had emerged successfully from our ordeal. To call it an ordeal was of course something of an exaggeration. After all, we hadn't been murdered. We hadn't been raped, or beaten, or stabbed, or robbed. We had only been slapped. Even so, we had been invaded, had we not, we had felt threatened in our streets and homes, we had been violated in some definite though enigmatic way. Therefore, when the attacks appeared to be over, we felt that we had emerged from an ordeal, though we were still uncertain how we felt. Sometimes it seemed to us that the stranger with his angry eyes had known something about us that we ourselves did not know. Sometimes we wondered whether he was right about us, even though we did not know what it was that he was right about. More often we dismissed such thoughts and reproached ourselves for our failure to catch him, our failure to prevent him from repeatedly attacking us. At about this time an editorial appeared in the *Daily Observer.* Signed THE EDITORS, the article discussed the episode of the stranger and concluded by saying that it was over now and that we ought to "learn from it and move on." The editors did not tell us what we might learn, unless it was that we needed a larger police force in our town, nor did they tell us in which direction we should think of moving. Therefore our sense of relief, when the attacks appeared to have ended, was also a sense of unrelief; our feeling of success was also a feeling of failure. Now, that is not the way things are, in our town. Here, success is success, failure failure. There is no confusion between the two. Success that is also failure is nothing at all. We don't know how to take hold of it. And so we wonder: What have we learned from it all? We know only that something has happened in our town that can never unhappen. On a fine spring day, when all this is far behind us, we may be walking down a street, under branches of budding maples and lindens. On the porches, reflections of porch posts and tree branches show in the glass front doors, which haven't yet been changed to screens. The thought comes: He could be standing behind that tree. Then we look more carefully at the root rippling toward the sidewalk, at the place where the bark-edge stands clear against the background of grass, street, and distant houses, and where, at any moment, a shoulder might emerge, an arm rise, a hand swing violently toward our faces, as we walk along, under the budding branches, with their yellow-green flowers against the blue sky.

Tales of Darkness and the Unknown, Vol. XIV: The White Glove

1

In senior year of high school I became friends with Emily Hohn. It happened quickly: one day she was that quiet girl in English class, the next we were friends. She had passed in and out of my attention over the last year or so, and it was as if I suddenly turned my head in her direction. I liked her calmness, her unruffled sense of herself, her way of standing as if she could feel the ground under her feet. As for me, I was a floater, a cloud-man, tense, jittery, cat-wary, all nerves and bone, and I'd spent the last year so desperately in love with another girl, so whipped-up and feverish, that even my happiness had felt like unhappiness. Emily Hohn's quietness drew me in as if it had been waiting for me all along. It wasn't only her calmness that attracted me. That would be unfair. I liked looking at her—at her thickish brownish shortish hair shot through with lighter strands that caught the sun, her small neat hands with close-cut nails, her round wrists, one of which had a pale chicken-pox scar, her slightly lowered eyelids that made her look a little sleepy, her slow smile. She reminded me of things I liked: streetlights at night, a peaceful room. I liked her clothes—the trim fresh-smelling pastel shirts, the knee-length skirts in black or dark green wool, the cardigans worn open with the sleeves pushed halfway up her forearms, the broad leather belts, dark red or black, with big square buckles that made me think of picture frames. I liked watching her crinkle her eyebrows when she tried to figure something out. I liked the way she sometimes reached over and scratched the back of her left hand with two fingers of her right. Most of all, I liked that she didn't stir me up—didn't move her body a certain way. I was sick to death of all that. I wanted something I could count on. I was grateful for stillness.

I walked her home from school one day, a warm October afternoon that felt like summer. Under branches of sugar maple and red maple we walked through flickers of sun and shade—here and there, in the still air, a yellow-red leaf came drifting down. I carried my books against my hip and my autumn jacket slung over one shoulder. Emily had tied her burnt-orange sweater around her waist, like a backward apron, and she carried her blue pebbly three-ring binder and her crisply covered schoolbooks in an upward-tilted pile against her white blouse. Speckles of sunlight danced on her as she walked, as if bits of light were being tossed at her through the leaves.

She lived in an older neighborhood, on a street where the houses had wide front porches, and tree roots pushed up chunks of sidewalk. On her porch sat a glider with faded flowery pink cushions, beside a green wicker table that held a glass of lemonade. A rake stood up against a window shutter; a bicycle leaned against a cushioned wicker chair. Everything about the house pleased me—the tarnished brass knocker on the gray front door, the living room with its dark blue couch and its deep armchair next to a pair of old moccasins, the scent of furniture polish mixed with a bready sweetish smell of baking, the sunny yellow kitchen with its bright porcelain rooster on the windowsill. On top of the refrigerator sat a cookie jar shaped like a bear hugging his belly. Emily's mother was standing at the sink, washing a big breadboard sticky with dough. Over a flowered dress she wore an apron decorated with richly red apples, each with two green leaves. She turned and began wiping her hands briskly on the apples. "Oh my, I can't shake your hand or I'll—Emmy, take the young man's jacket, why don't you. I'm Emily's mother, and you must be—Will. Well, Will. Would you like a soda? A piece of raspberry pie?"

I spent that afternoon creaking in the glider in the warm shade of the front porch, sipping root beer and eating raspberry pie. Emily sat next to me with an open French grammar facedown on her lap, pushing with one leg to keep us gliding—into the sun and back into shade, into the sun and back into shade. From time to time her mother opened the front door and asked if I'd like another piece of pie or a brownie with walnuts or an oatmeal cookie. Some girls were jumping rope across the street; farther off came the quick clean sharp bursts of a basketball against driveway tar. At the same time I heard the scratch of a rake pulling over leaves. I could feel myself settling into those sounds as into my own childhood—and the warmth, the slap of the rope, the creak of the glider, the dripping sunny hands of Mrs. Hohn, the square porch posts, the dip of the telephone wires between poles, all seemed to me, as I half closed my eyes, to be part of Emily herself, as if she were flowing into the peacefulness of an October afternoon.

2

I began walking home with her every day, dragging my feet through unraked leaves that sounded to me like waves drawing back on a beach. As the weather grew colder we moved indoors—sometimes to the living room, where we sat on the dark blue couch beside the armchair, sometimes to the kitchen table, with its maplewood chairs that had floral-patterned cushions tied to the seats. After a while we'd go upstairs to Emily's room, where I straddled the wooden desk-chair and faced Emily, who sat on the big bed with her back propped up against the headboard and her legs stretched out on the pink spread. I admired her desk, an old-fashioned one with pigeonholes and a writing surface that swung out on brass hinges. In one corner of the room sat a small bookcase no higher than my waist. It held a pale blue leather jewelry box, eight or nine books, a Ginny doll with one arm, and many boxes of puzzles. The small number of books surprised me, since I had two large bookcases in my room, a row of books on my dresser, and piles of books on the floor by my desk. But I quickly came to connect the absence of such things with Emily's calmness, as if books and edginess belonged together. We talked, we laughed, we did homework—I at the desk, she on the bed. Sometimes, turning over my shoulder, I would simply look at her, as she sat reading calmly on the bed with her black flats on the floor and her ankles crossed, reaching now and then to scratch the back of her left hand with two fingers of the right.

At 4:00 there would be a knock on the half-open door and Mrs. Hohn would sweep in with a tray bearing glasses of milk and a plate of chocolate chip cookies. At 5:30 I would hear Emily's father opening the two front doors, the storm door and the wooden door, and ten minutes later he would drive me home. Mr. Hohn was a mild, balding man with large melancholy eyes and a rueful smile. He did something in insurance, collected plate blocks and first-day covers of every newly issued American stamp, and liked to ask me serious questions about whatever book I was reading. He said things like "Can you hand me that thingamajigger?" and "That's for darn sure." I felt so welcomed by the Hohn family, so bathed in their atmosphere, that when I entered my own house, with its bookcases and its polished dark piano with piles of yellow music books and its faint sweet odor of pipe tobacco, it was always with a slight shock of estrangement, before familiarity settled over me.

I kept planning to invite Emily to my house, but I never did. At my place, we would have done my kinds of things—I'd have shown her my books, and my records, and my twin-lens reflex, and my collection of labeled minerals from quarries all over Connecticut. I would have played the piano for her, a piece by Chopin or Debussy, and then, to show that I wasn't stuck up, a boogie-woogie by Clarence Pine Top Smith. My parents would have welcomed her and made her feel at home. And as I imagined these things, all of which had happened many times before, a tiredness came over me, as if I were rehearsing for a play that I'd just finished performing in. It was as if, in my house, I could feel a continual soft pressure on me—emanating from the piano, from the reading chair in my room, from the mahogany bookcase in the front hall—to be the person I was, the one I felt I somehow had to be. What I liked about Emily's house was that I didn't have to be anything at all.

On weekends my father graded papers at home and let me have the car. When I asked about a curfew, he looked up from the armchair by the lamp table and said, "Your mother and I expect you home before the year is out." Every Friday night I would drive over to Emily's house, and every Saturday I would drive over in the late morning and stay past midnight. We did homework in Emily's room; I helped Mr. Hohn rake leaves and clean the roof gutters; I sat in the kitchen peeling carrots and cutting the ends off string beans while Mrs. Hohn prepared the pot roast or the roast lamb. After dinner, Emily washed the dishes and I dried them with a thick dish towel decorated with little bluebirds. Then the four of us would play Scrabble at the dining room table, under a small brass chandelier with narrow bulbs shaped like flames. Mrs. Hohn liked to press her hand to her chest and say that, good gracious, with me around, who needed a dictionary, but she was a skillful and relentless player and usually won—the two of us always came in first or second, while Emily and her father trailed far behind. Something gentle and unaggressive in Mr.

Hohn's play, which reminded me of his melancholy eyes, seemed to invite defeat; but I was merciless. "I can't believe these letters," Mrs. Hohn would say, or "Em, don't do that," as Emily reached over to scratch the back of her hand. Mrs. Hohn liked to win; we inspired in each other a spirit of friendly fierce combat. At times, lashed to competitive fury by Mrs. Hohn, I glanced at Emily as she sat staring mildly at her tiles. For a moment her calmness baffled me, as if we were playing different games. Then the battle was over, with laughter and headshakes, and Mrs. Hohn served cookies and cider and apple crumb cake, while outside the winds of November rattled the dining room windows.

One Saturday afternoon when I was in the backyard helping Mr. Hohn repair a wood-framed storm window that we'd taken down and set against the house, he looked up and said, "Looks like we need a plane. Wait here and I'll—or heck no, come on down." He opened the sloping door, led me down six steps, and reached for a key hidden on the ledge above the red cellar door. In the deep basement he led me past the furnace and boiler to a shelf that held a ball-peen hammer, a spirit level, and a shiny black plane with a wooden knob. "Since we're down here," he said, and motioned me along with two quick curls of a forefinger. We came to a wall piled high with boxes; a tall metal cabinet with two doors stood in a corner. Mr. Hohn opened the metal doors. I saw a row of little dresses all hanging on small white plastic hangers. "Emmy's," he said. He took one out, on its hanger, and held it up for me—a little blue dress with a white collar. "Three years old." He shrugged, rubbed the back of his neck, and hung up the dress. "We kept planning to give them away, but somehow—" He sighed. "Well!" he said, and closed the doors. Turning abruptly, he led me back up the steps into the backyard.

Meanwhile, in school, I waited for the day to end so that I could walk home with Emily. I liked to look over at her, in the classes we took together. Unlike me, always restless, always a little bored, Emily gazed at the teacher with full attention, or else bent her head over her notebook and wrote steadily. Sometimes she would give a subtle yawn, which revealed itself as a slight stiffening of her under-eye skin. Sometimes she would reach over and scratch the back of her left hand with two fingers of the right.

One day as I sat down in the cafeteria with my shepherd's pie and my Devil Dog, I noticed that the back of Emily's hand was a little red. "How's your hand?" I asked. She immediately placed it on her lap. "It's fine," she said. "It's this dry heat." She pointed to a hissing radiator.

3

On a dreary Monday morning shortly before Christmas break, when the sky was so gray and dark that the school windows glowed, as at a night dance, I arrived late at the lockers and rushed into homeroom seconds before the bell. Emily's seat was empty. Her desk, without her, seemed to be drawing attention to itself, like a lamp without a shade. It struck me that she'd never been absent before—it wasn't the sort of thing she did. All that day her absence pressed on me. She seemed, absent, more insistently present than when she was actually there. Under the fluorescent ceiling lights I had the sensation that she was visibly, luminously, missing. At my house I let myself in with my key. I dropped my books on the kitchen table, where they slowly began to topple, and dialed Emily's number. Mrs. Hohn answered the phone as the books slid along the tabletop. Emily was fine, there was nothing to worry about. She had gone to the doctor for a checkup. She was resting now, she'd be back in school probably tomorrow. Could I think of a six-letter word for "enliven"?

When I entered homeroom the next morning, Emily was sitting at her desk. Her ankles were crossed under her chair. The yellow collar of her shirt lay neatly on her dark green sweater. On the back of her left hand was a small white square of gauze, taped on all four sides.

On the way to English she said, "He doesn't want me to scratch it." She gave a little shrug. "Some sort of skin thing. It's embarrassing."

"No it isn't," I said. "No way. Absolutely not."

During Christmas vacation I spent so much time at the Hohns' that my mother started saying things like "We hardly see you anymore" and "I hope you aren't wearing out your welcome over there." Once she looked sharply at me and said, "Is everything all right, Will?" Every morning I took the long cold walk to Emily's house; I returned only at night, driven by Mr. Hohn. Late one afternoon the sky turned dark and a heavy snow began to fall. I was invited to spend the night in the upstairs guest room, under a sky-blue quilt covered with pictures of gray cats and red balls of yarn. I wore a fresh-laundered pair of Mr. Hohn's flannel pajamas, too wide and too short, striped white and dark blue. Emily, looking in on me, said, "You look—you look—" and gave a whoop of laughter, then covered her mouth with her hand. "Just let me know if you need anything," Mrs. Hohn said, and closed the door.

I lay in bed, in the quiet house, under the thickly falling snow. A novel by Turgenev rested open and facedown on my stomach. On the dresser stood a little porcelain man playing a fiddle, a blue glass bird, and half a dozen tiny dolls seated on two wooden benches, facing a miniature teacher standing at a blackboard. Over the dresser hung a painting of a deer in a forest, drinking from a sunlit stream. When I turned out the lamp on the night table, I could sense, behind the drawn shades, the snow falling in slanting steady lines. I imagined the streetlights shining through the falling snow.

For a long time I lay awake and peaceful in the dark, listening to quiet bursts of warm air coming through the vent at the base of the wall and a faint creak of floorboards in the attic. When at last I went to a window and pulled aside the heavy stiff shade, with its strip of wood in the cloth above the shade pull, I was startled to see a clear night sky. In the light of streetlamps, a glowing snow lay over sidewalks and bushes. It covered the fire hydrant across the street, rose thick along tree branches, swept up to the top of a corner mailbox.

Late the next morning I sat in the warm yellow kitchen peeling potatoes onto a paper towel, while Mrs. Hohn reached into a chicken and pulled out glistening dark innards, like wet stones. Emily and her father were out doing errands. "You know," I said, "I can't help thinking about Emily's hand. I was wondering—"

"There's not a thing to worry about, Will," Mrs. Hohn said. "It's just a pesky rash. Be a dear and fetch me down that platter, the bone-china one with the windmills. I don't know what those people were thinking, putting up shelves fit for a giant."

4

School startled me. It was as if I'd forgotten all about it during that snowy vacation, composed, it seemed to me, of long evenings playing Scrabble with the Hohns under the flame-shaped bulbs and one brilliant blue afternoon in the backyard building two snowmen with Emily: one with a wide-rimmed red hat on its head and a paper rose stuck in its chest, the other with a pipe in its mouth and an empty can of Campbell's tomato soup on its head. School was a clash of olive-green lockers, a scraping of many desks. Already I was looking forward to summer. I would be sitting near Emily in the warm shade of her backyard, in an aluminum chaise longue with six adjustable positions, reading a library book whose stamped card served as a bookmark, while beside me, on a round white wrought-iron table with an openwork top, a glass of homemade lemonade with a slice of lemon in it stood next to a plate of fresh-baked brownies with walnuts.

One morning toward the end of January I stepped into homeroom and saw that Emily wasn't there. I could feel disappointment spreading in me like tiredness. And yet, at the very center of my disappointment, I was aware of a prickle of satisfaction—for hadn't I known she was bound to be absent again? All that day I tried to savor her absence. It would, I told myself, make her presence all the more vivid and dramatic. The next morning, when I entered homeroom, I didn't allow myself to look in the direction of her desk. Instead, I imagined Emily seated there in her dark green or burnt-orange sweater, with the sleeves pushed halfway up her forearms and the collar of her shirt lying on both sides of her neck. When, overcoming my reluctance, I turned to look at her, I was so shocked by the sight of her empty desk that I glanced down at my watch, as if to see how much time was left before she really wasn't there.

At home I sat on the wooden steps between the kitchen and the back porch, with the telephone cord squeezed in the closed door, and called Emily. Mrs. Hohn answered. Emily was fine. She'd had to have a little work done on her hand; she was resting now. I wanted to know what kind of work. "Some minor surgery—nothing to worry about, Will. She came through with flying colors. I'm so proud of her. She's resting now. She ought to be back to school in a couple of days. I'll tell her you called. She'll be so pleased." Only in my room, as I sat bent over my typewriter on its rattly metal table next to my desk, did I understand what I'd wanted to say to Mrs. Hohn. Why didn't you tell me? Why? In my mind I shouted into the telephone. Anger burned in me like fever.

She was absent the next day, and the next. I called each afternoon; always Mrs. Hohn assured me that Emily was resting. The medication had left her feeling a little woozy, Dr. Morrison had said it might have that effect, she'd be up and about in no time. The next day Emily was absent again. At home I sat on the wooden steps, on the cold porch, with the phone in my lap, and did not call. I understood that Mrs. Hohn would tell me nothing—that my questions disturbed her. I called my friend Danny and invited him over for a game of chess.

The next day she wasn't at her locker. I was unsurprised—so deeply unsurprised that I felt no disappointment—and as I entered homeroom I glanced wearily in the direction of her desk, which when it was empty always stood out sharply, like a chair in an old View-Master reel. Emily was sitting quietly there. I'd been so certain of the empty desk that for a moment I became uneasy, as if I were in one of those TV dramas where you open a familiar door and enter another world.

She was sitting very still. Her books rested in two neat piles on the rack under her chair, and her forearms lay on the blond writing surface. She was wearing a pleated tan skirt and a dark red wool pullover with the sleeves pushed halfway up her forearms. On her left hand she wore a white glove. The glove was tight at the wrist and then flared out a little. Her gloved hand lay motionless, the fingers curved and slightly spread, facing down. She sat upright and stared straight ahead. The whiteness of the glove, the stillness of her arms, the slight tension I could see in her neck, all this made me think that it must be another girl, who was wearing Emily's clothes and taking her place in class, so that the other Emily, the one who didn't wear a white glove, could continue to lead her life elsewhere, for reasons she would later explain to me.

I sat down and looked over at her. She sat to my right and two seats up. She did not glance over to me. Her hair, thick with complicated small waves, concealed most of her face, except for her small rounded chin and the sharpish tip of her nose. I wondered who she was, this statue-girl with her one white glove. I glanced at the clock. I looked down at my own left hand, which had assumed the position of the gloved hand, and glanced back at her. She had turned her head in my direction and was giving me one of her slow smiles—and I felt so filled with gratitude that it was as if I had wronged her and been forgiven.

In the hall I nodded casually toward the glove. "So what's that all about?"

"It's nothing," she said. "Just some minor surgery. No big deal. He wants me to keep it covered." She shrugged her right shoulder. "Nothing to worry about."

I waited for her to say more, as though she'd stopped in the middle of a sentence.

"Then I won't worry about it," I said, and in my mind I heard my father saying: "Case closed."

Emily said nothing. I shrugged and said, "Case closed."

And as I walked home with her that day, wearing thick blue gloves of my own, I didn't worry about it. I didn't worry about it when I stepped into the warm yellow kitchen and greeted Mrs. Hohn, who smiled radiantly at me and said, "Welcome back, Will—this place hasn't been the same without you." I was back from exile, back in the peaceful place, after Emily's minor surgery that was already a thing of the past, though recent enough to require a protective covering; there was probably a bandage of some sort underneath, which would have attracted its own kind of unwelcome attention; already the white glove seemed less strange, like a new hairdo that took a bit of getting used to.

Upstairs in Emily's room I straddled the wooden desk-chair, with my forearms resting on the back, while she lay on the bed against two pillows. Her white-gloved hand rested beside her on the pink spread. I tried not to look at it. She wanted to know everything she'd missed in English and Problems of American Democracy, and I went through the classes day by day, after which I told her about Larry Klein's latest antic: he had skipped class and was found seated in the empty auditorium, and when he was brought to the principal's office he said he thought seniors could skip class at their own discretion. "That's what he said: 'at their own discretion.' Sanders just stared." The glove didn't move. There was a knock at Emily's door. Mrs. Hohn entered, with a tray of chocolate chip cookies and two glasses of lemonade. "Now you two just relax and enjoy yourselves," she said. "And if you want anything, just holler." At 5:30 I heard the opening of the storm door and the wooden door. The glove shifted slightly. I stood up and gathered my books. "See you tomorrow," I said, and glanced at the glove, which had moved from the spread to Emily's lap.

Mr. Hohn drove me home. The streetlights had come on, though there was light left in the sky; on one side of the street it was nearly night, and on the other it was still late afternoon. Through lamp-lit porch windows I could see parts of couches and table lamps and shimmering television screens. Mr. Hohn gripped the wheel with a pair of yellow-brown leather gloves that had a pattern of little holes on the back of each finger. "I was wondering," I heard myself say, as I stared at the bent fingers, "about Emily's hand."

"The operation was successful," he said, with his eyes on the road, "which is one good thing, let me tell you"—and at the word "operation" I imagined Emily's hand streaming with blood.

"Mr. Hohn," I said as we entered my neighborhood. "What exactly is wrong with Emily's hand?"

"Now *that,*" he said, keeping his head motionless but swinging toward me his melancholy gaze, "is a good question." He swung his gaze back. "A very good question."

5

We returned to our old ways, Emily and I. It was as if nothing had changed. But I was aware at every moment of the white intruder, drawing attention to itself, demanding awareness. At the wrist it was fastened by two small white buttons. They looked like ordinary buttons, with a glimmer of iridescence when they caught the sun. On their left was a small overlap of cloth, which formed a shadowy opening that revealed nothing. The glove seemed tightly bound, as if it were meant not to slip out of place, so that I imagined Emily had trouble bending her wrist, or even moving her fingers. I wondered whether she took the glove off at night—whether she took it off at all.

In class I watched her sit down at her desk. I noticed that she rested her gloved hand very carefully on the writing surface, where she left it motionless for as long as possible. Once, after a pencil rolled off the edge and struck the floor, she bent over to retrieve it, leaving her left hand in place. Her body, for a moment, was twisted unnaturally.

It struck me that the glove was harming Emily's grace of movement, penetrating her with a slight clumsiness. When she walked with her books cradled in her arms, she was careful not to let her gloved hand touch them—she supported the weight a little awkwardly with her left forearm. Now and then I saw a red mark on the underside of her forearm, from the edge of her notebook. At home, when Mrs. Hohn brought in sugar cookies and lemonade, Emily would lift the glass with her right hand, take a sip, set down the glass, and pick up a cookie. Her gloved hand, with the slightly curved fingers, lay rigidly in her lap.

I quickly came to know every detail of that glove. It fit snugly over the thumb but less tightly over the fingers. The left edge, where the white glove often rested, was faintly darkened. A triangle of small creases was visible in the place where the thumb joined the forefinger. A spot of blue-black ink showed on a knuckle.

Sometimes, staring at the glove in class, I could feel, on my own hand, the white cotton binding me. Then I would wriggle my fingers rapidly, or massage the back of my left hand, over and over, with the palm of my right.

But there was something else about the glove that troubled me, beyond the sharp fact of its presence. Ever since I'd become friends with Emily, I had felt an easy flow between us, an openness, a transparency. This restful merging, this serene interwovenness, was something I had never known before, something that reminded me of her porch in sunlight, or the night of the snow shining under the streetlights. The glove was harming that flow. It was, by its very nature, an act of concealment. Emily herself, by eluding the question of her hand, by refusing to reveal whatever it was she was hiding under the white cloth, was forcing me to think about her in a secretive way. It occurred to me that the glove was changing her—turning her into a body, with privacies and evasions.

But if the glove was creating a new Emily, a hidden Emily, it was also doing something to me. The peace I'd always felt in her presence was being replaced by wariness, by an almost physiological alertness, as if my body were warning me to watch her closely. At the same time, I was no longer able to look at her whenever I wished. Before the glove, I could turn my head frankly in her direction. Now, I felt compelled to throw furtive glances at her, like a stranger yielding to a forbidden desire.

One afternoon as we were making our way along an aisle of the auditorium, where someone was scheduled to bore me to death with a speech about career choices, I noticed Emily's white glove knock lightly against the back of a seat. Her body stiffened; for an instant she closed her eyes. Then she continued forward, holding her left hand in front of her as, with her right hand, she smoothed back her hair, in little quick movements, again and again.

Now and then an image would surge up in me, of her hand under the glove—the skin a burning red, or purple and yellow, as if recently crushed by a rock. Maybe there was some sort of scar, a harsh red line slashing across the back of the hand like a trail of fire. Maybe it was worse—a raw shiny pink wound sunk into the flesh. I understood that I was fastening my attention on Emily Hohn in a way I had never done before; that what drew me was no longer her stillness, or her gentleness, but the thing hidden by her glove; and I imagined myself tearing off that white disguise and beholding, in terror and exhilaration, her mangled hand.

A warm day came, taking everyone by surprise. Through the open windows we could hear the engine of a crane as it lifted steel beams at the back of the school. Later that day the weather grew cold, but we knew the turn had come. Icicles on eaves glistened and dripped. The last snow began to melt in the shadows of garages and under bushes hung with brown leaves. Willows, still yellow, glowed in the sun. The white glove, resting in a bar of sun on a desk beside a window, was so fiercely white that it hurt my eyes. Within the whiteness I could see the creases plainly, the faint discolorations, a small darkish stain beside one button. Somewhere a dog barked. And a restlessness came over me, the restlessness before spring, when the world, in that in-between season, is waiting for something to happen.

6

One night I woke in my warm room. I could hear the heat blowing through the vent at the base of the wall. It seemed to remind me of something, and all at once I saw the blue-and-white-striped pajamas, the tiny dolls on their wooden benches, the glowing snow stretching away. Emily lay in her room, fast asleep. Or was she also awake? Perhaps she had taken off her glove, which rested on the covers, the five fingers slightly curved. At the thought of the glove I felt a pressure in my head, like a thumb pushing against my temple, and when I swung out of bed and thrust aside the white blinds, which rattled like coat hangers, I saw that the sky was a deep and glowing blue, the blue of warm spring evenings.

I opened the front door and stepped outside. The chill startled me—it was a blue brisk night, with a big white rippled-looking moon that made me think of refrigerator frost. I turned up my shirt collar and walked quickly under that moon, a heavy cold stone that at any moment was going to rip out of the sky with loud tearing sounds. In the distance I could hear the trucks on the thruway like low rumbles of thunder.

It was a long walk, and for a while I forgot everything but the clear black lines of television antennas against the blue night sky and the curved shadows of telephone wires like strips of black typewriter ribbon stretching across one side of the road. After a while I came to a familiar neighborhood. Porch screens, catching the moonlight, became for an instant opaque aluminum walls, which suddenly vanished to reveal shadowy wicker chairs and leaning bicycles. The windows of Emily's house were dark. I walked along the strip of grass between the side of the house and the driveway of cracked tar. In the backyard I opened a sloping door and descended six steps. At the cellar door I reached up for the hidden key.

I made my way slowly through the dark cellar, lit here and there by long rectangles of moon-glow, and climbed the wooden stairs to the upper door. It opened onto a small space off the kitchen. A single plate leaned in the dish rack. I passed into the living room and turned onto the carpeted stairs. Halfway up I stopped, with one hand on the banister. Until that moment it hadn't struck me how easy my break-in actually was. The sheer ease of it exasperated me. Shouldn't the house have protected itself against intruders? The house trusted the world—it believed that it was safe from harm, that darkness was the beginning of rest. But things were no longer that way. Harm walked in the night. The glove was up there, in her room. It was always with her, always touching her—the white companion.

I continued up the stairs to the almost black landing, where I thought I recalled a painting of a red barn, and climbed the final three stairs. Then I seemed to remember that the painting showed not a barn but a barnyard, where a woman was flinging feed from her apron at white chickens. In the darkness of the upstairs hall I passed the Hohns' bedroom and felt along the wall for Emily's door. The familiar doorknob turned with ridiculous ease, and the door opened without a sound.

The shades on the double window were drawn, but a blurry bar of light lay at an angle on one wall. Emily was asleep on her back, her head turned to one side. On the bedspread her right arm was flung across her stomach. Her left hand, still bound in the white glove, lay beside her on the pillow. The palm was up, the fingers slightly curved. Quietly I closed the door behind me.

I came up to the bed and bent slowly over Emily. As I did so, I had the sense that I was introducing myself with a formal bow. The glove lay motionless. It seemed to be holding its breath. In the darkness made less dark by the blurry bar of light, I could see the two buttons at the wrist. I realized there were three of us in the room: the glove, Emily, and me. If

I undid the buttons and pulled at the white fingertips, only the glove and I would know. "Emily," I whispered, "are you awake?" But Emily was far away.

The glove lay very still on the pillow. It seemed to be expecting me, seemed almost to mock me a little: Here we are, you and I, what are you going to do about it? I reached out and touched the lower button with the tip of my forefinger. It felt like an ordinary button, with a slightly raised rim and a depression in the center. I could see the four holes and the tight lines of white thread crossing. The buttonhole was nearly concealed by the button. I would have to press the button through the taut slit, while at the same time I was careful not to push down on her wrist. If, with fanatical patience, I succeeded in forcing the button through without waking Emily, I would have to repeat the operation with the second button. But the glove, which fit tightly, would still be on her hand. I would have to remove it with extreme care, holding her bare wrist with one hand while I pulled at the cloth fingers with the other. At any moment her eyes might begin to open. She would see a dark figure bending over her, she'd feel a hand on her skin. The glove sat there, exposing its two buttons. They were looking at me. They were daring me, with little white smiles, to get on with it. And an anger came over me—at the grinning white buttons, and the smug white glove, and the fat white moon, and the careless house, which entrusted itself to the night, and at innocent Emily, lying there too peacefully, though with a slight look of strain between her eyebrows, and at the sky, and the stars, and the rushing-apart universe, and the vain fool who stood in the dark bedroom like a killer with an upraised knife—like a strangler with a cord in his hands—like a boy lost in a forest. "Emily," I whispered, "I wasn't here," and fled into the night.

7

Spring came. Under budding branches I walked with Emily along squares of sidewalk that sometimes showed the imprint of numbers or the swirl of a trowel. The sides of roads were dusted by maple flowers, dark red and yellow-green. On some afternoons it was warm enough to sit out on the front porch, which Mrs. Hohn had swept clean of brown, crackly maple wings left over from the fall. Emily and I never spoke of the white glove. One day she was absent; after school I didn't call. The next day she appeared with a new glove, white and clean, exactly the same as the first, its two buttons faintly iridescent in the sun. She held her arm very carefully and lowered it slowly to the desk. As we walked home in hot sunlight, I watched the glove pass through new leaf-shadows and patches of sun. On the porch Mrs. Hohn served us rhubarb pie and a fruit-juice punch. She set down the plates and glasses on the green wicker table. "Not yet," she said, holding up a handful of mail like a fan of cards. Emily and I were still waiting to hear from colleges. The idea of college seemed so remote that it was like a game I had played in childhood, in which you pretended to be a famous person, like George Washington or Babe Ruth.

I remained watchful—it was all I could do. I saw the glove resting motionless on the desk, in a band of sun. The fingers, slightly curved, lay in shade; suddenly the glove darkened; beyond the window, a shadow spread across the grass; a moment later the glove glowed brilliant white. Or it lay on its side across Emily's lap, as she sat in the glider with her legs tucked under and sunlight on her knees.

It stayed so still that sometimes, as I watched it lying there, I imagined it contained an artificial hand, stiff and shiny, like the one I'd seen a few years ago in a department store window, lying on the floor next to the foot of a mannequin with red hair. At other times, when she lowered it carelessly, I would see her lips tighten and small lines appear between her eyebrows. Then I would imagine sharp strokes of pain branching through the hand, like flashes of lightning.

Once, as she sat reading, I saw her right hand move across the desk to the back of the gloved hand and begin to scratch. As if startled awake, she snatched away her hand, glancing about as if she'd been caught in a shameful act. And once, when I left her on the porch to get a glass of water in the kitchen, where I sat talking with Mrs. Hohn, I returned to find Emily scratching furiously at the back of the glove, raking her close-trimmed nails across the cloth, over and over, while a flush showed at the top of her cheek and a coil of hair shook on her neck.

One warm afternoon I was sitting on the glider, holding a book open on my lap as I gazed across the street. Emily sat beside me, with her gloved hand resting in her lap. Beyond the porch posts it was a brilliant blue day. Across the street a small group of girls were jumping rope; the rope slapping the sidewalk sounded like sharply clapping hands. A squirrel skittered across the porch roof. Emily shifted her legs. I glanced at the glove, which hadn't moved, and looked back at the street.

"You're making it worse," I heard her say, in a voice so quiet that I wondered whether she had spoken at all. The glider creaked.

"Worse!" I whispered. "How could I—"

"By thinking about it," she scarcely said. I could feel her looking at me, as if she were touching my face.

"I never think about it," I said, turning suddenly, but Emily was leaning back with half-closed eyes.

That night, as I sat at my desk, it struck me that her words, which had barely crept out of silence, might have had another meaning. I had thought she meant that I was making it worse by drawing attention to something she wanted to forget. But now I wondered whether she'd meant that I was literally making it worse—harming her hand by my thoughts, which she could feel pushing painfully against it, like sticks.

A few days later, Emily and I were walking home under the maples. I was talking and gesturing with my right hand, which suddenly struck Emily's left elbow. "Sorry!" I almost shouted.

Emily smiled at me. "You didn't exactly kill me, you know," she said, with a little laugh.

I gave a little laugh of my own. "So tell me," I said. "What does the doctor say?"

Emily stiffened. In the silence I could hear her wide leather belt creaking as she walked.

"Nothing," she said.

"Nothing? The guy just stands there, like an idiot?"

"Nothing good. Nothing that helps. They don't know anything. Anything anything anything."

"All right," I said. "All right."

One night I dreamed that Emily held out her gloved hand to me. "I can't get it off," she said. I fumbled with the buttons, which wouldn't come undone, and as I unrolled the glove clumsily, for it clung tightly to her skin, I uncovered a smooth, pink, perfectly formed foot.

I could sense a change. In class she would lower her hand hesitantly to the desk, as if the slightest touch were more than she could bear. When she walked in the corridors, she cradled her books clumsily with her right arm, so that they were crushed up against her. Sometimes a book would slide slowly from the pile and fall to the floor with a sharp noise, like a shot. Then, before I could get to her, she would crouch down quickly, sitting awkwardly on her upraised heels, with one knee higher than the other, and balance her books in her lap while she reached for the fallen book with her right hand.

That was what I saw; but there must have been many things I didn't see, small embarrassments and humiliations. She had already withdrawn from typing class; she no longer went to gym. When I passed her in the halls, she was always walking alone. People gave her a little distance. No one wanted to brush against the white glove. It was easier to pretend she wasn't there.

I watched her—watched that glove. It clung to her hand like a growth on her skin. Emily was right: I could feel my thoughts scratching at the whiteness, like fingernails. Sometimes, glancing over, I would see a white wound, a bright gash in her flesh—and I would reproach myself, for after all, it was only a glove.

One rainy Saturday night I was sitting on the couch beside Emily in her dark living room, watching a black-and-white movie. A man in a rumpled suit and a dripping hat was walking along a deserted road at three in the morning, in a splattering downpour that seemed to be part of the rain outside. I had driven over after dinner in my father's Dodge; Mr. and Mrs. Hohn had retired upstairs after the ten o'clock news. When her parents left, Emily had turned off the lamp on the table between the couch and the armchair, for her father always liked to have a light on when he watched television. The room wasn't entirely dark; television light flickered on the mahogany lamp table, and light from a streetlamp entered beneath two slightly raised shades and lay in dim stripes along one wall. Emily sat on my left, with her cordovan loafers off and her legs tucked under. Her knees were toward me; the white glove lay stretched along her thigh. The whiteness grew brighter and dimmer as the movie changed.

I could hear the rain falling on the porch roof and dripping along the side windows, and I could hear the movie rain beating against the deserted road. Now and then there was a crack of thunder, which might have come from either place. It was the sort of night I liked best—the sound of movie rain, the different sound of real rain, the dark room touched by streetlight, Emily sitting quietly beside me with her legs tucked under, the peaceful house. But the glove lay there, invading the night, disrupting the dark with its irritating whiteness. I wished that she'd covered it with a blanket, or held it farther away. It was so close that I could have reached over and unbuttoned it without shifting more than a shoulder.

The movie ended. The last scene showed a close-up of the man, who was sitting at a bar with rain dripping from his hat. Emily rose, walked over to the television, and turned it off. She came back to the couch and sat down, stretching her legs out on the coffee table. Her ankles lay next to a little porcelain man playing an accordion. In the dark living room I could hear the rain, which was coming down quite hard, and it occurred to me that the exaggerated sound of the movie rain had actually been the sound of the real rain striking Emily's porch roof and dashing itself against the bushes by the windows. We sat in the dark, as we often did, and Emily said, "It's nice, sitting in the dark." "Yes," I said, "it's nice." The gloved hand lay in her lap. It rested on its side, the palm facing me; a dim streak of light touched her bare forearm and the wrist of the glove. I could see the two buttons very clearly.

"Look at that," I said, and lightly touched her forearm where the dim light lay across it. She looked down at her arm, where my two fingers rested. I moved my fingers slowly down her forearm until the side of a finger touched the edge of the glove. Slowly I lifted one finger and stroked the white cloth. It was softer than I had imagined. "What are you doing," Emily whispered. "Nothing," I said. I began stroking the part of the glove that lay over her wrist. Emily's right hand descended onto my fingers. She lifted my hand and placed it on her collarbone. With the fingers of her right hand she unbuttoned the top button of her shirt. Then she undid the button below. I felt the sudden edge of her white bra and the skin below her collarbone; my thumb touched the small connecting strap that joined the parts of the bra. I understood, with absolute clarity, that she was offering me her breasts in place of her hand. An immense pity came over me, for Emily Hohn, for the two of us sitting there like sad children, for the dark room and the spring rain, before anger seized me. She was hiding something from me—trying to put me off the scent. I reached down and began to unbutton the glove. Emily cried out—a single high sharp note, like the wail of an animal—then knocked my hand away and swung out of the couch. In the dark her hair looked wild, and for a moment, as she loomed over me, I had the sense that she was standing in the rain, glaring down at me, her hair dripping, her face shining, as I lay in a puddle at the side of the road with the rain beating against my face.

8

She was absent the next day. At home I dialed her number and hung up after the first ring. I was angry at myself in every way, but it was more complicated than that—I felt I'd been driven to the edge of what I could bear by the oppressive white glove. In all this, Emily wasn't innocent—she knew something and refused to speak. Exactly what I'd hoped to accomplish by removing the glove was no longer clear to me. But the glove had disturbed the harmony between us, had introduced a note of uncertainty, of opacity. If I longed to see what lay underneath, it wasn't simply in order to gratify a by now ferocious curiosity, but to release Emily and me from the spell of secrecy, to return us to peacefulness—for there was no peace between us anymore, only the mocking white glove. I hated that glove, hated the way it sat there without doing anything. I wanted to tear it off and set it on fire. Better yet, I would bury it in my backyard. Then a tree would grow, and every spring, when the maples put out their yellow-green and dark red flowers, the buds of my tree would open into white gloves.

When she appeared at school the following day, she rigorously avoided my gaze. She looked tired and drawn; her anger, if it was that, seemed a kind of sadness. I stayed out of her way. It was all fine with me—fine to smash things up, fine to be done with it all. High school would end, I would drag my way through the stupefying summer, then off to college and a new life, hey ho. It was all fine: dead and fine. She was already a memory—the girl with the white glove.

A week passed, the weather grew warmer. On the way home from school I heard the sound of hedge clippers and electric edgers. Someone was tarring a driveway. The smell of fresh tar mingled with bursts of cut grass. In school the windows were wide open and I could hear the dark cry of a mourning dove and the leathery smack of a baseball against a glove. One afternoon at my locker I heard a voice say, "Are you angry at me?" and I felt as if a hammer had struck the side of my head.

"Angry! No, why would I, not really, I thought you—"

"So would you like to"—she shrugged—"I don't know, come over?"

Then I was walking home with her, through flickers of light and shade.

On the front porch we sat on the glider. Mrs. Hohn brought out a plate of sugar cookies, each with a dab of jelly in the center, and glasses of iced tea. It was as if nothing had happened—had anything happened?—but I felt something unspoken in the air, like a heaviness. I glanced at Emily. She was staring straight ahead and holding a cookie in her hand, stroking it with her thumb. Sugary granules fell in her lap. I stared out past a square porch post, one side in sun and one in shade. Shadows of maple leaves moved on the sunny part. Emily said, "I've been meaning to tell you. I've been doing a lot of thinking."

"Thinking?"

"About—you know." She shrugged her right shoulder—a quick impatient little shrug, which made the right side of her collar lift and fall. "I'm ready now."

"Ready! I don't know what you—"

She looked at me. "To—you know—show you."

Her eyes burned at me—I had to look away.

"Only if you—" was all I could say.

It was to take place Saturday night. Her parents were going out and they wouldn't be back before midnight. She'd been thinking about it, ever since that night, and she now saw that it was the right thing to do. She had feared I would never visit her again, once I knew. She'd been afraid, she'd been ashamed, but she was no longer that way. Her mother wanted it kept a secret. Her mother would kill her. But Emily trusted me. It was meant to be.

"There's just one thing," she said.

"Which is?"

"Whether you're really sure."

"You mean whether I'm sure you—"

"I mean sure you really want to."

"What makes you think—"

"It's just that it's not—it isn't what you think."

"I don't think anything."

She threw me a look. "I mean it might really bother you. I mean more than you think."

"But you—you're the one—"

"It's you—it's you—you don't like it when things—you know, when things—"

"When things—"

"When things aren't—when they're not—not the way you—"

And an irritation came over me, for it was as if I were the one being tested.

"Oh, don't worry about me. But are you sure you—"

"Oh yes—yes—I mean if you're sure you—"

This was on a Tuesday. During the rest of the week we fell into our old habits with a kind of gratitude. It was early June; under the maple leaves Emily walked through trembling spots of sun with a light jacket tied around her waist. From the porch I watched the girls across the street jumping rope. Overhead a squirrel scampered across a telephone wire and leaped onto a branch. In the warm summery air I could hear the smack of the rope, the soft clatter of a basketball against a backboard, the slam of a wooden screen door. Beside me, on the glider, Emily sat with her legs tucked under. Her black flats rested on the floor of the porch and her gloved hand lay in her lap. She was wearing a rose-colored shirt with the sleeves rolled neatly above her elbows and a tartan-plaid skirt held in place at the side by a gigantic safety pin the size of a pocket comb. On the green wicker table, a black tin tray painted with pink flowers held a pitcher of pale yellow lemonade in which dark yellow slices of lemon floated. We talked about a paper for English, and her friend Debby's troubles at home, and the summer. She wished she could go on a family trip the way she used to in her childhood—she missed that camp in New Hampshire—while I argued that summer was a perfect time for doing absolutely nothing. "What do you mean by 'nothing'?" Emily asked. The rope slip-slapped. In the gleaming windshield of a parked DeSoto, I could see a perfect reflection of green leaves, brown branches, and blue sky. "Nothing," I said, "is the least amount of effort over the greatest amount of time." "That," said Emily, "is so—" and burst out laughing. The glider creaked. The sun shone down.

9

On Friday night I played Scrabble with the Hohns on the dining room table, under the little brass chandelier with six bulbs shaped like flames. Beside the table stood a wheeled cart on which lay a plate of homemade peanut butter cookies and four glasses of limeade, each at a different level. "Don't," Mrs. Hohn said, glancing at Emily. I stared at my tiles, which were not promising. Later, when it was time for me to go, all three of them stood in the little front hall. The wooden door was open, and through the screen door I could see dark leaves shining green beside a streetlight, and a pale band of sky over the black rooftops. "Night, Will," Mr. Hohn said. "Drive safe, now." "Good night, Will," Mrs. Hohn said, raising her hand shoulder-high and bending her fingers twice. "And thank you for keeping Em company tomorrow night. Not that she isn't perfectly capable of taking care of herself, Lord knows. My big girl." She placed an arm around Emily's shoulders and looked at me fondly. "You're all so grown up now! I can hardly believe it."

When I drove over to the Hohns' on Saturday evening, Emily opened the door. Her parents had already left. For a while we sat on the faded pink cushions of the glider, in the warm dusk. It was the time of day when leaves are dark and the sky is watery pale. The world seems unable to make up its mind, as if at any second it might become deep night or a new day. Suddenly the streetlights came on. "I've never seen that before!" Emily cried. I said, "I can't really remember whether I have or not. It's strange. Wouldn't I remember something like that?" "When I was little," Emily said, "I once saw it raining on one side of the street—right over there—and not on this side. It was magical. I ran over to touch the rain and then I ran back into the sun. And then, a few years later, maybe seventh grade, when I remembered it, I couldn't be sure it had really happened. I couldn't *feel* the memory, you know what I mean? And I still can't be sure, even though"—she waved her hand rapidly in front of her eyes—"oh, let's go inside, I hate these idiotic bugs."

I followed her into the living room and sat down next to her on the dark blue couch beside Mr. Hohn's armchair, with its slightly sagging cushion and its yellow hexagonal pencil lying on one arm. On the coffee table stood the little accordion player. His head was tilted to one side and he was looking at me with a mad grin. I leaned back, but Emily stood up and said, "Let's go upstairs!" I followed her up the carpeted stairs, sliding my hand along the dark banister. At the landing I glanced at the painting, but it was hidden behind the glare of its glass. For some reason I thought: Now I will never know. In Emily's room I pulled out the wooden desk-chair and sat with my arms crossed on the back. Emily sat on the side of the bed. Her feet hung just above the floor. The gloved hand lay in her lap.

She patted the bed beside her and said, "Sit over here." Carefully I made my way to the bed and sat down. "There's no use waiting," she said. Her voice sounded excited and weary at the same time.

She lifted the gloved hand slowly from her lap, as if it weighed a lot, and turned her forearm so that the two white buttons were exposed.

"All I ask," she said, "is that you promise me one thing."

I thought about it. "All right, I promise." I looked at her. "So what do I have to—"

"That you won't hate me."

"Hate you!" It struck me that I shouldn't be having this conversation, that things were taking a wrong turn. "Why would I—"

"Because it's bad. It's not what you think. It's—wrong."

"Wrong? That's a strange thing to—"

"I didn't want you to know. But you want to. You want to."

"But not if—"

"You're always thinking about it. Judging me. Holding it against me."

"That's not—I'm not holding—"

"Always looking. Making it worse."

"But that's—"

"Promise."

"I promise—I promise—but listen—Emily—" I stood up and began pacing up and down in front of her, like a man in a hotel room in a movie. "You don't—not if you—I mean, I don't have to—"

"But you do. You do. You have to. I know you. That's—who you are. You have to. Everything was so fine, and now—"

"It's still fine. And you're bound to get better, I'm sure the doctor—"

"It's not like that—you don't know. You want everything to be a certain way. But it isn't. It isn't. Look. Look. I'll show you."

Swiftly, angrily, she undid one white button. The glove seemed to expand slightly, as if it had been closed very tight. She began fumbling with the second button, the one closer to her hand. "Don't just stand there," she said fiercely. "Help me." I sat down next to her and began working the button through the hole, which was stretched to a thin line. The glove was bound so tight that it must have chafed her wrist, which looked a bit red, unless it was my tugging and pulling that was bringing the blood to the surface.

"I think I've got it—wait—Emily—just a—there!" The glove was now open at the wrist, though I could see nothing of the hand itself. "That must be a relief. Do you want me to—"

"Just help me get this—"

The glove seemed to be moving, rippling a little, as if, released from the buttons, it was stretching its muscles. I grasped the edge near the bottom, while Emily pulled at the fingers. The glove seemed stuck, and I imagined that it would always be like this—the glove on the hand, the frantic tugging and pulling, Emily and I on the edge of the bed, day after day, forever—but all at once something gave way and the glove slipped quickly from the hand.

"See!" she said, holding her head away, as if her hand might do something to her.

The hand was thickly covered by crinkly dark hair, which grew more sparsely on the fingers and the palm. Through twists of hair, the skin on the back of the hand looked raw and shiny, as though it were wet. Smaller, tightly curling hairs grew in the spaces between the fingers and in the grooves of the finger joints. An ointment or secretion glistened on the thumb knuckle. Not far from the hand, the glove lay on the bed, its bottom wide open, like a mouth.

"Now you'll never—" she cried. For a moment I thought she was going to swing her hand against my face. I leaned away from her, keeping my eye on the glove, in which I could see bits of hair and wet-looking stains. "You hate me!" she said bitterly, and when I raised my eyes I saw in her face an appalling sweetness, as if she were asking me to forgive her.

10

I woke late Sunday morning with a tickle in my throat; by mid-afternoon my eyes were burning and I had a temperature of 102. All that week I stayed in bed, shivering and sweating. Through heavy-lidded eyes I saw my mother's delicate fingers holding before me a glass thermometer with a silver tip. Worst of all was a sensation of itching all over my body, as if clumps of hair were growing. Then it was over, through my window screens I could hear the sound of two separate lawnmowers, and I returned to school on Monday, nine days after my visit to Emily. When I entered homeroom I saw her sitting there the way she always did, staring straight ahead. Her gloved hand rested on the desk. I tried to catch her eye but she did not turn her head. In English I kept looking over at her, but she was always turned away; at the lockers I started toward her but stopped. In her room that night I hadn't known what to do. After a while I'd helped her on with her hideous glove and buttoned it tight. My hands itched, and I had the sensation that my fingertips were cracking apart, bursting with hairs. "I have to go," I said suddenly, and didn't move, then abruptly left. At home I took a shower and rubbed my hands and body hard with a scratchy washcloth. When I looked at myself in the mirror, my chest was red and raw-looking.

School was nearly over. For the next week and a half I saw her always partly turned away, as if she'd become a profile. At home I studied intensely and without interest for final exams. I was tired of my room, tired of the town, sick of everything—I wanted high school to end. One hot night I woke suddenly in the dark. It was nearly two in the morning. I dressed quickly, crept out of my room and into the attached garage, and slowly raised the door. At Emily's house all the windows were dark. They shone like obsidian in the glow of a streetlight. Had I expected her light to be on, had I wanted her to be waiting for me? I thought of the night when I'd broken into her house and entered her room, and as I watched the front porch from my father's car I understood that this time I had come out only to sit awhile, as if I were looking for something that had once been there.

One afternoon in August I emerged from a new bookstore in the center of town and saw Emily across the street. I stepped back into the shade of the entranceway. She was walking with a girl I knew. They were wearing jeans rolled up to mid-calf, low white sneakers without socks, and plaid shirts with the sleeves rolled up above the elbows. Emily had on a straw sun-hat I had never seen before. She was laughing—a carefree, easy laugh. On her left hand she wore the white glove. I wanted to run across the street and shout at her that everything was all right, she could stop hating me now, things were still the same, weren't they, we could walk along the sidewalk under the maple trees through spots of sun the way we always did and sit on the glider in the warm shade of her front porch forever, but Emily and her friend turned under an awning and entered a store, and later that afternoon, as I leaned back on my elbows at the beach and stared out at a sandbar with a white-and-red beach ball on it, I felt that I was about to understand something of immense importance, everything was about to become clear to me, but a boy came running along the sandbar and kicked the beach ball and I watched it fly lazily into the blue air, rising slower and slower until it stopped and seemed to float there before falling toward the shallow green-brown water.

Getting Closer

He's nine going on ten, skinny-tall, shoulder blades pushing out like things inside a paper bag, new blue bathing suit too tight here, too loose there, but what's all that got to do with anything? What's important is that he's here, standing by the picnic table, the sun shining on the river, the smell of pine needles and river water sharp in the air, somewhere a shout, laughter, music from a radio. His father's cleaning ashes out of the grill, his mother and sister are laying down blankets on the sunny grass not far from the table, Grandma's carrying one of the aluminum folding chairs toward the high pine near the edge of the drop to the river, and he's doing what he likes to do best, what he's really good at: standing around doing nothing. Everyone's forgotten about him for a few seconds, the way it happens sometimes. You try not to remind anybody you're there. He loves this place. On the table's the fat thermos jug with the white spout near the bottom. After his swim he'll push the button on the spout and fill up a paper cup with pink lemonade. It's a good sound: *fsshh, psshh.* In the picnic basket he can see two packages of hot dogs, jars of relish and mustard, some bun-ends showing, a box of Oreo cookies, a bag of marshmallows which are marsh*mel*lows so why the *a,* paper plates sticking up sideways, a brown folded-over paper bag of maybe cherries. All week long he's looked forward to this day. Nothing's better than setting off on an all-day outing, in summer, to the park by the river—the familiar houses and vacant lots no longer sitting there with nothing to do but drifting toward you through the car window, the heat of the sun-warmed seat burning you through your jeans, the bottoms of your feet already feeling the ground pushing up on them as you walk from the parking lot to the picnic grounds above the riverbank. But now he's here, right here, his jeans tossed in the back seat of the car and his T-shirt stuffed into his mother's straw bag, the sun on one edge of the table and the piney shade covering the rest of it, Grandma already setting up the chair. And so the day's about to get going at last, the day he's been looking forward to in the hot nights while watching bars of light slide across his wall from passing cars, he's here, he's arrived, he's ready to begin.

Though who's to say when anything begins really? You could say the day began when they passed the wooden sign with the words INDIAN COVE and the outline of a tomahawk, on a curve of road with a double yellow line down the middle and brown wooden posts with red reflectors. Or maybe it all started when the car backed up the slope of the driveway and the tires bumped over the sidewalk between the knee-high pricker hedges. Or what if it happened before that, when he woke up in the morning and saw the day stretching out before him like a whole summer of blue afternoons? But he's only playing, just fooling around, because he knows exactly when it all begins: it begins when he enters the water. That's the agreement he's made with himself, summer after summer. That's just how it is. The day begins in the river, and everything else leads up to it.

Not that he's all that eager to rush into things. Now that he's here, now that the waiting's practically over, he enjoys prolonging the excitement of moving toward the moment he's been waiting for. It isn't the swimming itself he looks forward to. He doesn't even swim. He hangs on to the inner tube and kicks his legs. He likes it, it's fine, he can take it or leave it. No, what he cares about, what thrills him every time, is knowing that this is it, the beginning of the long-awaited day at the river, as agreed to by himself in advance. Everything's been leading up to it and, in the way of things that lead up to other things, there's an electric charge, a hum. He can feel it all over his body. The closer you get, the more it's there.

Julia, thirteen, isn't like him in that way. Soon as she's finished laying out the three blankets, she'll run over to the edge of the drop, scamper down, and cross the short stretch of ground to the river. She's always been like that, throwing herself into things—piano lessons, blueberrying, hiking a trail, the bumper cars at Pleasure Beach. She thinks he's cautious, too held-back, timid even, and it's probably true, but it's also something else: he likes things to build up slowly, because when it happens that way, everything feels important. Does this mean there's something un-grown-up about him, something that'll go away one day, like his stick-out shoulder blades and his knobby anklebones?

"Come on, give us a hand, Cap'n," Julia says. He's not invisible anymore. Julia doesn't like people standing around doing nothing. He takes a blanket corner and before he knows it she's off around the table toward the pine where Grandma's sitting, she's scrambling down the drop and out of sight. A second later her head appears, then she's all there except for her feet, then she's got heels, toes. She doesn't stop, goes right in past her knees, bends to splash water on her arms. He can see the reflections of her red suit broken up in the water. The river has little ripply waves, maybe from a speedboat out beyond the white barrels. His father once told him the Housatonic's a tidal river. He remembers the word: tidal. Could that be the tide he's looking at, those ripples? The Housatonic. He likes saying it, likes leaning into that "oooo" sound, which reminds him of a train coming around a bend at night in an old movie. Julia throws herself in, begins swimming out to the barrels.

"You run along now, Jimmy," his mother says. "I'll be fine here." He knows it's time to get started, you can't delay things forever. He goes over to the sunny inner tubes, lifts up the one lying on a slant against the other, squeezes the warm dusty rubber to make sure it's tight. Then he begins rolling it bumpily over the grass around the end of the picnic table toward the pine where Grandma's sitting.

It's a short walk, in deep shade broken by spots of sun. He's stepping on soft-crackly pine needles and spongy pinecones, which press up into the soles of his feet as though he's walking on rolled-up-sock balls. The earth feels bouncy and hard at the same time. Grandma's sitting next to a high pine that's leaning a little forward, as if one day it started to fall then changed its mind. To the left there's another pine, also leaning forward, and the two trunks form a kind of frame around the sunny river and the wooded hills on the far side. Everything's alive with interest: that big pinecone in dark shade with one end glowing in sunlight, that cherry-stained Popsicle stick lying next to a bumpy root. Grandma's chair isn't the heavy long one from the porch, with adjustable positions, no, she's got the small one with a straight back that unfolds with one easy pull. She's wearing her dark blue bathing suit and a pair of straw sandals, toenails polish-pink, her thick hair a strange sort of whitish yellowish orange. She's always laughing about her trouble with hair dyes. She's sitting in the shade near the edge of the drop, legs in sunlight, book in her lap. Her fingers are bent at the knuckles. She likes holding them up and showing them to him. See: arthritis. The crisscross strips in the chair are white and lime green. As he comes up to her, she turns her head, places a hand in her open book to keep it from closing.

"So, my good man, you're going in? Look at Julia out there." He brings this out in people, who knows why: Cap'n, my good man. It's something about him. His sister's by the barrels now, swimming on her back, kicking her feet, sweeping up both arms. "That's right, my good woman," he says, and Grandma does what he wants her to do, gives a deep-down scratchy laugh, a laugh with approval in it. It's a witty family, you have to be on your toes. If he gets up late in the morning his father says things like "Out drinking again last night, eh, Jim?" or "Behold, the son is risen." Standing beside Grandma, balancing his inner tube with his fingertips, he takes it all in: the two bracelets on Grandma's wrist, one turquoise and one silver, her fingers puffy, her knuckles bumpy, the clumps of hot-looking droopy grass on the few feet of ground that go past the chair to the edge of the drop, the thick pine-root twisting out of the slope. A piece of white string hangs over the root. These are good things to look at, but sometimes you don't see them. You see them when they're leading up to something.

He takes a few steps to the edge of the drop, the edge of the world. Behind him's Grandma in her chair, the floor of pine needles, the picnic table. Behind that, the sunny blankets, a field—but why stop there? Connecticut's stretching away at his back, the monkey cage in the Beardsley Park Zoo, the Merritt Parkway with its stone bridges, then comes Grandma's apartment on West 110th Street, and if you keep going, the Mississippi River, Pikes Peak, California. This is fun. You can do it in both directions. In front of him the slope, the sandy-earthy place at the river's edge, Julia on her back. Then the white barrels, the wooded hills on the far bank of the river, and beyond the hills the other side of Connecticut, the trip to the whaling ship at Mystic Seaport, somewhere out there Cape Cod, the Atlantic Ocean, Africa. He likes standing here, thinking these things. He likes the picture of himself in his own mind as he stares out sternly over the river, frowning in sunlight, his fingertips resting on top of the inner tube, his other hand on his hip, Huck Finn on the shore of the Mississippi, an Indian brave with a quiver of arrows on his back, getting ready to go down to the canoes.

But he can't stand there all day. Julia's looking at him from where she's resting against a barrel. She's shading her eyes with one hand and waving him on with the other. Come on, Cap'n! Grandma's looking up from her book to watch him. And besides, he wants the day at Indian Cove to begin, he really does, even if all he's been trying to do since he got here is hold it back for as long as possible. There're two ways down to the river: the hard dirt path on the other side of the pine, where the grown-ups go, or straight down the soft, crumbly slope. Gripping the inner tube under his arm, he steps over the edge and half slides half stumbles down, feeling the warm sandy earth spilling over the tops of his feet. It reminds him of salt sprinkled into his hand. He's there—he's made it—he's standing on the patch of orangey sandy dirt that's too small to be a beach. The beach they go to has real sand, lots of it, with blankets and beach umbrellas, salt water, a refreshment stand, seagulls, dead crabs, sandbars, waves. This is the shore of the river, and it's different in different places: here the sandy orange earth, farther down some boulders and cattails, elsewhere trees and grass right at the water's edge. This no-name place is gentler than a beach, more quiet, more shut away, with the slope behind him, the green-brown water in front of him, the white barrels moving up and down a little, as if the water's breathing.

He starts forward, rolling his inner tube. Nine or ten steps and he'll be at the water's edge. He can see ripples there, like very small waves: a tidal river. If he didn't know it was a river, he'd think he was standing by a lake. Tree branches bending down to the water hide the turn of the river on both sides, and what you see is a lake with wooded hills, a few little houses on the far shore, a pier with a tiny man fishing. He rolls his tube over the warm sand-dirt. There're pebbles here, but no rubbery piles of seaweed, no purple-black mussel shells. A green Coke bottle, empty, stands upright and looks out of place. It belongs on the beach, tilted in the sand next to a blanket. It's got a green shadow. Blurred footprints, a smooth flat stone good for skimming. The excitement's building. He's almost there.

At the water's edge he stops. He makes sure the little waves pull back before they can touch his toes. Through the water he can see ripply sun-designs on the river bottom. They look like a chain-link fence made of light. The river is it, the beginning of his adventure, and here at the final place he stops for the last time.

Everything has led up to this moment. No, wrong, he isn't there yet. The moment's just ahead of him. This is the time before the waiting stops and he crosses over into what he's been waiting for. He inhales the river-smell, takes it deep into his nostrils. He's been moving toward the moment that's about to happen ever since he woke up this morning, ever since last week, when his father came home from work and with his briefcase still in his hand said they'd be going to Indian Cove on Saturday if the weather held. Every day he could feel it coming closer. It was like waiting for the trip to the amusement park, like waiting for the circus tents to rise out of the fields the next town over. In another second the waiting will end. The day will officially begin. It's what he's been hoping for, but here at the edge of the river he doesn't want to let the waiting go. He wants to hang on with all his might. He's standing on the shore of the river, the brown-green ripples are breaking at his toes. The sun is shining, Julia's waving him on, the white barrels are rising and falling gently, and what he wants is to go back to the wooden sign with the tomahawk and start waiting for the shore of the river.

What's wrong with him? Why can't he be like Julia? He loves this day, doesn't he? Any second now he'll be standing in the water up to his knees, swishing his hands around. He'll go in up to his bathing suit. He'll wet his chest and shoulders, hop on the tube and paddle out to Julia. He'll laugh in the sun. Later he'll throw himself on his blanket, feel the sun drying out his wet suit. He'll eat a hot dog in a bun, drink pink lemonade from the jug. He'll be sluggish with sun and happiness. At the end of the day he'll change out of his suit in the creaking wooden bathhouse, he'll fall asleep in the car on the way home, under the streetlights. But now, as he stands at the end of waiting, something is wrong. He's shaken deep down, as though he'll lose something if the day begins. If he goes into the river he'll lose the excitement, the feeling that everything matters because he's getting closer and closer to the moment he's been waiting for. When you have that feeling, everything's full of life, every leaf, every pebble. But when you begin, you're using things up. The day starts slipping away behind you. He wants to stay on this side of things, to hold it right here. A nervousness comes over him, a chilliness in the sun. In a moment the day will begin to end. Things will rush away behind him. The day he's been waiting for is practically over. He sees it now, he sees it: ending is everywhere. It's right there in the beginning. They don't tell you about it. It's hidden away in things. Under the shining skin of the world, everything's dead and gone. The sun is setting. The day is dying. Grandma's lying in her coffin. Her crooked hands are crossed on her chest. His pretty mother's growing old. Her fingers are thick and bent. Her brown hair is stringy white. No one can stop it. Julia's dying, his father's dying, the Coke bottle's crumbling away to green dust. Everything's nothing. If he stands still, if he doesn't move a muscle, maybe he can keep it from happening. Things will stop and no one will ever die. His body's shaking, he can't breathe, here at the water's edge he's at the end of everything. You can't live unless there's a way to hold on to things. He can't go back because he's already used it up, he can't go forward because then it all begins to end, he's stuck in this place where nothing means anything, it's streaming in on him like a darkness, like a sickness, he's seen something he isn't supposed to see, only grown-ups are allowed to see it, it's making him old, it's ruining everything, his temples are pounding, his eyes are pounding, he feels a scream rising in his chest, he's going to fall down onto the sandy orange earth, "Ahoy, matey!" shouts Julia, and with a wild cry that tears through his throat he steps over the line and begins his day.

The Invasion from Outer Space

From the beginning we were prepared, we knew just what to do, for hadn't we seen it all a hundred times?—the good people of the town going about their business, the suddenly interrupted TV programs, the faces in the crowd looking up, the little girl pointing in the air, the mouths opening, the dog yapping, the traffic stopped, the shopping bag falling to the sidewalk, and there, in the sky, coming closer . . . And so, when it finally happened, because it was bound to happen, we all knew it was only a matter of time, we felt, in the midst of our curiosity and terror, a certain calm, the calm of familiarity, we knew what was expected of us, at such a moment. The story broke a little after ten in the morning. The TV anchors looked exactly the way we knew they'd look, their faces urgent, their hair neat, their shoulders tense, they were filling us with alarm but also assuring us that everything was under control, for they too had been prepared for this, in a sense had been waiting for it, already they were looking back at themselves during their great moment. The sighting was indisputable but at the same time inconclusive: something from out there had been detected, it appeared to be approaching our atmosphere at great speed, the Pentagon was monitoring the situation closely. We were urged to remain calm, to stay inside, to await further instructions. Some of us left work immediately and hurried home to our families, others stayed close to the TV, the radio, the computer, we were all talking into our cells. Through our windows we could see people at their windows, looking up at the sky. All that morning we followed the news fiercely, like children listening to a thunderstorm in the dark. Whatever was out there was still unknown, scientists had not yet been able to determine its nature, caution was advised but there was no reason for panic, our job was to stay tuned and sit tight and await further developments. And though we were anxious, though quivers of nervousness ran along our bodies like mice, we wanted to see whatever it was, we wanted to be there, since after all it was coming toward *us*, it was ours to witness, as if we were the ones they'd chosen, out there on the other side of the sky. For already it was being said that our town was the likely landing place, already the TV crews were rolling in. We wondered where it would land: between the duck pond and the seesaws in the public park, or deep in the woods at the north end of town, or maybe in the field out by the mall, where a new excavation was already under way, or maybe it would glide over the old department store on Main Street and crash through the second-floor apartments above Mangione's Pizza and Café with a great shattering of brick and glass, maybe it would land on the thruway and we'd see eighteen-wheelers turn over, great chunks of pavement rise up at sharp angles, and car after car swerve into the guardrail and roll down the embankment.

Something appeared in the sky shortly before one o'clock. Many of us were still at lunch, others were already outside, standing motionless on the streets and sidewalks, gazing up. There were shouts and cries, arms in the air, a wildness of gesturing, pointing. And sure enough, something was glittering, up there in the sky, something was shimmering, in the blue air of summer—we saw it clearly, whatever it was. Secretaries in offices rushed to windows, storekeepers abandoned their cash registers and hurried outdoors, road workers in orange hard hats looked up from the asphalt, shaded their eyes. It must have lasted—that faraway glow, that spot of shimmer—some three or four minutes. Then it began to grow larger, until it was the size of a dime, a quarter. Suddenly the entire sky seemed to be filled with points of gold. Then it was coming down on us, like fine pollen, like yellow dust. It lay on our roof slopes, it sifted down onto our sidewalks, covered our shirtsleeves and the tops of our cars. We did not know what to make of it.

It continued to come down, that yellow dust, for nearly thirteen minutes. During that time we could not see the sky. Then it was over. The sun shone, the sky was blue. Throughout the downpour we'd been warned to stay inside, to be careful, to avoid touching the substance from outer space, but it had happened so quickly that most of us had streaks of yellow on our clothes and in our hair. Soon after the warnings, we heard cautious reassurances: preliminary tests revealed nothing toxic, though the nature of the yellow dust remained unknown. Animals who had eaten it revealed no symptoms. We were urged to keep out of its way and await further test results. Meanwhile it lay over our lawns and sidewalks and front steps, it coated our maple trees and telephone poles. We were reminded of waking in the morning after the first snow. From our porches we watched the three-wheel sweepers move slowly along our streets, carrying it off in big hoppers. We hosed down our grass, our front walks, our porch furniture. We looked up at the sky, we waited for more news—already we were hearing reports that the substance was composed of one-celled organisms—and through it all we could sense the swell of our disappointment.

We had wanted, we had wanted—oh, who knew what we'd been looking for? We had wanted blood, crushed bones, howls of agony. We had wanted buildings crumbling onto streets, cars bursting into flame. We had wanted monstrous versions of ourselves with enlarged heads on stalklike necks, merciless polished robots armed with death rays. We had wanted noble lords of the universe with kind, soft eyes, who would usher in a glorious new era. We had wanted terror and ecstasy—anything but this yellow dust. Had it even been an invasion? Later that afternoon we learned that scientists all agreed: the dust was a living thing. Samples had been flown to Boston, Chicago, Washington, D.C. The single-celled organisms appeared to be harmless, though we were cautioned not to touch anything, to keep the windows shut, to wash our hands. The cells reproduced by binary fission. They appeared to do nothing but multiply.

In the morning we woke to a world covered in yellow dust. It lay on the tops of our fences, on the crossbars of telephone poles. Black tire-tracks showed in the yellow streets. Birds, shaking their wings, flung up sprays of yellow powder. Again the street sweepers came, the hoses splashed on driveways and lawns, making a yellow mist and revealing the black and the green underneath. Within an hour the driveways and lawns resembled yellow fields. Lines of yellow ran along cables and telephone wires.

According to the news, the unicellular microorganisms are rod-shaped and nourish themselves by photosynthesis. A single cell, placed in a brightly illuminated test tube, divides at such a rate that the tube will fill in about forty minutes. An entire room, in strong light, will fill in six hours. The organisms do not fit easily into our classification schemes, though in some respects they resemble blue-green algae. There is no evidence that they are harmful to human or animal life.

We have been invaded by nothing, by emptiness, by animate dust. The invader appears to have no characteristic other than the ability to reproduce rapidly. It doesn't hate us. It doesn't seek our annihilation, our subjection and humiliation. Nor does it desire to protect us from danger, to save us, to teach us the secret of immortal life. What it wishes to do is replicate. It is possible that we will find a way of limiting the spread of this primitive intruder, or of eliminating it altogether; it's also possible that we will fail and that our town will gradually disappear under a fatal accumulation. As we follow the reports from day to day, the feeling grows in us that we deserved something else, something bolder, something grander, something more thrilling, something bristling or fiery or fierce, something that might have represented a revelation or a destiny. We imagine ourselves surrounding the tilted spaceship, waiting for the door to open. We imagine ourselves protecting our children, slashing the tentacles that thrust in through the smashed cellar windows. Instead we sweep our front walks, hose off our porches, shake out our shoes and sneakers. The invader has entered our homes. Despite our drawn shades and closed curtains, it lies in thick layers on our end tables and windowsills. It lies along the tops of our flat-screen televisions and the narrow edges of our shelved DVDs. Through our windows we can see the yellow dust covering everything, forming gentle undulations. We can almost see it rising slowly, like bread. Here and there it catches the sunlight and reminds us, for a moment, of fields of wheat.

It is really quite peaceful, in its way.

People of the Book

My dear young scholars: welcome. Today you have completed the thirteenth year of your lives. On such a day, a day on which you have left your old selves behind forever, it is fitting that I should reveal to you a momentous secret. For by the laws of our forefathers you are no longer children, as you were yesterday, but young men and women, entitled to the fullness of adult knowledge. Now, I have no doubt that you are wondering, as you sit here before me, on this day of days: What is that momentous secret of which I speak? It is nothing less, my dear ones, than the secret of our people. It is the secret that distinguishes us from all other people. It is the secret that makes us what we, and only we, supremely are. You are well aware, my dear young scholars, that throughout our long history we have called ourselves People of the Book. Today I ask you to consider those words carefully. What do they signify? They signify, to begin with, that we revere books; that for us the study of books is the highest of callings; that we hold all books to be a reflection, however dim, of the First Book of all; that we consider every moment spent away from books a punishment and a desolation of spirit; that we believe, in every fiber of our being, that books, far from leading us away from life, lead us directly to the center of life, to all that is vital and everlasting.

But that is not all we mean, that is not even primarily what we mean, when we call ourselves People of the Book. For by that proud title we mean that we trace our beginnings to books themselves. We mean, my dear young scholars, that we originate from books. We mean, if I may speak to you even more plainly, that books are our ancestors. And by "our ancestors" I wish you to understand, in the broadest sense, all those books that have been born in the world up to the present day, and, in the strictest sense, those first Twelve Tablets from which all others spring.

You are of course familiar, my dear ones, with the Book of Legends. You have studied its stories. You have discussed the six levels of meaning under the guidance of learned teachers. Now, it happens that within the many volumes of the Book of Legends there are pages you have not yet seen. You have not seen them because until today you were children and therefore shut away from forms of knowledge not suited to your years. Among those pages is the Excursus in the seventh volume, which in its full title is known as the *Excursus on the Copulation of Books*. There we are told that in the beginning, when the earth was without form, and void, and darkness was upon the face of the deep, the Creator breathed forth the first words onto Twelve Tablets of stone. In this manner the First Book was born. Mark well, young scholars, that I have been speaking to you of the first day of creation, before the light was divided from the darkness. I have been speaking to you of a time before the creation of man. Now, those Twelve Tablets, into which the Creator breathed the breath of his incomparable being, were living things. And as living things they possessed the powers that rightly belong to living things, among which are numbered locomotion and copulation. Thus it came to pass, in those days, after the earth brought forth its creatures, and all living things flourished and multiplied, that when one tablet lay upon another, a new tablet was born. So began the coming forth of books, each one reflecting the original tablets, but more and more faintly. The reproductive virtues of the original tablets were passed on to their offspring, who in turn brought forth new books, each giving back a less perfect reflection of the first ancestors.

My dear ones, listen. As the generations of man began to multiply and spread throughout the land, a great discovery was made. It happened one day that a scholar, reading in a garden, under the shade of a pomegranate tree, grew tired in the warmth of the afternoon. And laying aside his tablet of stone, he fell into a deep sleep. It chanced that a maiden, the daughter of the house at which the young man was teaching, entered the garden. And seeing the stone tablet, which lay in the grass, she picked it up and looked at it curiously. Then the maiden sat down in the grass, and placed the tablet on her lap; and in the heat of the sun, she soon fell asleep. And behold, the divine spirit, which breathes through the generations of books, was present in that tablet of stone, and passed into the womb of the maiden. Thus she grew big with child. In this manner our race was born.

You see by this story, my dear young scholars, that our ancestors were born of a union between a tablet and a maiden, which is to say, between the spirit and the body, the word and the flesh. Now, you may well ask whether this method of generation is in use among us today. Although stories of such couplings are told, yet we read in the Commentaries that the power of generation was lost long ago, when the offspring of tablets, though bearing within themselves a dim spark of the living breath that had animated the ancestors, no longer retained that fructifying power. But do not despair, young scholars. For the power of passing on that original breath is the gift of our people; and as we grow fruitful and multiply, we who derive, however slantwise, however remotely, from those first tablets of stone on the first day of creation, so we participate in the animating spirit of the universe, of which we are the guardians and the perpetuators.

Since the birth of our people we have spread to every corner of the earth, where we mingle with ordinary men and women. How then shall we know one another, we who are one people, yet live scattered among far-flung races? My dear ones, we are known to one another by the outward signs of our inward devotion: the intense application to study, the habit of inattention to the physical world, the rejection of external distraction, a fanaticism of the desk. By our signs you shall know us: the back laboriously bent, the neck frozen, the head immobile, the eyes burning, the arms still as stone. Only the fingers occasionally move—just enough, and no more, for the turning of a page.

But how, you may wonder, shall such a people, devoted as they are to the perpetual act of study, carried on single-mindedly during the course of an entire lifetime—how shall such a people, who seek each day, in the faded reflections of multitudes of generations of books, the original splendor of the lost Twelve Tablets—how shall such a people live? How shall we conduct our lives? How shall we, with our furious dedication to the word, pursue a life in the world, with its myriad distractions and temptations? In the Histories we learn that in ancient days the practical duties of life were given over to the care of women and failed scholars. In this way the gifted among us were able to pursue their studies without worldly distraction, at long tables in communal libraries, interrupted solely by two sparse meals taken in silence, and by four hours of sleep at night. But even in those days the authority of women, although limited, was by no means slight. Exiled from the entirely masculine world of study, forbidden to strive for the highest reaches of the human spirit, they were nevertheless so completely in charge of the practical world that the scholars in their libraries were dependent on them for their very lives. In more recent times, of course, young girls have been permitted to engage in study side by side with boys, and are no longer prevented from attaining the highest degree of worthiness, while the duties of practical life have fallen to those of both sexes who, after the fifteenth year, have proved unable to live in the loftiest realm of rigorous learning, and so devote themselves to the useful tasks that sustain and nourish our people.

But even those men and women who serve the demands of daily life spend every spare moment bent over a book, since all of us have been trained to arduous study during our first fifteen years. Thus it may truly be said of us that even outside the highest domain of learning, we are all, in a very real sense, people of the book.

Because of our fervent devotion to books, my dear ones, it is necessary that our relations with them be clearly established by law, so that the spirit of excess, so visible in the history of our people, so desirable in all matters pertaining to the higher realms of existence, shall not be applied harmfully to the physical forms that bear upon them the outward signs of the indwelling spirit. You are all familiar with the vast Book of Laws. You have all memorized many passages. You know that the Book of Laws contains prohibitions which govern the relations between human beings and books. Now, the First Prohibition is this, that thou shalt not destroy, or mutilate, or in any way injure, a book, or any portion thereof. And this law, my dear ones, has been taught to you from your earliest years. But there is a second prohibition, which you do not yet know. And the Second Prohibition is this, that thou shalt not copulate with, or perform any manner of procreative act upon, a book. For although the books of our time no longer possess the capacity to engage in acts of copulation, as they did in ancient days, as recorded in the seventh volume of the Book of Legends, still it happens that a young person, or less frequently a person of mature years, feverish with the desire to learn, conducts himself or herself improperly with a book, as, for example, by laying the body with lascivious intent upon or beneath a book, or the open pages thereof, and must be punished. Now, the punishment for violating the First Prohibition, or the destruction of a book, is death. For a book is a living thing, as I have said. And the punishment for violating the Second Prohibition, or copulation with a book, is mutilation of the sexual parts. It therefore behooves you, my dear young scholars, to maintain proper relations with books, which is not to say that you should tame your fervor, but that you should direct it toward its proper end.

And having mentioned death, I would like to speak to you for a moment about the meaning of death, for us who burn with a desire to find our way to life, to the breath of the Creator breathed into the First Book of all. My dear young people, listen. Today you have completed the thirteenth year of your lives. And yet, if I may put it so, you already lie on your deathbeds. Your hands shake. Your eyes grow dim. Your ears admit no sounds. You are old, my dear ones, you are old. Birth, it is said, is the beginning of death. But it is not only the beginning of death. It is also the continuing of death, the continuing of all the deaths of all those who have come before you, since the sixth day of creation. When you are born, you are older than Adam, who lived nine hundred thirty years. You are older than Noah, who lived nine hundred fifty years. Methuselah, compared to you, is a baby who shakes his rattle. You are old, my dear ones. You are dying. You are already buried in the ground. You are born wailing, and why? Because when you open your eyes, Death grins at you from your mother's face. You come into the world with a knife in your neck. Your mother rocks you in your coffin. You learn to crawl inside a grave. The worm is your brother. Dead men's bones are your sisters. Who is the bridegroom? Who is the bride? Behold the two skeletons, kissing under the canopy. What is life? A sickbed in a hospital. The nurses are busy. The doctor is dying. No one will ever come.

Why then, my dear ones, should we live at all? What is the meaning of this dying that surrounds us on all sides, that lies in wait for us, day and night? And when you are mindful that it is not you alone who will die, but all those who are dear to you, your mother and father, your sister, your brother, your beloved friends, your revered teachers, your unborn sons and daughters; when you are mindful that all those who once were living are now dust in the wind; then it seems difficult, not simply to bend your mind to a lifetime of study, but even to rise from bed in the morning, in order to begin a new day.

But, you ask, can we not take pleasure in multiplying our kind? Can we not delight in passing on to the next generation our special task? For we do not live for ourselves alone: we live for our people, for all those who have yet to come into the world. Alas, in the Book of Prophecies we read that our people, so rich in wisdom, so rich in suffering, chosen above all others to find the undiscovered words, are destined to come to an end. There we read that the mountains will fall. The sky will grow dark. All mankind will cease. And a time will come when it is the seventh day, and then the sixth day; the fifth day, and then the fourth day; the third day, and then the second day; and behold, the last day of all; and thereafter it will be as it was before the beginning of days. That is what we are told in the Book of Prophecies.

Why then should we not despair, my dear ones? Why should we continue for another day? Another hour? Why should we devote ourselves to a long life of spiritual striving, in the full knowledge of our inevitable nothingness? My dear young scholars, I will tell you why. I will tell you that in the same Book of Prophecies, we learn of a way through the darkness. The cellar has a stairway. The grave has a door. Yes, my dear ones: yes. For just as that First Book, filled with the breath of the Creator, can never cease to be, so is it with all books touched by that life-giving power. My dear ones, my lovely ones, listen to me. Listen as I tell you of the Paradise of Books.

In the twelfth volume of the Book of Prophecies, we learn that books, like all things on earth, live out their years and die. Now, when a book dies; when, that is to say, a book crumbles to dust, or is destroyed by fire, or by water, or by pestilence, or by any of the innumerable accidents that can befall the creatures of this earth; when, for any reason, a book ceases to sustain its material shape: then, in the space of a single breath, it ascends to the Seventh Paradise, which is known to us as the Paradise of Books. There you may find the eternal and unchanging shape of every book that has ever been born. There you may find the generations of descendants of those first Twelve Tablets, whether they be of stone, or papyrus, or parchment, or paper, or any other word-receiving form. There, we are told, if you are among the most fortunate, you may come upon the First Book of all. Now, the Paradise of Books is the Seventh Paradise, as I have said. It is the place to which only scholars and writers of the highest spiritual striving can ascend. But all of us, by virtue of our origin, are entitled to approach the judgment seat, at the gates of that heavenly place. Therefore study diligently, my dear young scholars, and bend your minds away from worldly things, so that when you complete your dying, you will ascend to the Paradise of Books and live in joy forever.

And now you will understand me well, my dear ones, when I say unto you: Welcome to death!—by which I mean, Welcome to life, welcome to the breath that blows through all things, welcome to the Paradise of Books. The study and the library, in which you will spend your days, are emblems of that Paradise to which we all aspire. For though the way is dark, the end is dazzling bright. And I say unto you, my dear ones: Remember well the words I have spoken to you on this day, when you have completed your thirteenth year of life, of death. Now, let me ask you to close your eyes. Let me ask you to close your eyes and *see*. See the study-room. See the long tables. See the scholars at their books. Do you see them, the scholars in their clothes of black and white? They do not move. They make no sound. My dear ones, I ask you: What do they look like, when you see them there? What do they resemble? Are they not, by their stillness, by their inwardness, the very sign and symbol of a living book? Are they not tablets of breathing stone? For these are your people, whose origin you now know.

Then bless you, my dear young scholars, and be mindful, as you set forth on this memorable day. For on this day I have revealed to you the secret of our people. On this day I have shown you the meaning of death. For before the beginning *was*, the First Book *is*. That is the sum of all wisdom. That is all you need to know. My dear ones, my delightful ones, tomorrow is a new day. Tomorrow you will begin your long journey through the Commentaries. It is a journey that will last seven years. Some of you will fall by the wayside. The rest of you will persevere. At times you will grow tired. Your minds will grow perplexed. All life, all death, will seem to you a great riddle, which you can never solve. A darkness will come over your spirit. You will search for a way out, and there will be no way out. But in that hopeless place, in that blackness without light, remember what I have told you here today. Remember the secret of our people. Remember the Paradise of Books. And when you rise from the study-room, bowed down with weariness, then I say unto you, my dear ones: Lift your eyes to the heaven-shelves on every wall, lift your eyes to the living and breathing words that surround you, to the books that soar over you, lift your eyes in rapture, and know who you are: for behold, they are the Ancestors, row on row.

The Next Thing

1

The new structure rose on the outskirts of town, in the field next to the mall. It isn't true, as some have said, that we knew nothing about it at the time and were later taken by surprise. How could that have been possible? It was right there, next to the mall, a big operation only partly concealed by a high fence, with trucks going in and out every day, to say nothing of the ads in the local paper, telling us to get ready for the big event. I even seem to recall a sign somewhere in the area of the dig, with diagrams and pictures, though I can't swear to it now. So it just isn't true, as some say, that it took us by surprise, as if we were innocent, that it sprang out of nowhere, like a miracle. What they mean, in my opinion, is that we didn't really care all that much about it, at the time. The fact is, we knew places like that, we'd been going to them for years. Why should we care about another? And then there was the name itself: The Next Thing. That was a name that irritated a lot of us, made us skeptical and even resentful. It was the sort of name that seemed to smile at you and say, "I know you can't resist me," all with a sly wink. So I suppose it isn't entirely true that we didn't care about it, since our not caring was mixed with an irritation, a resistance to being treated a certain way. But I think it's accurate to say that many of us were in no hurry to go out there, once the doors finally opened.

Of course, those of us who stayed away were bound to hear things, there was no getting around that. It wasn't as if we were making it our business not to know anything, the way we might if we really hated it. What was there to hate? It was just another one of those places on the outskirts of town, with its opening-day hoopla and its vague promise of a better life. We hardly listened to the talk, though it's only fair to say that a few things did stand out as peculiar. When you entered the doors, people said, you found yourself in what looked like an immense office, with many cubicles, each with a person inside, and aisles going off in all directions. Another thing we heard was that the place itself was down below, in the basement. It struck us as an odd way to arrange things, the cubicles on the main floor, the shelves below, and that's mostly what we thought about, when we thought about it at all, in the days before we actually drove out for a look.

And we did go out there, as we'd always known we would, partly to see for ourselves, and partly I suppose to prove to ourselves that we weren't staying away in order to make some kind of point. A few did just that, of course; they had their reasons, the same reasons they always had; but for the rest of us, the ones who hadn't yet seen the place, it wasn't like that. We weren't in a hurry, that was all. What we found was the usual parking lot, the usual long flat stretched-out building with jutting wings and many glass doors. The first thing that struck us was the cubicles. I for one had imagined them very differently. They weren't formal and overorderly, as I had pictured them, but casual and almost festive, grouped in sections with wide aisles leading to down escalators. Each cubicle had three colorful glass panels and an open side, so that you could see into them and over the tops. What surprised me was the insides, which looked very comfortable and inviting—some had a few armchairs or small couches, some had a table and chairs, but all had little homey touches that caught your eye, like a table lamp with a fringed shade, or children's drawings, or a bowl of tangerines. So as you walked past the cubicles, you had a desire to enter, to look around. Here and there you could see a couple, leaning forward intently as a man or woman spoke to them. Even on that first visit, as I walked toward an escalator, I remember thinking that I ought to take a moment to step into one of the cubicles, see what they were all about.

The escalators went down, way down, crossing other escalators going up. During that long ride, you had the sense of shelves rising up all around you, higher and higher, until they were lost in the lights. If you held your eyes a certain way, you could make it seem that the shelves were moving and you were standing still. This was in the very early days of The Next Thing, but already the basement had a nickname: the

Under. People would say, "Have you been to the Under?" instead of "Have you been to The Next Thing?" So as I rode down, that first time, I thought: Now I'm seeing it, the Under. At the bottom, there was a feeling that you were standing on the floor of the ocean, trying to see up to the sky. The ceiling itself, I later learned, was one hundred and eighty feet high. You could tell that the architects had done what they could to counter the depressing effect of all that height—the aisles were wide, almost like streets, and here and there the management had set up Relaxation Corners, open spaces with couches and armchairs, where people sat reading newspapers or drinking mocha and hazelnut coffee from machines. Some of the crowd couldn't help staring up, like small-town kids in the big city. I stared too—it didn't bother me what anyone might think. The place seemed to have everything you might ever want, but a lot more of everything than you'd find anywhere else. I liked watching the big loading platforms that moved up and down the shelves from floor to ceiling, at intervals of maybe twenty or thirty feet. They looked like freight elevators open on all sides. There were also railed walkways, high overhead, that ran parallel to the shelves. Way up there, almost out of sight, clerks in yellow uniforms were unloading goods onto the platforms. Down below, youthful clerks in tan shirts and dark green ties walked through the aisles, trying to catch your eye, trying to see what they could do for you.

But I wasn't there to have anything done for me. I was there to—well, it would have been hard to say. I suppose I was there to look around. One thing you couldn't help noticing was the shopping carts. They were wider and deeper than the usual kind, painted bright red, with special flaps that folded out in front if you needed more room. Even better were the double-decker carts, high rumbly things that came up to your chest. You had the feeling that the people who ran the place had thought it all out, the big picture and the small. I think I was wondering what else they had to show for themselves, down here at the bottom of the ocean.

It turned out they did have something, though it wasn't anything like what I might have expected. I was walking along, going from one aisle to another, the way you do in a place like that, when all of a sudden things stopped. I don't know how to put it any better than that. The shelves just stopped. I don't mean I'd come up against a wall. That at least would have been something. I mean there was an emptiness, a darkness. You could see a pretty good way into it, because of the fluorescent lights in the high ceiling above the shelves, but after that came sheer nothing—blackness. About a hundred feet beyond the shelf-ends was a construction fence, and beyond the fence I could make out the top halves of excavators and dump trucks. Between the shelves and fence I saw dirt, rocks, a few sawhorses, an orange hard hat resting on the ground. You had the impression that the place was getting ready to expand, as it eventually did, though even at that time there were rumors of cellars being dug, of lots being marked off, out there beyond where you could see.

2

I came away from that first visit not knowing what I felt. That in itself was worth thinking about. I'm not much for the big noisy places, all things considered, though I'll visit them when they've got something I want. But this place—this place was so big that it was bigger than big; it was so big that big no longer made any sense. It meant the old words didn't apply—you needed new ones. You needed new feelings. You couldn't just know right off what to make of it, as you might have done with another place.

And so I wondered about it, tried to sort it all out, over the next days and weeks. One thing I knew was that I was curious about the cubicles. I liked their style, their air of patiently sitting there waiting for you to step into them. Come on, they said. Come see what I've got for you. And I kept remembering the slow ride down into the Under, with the shelves rising up, and the way it all ended in the dark, with a kind of promise of more to come. What I hadn't liked was the terrible height of all those shelves. I hadn't liked feeling that I was at the bottom of a place I might never get out of. But what bothered me most, I think, was knowing I would return. That isn't it, exactly. I didn't mind knowing that I'd be visiting the cubicles again, or riding back down the escalators. What I minded was that the place itself seemed to know I'd be back. It was very sure of itself, The Next Thing, very aware of its effect on people. That was the main reason I stayed away, longer than was natural, before paying my second visit.

In those days I worked at Sloane & Wilson, in the claims department. At lunch one afternoon, a colleague of mine told us she'd just switched all her shopping to the Under. She'd thought about it, she said, and decided it was the most convenient thing for her to do. A lot of people felt that way, she said. Someone said he didn't see what was so convenient about it, since the only way you could get down there was through the cubicles. Then someone else said he thought the cubicles were the whole point of the place. When I asked him what he meant by that, he came back with "Oh, you know what I mean," and wouldn't say any more.

That was the other reason I stayed away. You couldn't step out of your house, you couldn't walk down the sidewalk, without hearing about the place. They really were helpful down there, people said. The Under was always improving, people said. Already the loading platforms were being replaced by something better, new departments were opening every day, carpenters were hammering up a storm, out there in the dark. I listened to the talk, the way you do, but at the same time I didn't listen, I resisted it. I thought of other things. I knew it wasn't good to get swept up in all that.

Then one day I returned, there was no reason not to. What I hadn't expected was a new development on the outside. Covered walkways now stretched from the glass doors deep into the parking lot, as if to meet you and draw you in. The supporting columns were hung with surveillance monitors that showed people walking along, and between the columns, high up near the arched roof, white pots overflowed with pink and yellow flowers. Inside, the cubicles were pretty much as I remembered them, though busier than before. But either the arrangement had changed, or I had come in at a different door, because I'd gone only a short way before I became aware of a broad open space that looked like a park. There were clusters of trees, maples and oaks and some I didn't recognize, and picnic tables scattered about, and a stream with stones, and here and there you could see food stands with open windows. This was the Food Park, where you could buy a rack of ribs or a plate of pad thai or an ice-cream sundae with chopped walnuts and eat it at a picnic table under a tree, or take a stroll along one of the winding paths, which had places that widened out to make room for a wooden bench. You couldn't see the cubicles from the Park unless you were near the edges. Families sat eating under the branches of trees, kids were wading in the stream, and there was a relaxed, peaceful air about the place that reminded me of picnics with my parents by the river, under the pines, back in my childhood. You could see right away it was the kind of thing that would attract people, like a shady awning over a sidewalk on a hot summer day. I felt that I wanted to sit down by the side of the stream and rest awhile, like a traveler who has come a long way. Then I forced myself to turn back, before the shade could draw me in, since really I hadn't come a long way, not a long way at all.

I was startled to find myself back among the cubicles. There they were, one after the other, as far as you could see. As I made my way along, I noticed that many of the panels had small signs hung on them, with slogans like WE NEVER STOP or ALWAYS BETTER, ALWAYS BEST. Not all the signs were like that—some were more restful, like WE WILL TAKE CARE OF YOU or LEAVE YOUR WORRIES WITH US. I began looking for something in between, something that wasn't trying to convince me of anything, and finally I entered a cubicle with a small sign that said: WELCOME TO THE NEXT THING.

A young man of about thirty, wearing a light sport jacket and plain tie, rose from a table to greet me. He invited me to sit down, on a small couch with soft cushions. Still standing, he explained that The Next Thing took a close interest in the welfare of visitors and wished to serve us in every way possible. Would I care for a cup of coffee? I was, he said, free to ignore what he had to say to me, but he promised it would be worth my while to hear him out. At this point he sat down. He said he hoped I wouldn't mind if he spoke frankly to me. I told him go ahead, it was fine with me. People, he then said, could be divided into two classes: those who were unhappy with their lives, and those who were happy. The unhappy wanted to be happy, and the happy wanted to be happier, since even the happy had little pockets of discontent that limited their happiness and made them feel incomplete. The Next Thing, he said, was prepared to help both groups achieve their objectives. As he spoke, he looked directly at me, with an energetic and friendly attention, though once or twice he turned his head a little to look off as he searched for a word or paused before a phrase. This habit, I noticed, added a sort of drama to what he was saying, an effect that got stronger when he swung his head back. I saw that he was very good at what he was doing, whatever that was, and as he spoke I asked myself whether I was an unhappy person who wanted to be happy, or a happy person who wanted to be happier, or maybe a person somewhere in between the two, if that was possible.

He hoped, he then said, in a very polite voice, that I would permit him to put a few questions to me. I gave him a shrug and a sure, why not, and he proceeded to ask about my work, my home, my health, my retirement plans, and the degree of happiness I felt, when I contemplated my life. There were many opportunities, he said, at The Next Thing, for improving the quality of your life, each day and over the long haul. Some people moved directly from their current line of work into the same line of work at The Next Thing, at a higher salary and with a wide range of investment opportunities. Others preferred to enter one of the many training programs available at all levels. Still others were unsure, or afraid of change, and for them there were programs that addressed their fears and uncertainties. He himself, he said, had at first resisted the chance to improve his life, so he knew the kinds of fear that could get in the way. He asked me to fill out a form, which included questions about my salary, the estimated worth of my home, and the degree of happiness or unhappiness I felt, in my work and in my personal life. I would receive a letter within three weeks. At the end of the interview, if that's what it was, he stood up and shook my hand. "We believe we can help," he said. When I smiled and replied that I didn't need help, he gave me that direct look of his and said, "That's exactly what we mean."

I thought about those words on the escalator, but even on the way down I was distracted by signs of change. Below me, on each side of the escalator, I saw an arched surface stretching from aisle to aisle. Only at the bottom did it begin to make sense: each arch was a roof, spread overhead at a height of some twenty feet. The arched roofs, which covered every aisle, were attached to the edges of shelves and had been fitted with track lighting. The roofs, I knew instantly, were an attempt to overcome the oppressive height of the shelves, and it pleased me to see that The Next Thing had understood its mistake and done something about it. I say it pleased me, but that isn't all of what I felt. It bothered me, too—bothered me, I mean, that it was making an impression on me, bothered me that it pleased me, if I can put it that way.

Then I became aware that the new roofs had brought about another change. The loading platforms had disappeared. In their place, along the stretch of shelves that were waist high, was a series of black squarish panels. Each panel was supplied with a screen and two buttons, one red and one white. A clerk stepped over to me and explained how it worked. When you pushed the red button, rows of simple pictures—a clock radio, a floor lamp, a desk organizer—appeared on the PD screen. PD, he said, stood for Product Display. When you touched a picture with your finger, different versions of the item were shown on the screen. You selected the version you wanted by touch. Then you punched the white button, and the item was released from its upper shelf to a bin at your feet; the bin was flush with the shelves and had a handle at the top that allowed you to pull it open. The panels, called Virtual Boxes, were activated by a smart card, available to members of The Next Thing.

There were lines of people at the PD screens, and an air of confusion here and there, but all in all the replacement of the loading platforms struck me as a good idea. The aisle-roofs made you forget the towering shelves, the bins opened easily, and the PD screens were simple to use, once people got the hang of it. I figured the design engineers must have invented some way of cushioning the fall of high-up goods. Then I saw that I was getting drawn into things—I who had no interest in such places. But even as I drew my mind back and warned myself against the pull of the Under, I found myself walking along, listening to the sound of items dropping into the bins, searching for the place where it all came to an end.

For a while I felt lost in the aisles, which never ran for long distances but were always being intersected by systems of shelves at right angles. This, I thought, was like the new aisle-roofs—it was intended to keep you from feeling uneasy in the presence of vast spaces. You could see they wanted to tame the bigness, break it into little neighborhoods. As I continued left and right, I became aware of separate groups of checkout counters, scattered through the Under. And a question came to me, one that I was surprised I hadn't thought of before. How did people get their carts back upstairs? You could see shoppers on up escalators, holding bags, but what about the larger items, the lawnmowers and charcoal grills, the exercise bikes and Adirondack chairs, what about the heaped-up carts? A clerk in a tan shirt and green tie, who must have noticed my puzzlement, came up to me and asked if he could be of help. On hearing my question, he led me to a group of checkout counters. Behind them stood a row of what he called Returnways. These, he explained, were specially designed escalators with broad steps built to hold large items and entire shopping carts. The exit points of the Returnways, he said, were all located outside the perimeter of the upper building. You rode up to a system of moving walkways, which carried you over to the parking lot.

As I made my way through the aisles, I noticed that I was passing many Relaxation Corners, which seemed to have multiplied since my first visit. Some of the RCs, as people were calling them, now contained odd-looking structures: broad six-foot-high cylindrical columns, with wraparound screens showing views of different regions of the Under. On the screens you could see people filling their carts, checking the Virtual Boxes, moving along. The columns, a clerk informed me, were called Viewing Towers. They were there to help aisle coordinators check traffic flow. I thanked him and continued on my way. I was thinking about the towers when I suddenly found myself at the end of an aisle, looking out again into tracts of dark. But things had changed, even here.

The barren stretch of dirt was level and smooth, a smell of tar was in the air, and in the shadows I saw a yellow asphalt-paver moving slowly along, with a big roller behind it. The construction fence was gone. Farther away I saw a stand of black trees, with a faint glow over them. Through the trees, deep in the dark, I could make out a play of lights. They seemed to flicker, the way lights do when you see them through leaves. For some reason, probably because of the rumors, the flickering lights seemed to me the lights of streetlamps and house windows, in an invisible town, out there in the dark. And I seemed to hear, along with the clatter of shopping carts, and voices in the nearby aisles, the dim sounds of a summer night: laughter on a front porch, dishes rattling through an open kitchen window, a shout, a screen door shutting, a thrum of insects.

I turned back into the Under. It was very bright. There was a steady sound of goods dropping into bins, and all up and down the aisles you could see people lifting items out of the bins and putting them in their carts. Then it seemed to me that I was about to understand something, as I stood there watching the shoppers and listening to the unheard sounds of an invisible town. It was the sort of feeling you can get when you're standing on a beach at night, looking off at the dark waves, out toward where the night and the water come together, except that I was standing one hundred and eighty feet under the ground at the edge of the Under, looking down the length of an aisle, and what I was about to understand had something to do with the sound of goods falling into the bins and the flickering of those lights through the trees, but whatever it was I lost it, there at the edge of things.

I returned from my second visit as if I had voyaged to another country and come home to the familiar chair by the familiar lamp. The meeting in the cubicles, the Food Park, the PD screens, the lights flickering through the trees, all this seemed strange and unlikely in the clear light of a Saturday afternoon in summer. On my block, kids were playing catch. You could see sprinklers on the lawns, and in the air you could hear blue jays, electric hedge-trimmers, the bang of a hammer. Had I really been where I'd been? The whole visit was shot through with another feeling, an impression that is difficult to pin down. I think it was an impression of wariness, as if I didn't know what it was I'd just seen. Oh, I knew what I'd seen. I don't mean that. But there was some other thing I hadn't seen, something behind or within the things I was seeing. How can I explain it? The cubicles, the Under, it had all begun to work on me—that was clear enough. But I knew I wasn't going back there, not for a while. It's impossible to say why. But it was as if the place was too powerful, so that if you went back you'd be caught in some way.

3

It was during this staying-away period, when I was sorting through my impressions, that a letter arrived in the mail from the offices of The Next Thing. I was spending so much time trying to make sense of what I'd seen that I had entirely forgotten about the form. The truth is that I hadn't forgotten it, not entirely. It was still there, waiting for me, right next to other things in my mind, but I was doing my best not to pay attention to it, I was looking off to one side. A copy of the form was there in the envelope, along with a letter from an assistant manager. The letter stated that after studying my work experience, my salary, and my life wishes, the management was prepared to offer me a job similar to mine, in the Information Division, at a considerably higher salary. There was an on-the-job training program, in which I would learn how to gather information about hourly rates of sales in the housewares department and feed it into a database. Promotion to a higher level, at higher pay, with higher benefits, was open to me after two years of service.

The letter made the same impression on me that my second visit did. It interested me, it did more than interest me, it stirred me up, but at the same time it made me wary. The truth of the matter was, I wasn't all that happy with my job at Sloane & Wilson, where the hours were long, the rules of promotion blurry, and the future unclear. Over the last six months the company had been laying people off left and right. So it isn't hard to see why the letter produced an uneasiness in me. It was like having someone whisper something in your ear. It made me want to pull away—it made me want to wait. And it wasn't as if the letter was the only thing I had on my mind, at the time, since this was the period when we first began to hear about the house sales.

Houses in our town, we heard, were being sold to The Next Thing. They in turn sold them to their higher employees: product marketing managers, merchandising supervisors, purchasing trend analysts, customer taste engineers, package design coordinators, consumer desire directors, people like that. Now, there was nothing surprising about this, in itself. The housing market was in good shape, homes were being bought and sold all the time, it made sense that people who worked in our town should live in our town. Still, there it was, a fact to think about, a piece of information to turn over in our minds. The first thing we learned was that the people who were selling their homes had all recently been hired by The Next Thing. They had taken mid-level jobs as information gatherers, customer behavior profilers, product display developers, and shopper satisfaction regulators, as well as low-skill jobs as floor clerks, shelf loaders, aisle cleaners, counter helpers, screen watchers, and security facilitators.

The second thing we learned was that the people who sold their houses were moving into homes down below, which were being leased to them at very reasonable rates. It made sense, if you thought about it—the new workers were now much closer to their jobs in the Under. No longer did they have to drive to the upper parking lot, walk past the cubicles, and take a long escalator ride down to the shelves. Instead they could always stay on the same level as their work. Even so, we couldn't help wondering, those of us who lived above, how you could give up a home in town to live under the ground. When we tried to imagine it, we saw darkness down there, darkness and gloom. Then we heard—but this was still in the rumor phase—that the homes down there had certain advantages over the ones above. The new houses, it was said, had state-of-the-art kitchens with smooth-top ranges and granite-topped islands and hands-free electronic faucets, finished cellars, big-screen entertainment centers, hardwood decks with cedar furniture. As part of the lease arrangement, the landlord maintained the specially developed lawns, took care of the plumbing, repaired light fixtures and electric baseboards. Down there, the temperature was always mild, rain never fell, and no ice would ever cover your front walk. There was even some talk of benefits to your health, since you wouldn't have to worry about things like basal-cell skin cancer from overexposure to sunlight. All the same, we had trouble imagining a life lived like that, out of the sun, though we heard that the lighting was exceptionally good, and of course you were free to come up into the sunny world on your lunch break, or after work, or on your vacation.

When I look back on it now, it's difficult not to think there must have been a moment when things were at a point of balance, when they could have gone either way, so that if we had been more perceptive, more alert to what was happening, we might have kept things from going too far. Many of us believe this, and some even say it aloud, from time to time, in the company of trusted friends. I myself once thought the same thing. But now, when I think about it at all, it seems to me that there never was that decisive moment, which we somehow overlooked, but rather that things were set from the very beginning, and nothing we might have done, nothing at all, would have mattered, in the long run.

It's hard to remember exactly what took place when, but I'm fairly certain the next thing we heard about was the Discovery. It wasn't called that at first. At the time, it was just another thing people were talking about, in the streets and restaurants and bedrooms of our town. Three teenagers had wandered around the back of The Next Thing, where there were piles of wooden pallets and a coming and going of delivery trucks. The boys were chased away by a guard, but not before they saw large crates the size of refrigerators descending slowly into the ground. That in itself was nothing special. We knew the goods had to get down to the shelves one way or another. It became worth speculating about when a second elevator was spotted behind an old warehouse, at the far end of town. In the course of the next few weeks a third and fourth elevator were discovered, one behind an abandoned mill on a different side of town, the other in a clearing in the north woods. One thing that struck us was the great distance apart of these delivery elevators. Could there be others? We imagined a system of underground tunnels, along which the goods were transported. Or maybe, some of us thought, the elevators led directly to unloading stations in the town below.

Whatever it was, people in our town began to grow uneasy. Who owned the land below us? we wanted to know. Was The Next Thing buying up the ground right under our feet? We held town meetings, where tempers flared. Some people claimed that if you owned a quarter-acre lot, you owned the quarter acre of land under your land, all the way down, as far as you could go. One skeptic asked whether that meant you owned the earth all the way down to its molten core and up the other side. It was decided at last that the land below the town, starting at a depth of eighteen feet, belonged to the town and could be sold or leased. Large portions had already been leased to The Next Thing, and the revenues had benefited our town in every way. It was true that three members of the Board of Selectmen were already employed as consultants by The Next Thing, and this caused more meetings. At a referendum, citizens turned out in great numbers to vote in favor of continuing the lease, which was said to serve the interests of both parties.

Meanwhile houses all over town were being sold to The Next Thing, who continued to sell them to upper-echelon employees. The new owners maintained the grounds and exteriors but gradually transformed the houses into places of business, with offices where the living rooms used to be. Now it became possible to speak to a representative in your own neighborhood, instead of driving across town to the cubicles. A further advantage was that any item purchased at the Under could conveniently be returned to any of the new offices, just a few blocks away.

As these events were taking place in every neighborhood, I tried to make sense of it all. I knew that a great shift was under way, all through our town, but I didn't know whether it was good for us or bad. All I felt certain about was that everything was moving too quickly. I wanted the old slow feel of things, before all the motion set in. I had even stopped going out to the mall, which stood so close to The Next Thing that it seemed to be there only to draw attention to its rival. Besides, the mall was changing. It was beginning to have the half-deserted look of rundown amusement parks at the end of summer, of old movie theaters with springs poking through the seats. Empty shopping carts stood at different angles in car spaces on the lot. Even the old supercenter where I shopped, on the other side of town, struck me as shrunken, diminished, drained of life, a place where gloomy people wandered sluggishly, shuffling their feet. In pharmaceuticals, a bottle lay on the floor, in a thick red ooze; in an aisle in men's clothing, an overhead light flickered madly, like heat lightning on a summer night.

4

Late one Saturday morning, I drove out to The Next Thing. The building had changed. New wings and extensions had sprouted everywhere, and large doorways had sprung up, with sheets of glass stretching from the lintels to the roof. The whole was flanked by high white towers that had notches at the top, like the tops of castles. A blue flag flew from each tower, showing the letters NT in white. In the new wings and entranceways stood booths and counters marked for services: banking, mortgages, universal life insurance, eye care, funeral arrangements. The old cubicles were farther in, but many now had signs like LOANS and INVESTMENT COUNSELING.

After a while I came to the place where the old Food Park used to be. It was now a much larger park, surrounded by a wrought-iron fence with spiked pickets. Inside you could see fountains, pavilions, restaurants, gazebos, a merry-go-round, even a small zoo. A sign on an entrance gate said that access was restricted to employees of The Next Thing and their immediate families.

Down below, in the Under, shoppers moved from screen to screen, selecting their items, which tumbled into the bins. A few innovations caught my attention. On the row of shelves above the PD screens, I saw small stainless-steel disks the size of coat buttons. These, I learned, were audio surveillance units, or ASUs, which permitted personnel in distant listening stations to overhear and record customer responses to merchandise. Here and there, at aisle-ends or open plazas, I noted another development: red metal posts, about the size of parking meters, with a top panel containing a slot for a card. If you entered your Menu Card—which could be obtained for a reasonable fee in any of the cubicles—your purchases would be selected for you by computer. The selection was based on your shopping history and your answers to a detailed questionnaire submitted at the time of application for a card. Though the system was still in its early stages, I was struck by the vision itself: customers were invited to experience the atmosphere of shopping without any of the tiring effort associated with the act itself. You picked up your filled cart at an area near the cashiers, at which time you could remove items you didn't care to buy. Between the insertion of the Menu Card and the pickup of your cart, you might have a pleasant sit in a Relaxation Corner or wander toward the ends of the Under, where deep changes were in progress.

The rough area beyond the shelves had vanished. The ground was paved over and reached all the way back to the line of dark trees, with the lights flickering through. To my left and right, the asphalt stretched off as far as I could see. Men were working all around, setting up surveillance cameras on poles, putting finishing touches on curbed islands planted with bushes, erecting roofed walkways that led directly out from the broad aisles. I questioned one worker, a young man in a dark blue uniform, who told me that opening day was in a week. When I expressed surprise, he explained that people who lived down here—he swept his hand toward the trees—would soon be able to drive directly to any part of the Under, park in the lot, and enter without the obstacle of a door. Some sections of the lot were already in use. The aisles would be kept open round the clock, so that the bright-lit shelves would always be on display, but doorless openings at the aisle-ends would be supplied with security-tag detectors to prevent theft. The paved area entirely surrounded the Under, and the town was on all sides, behind the trees.

When I asked whether it was possible to see the town, the young man laughed and said I was already in it. The Under was the center of town down here, and folks lived all around. At this point he swept out his arm in a wide gesture, which seemed to take in the trees, the flickering lights, and all the dark. But I could see for myself how things looked down here, if I wanted to—all I had to do was walk across the pavement into the trees. Folks did it all the time.

It turned out that the trees formed a small wood, with winding paths and a road going through. Here and there, lanterns with glass panes hung from branches. On the other side, I stepped into a well-lit street that ran parallel to the line of trees, with other streets going off at right angles. I saw homes with glowing porches and bright yards, where kids were playing Wiffle ball or running under sprinklers. In the yards, bordered by white picket fences, lanterns stood on posts. Floodlights shone down from every house, and I noticed that long fluorescent lights ran under all the eaves. A dog lay in a driveway; a young mother was pushing a stroller along a sidewalk. Despite the darkness, I realized that it was the middle of a summer afternoon. High overhead, recessed lights shone down. A man stood in a floodlit driveway, hosing off his car. Telephone poles with crossbars lined the streets, and the wires that ran from the poles to the house sides glittered in the light of streetlamps.

Except for the day-feeling mixed in with the night lights, it all felt very familiar: kids playing, sprinklers turning, a boy riding by on a bike. It wasn't our town, since the houses and yards were a little different, but it felt like a version of our town, a town born from our town, a town more at peace with itself than ours could ever be. You could tell that some of this came from certain effects worked out by the planners, like the old-fashioned telephone poles with glass insulators on the crossbars, instead of the new metal poles you see everywhere, or the streetlamps with glass globes, nothing fancy, but reminiscent of better times. Most of the porches had old-style gliders, and I even saw milk boxes by the front doors. They were trying to take you back, you could see that, and you couldn't help admiring the general effect, even as you saw what they were trying to do. But that wasn't all of it. Up there, in our town, even at the best of times, you could feel a sort of worry, a tension, which flowed from the houses out into the streets and up into the leaves of the trees. I don't know where it came from, that worry, but there were times you could almost hear it, like a hum in a wire, on hot summer afternoons under a blue sky, or on spring evenings at dusk, in the stillness between the slam of a front door and the ringing of a telephone. It was just an impression, of course. But down here, it seemed, you could get away from all that and lead a different kind of life.

I came to a corner where two small girls with blond braids sat at a table lit by a streetlamp. They were selling lemonade, which stood in a gleaming glass pitcher that made you think of aprons and cookie dough. I was thirsty—they filled the paper cup to the top. As I drank, I looked up at the sky, with its soft-glowing recessed lights. I wondered whether the lights were dimmed at night, or whether they stayed the same all the time. I put the cup down and glanced back in the direction I had come from. Over the line of trees I saw the vast shelves of the Under, fiery with light, rising up in the darkness, like a city on an ancient plain.

5

I returned to the Under, rode up to the cubicles, and walked out into the parking lot. The sun was so bright that I had to shade my eyes with my hand. Heat rose from the asphalt and from the cars, brilliant in sunlight, sitting there row on row. I remembered how, not so many years ago, the parking lot had been a field of high grass and wild asters, next to the mall. Twenty years back, the mall itself wasn't there, this part of town was still farm country, and before that, who knows, bobcats and Indians. Things were always changing, there was no stopping it, and as I walked toward the car I had the feeling that if I looked over my shoulder I would see machines tearing down the building behind me, erecting steel columns, lifting sheets of glass high into the air.

For the next few days I went about my business, without thinking about anything. But I must have been turning things over in my mind, because a few days later I accepted the position offered in the letter. Two weeks after that I started my on-job training program. This took place on the ground floor, in a small office in one of the new extensions. About a week into the program I sold my house to The Next Thing at better than market value and signed up for one of the houses in a new neighborhood down below. It was a good location, away from the delivery depots. The lot was smaller than what I was used to, but the house had a granite-topped island in the kitchen, airtight triple-track windows, and a front porch with a glider. It cost me nothing except a security deposit and the first month's rent, and they even threw in the moving costs. It was difficult for a while, driving each day from my new neighborhood to the parking lot on the other side of the trees, entering the Under, riding an up escalator, and making my way to the office in the extension, but on the positive side I was able to go shopping without changing levels, the training program was expertly run, and I knew that life would improve once I began my new job.

In those days I still sometimes visited the old town, where things were changing. The small stores on Main Street were gone—Politano's Variety, Klein's Men's Shop, the tobacconist's and the newsstand—but the street had shaken off its slump and was flourishing: the old places were now specialty outlets of The Next Thing, with big plate-glass windows and new awnings, where people in the upper town could do their shopping without having to go down to the Under. On the outskirts of town, the mall had been transformed into a suite of NT offices with a new main entranceway and a second floor. Next to the mall, the old building of The Next Thing was closed for renovations, except for a single door where you could enter. Inside, I saw workmen bolting steel beams to columns as they blocked out the inner walls of a new five-story office building. On the ground floor, past the open door, only a few of the old cubicles remained. Through the wrought-iron fence I saw a flat expanse of dirt stretching away.

The houses in town were changing, too. All but a stubborn handful now belonged to top-level employees, who were building wings, adding floors, erecting upper balconies and decorative towers. I saw three-car garages, front walks flanked by stone lions, porches with high white columns, doors with stained-glass sidelights and Victorian fanlights. Birdhouses shaped like hotels hung from the branches of shade trees. Gardeners kneeled beside beds of geraniums.

I began work a few weeks later, in an annex built out from two aisles of the Under. That was fifteen months ago. The hours were a little longer than I'd expected, because apart from the official workday, nine to six, there was the scheduled work that had to be completed each day before you went home, so that you expanded your hours to fit the work in. Luckily it was possible to save time because of the short drive home. Since I had to pass through the Under on my way to and from work, I picked up what I needed during the week. On Sundays I sometimes visited the upper town for an hour or two, though I was usually so tired that I just paid bills and did the crossword puzzle.

Last time I was up there, I paid a visit to the old neighborhood. On my block I barely recognized my house, with its third story and its bay-windowed wing off the bedrooms. Across the street some high school boys were playing basketball on a driveway, with a high white house rising up behind. I watched them from the curb. They were tall, quick-moving, their hair shining in the sun, but what struck me was the grace of their bodies, the easy flow of their movements. Then I became aware of something else, which must have been there all along—a steady banter, a light playfulness, that seemed to grow out of the flowing motions, unless it was another form of the same thing. It occurred to me that I hadn't heard that sound for a while, down in my town.

As I stood there watching, a security guard in a dark green uniform strolled over from around the corner. He asked to see my Employee Number. "Planning to stay long?" he said as he handed back my card. He thrust his fingertips under the wide black belt around his waist and looked at me curiously. "We don't get many of you up here," he said.

These days my work keeps me busy. I usually don't get home till after eight, and there's a lot of pressure to do more, to show them what you're made of. It's what you've got to expect in an expanding organization like this. They want you to work hard, they believe in hard work, and if you slack off you get a warning. Three warnings and you're out—out of a job, and out of a house, since they won't renew the lease. You have to move to some other town and make room for the next employee. They mean business down here. After a long day of entering sales rates from housewares, electronics, and building supplies into a database, I like to come home and stretch out on the sofa, where I sometimes fall asleep in front of the TV before I make dinner. I work a half day on Saturday and generally go in for a few hours in the afternoon, and on Sunday, my day off, I do my catch-up shopping and my household chores.

Sometimes, when I'm wandering the aisles of the Under with my cart, or sitting on my glider on my lamp-lit front porch on a Sunday afternoon, I'll have a sudden memory of the town up there, where I used to live. I can see my childhood home, with its deep cool cellar and its sunny kitchen, and the later house, with the screened back porch that looked out at the catalpa tree. I remember the big rubbery leaves of the catalpa, the green cigars hanging down, the play of light on the porch screens. I like thinking of those houses, but that isn't the same as wanting them back. They're part of another time, that's all. Some people talk about that time the way they talk about everything in the past, as if it has a special glow. Well, it does have that glow. It's the glow of something you can't get to anymore, the glow of something no longer there. If you reach out for it, you won't feel anything at all.

Things have been pretty steady down here, though there have been some changes. The old Returnways were shut down about six months ago, and the last of the escalators stopped running fairly recently. People complain about it, but why should the escalators run if no one up there comes down to the Under, and besides, you can still climb the stairs if you want to get out for a while. Some of the neighborhoods down here aren't kept up the way they should be, especially the run-down ones near the delivery depots, where goods come down at all hours and trucks are always on the move. Sometimes there's a run on some item in the Under, like gas grills or grow lights, and they don't restock as fast as they used to. You can go to the Complaint Department and fill out a form, but the place is hard to get to and the lines are long.

You hear people say things are better up there, but I don't know about that. Isn't that what people always say, about someplace else? I've even heard talk about how we look different, down here. I suppose there's a certain truth to that. We're bound to grow pale, living the way we do, it's only to be expected, except of course for the ones who turn wrong shades of dark with their tanning lamps and their skin creams. In thirty years, some say, we'll all be soft white squishy things with fat legs and little squinty eyes. These are people who are usually trying to get you to join their gym or take some miracle health remedy. It's true there's a tiredness about us sometimes, a heaviness. You can see it in the Under. The other night I saw a woman from my annex just standing there, in the middle of an aisle, with slumped shoulders, not moving, her eyes not looking anywhere, her hands hanging down. But what do you expect, after working a long shift every day, six days a week? That explains a lot of the faces, with their dead eyes, their saggy mouths. People are tired, that's what it is. They move slowly, when they're not working. Chins hang low. Flesh builds over the hips, moves down over the tops of shoes. There's no escaping it. And if, as some say, people down here fall sick all the time with headaches and upper respiratory infections and what have you, well, they can go straight to the new infirmary built out from the Under and make up the work later. You'd think people never fell sick up there. You'd think people up there never had problems of their own. As I see it, there's nothing to be gained by wishing you had something else. Maybe it's true that things are different up there, maybe people up there get through life in a different way, without our troubles. Speaking for myself, I'm no worse off down here than I was up there, with more money in the bank from the sale of my house, though the hours are longer than I thought and the streetlamps keep flickering out. When a tree falls over you can wait weeks before a truck with NT on the side comes around to pick it up, and there's no denying they're behind on street repairs. Sometimes you hear talk about improvements, like an elevated monorail system that would eliminate ground traffic, but I'm not holding my breath. I don't care for the fortune-telling parlors that are springing up all over, or the fad for ghosts and spirits, or the new cults you keep hearing about, like the Fourth Millennium and the Prophets of Doom, though I suppose people need something to do when they're not working. Things may not be exactly what I thought they'd be, back then, but things weren't perfect up there, not by a long shot. As for work, everyone works, you work till you drop, it's how things are. In nine months I'm up for promotion, with a good chance of moving to the office next to this one, with a big window looking out at the lot.

The other day we heard that the last house was sold in the Over, which is what we down here call the upper town. Rumor has it that field personnel from the Contact Office have been seen in nearby towns, visiting malls, taking photographs, and questioning shoppers. There's talk of plans for new underground neighborhoods. You hear about bigger and better Unders, connecting tunnels, a town beneath our town. It's hard to know what to make of all that. These are interesting times.

We Others

1

We others are not like you. We are more prickly, more jittery, more restless, more reckless, more secretive, more desperate, more cowardly, more bold. We live at the edges of ourselves, not in the middle places. We leave that to you. Did I say: more watchful? That above all. We watch you, we follow you, we spy on you, we obsess over you. We crave your attention. We hunger for a sign. We humiliate ourselves—always. Hence our scorn, our famous bitterness. But what's all that to you?

My name, if I still have a name, is Paul Steinbach. I was born in Brooklyn Heights, in the middle of the last century. Of my childhood apartment on Joralemon Street I remember only a kitchen so narrow that I had to squeeze past my mother's legs, a little balcony behind a high window that I was forbidden to open, and a mahogany oval table covered with puzzle pieces. I can still see my father sitting next to me on a rug, opening a squeaky black bag and drawing from it, very slowly, a long snaky thing with a silver circle at one end. He raises the object solemnly toward my face, fastens something to each of my ears, and presses the cold circle against my chest. "Listen," he says gravely. "That is the sound of your life."

Shortly after my fourth birthday we rode in a train away from Brooklyn and never came back. Our new home was in a small town in southern Connecticut, where my bedroom looked down on a backyard with a clothes pole and two crab-apple trees. My father, who worked from an office in our house, struggled at first but gradually established a successful practice, represented in my mind, even then, by our move across town to a tree-shaded house with two porches: an open front porch with wicker chairs and a glider, and a screened back porch with the Brooklyn couch and my grandmother's armchair with lace doilies. I was a happy child, well liked by my friends, adored by my mother, and encouraged by my father in all my pursuits. My favorite pastimes were collecting minerals, building model ships with masts and rigging, and taking photographs with my own twin-lens reflex that hung on a strap around my neck. I want to emphasize that from the beginning I was a normal, ordinary, well-adjusted boy, without a trace of anything that might account for the fate that lay in store for me. In eighth grade I joined the Science Club and had a crush on Diana Aprilliano. In high school I joined the swim team, learned to ice-skate, and kissed Margaret Mason on the mouth at a Halloween party. In college two things happened to me: I fell in love with a girl I had known in high school, and after a brief flirtation with English literature I switched to pre-med.

With the help of a scholarship and a federal loan I went on to medical school in Boston. Let me be clear: I did not have strange ideas. I did not spend my time brooding over the mysteries of the universe. After a three-year residency I started my own practice, paid off the loan, and married the girl from high school. A year later I put a down payment on a house in our town, not far from the old neighborhood. We were happy for a time, then less happy. There was a miscarriage; after the second one we were told it would be dangerous to try again. She became moody, withdrawn; the joy of life seemed to go out of her. I could feel her floating away, like a balloon on a string that slips through fingers trying to hold on. One day she left to spend a few weeks with her parents in Florida and never returned. After a period of unhappiness I came to understand that it had to be this way. I was able to throw myself into my work and soon became active in community affairs. I even came close to marrying a second time, but something felt wrong, I pulled back at the last moment. Over the next years my practice continued to grow. My friendships remained strong. My health was excellent. Not long after my forty-sixth birthday my father had a triple bypass that left him weak and barely able to walk; he died from a second heart attack six months later. My mother did not survive the year. I sold the family house, consulted a financial advisor, and invested the money in a portfolio of mutual funds and treasury bonds that earned a steady seven and a half percent. At no time did my thoughts take a peculiar turn. My nature was practical. I moved my office to North Main Street and the following summer delivered a series of well-received talks on medicine and morality to the Ethical Culture Society. In this and all other activities I concentrated on the here and now. The riddle of the universe was of less concern to me than the prevention of a flu. I was invited to picnics and dinner parties, widened my circle of friends, and served on the Board of Health and the Regional Planning Commission. At the age of fifty-two I felt almost like a young man. My outlook was hopeful, my income excellent. I began to entertain the idea of marriage again. One evening toward the middle of September I experienced a slight episode of dizziness. I went to bed with a feeling of uneasiness and a heaviness on my chest. I immediately took out my stethoscope and listened to my heart and lungs. As I did so I recalled my father pressing the cold circle against my chest and saying: "That is the sound of your life." I vowed to stop working so hard, to take some time off; I hadn't had a vacation in a long time. I soon fell into a restless half sleep.

I woke in the early dawn with a pleasant sense of lightness, as if the weight had lifted not only from my chest but from my entire body. At the same time there was an odd kind of airiness in my mind that I had never experienced before. It wasn't a dizziness but a bizarre sort of clarity, as if I were able to perceive objects with unusual distinctness, while at the same time I felt sharply separate from them. I saw the lamp on the night table, the digital clock, myself in the bed. It struck me as strange that I should be able to see myself in the bed, and I wondered whether I was suffering from a disorder of the visual system. I was in the bed and I was outside the bed, watching myself in the bed. The figure in the bed did not move. I bent over and saw that I was no longer breathing. I remember seeing the tendon of my neck protruding, my hand rigid on the spread. On the night table my eyeglasses lay folded on a mystery novel with a cover showing a black gun and a blood-red rose. I thought: Now there is no one to return my book to the library. At that moment an understanding began to grow in me, like a ripple of terror, though even then I couldn't have said what it was that had happened in that room.

2

Let me linger over that moment. A sensation is growing within me—a sensation that I'm about to understand something. I pose a hypothesis: I,

Paul Steinbach, am suffering from a form of mental derangement that causes me to experience myself as two beings. My very ability to form this hypothesis makes me doubt its validity. I feel that it is extremely important for me to trust my senses, even though they may be misleading me. My senses inform me that I am observing my lifeless body on the bed. But who is this observer? I consult my memory. I see the oval table in Brooklyn, with its scattering of puzzle pieces. I see the screened back porch in Connecticut, the sunlight streaming through the venetian blinds in my boyhood room that looked down on the crab-apple trees. There can be no doubt at all that I am Paul Steinbach. Yet there he lies, Paul Steinbach, in his bed. I can see the familiar hand lying on the bedspread. The nail of the fourth finger needs to be cut. He is not breathing. I try to observe what I can of my other self, the one who's standing beside the bed, and I see a vagueness, a sort of ripple or waver. At this instant my understanding takes a leap forward, and without exactly knowing what it is I'm doing, I burst into a laugh.

That is what we do, we others: we burst into a laugh. It is the brash, uneasy laugh of one who is about to understand. There is another laugh that we reserve for the moment of understanding itself.

I fled. There was no reason to remain. I was about to understand, but I didn't want to understand. I wanted only to be elsewhere. How familiar I was to become with that desire!—the desire to be elsewhere. It is our nature. That, and the desire to hover, to remain.

I fled downstairs and out into the backyard. All my senses, such as they were, warned me to keep out of sight. The sky was a darkish luminous gray, the exact color of a smoky quartz crystal. A band of pallor showed in the east. At any moment the sun would leap up with a shout. I made my way through the tall hedge and entered the Delvecchio backyard, with its flagstone patio shaded by a canvas top. On the black-green grass a soccer ball sat beside a yellow sprinkler, silent in the dark dawnlight. Through hedges and fences I passed from yard to yard, under cover of a day not yet begun. Now and then I would hear a voice from a radio, the clatter of a dish. A length of downspout lay in the grass by a cellar window. I crossed Myrtle Street, disappeared between two sleeping houses, hurried from yard to yard as if I were being pursued. Once a cat on a porch arched its back and hissed at me as I passed. I fled across other streets, made my way into little-known neighborhoods. Here and there I saw a sudden figure standing in a kitchen window. In the east, the whitish band was turning pale blue. I soon found myself in an older part of town. Mailboxes with red reflectors that looked like gigantic lollipops sat at the ends of driveways. Here the houses were set deep among pines and oaks. I crept along the side of a garage, crossed a back lawn, slipped through a stand of spruce, and entered a backyard where a wooden swing hung down from the branch of an old sugar maple.

It was dark under the leaves. A coil of hose hung from a hook beside a porch with a sloping roof. A shovel leaned up against the railing. Night reigned in the dark yard, though day was breaking out above.

I climbed onto the porch and entered through the screen door, the wooden door. In the kitchen a single cup and a single dish sat in the dish rack. The living room and dining room were empty. The stairs were covered with a faded carpet. In the upstairs hall I found what I was looking for: a door that opened onto a flight of wooden steps. At the top of that stairway I stopped. I looked at the dark rafters, at the old bookcases filled with glassware and toys, at the dressmaker's dummy beside the sewing machine, and in the dark and permanent dusk I felt, for the first time that day, that I might be able to rest awhile.

3

For three days I remained in that attic, as if I'd been flung into prison. At some point during the second day I burst into another laugh: the short, bitter laugh of one who knows. Otherwise I was silent as a fog. When light streamed through the small window, I sought the dark corners; at night I prowled restlessly. An attic is the most seductive portion of any house, combining as it does the aura of the department store, the museum, and the ruined city, and I began to make myself familiar with its collection of objects. Here and there rose chest-high piles of brown packing boxes, each with its neat label printed in black marker: SWEATERS, BLOUSES, PLACE MATS, MITTENS AND GLOVES, GIRL SCOUT UNIFORM: 5TH GRADE. On a tilted wooden coatrack hung a broad-brimmed straw hat with pink plastic flowers, a knitted red scarf with white reindeer, and an extension cord. Beside an old carpet sweeper stood a twelve-room dollhouse with curtains on all the windows; four little dolls were seated at a table, leaning sideways in their chairs, as if they'd been shot. I saw bears, giraffes, elephants, an old black typewriter in a sewing basket, a tall porcelain vase that held a shiny metal tube from an old vacuum cleaner. At some point on the first day I heard a car pull up to the garage in back, a key turn in a downstairs lock. Footsteps struck the floor—a single pair of footsteps, as the one cup and saucer had led me to hope. Later that day I heard her voice on the telephone. It was a low voice, without much inflection. I could not make out the words. I became familiar with her sounds: the rush of water from the kitchen faucet, the whistle of a teapot, the knock of a spoon against a cup. She left by the back door in the early morning and returned in the afternoon, before other cars returned. From the attic window at the rear of the house I could see her car, a small silver hatchback, backing out of the garage in the morning and driving up in the afternoon.

I came downstairs on the fourth night. For when all is said and done, we are curious, we others, we simply cannot help ourselves. At the bottom of the carpeted stairway I saw her sitting on the couch in the darkened living room. She was watching television. A light in the kitchen had been left on; through the half-open door a glow came partway into the dark room. She was a stout mid-fortyish woman, with big pink eyeglasses and a small girlish mouth. Her hair lay in straight bangs across her broad forehead and fell to her shoulders. She was wearing some sort of flowered housedress with short sleeves. When she moved, a barrette gleamed above her ear. She looked like a little girl who had become a big matronly woman without ceasing to be a little girl. I stood watching her until she turned her head with a slight frown, as if she'd become aware of something in the room.

4

I began to come down nightly, during her television time. I wanted to observe her, I wanted to be near her, I wanted—oh, who knows what we want, as we stand there watching you and trying to make up our minds! There she sat, intently watching a crime drama or an office comedy while she sipped cup after cup of herb tea and nibbled on salted almonds in a dish. At first I was careful to stay at the bottom of the stairway and peer into the darkened room. Against the wall directly on my left stood a

CD player on a table. Then came a shadowy bookcase. The couch sat with its back to the bookcase, leaving a passageway.

After the first few nights I began to think about that passageway. Beyond the bookcase, in a dark corner near the half-open kitchen door, stood a lamp table and an armchair. It seemed to me that someone who was cautious but also deeply curious by nature could walk behind the couch in the direction of that armchair without attracting the attention of a person absorbed in a thrilling courtroom battle involving a beautiful defense lawyer and a corrupt judge. One night it happened. I walked along the passageway and sat down in the dark armchair. It was as simple as that. I was now closer to her and able to observe more of her: the other side of her head with its exposed ear, a moccasin sitting on a far cushion, her big pale knees. Had she turned her head, she might have seen him there—the stranger in the dark, waiting like a killer in a B movie. Did I want her to see me? Yes and no. After all, our condition is desperate. Ours is a savage loneliness of which you can know nothing. At the same time we are proud, haughty, unwilling to be known. For the moment it was enough to be in her presence.

Meanwhile I was getting to know quite a bit about her. Her name was Maureen, as I learned from the voice of someone on the phone. She taught second grade at the Collins Street Elementary School. She arrived home each weekday in the mid- or late afternoon, sometimes carrying small packages of groceries, as I could see from the attic window. She immediately climbed the carpeted stairs to her room on the second floor, where she changed out of her teaching clothes (scrape of hangers, bang of drawers) into her house clothes, which at night I saw to be either loose smocks printed with flowers, or oversized button-down shirts that hung down over baggy corduroys. Each night, at exactly eight by the mantelpiece clock—a white porcelain kitten—she called her mother and spoke to her while watching TV with the sound off. During these conversations she became tense and would rub her knuckles across her forehead or scratch her palm again and again with the curled fingers of the same hand. When she was through talking she would stride into the kitchen and return with a dish of malted-milk balls, which she devoured swiftly, as if angrily. The skin of her hands and face was very smooth, her nails short and polished. She fiddled a great deal with her eyeglasses, often removing them, holding them up toward the light from the kitchen, and returning them to her face.

It is not pleasant to observe someone secretly. For me at least there was in it no sense of exhilarating power, of mental or sensual freedom, as there might have been if I were a man of perverted appetites feeding on the sight of a seductive woman observed without her knowledge. What was it that I wanted, in that dark living room, in that lonely house, at the far end of town? To call it a desire for companionship would be to confuse it with more respectable realms of feeling. Our desire is infused with a darker, more ferocious longing: the desire for all that we have ceased to be.

I can't say when exactly Maureen became aware of my presence. At first there were small signs—a sudden tension in her neck, an abrupt slight shifting of her head, a pause in the movement of her hand, as if she were listening. I should explain that she was somewhat nervous in temperament, and it wasn't always easy to distinguish the new signs from her usual habits. Every evening she would get up to check the chain on the front door; she was always turning her head at the sound of a passing car. Sometimes she went to the kitchen, raised the shade, and peered out at the backyard. Once she called the police to report that someone was out there, behind the sugar maple—she'd seen something, she was sure of it. Every once in a while she sat up abruptly, rummaged wildly through her purse, and pulled out her cell phone, which was not ringing.

Now, it is my belief that these nervous natures, perpetually distracted by small disturbances in the outside world, are precisely the ones who prove unusually receptive to our kind. I began to sense a new alertness in her as I entered the room. Her body would become very still, her head would tilt slightly, her fingers stiffen, as if someone had crept up behind her and placed a hand gently on her shoulder. Once settled in my chair, beside the always unlit lamp, I would see her look around, very slowly. Sometimes she would stretch her arm across the back of the couch, place her chin on her forearm, and survey the part of the room behind her: the CD player, the bookcase, the lamp table and armchair in the dark corner.

One evening as I stepped from the bottom of the carpeted stairs and turned to enter the living room, I saw that something had changed. She was sitting on the couch, as always, but the television wasn't on. The remote lay on the coffee table beside the cup of tea. The room was dark, except for the light that entered through the half-open kitchen door. I sensed immediately that she was waiting—waiting for whatever it was that had begun to visit her. She sat motionless and alert, before the dead

TV. I hesitated. Wouldn't it be better to return to the attic, where I had made a home of sorts among the outcast objects of a life? Why risk the dangers of an unpredictable encounter? But we are curious, we others; we are driven by irresistible urges of a kind we ourselves can barely understand.

So for a long time I stood on that threshold, feeling both sides of an argument blowing through me like bitter winds, before I stepped into the room.

5

As I entered I reminded myself that she had become aware of something, over the last few days. Exactly what she'd become aware of I had yet to find out. At the very least she was aware that something wasn't right in her house, and she had taken steps to meet it head on. It was a show of courage that I acknowledged with a certain gratitude. My sense of her was that she was a lonely woman, a woman who might welcome companionship—even such companionship as mine. I was less sure of my own reasons for crossing the threshold. I suppose I craved simply to be in her presence, as someone shivering with cold might wish to be in the presence of a fire. But it was more than that. I could feel in myself a stranger desire: the desire to be seen. It struck me that I hadn't been looked at by anyone since the flight from my house, under the smoky-quartz sky, a trillion years ago.

The couch, as I've mentioned, stood in the middle of the room, where it faced the television. Beyond the couch, in the far corner, my armchair sat beside the lamp table with the unlit lamp. But there was a second armchair, a more sociable armchair, situated between the couch and the television, and facing neither. It was toward this chair that I now made my way, passing behind the couch and keeping my distance from the back of a head that suddenly struck me as a child's prank—at any moment I'd see the mop handle standing straight up between the couch cushions, the mop head peeping over the couch-back. At the end of the couch I swung around and made my way over to the chair. There I stood stiffly, facing her profile, with one hand resting on the back of the chair, like a bank president in a portrait.

She began to turn her head—not precisely in my direction, but in the direction of the empty chair beside which I stood. The fact that she'd sensed my presence, but had mistaken my position, filled me with a kind of nervous irritation that felt like an inward itching, and without caring what anyone might think I abruptly stepped around and sat down. But she had already begun to look past the chair, first toward the half-open kitchen door, and then toward a corner of the room that held a small table with a glass bowl on top. This second gesture filled me with such hopelessness that I had to turn my face away. At that moment I felt penetrated by the knowledge that this was how things were going to be from now on, this sensation of absence and emptiness, and that it would be far better for me to stop all the nonsense and return to my attic, where I would live like a spider or a bat. When I raised my head I saw that she was staring directly at me. One hand was pressed flat against the couch cushion and the other was raised to a point just below her throat. She looked like a woman who was protecting herself from a cold wind. I waited for her to leap up, to knock over the coffee table and send the cup of tea rushing across the rug, to stumble wildly from the room, but what happened next wasn't at all what I might have expected. Stricken with a sensation of awkwardness, of sorrow, and of terrible shame, I rose slowly from the chair, looked once in her direction, and made my way out of the room. During my retreat she remained sitting on the couch with one hand pressed to the cushion and one hand resting below her throat.

6

I remained shut up in the attic all the next day. During the whole of that time I paced fiercely—we know how to pace fiercely!—flinging myself down in corners, leaping up, moving about, collapsing onto a metal-trimmed trunk or a box of dolls. I was so furious at myself for my cowardly flight that I wanted to dissolve into ribbons of smoke. At the same time I kept summoning to mind the unfortunate moment in which I'd been seen. She had looked at me the way a woman in an alley at midnight might look at a man with a rag around his head who is holding a knife. It is not good to be looked at in that way. It's especially not good if one has come down from the attic in search of—in search of what? Shall we say, a pleasant encounter between two like-minded souls, in a suburban living room, of a September eve? And yet the craving to reveal ourselves spreads in us like a disease. It's also true that we long not to be seen, never to be seen, to live out our existence—our existence!—like growths of mold in the depths of forests.

At night I couldn't bear it anymore. I came down, but only to glance into the living room before escaping from the house. She was sitting there in the dark, waiting for me. She was waiting patiently—waiting tenaciously. I could feel that waiting like a distant storm. Outside, in the night, I felt a sudden sense of expansion, as when, as a child, after passing along the stream under the road by the side of the bakery, I came out onto a sunny field. Was it possible that I hadn't been outside in all this time? I turned defiantly from the almost dark house and strode out into the night.

We are always striking poses, we others. It's part of our unfortunate nature.

And yet I was happy enough, on my night journey. It was one of those summery nights in September when the sky seems to be the dark blue ceiling of an immense theater, which I had been allowed to enter even though it was long past closing time. Someone with a big pair of scissors had cut the moon exactly in half. I drifted from yard to yard with a sense of discovering new powers of movement. For though it's far from true that there are no barriers to our kind, nevertheless we range with a freedom that, under happier circumstances, might fill us with delirious joy. I made my way through hedges and fences with dreamlike ease, accompanied by inner ripples or flutters that felt like the very sensation of transgression. Now and then I strayed onto dark back porches, where I stretched myself out on a chaise longue or sat on a motionless glider before passing on.

Such pleasures quickly pall. I struck out beyond the world of backyards and soon found myself looking up at the stone pillars and tall windows of my old high school. Inside, I roamed along rows of olive-green lockers, drifted up the stairs, entered a classroom that I suddenly recognized as my English class of thirty-five years ago, though the desks had changed and something about the blackboards was all wrong. I had sat two rows over from Margaret Mason. I remembered the heavy sweaters she wore, dark green and brown-gold. From the high windows at the side of the room I looked down at the athletic field and the distant railroad tracks. I remembered the way she would push up the sleeves of those sweaters to reveal her long forearms. But already I felt a sharp impatience. What was I doing here, creeping around like a pale criminal in the teenage museum? Back in the corridor I found another staircase and headed down. As I turned into the first-floor corridor I became aware of a motion at the far end, as of a stirred curtain. With a feeling of revulsion, almost of outrage, I understood that I was looking at another of my kind.

Until that moment it hadn't occurred to me that I wasn't the only one. I had been feeling my way into the conditions of my new existence, brooding over my nocturnal visits to Maureen, accustoming myself to myself, in a manner of speaking—it had taken what energy I possessed simply to pass through the motions of my day. Now, all at once, I had the sense of stepping outside the narrow circle of my obsessions, into a wider realm. At the same time, as I've said, the feeling that seized me in the presence of my fellow outcast was not pleasant. Does the fat boy in gym class love the other fat boy in gym class? No, I kept my distance. It's that way with all of us. In time we tame it down, that quiver of revulsion, but it is always there.

What came over me now was a violent desire I didn't entirely understand: I longed to be back in the living room. Was it that, in the presence of my own kind, I longed all the more for what I could no longer be? The night journey had lost its power. I remember nothing of the way back.

She was still sitting there, like a marble monument in a park. I was aware of something awkward about her position and soon realized that she must have fallen asleep. She was leaning toward the far end of the couch, with her arm stretched along the couch-back and her head bent into her forearm. A pity came over me for this big girl-woman who had fallen asleep waiting for something—waiting for me—and I felt a momentary impulse to reach out my hand. It is not our way. It's never our way. I sat down at the other end of the couch and observed her closely. The pressure of her cheek against her arm pulled up one side of her mouth, so that she appeared to be snarling. Her free hand lay palm up in her lap, with the fingers open and slightly curled, as if she were holding an invisible tangerine.

For a long time I watched her as she slept—watched over her, I couldn't help thinking. I imagined that at any moment she would sleepily open her eyes. She would find me there—her protector, her brother. But we are sentimentalists, we others. She was dead asleep.

When at last I stood up to return to the attic, an awkwardness came over me as I loomed above her while she lay twisted against the couch in sleep; and suddenly, dramatically, extravagantly, absurdly, I bowed.

7

I thought about that bow the following night as I paced the attic wondering what to do. For though we'd established a rapport of sorts, I was reluctant to inflict on myself a repetition of our first meeting. Humiliation still flamed in me; to avoid another occasion for it seemed a kind of victory. Victory? For us there is no victory. For us there is only the sharper or duller savor of failure. We are the lords of desolation. We leave the triumphs to you.

Besides, darkness is our natural element, as Maureen herself had cleverly come to understand. Light harms us, like a shout in the ear. Instinctively we avoid the glare over the kitchen sink, the clock radio with its violent green numerals, the ominous night-light howling in its socket. We prefer the quiet place where the rafters slope down to the floorboards. In earlier times, before the fanatical multiplication of light, we were no doubt more present in the darkness of the world, more visible, more familiar, more woven into the fabric of things. I was pursuing this line of thought when I was startled by a flare of light that immediately went out.

She had opened the door to the attic—what I'd seen was the light from the hall—and immediately closed it. She was climbing the stairs in the dark. Maureen never entered the attic. That she had done so, and in the dark, was alarming and revelatory: she must have come in search of me. I was fortunately far away from the head of the stairs, well hidden behind a wicker hamper beside an old couch on which sat an enormous bear. Any movement might reveal me. At the top of the stairs she stopped. She stood there a long while—I could hear her breathing as if she'd run around the block. She took a step forward and stopped again. She stood motionless for a full five minutes before turning and descending the stairs.

I understood that I was in some sense to blame for having provoked this attic journey—that she was bound to search the house for a presence she felt had taken up residence. I understood another thing as well: it was in my interest to confront her on her own ground.

I listened for her footsteps in the living room before making my way down. She was sitting in the dark like a queen of the netherworld. This time I entered decisively, and as I did so I thought how rarely I had acted with decision since the moment I had entered this house. We are not decisive, we others. Or rather, our decisiveness is intermittent and erratic, with intervals of paralysis, so that what it most resembles is its opposite. Then I recalled that other life, where I hurled myself through obstacles with energy and certainty. But already I had crossed the room in front of her and was sitting down in the armchair that faced neither the couch nor the television.

I could sense the change in her, though she remained as motionless as the cushion she sat on. It was a sudden tension of alertness—a tightening that was also a readiness. All her senses had sprung open. I could see her face in the darkness, looking more or less at me but not precisely. Her eyes moved, as if trying to find someone there.

"What do you want?" she then asked.

I hadn't expected her to speak. In her voice I heard coldness, and anger—the anger of a woman whose privacy has been violated. I heard also a touch of curiosity. And there was something else I heard, something that seemed to me a kind of wary and distrustful hope. It was the hope of someone whose desperately dull life has at last taken a turn toward the unexpected—toward the unknown.

We do not like to speak, we others. We inhabit silence as we inhabit darkness—naturally. Even among ourselves, what takes place is a species of silent speech—but more of that later. At the moment I felt a dreary need to answer her.

"What I want," I said, and stopped. It was the first time I'd heard myself speak. I heard what sounded like a voice at a great distance—a faint, thin, rippling voice, a voice blown by a wind.

"What I want," I said again. "What I want—" The sound of those wavering words rang out in me like a cry. I felt a violence of wanting, a rage of bitter longing. The force of it frightened me, as if I had leaped out at myself in the dark.

"It's all right," she then said. "Everything's going to be all right." And I was grateful to her for those words, for she had felt my trouble; and I was angry at her for those words, for nothing was ever going to be all right.

8

She allowed me to sit there in silence—it seemed enough for her that I'd come at all. Nor did she object when I rose not long after to take my leave, though the look she threw at me seemed to say that I would find her there tomorrow, at exactly the same time. And so I visited her the next night, and the night after; it quickly became a habit. She would prepare carefully for these encounters. After dinner she changed clothes a second time—clash of hangers, thud of drawers—and sometimes there were long pauses, in which I imagined her studying herself before a mirror, or combing her hair with scrunched-up eyes. Back in the living room she would close the venetian blinds and take up her position on the couch, with her cup of tea and a book. Sometimes I heard a faint whirring or grinding sound: she was sharpening a pencil in the electric sharpener as she prepared a lesson plan or corrected a set of second-grade exercises. At eight o'clock she called her mother. After that came the malted-milk balls. I would hear low sounds from the television, and sometimes I could make out the clicks of turned-off lamps. Later in the evening I might hear a faint rattling sound: salted almonds spilling into a dish. At some point I heard her moving about the living room, drawing the long curtains across the windows. In the kitchen she turned off the overhead light, leaving only the fluorescent light above the kitchen sink. Only then was she ready for me. In the not-quite-dark darkness she would take up her position on the couch, drawing her legs under her, smoothing down her dress or fiddling with the knees of her pants, turning off the TV with the remote, and subsiding into stillness.

It was about this time that I would come down, for I too had been waiting. I would make my way over to the armchair and our evening would begin.

Maureen understood that I preferred not to speak, but she herself had a good deal to say. She spoke of her childhood in a small town in northern Vermont—she had read a lot, worn eyeglasses, and felt that her older, prettier, thinner sister was the one her mother really cared about. No boy ever gave her the time of day until senior year of high school, when Ron Olsen invited her to a party and left with another girl. She went to college at the University of Vermont and after graduation began teaching in elementary school in her hometown. At her school she fell in love with an older man, married him, and divorced him a year later when she learned he was carrying on with another teacher. She moved first to upstate New York, where she felt out of place, and then to Connecticut, where she'd been teaching for over twenty years. It was difficult for a single woman, the social life here was closed, her mother was always hounding her. She saw her sister once a year, at Thanksgiving, though she was close to Andrea, the older of her two nieces. Andrea was like a daughter to her, and visited her more than she visited her own mother—not that that came as a big surprise.

I listened with wavering attention to these revelations, wondering precisely what it was that I was doing there. It was true enough that I liked being spoken to—it hardly mattered what was said. Sometimes she would seize my attention by a sudden swerve in my direction. "I can't always see you," she might say, "but I always know you're here." Evidently we moved in and out of visibility, in accordance with laws that we ourselves have never understood. "Do you see me now?" I once said, in that quavering voice—for I sometimes broke into speech. "Oh yes," she replied. "I can see you real well. You've got your hair parted on one side—eyeglasses—strong chin—a distinguished-looking man. You're wearing a sport jacket—herringbone, I think—open—no tie. Your fingers are long." At other times she could make out my eyeglasses and my general form but without any detail. These are the things that obsess our kind. We cannot be told enough about ourselves.

I understood that what drew me to Maureen wasn't quite the same as what drew her to me. Though she was careful not to ask questions, I knew she was deeply curious about my history—she wanted to know me so that she could absorb me into her life. At times she behaved like someone who was engaged in the act of being courted. For me she was—well: one of you. I don't mean that I was indifferent to her. Not at all. There was a sweetness about her, a flirtatious innocence, that I knew how to appreciate. But I was what I was, and she?—she was everything I had left behind. We are drawn to you, we others, because you carry with you all that we no longer are. We are jealous. We're angry. We are filled with unbearable longing. It is not good for you to be with us. Maureen knew nothing of this. I could feel her terrible happiness.

Thus our evenings. After a longer or shorter while I would take my leave, silently. Her visible regret was appeased by the knowledge that I would return the next night. I could feel her anticipation opening in her like a wound. For my part, I was already restless. Back in the attic, I waited for her to creak into bed before making my way down the two flights of stairs and out into the night.

9

The pleasures of the night! I call them pleasures, those wistful wanderings, with their intimations of freedom, their little whiffs of forgetfulness, but really there should be another word. For me the night was a larger attic, in which my restlessness might more readily seek distraction. The dark was never dark enough. I avoided the streetlights that glared down at me even in rural lanes, the store lights in town, the warm-lit front windows. I was a wanderer in the forlorn byways of the night, a seeker-out of extinguished places. I welcomed the tilted headstones of unlit churchyards, the clusters of pines and picnic tables behind shut-down ice-cream parlors. There is a poetry of abandoned public places, and I became a connoisseur of the deserts of the night: the three dumpsters at the side of the car-wash, the piles of wooden pallets in the delivery lot behind the supermarket, the row of empty swings hanging from chains beside the slide in the forsaken playground. I was the companion of lawnmowers in toolsheds, of gas grills beside tarp-covered woodpiles. In the backyards of the night, rabbits sat like stone sculptures, then darted like leaping ballerinas across dark lawns. Raccoons peered out at me from behind fat garbage cans.

Let me confess it: I wasn't out only for poetry. The incident at the high school was with me still. Now and then I would come across one of them—a shadowy wanderer, a fellow seeker of abandoned places. We would acknowledge each other uneasily, abruptly, as our kind do, and pass into our separate solitudes. One night as I was returning home I entered a backyard and was startled to see two figures standing on opposite sides of the lawn. I say "see," but that isn't precisely the way we perceive our own kind. It's first of all an almost tactile sensation, as if one should enter a black room and know that someone else is there. You must understand that these are rough approximations at best, since there can be no question of the tactile with respect to us. Second, there is an immediate and absolute perception—perhaps that word will do—

of the other, which includes a knowledge of physical appearance. The distinction from seeing lies in our knowledge of certain aspects of appearance that cannot be gained from immediate sight—the back of the head, for instance, or the shape of a hand hidden in a pocket. It's as if, in the moment of perception, we experience the entirety of the other being, without the limitation of perspective that is characteristic of sight. So it is with us. I don't know why it should be so, only that it is so.

Two figures, then: one a man of about sixty, standing by the side of the garage in a rumpled suit, with the front part of his tie hanging out of his buttoned suit-jacket; the other a woman of perhaps thirty, in a blouse and knee-length skirt, with hair pulled tightly back, standing very erect under a tulip tree. They didn't seem surprised that I should have entered the yard. I stood by a corner of the hedge, well apart from both of them. There was nothing unusually awkward in this dismal meeting; I understood that they, that we, were waiting to enter the house.

Soon a figure emerged from the back door and stood on the porch. It was our sign to enter. He led us through the deserted house up to the attic. It was a much larger attic than mine, well cluttered, with high rafters and a series of subdivisions that formed smaller alcoves. It was the first time I had seen so many of our kind. Disposed on barrels and trunks, on broken chairs and old couches, here standing erect, there sitting on the bare floorboards, they filled the attic like an expectant audience at a theater. Indeed it was clear to me that we were all waiting for something to begin. Several new figures entered and made their way over to empty spaces. We are of course capable of occupying the same space, we others, but the idea is inexpressibly repellent to us. The slightest accident of that kind—an arm brushing through an arm—creates in us a sensation of nausea.

A figure of about forty, wearing a pullover and jeans, stepped onto a wooden box and addressed the group. But again I am giving a misleading impression. Among ourselves we never speak, we others. Our thoughts are projected, or emitted, silently and are immediately apprehended. It isn't a matter of having one's darkest secrets available to others; the thought, once formed into words, must be willed outward. This is the silent speech we use among ourselves.

The subject of the gathering was the nature of our being. Last week, he said, we had discussed whether or not we may be said to exist at all, and, if so, what the nature of that existence might be said to be. The discussion had ended inconclusively. This evening we were going to approach the issue obliquely, by considering one of the questions concerning our capacities or abilities in the world in which we find ourselves: namely, our relation to material objects. If, he said, as the evidence suggests, we are insubstantial beings, how is it that we are able to assume certain relations to objects—as, for example, a chair in which we have the power to sit? It is well known that we can pass through those very objects with which we can assume relations that appear to be substantial. It's also well known that we can rest for long periods in a manner bearing no relation to the material world. What then is our nature? What are our powers? Can we, as some have claimed, cause a material object to move? He had never witnessed it, himself, though he was open to persuasion. It seemed to him—and he'd thought about such matters for a long, long time—that although we were strictly insubstantial beings, we were, under certain circumstances, able to move in the direction of substantiality, or, more precisely, to adapt ourselves to the material conditions in which we found ourselves. Exactly how this came about was uncertain. More often than not, in his experience, it concerned the presence of them, in whose houses we took up residence.

I won't report here all that he had to say, or the discussion that followed. Suffice to say that I found myself drawn deeply into his words, which seemed to strike at the center of what I was. The gathering lasted far into the night before breaking up rather abruptly. I learned that gatherings were held once a week, in the attics of houses known to be empty for the night. For although we avoid others of our kind, we are also compelled toward one another by some inner command, which is perhaps no more than the desire of the freak to lift the flap of the sideshow tent.

Outside, the night had already lost its charm. I returned to my attic, from whose window a streak of dawn was already visible. As I settled into unrestful rest, wondering whether I was assuming a relation to the floorboards that might be called substantial, I could already hear the sound of Maureen moving from her bed to her closet, where she would throw on her robe before descending the stairs to the kitchen.

10

Let me pass briskly over the next three weeks. Things happen that way: an hour expands into centuries, three weeks collapse into the space of a sentence. My existence, to call it that, had begun to settle into a shape. At half-past nine by the mantelpiece kitten-clock I entered the darkened living room and sat with Maureen for an hour and a half. Afterward I withdrew to the attic, where I waited impatiently for the sounds of her bedtime routine. Then it was off into the night with me, as I sought out abandoned places and tried to come to grips with the unthinkable nature of my unspeakable existence—then up and away, as I fled that understanding and returned to the darkness at the top of the house before the first gray began to glimmer through the dusty attic window. Meanwhile I attended each weekly gathering as if I were a responsible member of a citizens' association concerned with neighborhood safety. Orderly in my habits, bourgeois even in my disarray, I could feel myself settling into my new unlife.

Not that the world was changeless around me. Fall was upon us, the trees—but what has that to do with the likes of us? We don't shiver, we don't require scarves and overcoats—those are for you. Nor does our melancholy have need of autumnal decors. Autumn, then: a fact, no more. What was changing was Maureen. Her waiting had become more charged with anticipation—I could feel it in the atmosphere. I could see it as well, for she now had a habit of changing into more elaborate clothes. One night I found her in a flouncy black dress that swooped down to her ankles, with a lavender shawl flung around her shoulders and big-loop earrings dangling like door knockers. Another night she wore a pleated mint-green skirt that came halfway down her thighs and a white V-neck sweater tucked into a wide red belt. Her hairstyles kept pace with her costumes: one night a frothy mass of curls, the next a tight updo with a French twist in back. Sometimes she talked in a rush, bursting into laughter and throwing her hands around; at others she sat silently and stared at me with an intensity that made me look away. Although she continued to honor my desire for silence, she began contriving ways to draw me into her talk. "I'm just going to ask you a question, and you just nod yes or no. Okay? Here goes. Do you find me a little—you know, attractive? I mean: this much?" Here she held up a hand, with the index finger one-half inch from the thumb. I wanted to tell her that, had we met at some other time, in some other universe—but what was the point? Her ardor made me restless. Did she really expect something of me? Was I supposed to take her out to dinner at the new bistro on South Main? I imagined the two of us sitting across from each other at a candle-lit corner table while people rose with their mouths open, their napkins falling, their wineglasses lying sideways on the red-stained white tablecloths. Even better: she would ask me to meet her mother. "Mother, this is Paul. Paul, say hello to Mother." I was elaborating this picture when I became aware of a change in the atmosphere. The air had become denser and was pressing against me. I saw that she was leaning toward me, slowly reaching out a hand. It's difficult for me to explain the sensation I then felt. It was a sensation of extreme alertness and above all of danger—as if something monstrous had entered the room.

I am not timid by nature and have never been afraid of the bodies of women. This fear was of a different kind—a warning that had flared up in every particle of my being. It wasn't a physical fear. It was the fear of a child alone in the dark.

I stood up. I stepped back. I fled.

At that time I still had much to learn about the relations it is possible for us to have with your kind.

She understood; she didn't attempt to touch me again. On her face, the next night, I saw only tiredness and gratitude—gratitude that I hadn't taken flight forever. For my part, I wondered with irritation why I'd come back. My position toward her was becoming impossible. What was I doing there? What was I doing anywhere? Banished from her kind, distant from my own, I was nothing—nothing at all. Even that wasn't true. If only it were! How I longed for the simplicity, the purity, of nothingness! Instead I was a something—a restlessness blown by a wind. I had sought her out for reasons still not clear to me, thereby awakening in her an absurd passion. I should have left that house, fled from that town, that solar system. But where was I to go? Besides, I was weak—we are all weak, we others. The weak are dangerous. Down with us.

During this time I hadn't neglected the gatherings. They had about them a touch of the Quaker meeting and a touch of the secret society. It was still necessary for me to overcome an instinct of aversion, but nevertheless I found my way up to those attics and sought out the empty spaces. Some held forth inanely and at wearisome length; a few struck at the center of things. I paid attention whenever the figure in the pullover rose from wherever he was sitting. He spoke more than once of the phenomenon of what he called "presence"—the showing forth of one of our kind to one of yours. The precise conditions of its operation remained, he said, unknown to us. It was clear enough that in order for the phenomenon to take place, a receptive temperament was necessary, though what constituted receptivity was far less clear. Some of us believed that only certain human beings possessed the temperament that permitted presence to operate, while others argued that any temperament was receptive under favorable conditions, even if it remained uncertain what those favorable conditions might be. But it wasn't only a question of the receiver. We too had a necessary part to play. We must, if he might put it that way, be receptive to being received. We must, in some sense, desire to be seen. It was true that there were cases in which we were seen unawares; such instances were uncommon, though not rare, and were not fully understood. There were also many cases in which the conditions appeared to be right, but presence was not achieved.

Such questions fascinate us, though they're of no particular use. I knew at any rate that I had become entirely visible to Maureen, with whom I continued my nightly visits. She kept her distance, a little too pointedly, as if to assure me, reproachfully, that I was safe with her. I accepted the reproach and was grateful in my own way that she continued to receive me. One night I sensed that she was distressed about something. Her hands kept fluttering up to her face, where she would touch her eyeglasses or push back strands of hair. Had I upset her again? There was no mystery: she poured out her trouble. Her niece was coming to stay with her for a week—a whole week. She'd be arriving tomorrow. Andrea visited from time to time, and they got on really really well, but now was definitely not a good time, as I could surely understand. She and Andrea always sat up talking—but now she couldn't bear the thought of sacrificing our evenings, since of course it was out of the question that Andrea should know anything about me. The only possible solution—she'd thought of many impossible ones—was for me to listen for Andrea's return to the guest room, after which I would come down and visit. She would stay up late, as late as necessary, so that at least she didn't feel she'd banished me—to say nothing about her own feelings of exile and the resentment she was bound to feel against Andrea, who to be fair was completely innocent and had problems of her own. She was the older of her sister's two daughters, and from the beginning she'd been a disappointment to her mother—a plain-faced little girl, given to fits of sullenness, withdrawn even as a child, which wasn't to say that she wasn't a wonderful girl with a tender heart, but her mother saw only the outside of things—and you could imagine what happened when Sandra came along, Sandra with those big blue eyes and blond curls, happy, lovely, laughing Sandra, who looked like a cheerleader even at the age of four. Oh, but that was nasty; that was cruel; Sandra was all right, really; it was her mother who spoiled her rotten, bought the beautiful clothes that, on Andrea, always seemed a little out of place. It was only natural that Aunt Maureen should have shown an interest in poor little Andy, whom her mother was all too willing to allow to be taken off her hands. And so a bond had grown up between them, the childless auntie and the unhappy niece, each with a sister so popular that there had been nothing left for anyone else. She'd seen her niece through the throes, and brother did she mean throes, of adolescence, when Andrea had begun therapy, and she'd been there for her on Christmas holidays, when sexy Sandra and the boyfriend of the moment came rolling into town—and even now, at the age of twenty-six, holding down a decent job at the ad agency and paying her own rent, Andrea would drop in on her old Auntie Maur from time to time, especially when vacations loomed with their promise of empty days. So here she was—arriving tomorrow. There was no way out of it.

At this point in the narrative she paused to look at me.

I willed myself into the expulsion of a few words, in that thin and distant voice that put me in mind of a mournful wind. I heard my voice telling her that I would follow her plan, that things would be—all right. She was leaning forward, listening intently, as if my words were difficult to hear. Gradually the tension left her face, though she continued to look worried. She leaned back, closing her eyes.

"A week," she said, and drew two fingers across her forehead. "Of course," she said, "with a mother like that." Her head slid slowly to one side, and I saw that she was asleep.

11

Andrea was for me a slower pair of footsteps, moving among the more energetic footsteps of her aunt. She spoke very quietly, with long silences and occasional coughs. All day she kept dragging her way up to her room on the second floor and dragging her way down again, as if she'd forgotten something but was in no hurry to find it. In her room, vague shufflings and pushings filled the silence. Later came the sounds of dinner, multiplied, interspersed with voices. The sounds moved into the living room: television, cups on saucers, low murmurs of talk. The night drew on. Slow footsteps climbed the stairs. Near the end of the hall stood a bathroom. Human beings turn a surprising number of doorknobs and faucet handles on the daily march to oblivion. The bed creaked. I went down.

"Do you think it's safe?" Maureen whispered, leaning toward me and jerking her head toward the ceiling. Without waiting for an answer she told me that despite Andrea's hard work, another girl had just been promoted to a position Andrea had every right to expect, it wasn't fair the way things seemed to go against her, and on top of all that her landlord had said something rude to her, something inappropriate, Andrea hadn't told her the exact words but it was the sort of thing that happened to women who lived alone, she'd have to look for another place, though that was easier said than done, what with rents being what they were, to say nothing of the expense and aggravation of moving, and of course Andrea didn't make things any easier for herself by her attitude, which wasn't hostile exactly but wasn't what you'd call friendly either, though who could blame her after an upbringing like that, and it didn't really help that she wouldn't listen to a word of advice, all of which she tended to interpret as flat-out criticism, even well-meaning advice from her Auntie Maur, who only had her best interests at heart. But good heavens, listen to her! The last thing she wanted to do was bore me to death with family troubles, in the precious time we had together, though one thing she did feel she wanted to say about her niece was that Andrea could be a little, what was the best way to put it, a little on the self-absorbed side, which was understandable enough, what with her problems growing up in that family, but still, it wasn't all that hard to imagine the needs of other people, who just might want a little time for themselves to unwind at the end of the day. Here Maureen took a deep breath and burst into tears. She immediately stopped herself and continued talking, as if her fit of weeping had been no more than a clearing of the throat.

As I listened to this rush of words, which came flying out of her like maddened bees, I contemplated my own relation to Maureen's niece. My whole existence had been thrown into an uproar by the presence of this shuffling stranger in the house. I was irritated by the ease with which my composure could be shattered. We become used to things, we unhappy ones—we resent the slightest change. I think it's because any modification of our precarious routine flings us up against ourselves, makes us glare at ourselves with a terrible clarity. At the same time we're helplessly curious about newcomers, who, even as they oppress us with the weight of the unfamiliar, attract our unwilling attention. I was curious about Andrea as a dangerous phenomenon in the house, as I might be curious about a flooded cellar.

When our sitting time was over I went out into the night. Far from experiencing a sense of release from the confusion of the house, I felt only that the night was a larger form of disorder. Those wild-looking trees with their billions of branches, that wobbly moon like a child's drawing . . . Back in the attic I could hear Andrea's mattress creaking like an old floorboard. She was a restless sleeper. I imagined her continually reaching out for something that wasn't there.

I heard her all the next day, moving slowly about the house while her aunt was at work. More than once she went up to her room and lay down. By the time Maureen returned home I'd begun to feel banished—driven into exile by those alien footsteps. I had also begun to feel a deprivation, as if I'd been condemned to experience Maureen's niece solely through the act of hearing. I felt—the word sprang up in me—haunted. Yes, I was haunted by this unseen creature who dragged her way through the house like an invisible monster in a tale for children. By dinnertime I could no longer stand it and had contrived a plan.

Andrea, as I've said, had a restless habit of climbing up to her room. My plan was quite simple: I would catch a glimpse of her in the upstairs hall. With that in mind I descended the stairs and positioned myself on the step just behind the attic door. I knew that she always turned the hall light on when she reached the top of the carpeted stairs and turned it off on the way back down. I listened for her slowly climbing footsteps, heard the click of the switch, saw the line of light under the attic door. The footsteps passed directly before me and down the hall to her room. She did something in her closet. The footsteps returned to the hall. For all I knew, Maureen's niece was a pair of ambulating feet without a body. The footsteps passed me and moved in the direction of the landing. The moment the light clicked off, I emerged from behind the door.

The hall was dark at one end and illuminated at the other by the light over the landing. I came out in time to see Maureen's niece standing at the head of the four carpeted stairs that led to the landing and the larger stairway below. She was wearing a loose-fitting long dark skirt and a dark sweater buttoned over a blouse. What struck me was the slope of her shoulders. It suggested a terrible weariness, the weariness of defeat—there was in it a whole history of disappointments, of failed expectations. She seemed to pause there, at the top of the stairs, her head slightly bowed, as if readying herself for the difficulties of descent. She reached out a hand to the wooden rail, stood motionless for a moment, and stepped out of sight.

I returned to the attic with the sense that I hadn't satisfied but only stimulated my curiosity. The glimpse I'd had of her was so brief that I would not have been able to recognize her in a photograph. Of her face I'd seen only a narrow pale streak, next to a broad dark streak of hair. She looked like a dashed-off sketch in an artist's notebook. I had planned to listen for her final return to her room and then go down to Maureen for my nightly visit. Now I decided to wait for her; to watch.

It is never clear to us how visible we are to you. I thought it best to keep out of sight, like the victim of a disfiguring accident. Not far from her room was a linen closet with shelves of sheets, pillowcases, and folded towels. I entered that closet and waited for her return.

She spent a long time with her aunt that night. Wisps of conversation drifted up to me like cigarette smoke. I was trying to decipher a sound that suggested a piece of wood tapping against glass when I heard her footsteps on the stairs. She climbed slowly, as if at the end of a long hard day that had drained her of energy, even though she'd gotten up only a few hours before her aunt returned from work. I heard the click of the hall light at the top of the stairs. I listened to her steps approach the linen closet and pass by. I heard her turn the doorknob and click off the light switch at her end of the hall. At that moment I emerged.

She stood with her hand raised against the partially open door to her room. I was much closer to her than I had imagined—some half-dozen steps away. Although the light from the landing was on, the hall was nearly dark where she stood. I could see her face in three-quarter profile: the tired anxious eyes, the mouth turned down at the corners, the fleshiness under her small chin. There was a heaviness about her—like her aunt, she had the look of an overgrown schoolgirl, with something mournful thrown in. Her hair was thick and heavy, and fell into a tangle of curls at her shoulders. She had so much hair that I wondered whether she liked to hide behind it. All this in an instant—she had already pushed open the door and was halfway through.

But now she stopped—abruptly—and glanced back into the hall, as if she'd sensed something behind her. Her gaze swept down the hall, toward the well-lit landing. Then she entered her room quickly and closed the door.

"At last!" Maureen whispered, as I settled into my chair. "I thought she'd never go!"

12

The next day, a Saturday, Andrea rose late and went off with her aunt for a drive in the country, to look at the turning leaves. I'd grown used to hearing her shuffle about the house all day in what sounded like very soft slippers, and the silence and emptiness irritated me—filled me with a devouring impatience. We are not good at whiling away the time, we others. We don't know how to take it easy. Loafing is not for us. Anxiety's our pastime, desperation our sport. For a long time I zigzagged back and forth across the attic like a bored beetle. At some point I discovered that I was moving down the stairs and out into the second-floor hall. For a moment I stood before Andrea's door, telling myself to go back, go back. Do not enter. Mistake. Go back. Sunlight filled the room like an angry crowd. At first I could barely see. Brightness lay over objects like a sheet. Then details began to emerge—a patch of pink, a swirl of blue. The curtains were pink and flouncy, drawn back with tasseled curtain ties. On the ruffled white quilt with its pattern of gigantic blue blossoms lay a big brown pocketbook and a roll of mints. On top of a chest of drawers I saw a white porcelain angel who rested one hand on the shoulder of a blue-eyed porcelain girl. A wooden clock shaped like an apple with a stem hung on one wall. On another I saw a framed painting of a girl with blond pigtails sitting on a swing and eating a pear. A dark blue suitcase sat in one corner.

From this bright and happy world I retreated into the black night of the closet. Two long skirts hung beside a fleece bathrobe. Wooden and wire hangers stretched away. A pair of fuzzy pink slippers sat on the floor.

A fine picture!—the stalker in the closet, waiting for the unsuspecting young woman to enter her bedroom. But that isn't at all what it struck me as being, at the time. At the time I felt curious, dissatisfied—I wanted to know more about her. That was all. For us, hiddenness holds no pleasure. It's nearness we crave—nearness and revelation.

I heard everything: the car pulling up, the footsteps leading to the back porch, the slamming of the screen door. Voices, a sneeze. A thump on a table. On the carpeted stairs her footsteps were heavy and slow. The sharp turn of the knob came a moment before I'd expected it. She was—as if suddenly—in the room. The bed creaked. I was puzzled by the next sounds, followed by a familiar thunk that explained things in reverse: she had untied a shoe and dropped it on the floor. People in rooms move around more than one might think. They pick things up, they put things down, they stride up and down like madmen, they look out of windows, they glance into mirrors, they push on. They never stop. A drawer slid open, changed its mind, slid back. A knock—a scrape—a creak of the bed. Many creaks of the bed. Had she picked up a book? Her breathing grew slow. I heard no turning of a page. I waited a little longer before I emerged from the closet.

The sunlight—the horrible sunlight—how can I explain? It was like a fistful of sand flung in my face. Even as I struggled against the glare I realized that it was softer than before—she had turned up the slats of the two blinds. Gradually I made out her form on the bed. I had expected to find her fast asleep, but she lay on her back with her eyes open. A book lay facedown on her stomach; it rose and fell slowly. She wore a long black skirt and a dark brown blouse. Her large bare pale feet were crossed at the ankles. I could see her broad face clearly: the somewhat petulant mouth, the heavy-lidded eyes, the large space between the bottom lip and the jaw. She wasn't what anyone would call an attractive woman. I cared nothing about that. I took her in gratefully, hungrily. We are greedy, we others. We can never have enough.

I'd been observing her eagerly, in a kind of daze of concentration, when I was startled into alertness. Andrea had sat up. She had sat up swiftly, violently, with a hand clutching the V of her blouse. She looked around the room in a series of quick sharp motions of her head, with startled pauses between. Even I looked about for a moment, in search of an intruder. She swung her legs over the side of the bed and sat suddenly motionless. She was leaning forward a little, as if preparing for a leap. Her immobility unnerved me more than her fierce movements. She turned her head—another abrupt motion. She sat there. She listened. She sprang up and was at the door. With her hand on the knob she looked back into the room—at the closet, at the window—and vanished.

I laughed: the short, bitter laugh that gives no relief. Then, without thinking, I stepped over to the bed, bent over, and inhaled deeply. Some claim that we have no sense of smell, we others, but I can tell you that I was penetrated by the odors curling up from that bed: the laundered, lemony smell of the white-and-blue quilt itself, the darker aroma of her clothes, the sting of a hand lotion, and the fresh-acrid scent of her body, which made me think of rye-bread toast and salted boiling water.

Behold the creature of bitter laughter!—bent over the bed in a posture of abasement. I glanced over my shoulder, as if to catch someone spying on me. But wasn't the whole point that she hadn't seen me at all?

I returned to the attic, where I roamed among cast-off things—my comrades, my companions in exile. Impatiently I awaited the sound of her footsteps on the carpeted stairs. That day she remained below. I waited through dinner, listened for the move into the living room. What did the two of them have to talk about? Hadn't they talked enough for one day? For a whole lifetime? I restrained myself, I crushed down my impulse to be a secret witness. Her footsteps climbed the stairs. She entered the room. After a suitable time, I went down to Maureen.

She was standing in the dark, smoking a cigarette. I had never seen her smoke before. "She suspects something," she said, in a conspiratorial whisper, and began to walk melodramatically up and down before the couch. As she paced, she held one forearm pressed across her stomach, with the hand cupping the elbow of the upright arm. She whirled and looked at me. "She knows."

13

What she actually knew was less clear than that she didn't want to know too much. Andrea had apparently told her aunt that she'd sensed something—something in the hall, something in her room—and had thought at first it might be an intruder before she'd realized that her mind was playing tricks on her. So much at least I gathered through the sharp bursts of cigarette smoke that erupted from Maureen like hisses of steam. At one point she turned to me and said in a fierce whisper: "We've got to be careful. She knows, she knows. Oh, she doesn't know she knows, but she knows. Hssst!" Here she held up a hand, turned her head sharply, listened. She shrugged. "I thought—" She listened again. "Do you think she's listening?" She waved at the smoke with swift short strokes of her hand, as if someone might be hiding in there.

Later, on my way to the attic, I lingered in the upstairs hall. Maureen had a habit of going to the refrigerator for a drink of bottled water and a bite of whatever lay at hand before she climbed the stairs to get ready for bed. In the unlit hall I stood before Andrea's door. A line of light showed under it. I could hear the turning of a page, the creak of bedsprings. My desire to enter the room was so powerful that I could feel it penetrating the door and coming out on the other side. But already I could hear Maureen's footstep on the carpeted stairs. Back in the attic I listened to her enter her room, across from Andrea's.

Please understand: it had been scarcely five weeks since I'd fled from my house through the dark dawn. I knew some things, but not many, about the conditions of my new existence. Even so, I recognized that my behavior had taken a turn toward the—well, toward the bizarre. I had always been a quiet man; a man of regular habits; a conventional man, if I may put it that way without the sneer that usually accompanies such a description. My relations with Maureen, peculiar though they might seem to an outsider, made entire sense to me. What didn't make sense was my behavior toward Andrea. I was no bender and sniffer, no lurker in ladies' closets. What had come over me?

Let me speak for a moment about the nature of our desire. We do not understand it, we others. Our relation to the world in which we find ourselves is murky at best. We possess the faculty of sight, though we see best in the dark. We hear, but the sound of our own voices is always disturbing to us. We are entirely without the sense of taste. Some of us are without the sense of smell, though I am not one of them. Many of us claim that we are without the sense of touch, though it's well known that we can adapt our shapes to the shapes of the world—we can sit on couches, stand on floors, climb steps. I would argue that we have a memory of touch, a shadow-touch that permits us to conform to your world. What then of desire? Our desire resembles yours in certain respects, with this difference: it expects nothing, it believes in nothing. Above all, it does not believe in itself. Why should it? We know who we are, we others. We are not-you. We have nothing to do with you. Which is to say, we have only to do with you—for without you, we are even less than ourselves, we are less than absences. Is this clear? Nothing is clear. A murky business, as I've said.

As for Andrea, I knew only that I craved to be near her—to be as near her as possible. I did not crave to see her naked body. Such desires have nothing to do with us. But the desire to be near, to be as near as possible, to be nearer than is possible, to mingle, to merge, to lose ourselves in the substance of a living creature—that is what we desire, when we desire.

After Maureen was safely in her room, I found myself in the upstairs hall before Andrea's door. I say "found myself" because I became aware of standing there without any memory of having descended the attic stairs. A moment later I was inside the room. It was entirely dark—she had closed and lowered the blinds and drawn the curtains—and it was only now, in that room, that I realized how very well I was able to see in the dark. She lay on her back with her head turned to one side and one arm lying across her stomach. The sleeve of her pajama top had been pulled back to the middle of her large forearm. I sat down on the end of the bed, next to the place where her feet pushed up under the covers. I felt gratified to be near her. I felt more than gratified, I felt soothed, as if my existence were a bleeding sore for which she—but this is a horrible metaphor. I leave it here as evidence of my agitation.

Andrea was a restless sleeper—I had known this before. What I hadn't known was how much, in sleep, she remained in motion. She moved each of her shoulders; her hands shifted position; her head turned until she was facing straight up. Then her whole body began to roll over. I had the impression that her body was a train traveling through the night, while she lay fast asleep on a berth somewhere inside. Now she lay on her outstretched arm. Now she turned again, onto her stomach. She took a deep breath, and was still—then rolled onto her back. She said, very distinctly, the syllable "nong." She sighed. She opened her eyes.

I hadn't expected her to open her eyes. She saw me—I saw her see me. She sat up violently, holding the collar of her pajama top against her throat. The gesture reminded me of her aunt. She held up her forearm, as if to prevent a blow to the face. I heard myself speak—that distant, despairing sound—and with a cry she leaped from the bed and rushed to the door, where she fumbled at the knob before escaping into the hall.

I continued to sit there, paralyzed with shame, while outside I heard Andrea tear open the door of her aunt's room and cry out "Oh god—oh god—" and as I rushed from that cry and hurled myself up the attic stairs, I could hear the women talking together, very fast.

14

In my high lair I paced and brooded. What else was there to do? I had seen the look of terror on Andrea's face and I could imagine with dreadful ease the dark thoughts of Maureen. I kept out of sight all day Sunday and came out only when it was safe. Maureen was waiting for me in the darkened living room. As soon as I appeared she whispered, "You scared the life out of her! She's practically—how could you?" She paced in a haze of smoke, waving her cigarette. "I told her it was all a dream. I think she—but she knows. She knows. I made her doubt her own eyes. I can't believe that you—in her room, of all places. What were you doing in her room?" I stood there stiffly while she shouted in whispers. Smoke swirled around her like river mist. Light from the kitchen caught her barrettes, her eyes. She looked like a creature in a chamber in hell. Jealousy flared in her like fire. "I thought we had an agreement—an understanding—" She flung herself heavily onto the couch. Her head lay against the couch-back. A hand fell to her lap.

I breathed out an apology and made an awkward exit. I had no excuses, nothing to say. Outside, in the night, I threw myself from one refuge to another, in search of calm, but there was no calm. I had terrified one woman and mortified another—it was time for me to banish myself to the ends of the earth. But where does the earth end? The earth never ends. Besides, where could I go, really? It was also true that I wanted desperately to return and set things right—I who was wrong in my very existence.

Back in the attic I paced and paused, paced and paused, like someone with a memory disorder who is searching for something that keeps vanishing from his mind.

Have I spoken of the dawn? We do not like the dawn. We object to its youthful radiance. We dislike its suggestion of new beginnings, of the uplifted spirit. We are creatures of the downward-plunging spirit, where hope perishes in black laughter. Some claim that at dawn we cease to exist, that we dissolve in light. Blissful thought! But that is pure superstition—or careless observation. No, we're there, always there, though in a weakened and faded way, like flowers that bloom only after sunset.

Dawn came. It was Monday morning: a school day. Maureen was soon stirring. When I heard her leave, I understood that I wasn't going to remain locked up in the attic like an insane relative shut away from the healthy part of the house. It was absolutely necessary for me to know that Andrea was all right. I understood that I was behaving foolishly, even recklessly, and that my desire to assure myself of Andrea's well-being was a mask for my imperious need to be in her presence.

I had known from days of listening that Andrea spent her time drifting about the house, but as I followed her—at a safe distance—I was impressed by the number and intricacy of her rituals of wasting time. In her long robe and big fuzzy slippers she sat at her late breakfast in front of an open newspaper that she folded carefully along the crease each time she turned the page. After this she folded the paper exactly in half and then in half again. Every few minutes she rose to go to the silverware drawer, or check the faucet in the sink, or look for something on the counter, or gaze out the kitchen window while she sipped her coffee. Later she brought her coffee and the newspaper into the living room, where she turned on the television and flipped through channels, never watching a program for more than three minutes at a time. She rummaged through her large pocketbook and removed a big comb that she pulled for a while through her hair. She went to the front door, opened it, and looked out. In the kitchen she rinsed one of her dishes and placed it in the dishwasher. In the living room she closed the blinds of each window and then partly opened them again. Once, in the kitchen, she looked around suddenly. I was standing closer to her than I had realized, but she saw nothing. She liked to rub the side of her nose, stretch out her arms, fling herself onto the couch. A moment later she would stand up and go into the kitchen, where she opened the refrigerator and peered inside with a studious frown.

Intermixed with her restless rituals was a different species of behavior, a nervous alertness or watchfulness that I observed with interest. She would turn her head suddenly, as if she'd seen something out of the corner of her eye. Or she would stop in the middle of a room, where she grew tense and still, listening with stern attention. It was as if she knew she wasn't alone, in that empty house, in the middle of the empty day. And an irritation came over me, for I had done my part, had I not, I had kept well out of sight, hadn't I?

At the sound of Maureen's car in the drive I retired to the attic. I could hear the vigorous sounds of their voices, crisscrossing far below. Perhaps they were arguing—what did I know of these women? For that matter, what did I know of myself? Of anything? Then I thought: My name is Paul Steinbach. I have fallen asleep in my bed. This is all a dream. Even as I welcomed the thought, I was repelled by its ludicrous triteness. There was nothing to do but wait. I waited. I waited for the sounds of dinner. I waited for the move to the living room. I waited for the slow, dragging footsteps on the stairs.

Scarcely had the door closed when I found myself rushing down the attic steps to the hall. In a moment I was at the landing. As I made my way down to Maureen, I became aware that I was moving more and more slowly, as if impeded by some substance in the air. By the time I reached the bottom I discovered that I had come to a complete stop—as in the old days, I couldn't help thinking. But these were the new days, weren't they? Maureen was sitting on the couch, in her storm-cloud of smoke. Ah, she was tired, desperately tired—she was coming unraveled before me. Her hair hung down carelessly. A button of her blouse was undone, revealing the bottom edge of a ghostly white bra. She sat there, a tired, middle-aged woman. I could feel harm flowing from me like ripples of heat.

I turned around and went back. Yes!—a coward. I confess it. Shall I say it again? A coward. She would have looked at me accusingly—pleadingly. I couldn't—I couldn't. In the attic I fell into a restless stupor. Dutifully I moved among her old things. Have I mentioned the porcelain cookie jar shaped like a panda? In a dusty green bowl lay an old eggbeater and a pink rubber ball. As I paced the floorboards I felt like an aging actor in an empty theater. At some point I heard Maureen's footsteps on the carpeted stairs. The footsteps irritated me, since they meant it was now impossible for me to go down to her. Even my irritation irritated me, for, when all was said and done, what good did it do me or anyone to know, with absolute clarity, that I had failed to rise to an occasion?

I was wondering how I would drag myself through the rest of the appalling night, while the two women in their big soft beds lay calmly out of it all, when the world burst open with a roar. That is to say: a sudden noise was followed by a jolt of light. The light swept across the rafters. It withdrew. I understood that the door to the attic had opened and a flashlight was shining up. She was climbing toward me. The beam of light wavered along the stairs like low fire. I saw her rising slowly into view like a creature from the sea. I slipped behind a child's bookcase filled with old puzzles and Golden Books. Through a crack in the flimsy back I could see her take two steps into the attic and turn off her light. "You're here, I know you are," she shouted in a whisper. "Are you here? Paul! Where are you? Why didn't you—" The flashlight burst into life—the beam swept across the floorboards, leaped to the rafters, rippled across the dressmaker's dummy and the old typewriter in the sewing basket. Off with the light—darkness swarmed back. "She told me there's something in the house—she's sure of it. She asked whether I'd ever—whether I'd ever seen—" She sighed. Then, in a fierce whisper: "Never!" She continued more mildly. "She won't sleep in her room anymore. Can you imagine? Too *haunted* in there, ha ha. Now she sleeps with me, like twenty years ago. A bit crowded in there, as I'm sure you can imagine. Well"—in a merry voice—"now you'll have to visit both of us! But you know"—here her voice dropped—"I'm so tired . . ." I heard her shuffle forward in the dark. "Oh, where are you? Paul? I know you're somewhere." The flashlight sprang on and she moved about, her beam of light held out before her like a sword. "You can't hide from me!" A moment later she said, "Please, Paul. What have I done? I'm sorry." Wearily she turned around. I could see the light shining on her moccasin slippers trimmed with red beads and white fur. She walked down the stairs, clutching the rail. I watched as she sank back into the sea.

15

At the sound of the attic door closing I felt a sudden stillness of relief. At the same time, in the center of that stillness, I could already detect the stirrings of the opposite of relief. That's how we are. Our rest is unrest, our peace is unpeace, our hopefulness has a heart of doom. Things were spinning out of control. I wanted to calm it all down, immediately, forever. Yes, I wanted to assure everyone that things would be all right, in the long run. If anyone had had the gall to assure me that things would be all right, in the long run, I'd have looked at them as one might look at an elderly woman in a nursing home who has said that she is waiting to join her dear mother in heaven. But there I was, eager to spread comfort wherever I could, even as I seemed to hear, behind my back, a howl of mocking laughter.

I hurried down the attic steps with no definite idea of what I was going to do. Or perhaps it's more accurate to say that I knew precisely what I was going to do but concealed it from myself cunningly. In my mind there was nothing but an image—those moccasin slippers, trimmed with red beads and white fur. There they floated, helpless and forlorn. It seemed to me that I needed to protect them, to save them from harm. Swiftly—like a cleansing wind—I entered Maureen's room.

She was sitting up in bed, in the dark, supported by a pillow that stood upright against a reading pillow with arms. "You can't—" she whispered, in that stifled shout. At the edge of the bed lay Andrea. She was on her side, facing the wall. Only her cheek was visible above the turned-back sheet. At Maureen's stifled words, Andrea opened her eyes and lazily turned onto her back. "What did you—" she said, and saw me. Clutching the sheet to her chest with one hand, she pushed herself back against the headboard and held up the other hand, as if directing traffic to stop. Maureen leaned forward in my direction, shaking her head and saying "No . . . no . . ." I looked at the two women sitting up side by side, their bodies touching, one pressed back against the headboard, the other straining forward, and what I most wanted, at that moment, was for one of them to move forward a little and the other to move back, so that both of them would be sitting shoulder to shoulder, looking at me with an air of quiet expectation, and in order to encourage this new arrangement I said, "What I want to say—" But at the sound of my voice, which startled me like a groan, Andrea held up a forearm in front of her face, while Maureen lifted her head alertly, raised both arms, as if she were offering me a tray of chocolate chip cookies, and let them fall heavily onto the spread, where they lay with the palms up. Unnerved by my voice, and by the sight of the two women, one staring at me from behind an arm held out across her face, the other looking sadly at me with her hands lying upside down on the spread, I felt like a man in a mask who had broken into a bedroom at night, and with a breath of apology, which sounded to me like the rattling of a distant chain, I left them there.

I left them there, but not so that I might disappear into the attic like another broken doll. No, the entire house now seemed to me a place of misery—I was eager to escape into the night. Exactly what I thought I might do, out there in the night, was as uncertain as my larger fate, but I found myself drifting from yard to yard, as on that first, fatal morning. After a while I saw that I'd come to a familiar neighborhood. I crossed a street, made my way through hedges and fences, and entered the Delvecchio backyard, with its flagstone patio shaded by a canvas top. The sprinkler and the soccer ball were gone, replaced by a leaf rake standing against the side of the garage. I passed through the tall hedge and stopped.

Nothing had changed. There stood my small back porch, with the four wooden steps and the white posts under the gabled roof. There was the cellar window with the taped pane. I wondered whether Paul Steinbach, M.D., was inside, asleep in his bed. I wondered whether he'd remembered to return that book.

In the kitchen I was startled by the refrigerator. It had become much larger in my absence. In the dish rack I saw a plate with a solid band of color along the rim, instead of the apples and leaves that ought to have been there. Somehow the old stove with its four burners had been replaced by one of those glass-topped ones. It was as if the house, in my absence, had decided to dress up in some way, like a child left alone in its parents' bedroom. Upstairs in the hall I lingered before a familiar door—his door. What, it occurred to me to ask myself, was I doing in this house, which had abandoned me long ago? But it was too late, already I was in the bedroom, where an alien chest of drawers stood against the wrong wall. In a bed with no headboard a man lay on his side. He had a straight sharp nose, with a raw pinkness at the bridge, where his eyeglasses must have rubbed. The rimless glasses rested on their wire temples on a book at the base of a new lamp. On the cover of the book was a photograph of a woman with a boa and a feather hat. Perhaps, I thought, I had fallen asleep many years ago and lay dreaming there. In my dream I had come to this place. And if I should wake?

The sleeper stirred. He muttered something, moved a shoulder, and lay still. An eye began to open. It fell languidly shut. It opened again. Now the man began a scramble, a sideways tangled sluggish rush among the bedclothes as he tried to twist away from me. One arm, caught in the sheets, beat about like a broken wing. I had the feeling that I was watching the antics of an amateur actor who exaggerated his effects. Something shattered against the wall behind me. I looked at the floor and saw the scattered pieces of a clock. Had he thrown it at me? "It's mine!" I wanted to shout, meaning the room, the house, his life. He was glaring at me with a mixture of wildness and wariness—a man in striped pajamas, rudely awakened in the middle of the night. In the morning he would recall his dream with bewilderment, with interest. There was nothing for me in this place.

Out in the yard I hesitated. I had fled from one home, only to be driven from another. I imagined searching for a new attic, in a new town, where I would start a new—but at this thought I could feel something stirring deep within me, and all at once I burst into a laugh. It was not a pleasant laugh, that laugh. But then, ours are not pleasant laughs. I turned and made my way through the hedge.

As I approached Maureen's neighborhood I became aware of a glow over the dark trees. I crossed a lawn, passed through the stand of spruce, and stopped in her backyard.

The house was ablaze with light. At any moment I expected to see flames bursting through the windows, leaping up toward the roof. By which I mean: all the lights were on—the kitchen overhead light, the sink light, the dining room light, the floor lamp and the table lamps in the living room, the stair light, the hall light, the bedroom lights, the bathroom lights. Even the back-porch light flung its harsh brightness across the lawn. Were they trying to drive me out by light? Like a crazed lover or father I stumbled across the brilliant grass into the blazing house. I rushed up the fiery stairway into the hall. The sharp light cut into me like splinters of glass. Behind the bedroom door I could hear them breathing quietly. I would never let them drive me from my attic. Even up there, the light was on—a single bare bulb that gave off a garish glow. Where there is light, there is dark. I made my way blindly toward a dark corner and threw myself down on the floor behind a row of peeling suitcases. A rag doll lay facedown beside me. Her yellow string hair streamed out like the rays of a child's sun. I tried to think what to do.

16

I was in the midst of imagining myself on the move, passing from attic to attic, across alien lawns, through unknown towns, in remote lands, as strangers in beds rolled wildly in their sheets and clocks shattered against walls, when the attic light went out. In the sudden darkness I heard the closing of a door. Footsteps shuffled in the hall below. It struck me that I had sunk so deeply into my thoughts that I hadn't heard the attic door open or the switch click off. Through the attic window the sky was black. For a while I lay there trying to make sense of it all. Was it still the same night? We are careless about time. We have too much of it. With a wary kind of suddenness I rose and passed across the attic and down the wooden stairs.

In the hall it was dark. I could hear the sound of breathing in Maureen's room and the sound of movement down below.

When I reached the bottom of the carpeted stairs I saw that all the lights were out. At one end of the couch, Andrea sat tensely upright in her bathrobe.

I entered the room and started to walk behind the couch, thought better of it, and passed in front of her. Without incident I reached my armchair and sat down.

"I'm not afraid of you anymore," she said quietly.

She glanced over at me and looked away. "I was afraid before," she said. "But I decided not to be." A pause. "I want to get to know you." She continued to sit upright, like a student in a principal's office.

Something about her awkwardness put me—I was going to say: at ease. But we are never at ease. It's more accurate to say that the unease which is my nature became a little less uneasy, like a fist relaxing slightly—the knuckles are no longer white, but the fist remains closed.

"I turned on all the lights," she said. "But later I went back and turned them all off." She raised a hand to her hair, wound a strand round and round a finger, then removed her finger and lowered her hand. She turned her head toward me and held it there.

She continued to hold it there as I began to speak. My voice sounded to me like the rustle of dry leaves. Even in my past life I was a man of few words, but on this night I told my story: the unbreathing figure in the bed, the dawn flight, the wooden steps to the attic, the visits to her aunt. It occurred to me, with surprise, that I really did have a story to tell.

When I came to the end I waited for her to pour out her own story, but she said simply, "Thank you." A sudden yawn, deep and shuddering, seized her. She thrust a hand across her mouth as if she were trying to stifle a laugh. "Oh god," she said. "That had nothing to do with—it's just so late. Look! It's practically morning." Through the drawn drapes I could see a faint lightness.

She stood up. "She'll worry about me." She looked at me. "I hope we can be friends now." At once she turned away, walking with great strides, swinging out of sight and thrusting herself heavily up the stairs.

Above, a door shut. I remained alone in the empty room. I imagined Andrea striding fiercely through the house, turning on light after light, faster and faster. When all the lights are on, she returns to Maureen's room. She lies down on the bed with her eyes open. She says nothing. After a while she gets up. She looks around. Then she walks back through the house, turning each light off, one after the other.

17

The next day it rained. It was one of those violent autumn rains that hurl themselves against roofs and attic windows, while through the water-sheeted glass there's nothing to see but the bleak dark sky and the branches bending in the wind. The attic was dusky-dark. A good day for solitude! That was the thought that presented itself to my mind as I made my way down the attic stairs in search of—something else. Through the storm I had heard Maureen's car backing out of the drive. I was struck by the gloom of the upper hall, as if the storm clouds had penetrated the house itself. Then I saw that the shade had been drawn on the window at the end of the hall and the two ruffled curtains pulled together. For some reason I thought: They have left me here, they have all gone away. When I reached the bottom of the carpeted stairs I saw that all the shades had been drawn and the curtains closed. A sullen day-darkness hung in the house. Andrea was sitting on the couch, in her bathrobe, erect but with half-closed eyes.

She raised an arm and swept her hand vaguely sideways before letting it drop to the couch cushion. It rose and came to rest in her lap. "I wanted you to feel—welcome," she said, without turning to look at me.

I walked past the couch in silence and settled into my armchair. The word "welcome" had irritated me, and I looked at her without pleasure. I wanted to shout: We never feel welcome!—but I sat there, listening to the windows rattling behind the closed curtains. I stared at her large hands resting awkwardly in her big lap.

She said, "Auntie Maur told me you like to—I don't know, sit with her at night, and I thought maybe if we—I like rain, rainy days." She paused. "It's all right if you don't feel like talking. We can just sit here."

After a while she said, "I'm going to make some tea now. I think a cup of tea would be nice. I'll be right back."

I watched her go slowly past my chair into the kitchen. There was strain in her face, and her stride was slightly wrong in some way, as if she were practicing a walk in front of a mirror. As I listened to her moving about in the kitchen, the thought occurred to me that now would be a good time to rise from my chair and pass out the door into the storm, never to return. I sat there thinking this thought and hearing the sound of the rain against the house, and of the teapot as she set it down on the stove.

All that dark morning she passed back and forth between the kitchen and the living room, carrying cups of tea, plates of crackers, glasses of juice. In the living room she would sit for a while over her tea, then stand up and go to a window. There she pushed aside a curtain and looked out at the rain. Moments later she would go over to the bookcase, take out a book, and bring it to the couch, where she opened it up and immediately put it aside. Sometimes she went into the kitchen, washed a cup, and set it in the dish rack to dry. Even when she sat still she was always in motion, stretching out her arms and interlocking her hands, or raking her fingers through her tangled hair. She rarely looked in my direction, but from time to time would utter a few words intended for me, such as "These rainy days are really something" or "I can see you better now." Even as she moved restlessly about, I was sharply aware of her awareness of me. I noticed that she was very careful to keep a good distance between us at all times; but it was when she was farthest from me, across the room or hidden away in the kitchen, that I most had the feeling she had somehow wrapped an arm around me and brought me with her.

At lunchtime she carried her plate with its sandwich and her saucer with its cup of tea into the living room, where she placed them on the coffee table. She ate bending over awkwardly, while repeatedly wiping her mouth with a napkin.

After lunch she brought her dishes back to the kitchen and returned to sit on the couch. She leaned back and closed her eyes. Slowly her mouth began to open; she covered it with a hand. "Days like this," she said, "make me sleepy." She shifted on the couch. Then she stood up, pushed a hand through her hair, and began walking toward the stairway.

There she stopped, glanced in my direction, and began climbing the stairs.

I listened to her clumping up the stairs in her fuzzy pink slippers. In the dusky light of the living room a restlessness came over me, and as I rose from the armchair I had the odd sense that she was watching me from the landing, even though she was no longer in view.

When I reached the top of the stairs, no one was there. I could hear the rain against the curtained window at the end of the hall. I made my way past the closed door of the attic to a door that stood partway open, and with a feeling of anxiety I entered Maureen's room.

The curtain had been drawn. Andrea lay on one side of the bed with an arm over her eyes. I sat down on the other side of the bed and then lay down. I have already mentioned the sensation of danger that flares in us when the distance between us and you grows too close. That sensation was leaping in me as I lay on the bed beside this young woman with the fuzzy pink slippers who lay on her back with an arm flung over her face. But I was aware of a second sensation as well. This might be described as a sensation of disobedience, a rebellion against the very warning that sounded in me like a cry. It's the feeling of a child who reaches toward the fire and, despite the heat scorching his hand, reaches farther. Was it perhaps only a desire to know? I forced myself closer to the flame, which in this case was also an icy wind. As I crossed the boundary I felt an unraveling, a fierce dissolution. Flesh stops at flesh—but we others, we mingle entirely, we invade and penetrate like rays of light, like dark smoke. I felt myself spreading through her like wind in a room. Who knows how long it lasted? At some point I found myself separate from her. I lay there unmoving. Tears of terror or tenderness lay on her cheek. Danger leaped along my side.

So I lay there listening to the rain against the draped windows. I became aware of pictures drifting before me: the book with the black dagger and the blood-red rose, Maureen raising her eyeglasses to the lamp, my father opening his black bag on the rug, Andrea standing at the end of the hall, her shoulders stooped and her head bent. Each picture seemed to contain a secret that eluded me. If I could grasp that secret, I would understand the universe. Then I became aware of my silence, as I lay there examining the pictures in my mind, and I recalled where I was, in the middle of an otherwise ordinary afternoon. I had the sensation that I was being looked at, and when I turned my head I saw a pair of dark tired eyes, much larger than I had remembered, looking at me with an air of expectation, as if it were my turn to say something in a conversation we had been having. Gradually her eyes changed, a dullness came over them, and she turned her head away. I was wondering what I ought to do to attract her attention when I became aware of a sound that was not the sound of the rain. It was at this moment that the door opened and Maureen entered the room.

She was stepping toward the bed and had begun to open her mouth, as if to address Andrea, for it must have seemed strange to her that the curtains were drawn in the living room and at the end of the hall, in the middle of the day, and in fact I detected in her face an expression of concern, as she looked at her niece lying in bed, in a darkened room. Her mouth was still opening when she saw me there. Her body stopped abruptly—she was leaning a little forward—and for a moment it looked as though every particle of her flesh had been replaced by a mineral deposit, as if she'd become a petrified tree, destined to remain there, leaning a little forward, with her mouth partly open, till the end of time. But gradually she came back to life, and straightening up, and raising a hand toward her cheek, without touching her face, she said, "No . . ." Then she began shaking her head slowly back and forth, like someone trying to get rid of a crick in her neck. Her "no," although spoken quietly, must have been heard by Andrea, who removed her arm from her face and half raised herself on one elbow as she stared at her aunt with large, nervous eyes. "No," Maureen said again, still shaking her head, and she began stepping backward toward the door. "Auntie Maur!" said Andrea. "It's all right, I was just lying here." But at this Maureen drew herself up and said in a loud voice, "I trusted you," and raising a hand she pointed a finger at her niece. Now it was Andrea who began shaking her head, while she ran a hand through her hair and started to open her mouth, which she closed at once as if she'd thought better of what she was about to say, before she lowered her eyes beneath her aunt's fierce stare. But now Maureen, like someone who had exhausted herself in a prolonged outburst, dropped her hand to her side, and with a distracted glance that swept across Andrea's half-lifted torso and the lower part of my face, she took a final step backward out of the room and closed the door. As the door shut, Andrea reached out her arm, as if to pull the door back open, and kept her arm suspended there, as if she'd forgotten it.

I understood that it was of vital importance for me to go to Maureen immediately, and with this end in mind I rose from the bed and stepped over to the door. Andrea was still leaning up on an elbow, but her extended arm had fallen a little, and the fingers of her outstretched hand had begun to droop. Her fuzzy pink slippers, her dark robe partly open at the throat, her broad pale neck, her big forearm on the bed, all this made me think for some reason of a sad queen who had lost her kingdom, and I tried to remember whether I had ever read such a story. But time was passing, I could already hear sounds coming from the stairs, and with a nod toward Andrea, who was staring at her feet, I hurried into the hall.

18

Behind the curtains of the living room, rain spattered against the windows like bits of ice. The couch and the chairs were empty. "Maureen!" I called, in a voice like distant rolling barrels. In the kitchen I found two plates in the dish rack, a white cup on the table. Around the dark table in the dining room, with its blue cut-glass bowl, four chairs sat neatly in place. Had anyone ever sat at that table? Then it struck me that the footsteps I'd heard had perhaps come from those other stairs, leading up to my own domain. Quickly I mounted the steps to the attic, where in the afternoon rainlight it was less dark than in the curtained living room. "Maureen!" I called, trying not to listen to my voice, but she was nowhere. I walked among the piles of labeled boxes and the old chairs, looked behind the dresser and the child's bookcases, but the attic was deserted. Then I went back downstairs and roamed the empty rooms, looking over my shoulder from time to time as though I suspected her of sneaking up behind me. From the kitchen I stepped onto the open back porch. Chimes near a porch post rocked in the wind. Gusts of rain blew across the floor. When I raised my eyes I saw Maureen striding across the stormy yard, carrying an aluminum stepladder toward the sugar maple.

I hurried down the porch steps and out into the fierce rain, but she ignored me or perhaps could no longer see me. She placed the six-step ladder beside the wooden swing that hung from a thick branch and began to climb. Over one shoulder hung a length of rope. I did not like that rope and I began to call out to her, but my words blew away in the loud wind. Her wet dress clung to her as she climbed, her hair darted up and down like flames, her skin was shiny as a seal's. On the fifth step she stopped, looked up as if she were peering into the rage of heaven, and flung an end of the rope over the branch. She looked like a big Girl Scout engaged in some woodland skill. She caught the loose end of the rope, tied a loop into it, and slid the other end through. When she pulled, the knot slipped upward and stopped against the branch. Then she began tying a second loop into the hanging end of the rope, while I shouted her name into the storm. Rain lashed her face. When she let the rope drop, a noose turned in the wind. She slipped it over her head and stood on the ladder, staring out into the rain. I waved my arms, shouted into the rain and wind. Then it seemed to me that, far from not seeing me, she saw me clearly and wished to be seen by me. I begged her to come down, I howled into the storm like a crazed dog. Desperately I ran to the ladder and began to climb, reaching out uselessly to her ankle, her leg. As if emboldened by my nearness she jumped, kicking over the ladder, which began to fall slowly, lazily, toward the soggy ground. The rope tightened around her neck and for a moment she hung there with her arms dangling awkwardly. Then the rope tore from the branch and she fell heavily to the ground. She lay on her side with the slick rope trailing from her neck like a monstrous artery.

I rushed over to her and knelt down. Somewhere a screen door slammed. Footsteps sounded heavily on the porch. Andrea came running down the steps into the yard and knelt in the sloshy grass beside her aunt, who was trying to push herself up. "I hurt my leg," Maureen said, wincing as she sat partway up. Andrea sat down in the wet leaves and the rain and threw an arm about her. "It's all right," Andrea said. "Everything will be all right now." She pressed her cheek against her aunt's cheek. I had moved a little away and stood looking down on them, as they leaned together in the storm like a wet marble statue commemorating a battle. Then I looked up at the rainy bleak sky, which seemed to be darkening into night. "Go away," someone said, and when I looked back down I was startled to see the two women staring up at me in rage and sorrow.

19

And so I have come to this place. No one will find me here. I ask no more.

I didn't once look back as I walked away through the harsh rain. I could feel their gaze following me, rising slowly above me, hovering in the heavens like a fiery sign.

We others have no business with the likes of you.

When the restlessness comes, like a ripple of madness, I seek out my own kind. I attend a gathering, where I force myself to crush down that little eruption of revulsion. In an abandoned attic we consider our nature, we brood communally over our fate. Then we melt away into the empty places of the night.

It is said that we haunt you. It is far truer to say that you haunt us.

Here in my retreat, here where the world ends, I return to Maureen on her ladder. What seizes me isn't her earnest awkwardness as she climbs, or her look of innocent and childlike stubbornness as she removes the rope from her shoulder and tosses it up to the branch. No, what I return to is the instant of the leap. For in that moment I detected in myself a little hot burst of envy. To know, at every second of your life, that you can kick over the ladder and jump into nothingness—what a glory that must be! For us there is no ladder, no leap. No way out.

I used to think of myself as a good man, who took care of his patients and protected them from harm. It may or may not have been so. But I can tell you that we are not good, we others. We bring harm to you. Already I have harmed two women. I offered one a false dream and drove the other to a rope and a tree.

And yet I maintain that they are far happier than we can ever be. For they will recover from my eruption into their lives. They will console themselves with hope. For that's what you do: you console yourselves with hope. You console yourselves with the hope of a new beginning, of another day. We others do not console ourselves.

One question that arises at the gatherings is this: Why? Why us? We all ask it. Why? Why me? Some say that we are random events, equivalent to any other random event in Nature—the birth of the first self-replicating molecule in the primal soup, the extinction of a species of lizard. Others argue that there are no random events and that each of us can be accounted for by means of scientific laws that have yet to be formulated. Still others make the claim that we are being punished, though there's disagreement over the nature of our crimes. I myself waver between the random-events theory and the theory of punishment, with a tendency to favor the second. For a time I believed we were being punished for not having lived fully enough, for having failed to seize the portion of life that was ours—hence our terrible longing. Now I have come to think that such an argument is too comforting, that it satisfies too readily our need for an explanation. No, if we are being punished, it's because we once thought of ourselves as good.

We are bad for you, we others. We bring unhappiness. We have no words of comfort for you. We bring no tidings of joy. Do not look for us. Cover your faces when we're near.

For we are always near. It's true that I have taken myself away, to this place. But we are weak, as I've remarked before. Sooner or later a time will come when I will deceive myself. I'll tell myself that I desire only a glimpse, a passing glance, no more. You will be sitting in your chair, or on your couch. You will sense a change in the room. Is it a draft? Can a window be loose? You will get up and go to the window, you will fiddle with the window lock. Then you'll return to your chair, your couch. It is a quiet evening at home. You can tell that you're feeling a little bored. You'll wish, just for a moment, that something new might come into your life. If only the telephone would ring! If only someone would knock at the door! That is when you will feel something in the atmosphere. It's as if a shadow has fallen across the back of your neck. It's as if all the streetlights have gone out. Is it possible that you're no longer alone in the room? You'll feel that someone may be watching you. Is someone standing behind you? You will want to turn around. You will want to look. You will want to know. Don't turn around. Don't look. Don't want to know.

SELECTED STORIES

from

In the Penny Arcade

A Protest Against the Sun

It was an absolutely perfect day. Her father at once objected to the word, looking at her over the tops of his glasses and nodding morosely in the direction of a loud red radio two blankets away. Elizabeth laughed, but she knew exactly what she meant. She meant the day was so clear that you could see all the way across the Sound to a tiny cluster of three white smokestacks on blue-green Long Island. She meant the far-off barge, moving so slowly it was barely moving. It was the rich dark color of semi-sweet chocolate. She meant the water, dark blue and crinkled out there, smooth and greenish brown between the sandbar and the beach. She meant that yellow helicopter, flying high over the water toward the Sikorsky plant. She meant that orange-and-white beach ball, that grape-stained Popsicle stick, that brilliant green Coke bottle half-buried in the sand. A white straw was still in it. She meant that precise smell: suntan lotion, hot sand, and seaweed. She meant the loud red radio. She meant all of it.

"Still," she added, shading her eyes at the helicopter, "I suppose it would be even more perfect with a blimp. Do you remember that incredible blimp? Nanny from heaven? What in the world ever happened to blimps? At least we still have barges."

It was her mother who took it up. "Oh yes: Nanny from heaven. I'll never forget the look on your face as long as I live." Her own face glowed with it; drowsy in sunlight, Elizabeth smiled. She was just exactly in the mood to be drawn into the circle of family reminiscence. But it really had been incredible: mythical. It was a summer day in her childhood. They had been on this same beach. She remembered nothing except the blimp. There it suddenly was, filling all the sky like a friendly whale—like a great silver cigar—like nothing on earth. It was better than balloons, it was better than a walrus. She had looked up, everyone had looked up, because really there was nothing you could do when a blimp appeared except look up. They always frightened her a little but they were so terribly funny: strange and funny as their name, which of course was the wrong name as her father patiently explained. But still. And so the blimp appeared. And suddenly, it was so wonderful, the sky was full of falling things. Swiftly they came slanting down out of the sky, and all at once the little parachutes opened up, green ones and red ones and yellow ones and blue ones: and slowly slanting down they fell far out in the deep water, and then close by in the shallow water, and then on the sand. People shouted, jumped up to catch them, ran into the water. Elizabeth wanted one so badly that she felt she couldn't stand it; she wanted to cry, or die. But she stayed very still, she was in awe. And then one landed near her, the little colored cloth at the end of the strings came fluttering down, and she pounced. And it was hers. And it was bread. Two slices of white bread in a little package. And her father said, "Nanny from heaven." And so she said, "Nanny from heaven."

"Have you seriously failed to deduce the connection?" said Dr. Halstrom.

Elizabeth turned in amazement. "What in the world are you talking about?"

Her father raised his eyebrows in surprise. "You asked what happened to the blimps."

"Yes? You know what happened to them? What happened to them?"

"Did something happen to the blimps?" said Mrs. Halstrom.

"You noted the absence of blimps," said Dr. Halstrom, "and you noted the presence of barges. It occurred to me, in the best manner of contemporary thought, to draw the inevitable conclusion. Consider," he continued, lowering his voice and leaning toward Elizabeth, "the shape of barges. Carrying off the blimps: you can bet your bottom dollar."

"What?" said Mrs. Halstrom. "I couldn't hear you. Bess! What did he say? Tell me what's so funny! Did something happen to the blimps?" Then she too was laughing, because there was laughter; but they wouldn't tell her what he had said.

It was a lovely day. The sun burned down. Elizabeth pressed her back and shoulders into the army blanket. Sand was wonderful: it was soft and hard at the same time. It was such a good idea to come to the beach. With momentary irritation she recalled how the trip had very nearly failed to come off. She was suddenly furious. The day had been on the point of foundering because Dr. Halstrom had a paper to finish. She had fretted away the whole morning, exasperated by the unexpected change of plan. It was unfair. He sat shut up in his study on a Saturday in August. It was outrageous. She had set her heart on it. He had been sharp at breakfast, sharp and withdrawn. By noon she no longer cared. She said she no longer cared, but she was desolate. But then he emerged at ten of one, apologetic and triumphant. They had thrown things in the car and left. The tide was out, but that was nothing. They had the whole afternoon.

Elizabeth lay on her own blanket, but she had carefully made the edge overlap the edge of her parents' blanket. She liked to lie down in the sun and they liked to sit on low beach chairs on their blanket while they read. The chairs were so low that her parents could stretch their legs straight out. But the books! It was absurd. Her mother had brought *Persuasion.* But she was afraid to get sand in it, because it was a present from Elizabeth, and so she had brought a library novel with a vase of red roses on the cover; she said it was awful. Her father had dragged along a fat seventeenth-century anthology, two collections of Milton criticism, and a library novel showing an airplane with a dagger going through it. She herself was no better: *Théâtre de Molière,* Volume II, and a paperback Larousse, really a ridiculous choice for the beach, and, because she had secretly known it was a ridiculous choice, a science-fiction thing called *Dune,* which Marcia had recommended, and which was even more ridiculous since she hated science fiction with a passion. But she liked Marcia. So she had brought *Dune.* It was all ridiculous. Her father had made a joke about carrying coals to Newcastle and *Dune* to the dunes. He had asked her how she was dune. I'm dune fine, she had said. Her three books lay in a neat pile near her straw beach bag, and her father's books lay scattered on the other side of her. It was ridiculous; absurd. She was lying on a sunny blanket in the middle of a library. Her mother had read for a while and then put aside her awful book, taking off her white beach hat with the broad brim and throwing back her head. Her beautiful hair in sunlight was the color of mahogany: but soft. And finally she had folded up her chair and lain down in the sun. Dr. Halstrom had continued reading, but at last he too had put his book aside, and sat with half-closed eyes looking out at the water. Elizabeth thought he was a dear to have come. He looked almost boyish with his little carefully groomed blond beard so lightly streaked with gray that you could scarcely tell. He had the fine smooth skin of a man not much exposed to weather. His face and forearms had color but his broad chest and upper arms were pale.

"You'd better put your shirt on, Dad. You don't want to burn."

"Oh, no. Thanks, Bess. I'm all right. I never burn, except with moral indignation. Plato was right: in a properly ordered republic, that radio would not be tolerated. The lack of consideration of that woman."

"I can ask her to turn it down."

"Unfortunately I believe in her God-given right to torment me. I was thinking, though, that your book looks rather forlorn. It ought to be called *Forlorna Dune.*"

"If you keep mocking my book I won't tell her to turn it dune."

And her father laughed, showing his boyish smile with the two handsome hollows in his cheeks like elongated dimples.

It was a lovely drowsy day. Elizabeth felt that her pleasure was probably excessive; her father said she shared with her mother a tendency toward the excessive. Even to Elizabeth the morning's anger and desolation seemed a little excessive. After all, she was no longer a child. It wasn't as if they couldn't have gone to the beach the next day, or even the next. But it was already late in August; she would soon be away at school again; somehow these little family outings had a way of being too casually proposed and too easily abandoned. If she hadn't fought for it, the day would have been lost. Lately, for no particular reason, Elizabeth had felt the absence of family occasions. Nothing whatever had changed at home: the treasured closeness was there. But she felt there was a carelessness, a danger, in just going on thoughtlessly from day to day. There were only a certain number of days in a lifetime, after all. She really didn't know how to express it, but she felt that just by existing, just by letting the days flow by, they were all threatened in some way: as if deterioration were bound to set in. She couldn't account for it. Maybe she was growing morbid. But there were times she felt like saying, as if she were old and they careless and young: Don't you realize that nothing lasts? That one day it will be too late? She had no idea what it would be too late for; she barely knew what it all meant. But she did know there were times when she needed to assert her family feeling.

Dark thoughts for a sunny day: she hoped she wasn't growing morbid. It was so nice to lie all lazy in the sun. The blanket warmed by the sun made her think of pajamas fresh out of the dryer: she liked to press them to her cheek. Elizabeth felt porous: penetrated by warmth. She wanted to lie there all afternoon. She wanted to lie there forever, under the blue sky of August, filling up with sunlight.

But it grew too hot, and Elizabeth sat up, a little restless.

"I don't know about you people, but I'm going down for a swim."

Her father seemed to come awake. For a moment he had a dazed look before his dark blue eyes sharpened to alertness. "You go right ahead. I'm content to sit here in lizardly contentment. Lil? Bess is going for a swim."

Her mother murmured something, half asleep, and Elizabeth, placing her hand on her father's arm, shook her head: Don't disturb her.

"You be careful," Mrs. Halstrom anyway said, half-sitting up with a worried look and shaking back her hair. They were none of them good swimmers. Elizabeth smiled. "I'm just going in for a wade. The tide's out anyway."

She stood up, feeling heavy with sun. Conscious for a moment of eyes on her, she strolled down toward the shallow greenish water. The sand was silky and scalding hot. He had said "content" and "contentment": not a good sentence. He had not been fully awake. A man with a little mustache looked hard at her as she passed, and Elizabeth felt pleased to draw his gaze. Then she felt angry at herself for feeling pleased. Who cared what some nasty little man thought of her? Let him rot. Let him die. But she was pleased anyway. The woman beside the man was thin and wore a red bikini. Elizabeth had a grudge against thin women in bikinis. She was a little heavier than you were supposed to be. She even knew the word for herself: buxom. She had known it at twelve. Skinniness was in fashion, so what could she do? She had big bones; she took after her mother. Her wrists were big. If she starved herself she would look awful. Flesh was no longer allowed, except in discreet doses. If your hipbones didn't stick out you were through. You might as well lay down and die. Of course there were exceptions. Elizabeth knew she had a good figure. She wore a two-piece suit but not a bikini. Those were her phrases: good figure, and buxom. Another was: a woman with a little flesh on her. Her father had once said to her in Howland's, "I like a woman with a little flesh on her." And he had looked at her admiringly. One of the two boys she had slept with, before renouncing promiscuity, had said to her, "You do that well." She hadn't done anything at all, but suddenly she was a girl who did that well. But he had looked pleased with himself, saying it. She had decided not to believe him, except slightly. She wondered if all women carried around their little phrases. Handsome, though not beautiful. Small breasts, but nice legs. A really warm person. A good cook. She does it well. She certainly wasn't fat, or even plump: just plain buxom. And she had a good figure. Men looked at her. And she was not a virgin. On her bad days she could look herself in the eye and say: Well, at least you're not a virgin. It didn't help at all: but still. She supposed it was some sort of accomplishment. But she was fussy about falling in love. Men without charm, brilliance, and spiritual perfection need not apply.

Suddenly she thought: Not lay down, but lie down.

The green-brown water between the beach and the sandbar was warm. Elizabeth turned and waved at her parents, who were watching her from the blanket. The nasty little man was also watching. Her mother was sitting in the chair again. Yes, watch me. Watch over me. Because one day it will be too late.

She waded up to her waist and stood for a while, turning her shoulders from side to side and dragging her fingertips along the top of the water. She half-remembered a game of her childhood, and cupping a hand she held it just under the surface. You tried to trap a little spot of sun. It was called a fisheye. She couldn't remember how to do it. It didn't matter, really. Maybe you needed a bit of seaweed. But even the seaweed didn't seem to help. No: there it was. A spot of yellow floating in her palm: a yellow eye. The man had stared at her behind. She hoped he enjoyed it: she had a good one. Men staring at women's behinds. She wished she had an eye back there: then she could wink at them. Just fine, thanks. And you? People standing around half-naked on beaches, looking each other over. Or pretending not to look, to be above it all. Boys looking over girls, girls looking over boys. But the real killer: girls looking at girls, women at women. It was the cruellest look she knew. A look of hungry, harsh appraisal. Her this is too that. Mine is bigger. Hers is better. One day she and Marcia had invented a wonderful new bathing suit. It would cover all the parts of the body left uncovered by old-fashioned bikinis, and expose all parts now covered. They called it the Negative Bikini. It was revolutionary. It was worth a fortune. It cracked her up.

Elizabeth waded out to the sandbar and walked along the wet dark shine to the firmer sand in the middle. A fat little girl was sitting in the mud, spreading it carefully over her arms. Even she was wearing a bikini.

Two boys raced; the sound of their feet on the solid wet sand was beautiful. It sounded like softly clapping hands. Beyond the sandbar people were swimming; the water was breast-high. Elizabeth waded out and went for a little swim. She swam poorly, but at least she knew how to swim. She had never been much of a beach person. She wanted to get her hair wet, she wanted to be wet all over. She wanted to dry out in the sun.

She came back up the beach toward the blanket, glancing at the woman in the red bikini as she passed. The man lay on his stomach, his face turned away.

Elizabeth stood dripping on the blanket; water streamed from her hair. She rubbed her head hard with the towel.

"Here, Dad," she said, and flicked waterdrops at him, laughing.

"Don't do that," he said sharply, jerking his face away.

"Did you have a good swim?" said her mother. "It's such a lovely day."

Elizabeth lay down in the sun. Farther up the beach, where a few scraggly trees grew in the sand, some boys were throwing a baseball back and forth. The smack of the baseball in the leather gloves, the shouts of children, the low waves breaking slowly in uneven lines and drawing back along the sand, soothed her like soft music. A faint tang of salt water rose from her skin. She smelled delicious to herself. Her father had wounded her for no reason. A sharp word was a knife. She lay grieving in the sun.

Dr. Halstrom said, "The tide seems to be coming in now, if I'm not mistaken. It's a good thing we didn't lay our blankets down by the water. We saw you bending over in the water, Bess. Were you looking for something?"

Then it was nothing. She was too emotional. Excessive.

"No. Yes, in a way. I was trying to make fisheyes: you know, those spots of sunlight? I did it, too."

"You used to think you could bring them back," he said. "You tried to bring me one, once."

"Oh, come on. I don't remember that. Really?"

"Absolutely. You thought they were pieces of gold. You kept holding the water in your hands and running up the beach. But when you arrived it was all gone."

"It sounds a little sad." She felt sad. The poor child! Gold running through her fingers.

"Not at all. It was a generous, noble, and beautiful thing to have done. Your mother and I were extremely touched. I explained to you that it was sunlight, and not gold, but that in another sense, a more important sense, it was gold, and that you had accomplished what you set out to do."

Elizabeth felt so full of love for this man, this father, who gravely called her noble and generous, that she knew she could only disappoint him. She was bound to let him down, in the long run. She felt that if he knew the truth about her he would never forgive her. And yet she had no particular truth in mind. It was just how she felt.

"A fine mouthful for a five-year-old child," said Mrs. Halstrom. "Poor Bess! She didn't know whether she was coming or going."

"I'm certain she understood what I said to her." As if aware of the sharpness he added, "Or else she pretended to." He laughed. "But that would have been nobler still."

It was an absolutely perfectly lovely day. The sun burned down, the baseball made smacking noises. The sun warmed her clear through, filled her with lazy golden warmth. She was a golden girl, lying in the sun. She thought of the slow barge lazily sunning itself like a great lazy cat of a barge, stretching out its great barge-paws, slowly closing its drowsy barge-eyes. Beside her she heard her father take up a book. The turning of a page was a beautiful sound. Under the hot blue sky Elizabeth felt a pleasant drowsiness. She felt more and more relaxed, as if some tightness were flowing out of her. She felt calm and clear as a glass of water. A page turned. The turning of a page was like a low wave falling. The sun shone down. To fall asleep in the sun.

Elizabeth seemed to start awake. "Good gracious!" It was her mother's voice. Her father was staring at the water with lips drawn tight. Elizabeth sat up and saw.

A boy who looked about sixteen was walking along the beach down by the water. He wore heavy bootlike shoes, black denims, and a dark, heavy parka fastened up to his neck. His hands were thrust so hard in his coat pockets that he seemed to be tugging down his shoulders. He walked quickly, furiously. Sweat streamed along his dark-tanned cheeks. He had black hair and black furious eyes. His face was so taut with fury that his high sharp cheekbones seemed to be pushing through the skin.

His tense tugged-down walk made him look as if he were holding himself tightly in place to keep from blowing apart. His black eyes looked as if a black bottle had exploded inside him and flung two sharp pieces of glass into his eyeholes.

"Imagine," said Mrs. Halstrom, "wearing a coat like that in weather like this. What on earth do you suppose is wrong with him?"

"Don't encourage him with your attention," said Dr. Halstrom, turning a page harshly.

All along the beach people turned to look at the dark parka. The boy tramped with hard angry strides along the firm wet sand at the edge of the beach. Water slid over his boot-toes but he tramped splashing on the water, indifferent, wrapped in his rage. Sweat glistened on his dark cheeks. Two girls on a blanket exchanged smiles. A little girl in the water pointed at him and yelled with excitement. On a blanket crowded with teenagers a muscular boy in tight turquoise-blue trunks stood up with his fists on his hips, but did not move or speak.

Down by the water the boy in the parka tramped past. For a moment his furious black gaze swept the beach. Elizabeth saw his lips draw back in mockery, in disdain.

"Don't stare at him," said Dr. Halstrom.

"I'm not staring at him," said Elizabeth, startled; angry. She was furious. Blood beat in her neck.

"It only serves to attract his attention."

And suddenly an extraordinary thing happened. The furious boy reached back over his shoulders and put up his hood. He plunged his hands back in his pockets and stared out of his hood with black broken-glass eyes, mocking and furious. Sweat poured along his face and shone in the sun. He tramped past. Rage consumed Elizabeth. She was a black flame. She felt the hood over her head, she tramped on waves. Sweat poured down her cheeks. Sun-people on beaches: laughter in the sun. Glittering people on beaches laughing. She swept them with her furious black gaze. The beach glittered in the sun. Hate welled in her heart. It was all a lie. Out with the sun! People on beaches caught up in the lie of the sun. Deniers! She mocked them. She trampled the water. Hate raged in human hearts. The beach lied. She was alone in the dark.

"Beach like that." Elizabeth was startled into her skin by her mother's voice. Her heart was beating quickly, she felt a little faint. Sweat trickled along her neck.

"I find the entire subject—" her father was saying.

The dark, hooded figure was far down the beach. People lost interest in him as he moved farther away. The excited little girl was sitting down in the water, splashing about and laughing. Far down the beach he seemed a small, dark animal on a brilliant expanse of snow.

"But why would anyone behave like that?" said Mrs. Halstrom.

"He wished to attract as much attention as possible and he succeeded admirably. The subject is not interesting."

When he reached the jetty he leaped up onto a rock and looked back at them: he was so far away that Elizabeth could no longer see his face. Then he climbed to the path at the top of the jetty and strode toward the parking lot. He was gone.

"I hope you locked the car," said Mrs. Halstrom, turning her head and shading her eyes.

"The parking lot is policed. I suggest we drop the subject."

"But why on earth," said Mrs. Halstrom, still shading her eyes.

"He was clearly disturbed. I asked you to drop the subject."

"I never saw anything like it. Never."

"I said drop it."

"He was mocking us," said Elizabeth.

Dr. Halstrom turned to her angrily. "Just what do you suppose you mean by that?"

"There's no call to be angry," said Mrs. Halstrom.

Dr. Halstrom closed his book. "Well, my day is ruined by this constant squabbling." His eyes were blue fire. Elizabeth felt tired.

"I meant he was mocking us—them—all this." She raised her arm and made a slow, sweeping gesture, including the sand, the water, and the sky. For a moment she looked at her arm held gracefully against the sky. Far out on the water the barge had moved on, quite a distance.

"All this? I trust you can be a little more articulate."

"All of it." She dropped her arm. She looked at her hand lying on the blanket. "He was protesting." It was impossible to go on. "Against all this. Against the sun." She was a fool. She had no words. She felt drained.

"Good heavens, Bess," said Mrs. Halstrom.

"Protesting against the sun, eh?" Elizabeth looked up. His voice was no longer angry. She didn't understand anything. "Well by God he didn't succeed very well." He pointed. "It's still there, I notice."

"What a conversation," said Mrs. Halstrom. She began to comb her hair.

"Though if it comes to that, I confess I agree with him. It's hot as blazes."

He laughed lightly, at ease, showing his boyish smile with the two handsome hollows like elongated dimples.

"Why don't you take a little dip, if you're hot?" said Mrs. Halstrom. "It's a good time of day." She pulled the comb slowly through her dark sunshiny hair.

"Your hair is so lovely," Elizabeth said.

"Why, thank you, Bess." She stopped combing. "What a dear thing to say. Yours is too."

A line of low waves fell gray and green and white along the far edge of the sandbar. Low slow water fringed with white slid lazily forward, stopped in different places, and silkily slipped back. A little girl in a brilliant yellow bathing suit stood looking down at her feet.

"Oh, Daddy," said Elizabeth suddenly, leaning back on the warm blanket and stretching out her arms along her sides, "do you know I can't even remember what brand of bread it was? Isn't that awful?"

"The tide's coming in," said Mrs. Halstrom, shaking out her hair. "You'll feel much better, after a dip."

"Silvercup," said Dr. Halstrom decisively.

August Eschenburg

YOUNG ESCHENBURG

At the age of eight, August Eschenburg spent long summer afternoons playing with a cruel and marvelous toy. It had appeared suddenly one day in the field down by the river, and it was to disappear just as suddenly, in the manner of all delights which reveal themselves too quickly and too completely. A hollow paper figure represented a clown, or a fireman, or a bearded professor. When you put a captured bird inside, the poor creature's desperate attempts at escape produced in the paper figure a series of wildly comic motions. August, who knew that the game was cruel, and who never told his father, tried more than once to keep away from the field by the river, but he always succumbed in the end. The other boys seemed to take pleasure in the struggles of the bird, but August was fascinated by the odd, funny grimaces of the tormented paper man, who suddenly seemed to come alive. This forbidden toy was far better than his music box with the slowly turning monkey on top, or his butter-churning maid who moved her arm up and down when you wound her up, or his windmill with sails that turned in a breeze. It was even better than his jointed yellow clown who all by himself could climb down the rungs of a little red ladder. August was relieved when school returned, and the cruel game in the field by the river disappeared as mysteriously as it had come, but he never forgot the sense of fear and wonder produced by those dangerously animated paper men.

He had always been fond of toys that moved, and for this love he considered his father in large part responsible. Joseph Eschenburg was a watchmaker by trade, and one of August's earliest memories was of his grave, mustached father removing from his vest pocket a shiny round watch and quietly opening the back to display the mysterious, overlapping wheels moving within. August could not follow the patient explanation, but he realized for the first time that the moving hands of a watch did not just happen that way but were controlled by the complicated wheels hidden away inside. Not long afterward, when his father took him to the North Sea and he saw waves for the first time, he was hurt by his father's gentle laugh when he asked whether the waves had wheels inside.

Young August was enchanted by the clocks and watches in his father's shop. He liked to step out of the busy street where it was always a certain time and enter a world where it was many times together and therefore, in a way, no time at all. He liked to open the glass doors of clocks that came in cases and to set the pendulum swinging with a finger, and he liked to hold the heavy pocket watches in the palm of his hand and feel the secret mechanism beating inside like the heart of a bird. He liked the gleaming porcelain clocks with their carved Cupids and shepherdesses, and he liked the clock dials that had scenes painted on them: a sunlit glade with dancing knights and ladies, a Japanese woman with a very white face and a very red fan, children skating on a pond with their scarves streaming out behind them. But most of all he liked the secret wheels within, which made the hands turn at different speeds and which formed a far more complicated and beautiful pattern than the carvings and paintings on the outside. From an early age he had begun to help his father in simple ways, such as carefully cleaning the tiny mechanisms that lay scattered on the worktable under the hot light, and soon he was learning to perform the less difficult kinds of repair. He learned that the secret of the motion lay in the coiled spring, which when it rested alone on the table looked terribly helpless and awkward and reminded him somehow of a dead fish floating in the water. He learned how the spring in its hollow barrel was made to coil tight when you wound the watch, and how it slowly unwound to turn the gear train, with its three wheels each turning more rapidly than the one before. The second of these three wheels moved eight times as fast as the first, making one revolution in an hour, and the third made one revolution every minute. This wheel was in turn geared to the escape wheel, and August learned to take apart and assemble the section composed of the escape wheel, the forked lever with its two tiny jewels, and the balance wheel with its hairspring. All these things his father patiently taught him, scolding him only when he was especially clumsy, and the time came when August was able to take apart a watch, lay out its precious contents on the table, and put all the pieces back together again. It was far, far better than his colored wooden puzzle called *Europe Dissected for the Instruction of Youth in Geography.* He understood that the same mechanism which turned the watch hands also drove the little men and women who on certain clocks would step stiffly forward and turn their heads from side to side, but those simple figures were of far less interest to him than the complex wheels themselves. Even the butter-churning maid that his father took apart for him failed to do more than satisfy his curiosity, perhaps because the motions of the toy could not equal the double wonder of minute hand and hour hand smoothly performing their flawless motions. Those motions were perfect and complete in themselves, whereas the motions of the clockwork butter maid were a very imperfect copy of human ones. Much later, when his life had developed in a way that felt like a destiny, August was to think it strange that never once during his childhood had he attempted to construct a clockwork figure of his own, as if his considerable skill as a watchmaker existed somehow apart from everything else, awaiting a certain fateful jolt before it revealed its inner meaning.

August's mother had died when he was so young that he could scarcely remember her. Although his feeling for his mother was tender and reverent, she existed for him only in the little silhouette in the oval frame that his father kept on the night table beside his bed: a two-dimensional mother with a turned-up nose on one side and masses of curls on the other. For a while the boy had longed to penetrate that blackness, but later he was pleased that she had left behind only her shadow, as if his ardent, expansive feeling for her would have been unduly limited by too precise an image. But Joseph never forgave himself for failing to preserve his beloved Magda in a photograph—a mistake he was determined would not happen again. It was shortly after her death that the watchmaker first took little August to a photographer, and the child never ceased to marvel at the stern brown-and-white picture of himself in curls and knee-breeches, on a stiff cardboard backing. The new art of photography was scarcely a quarter of a century old, and much later, when the full meaning and destiny of the art were revealed to him, the early picture was to seem yet another fateful sign.

But far better than the cardboard photograph was the funny painting he saw one rainy Sunday afternoon in an obscure corner of the Stadt-museum of a neighboring city, two hours by coach from Mühlenberg. He and his father had spent a long time admiring the splendid collection of clocks, the hall of dollhouse miniatures, and the three rooms of early toys—wheeled horses from Berchtesgaden, flocks of lambs from Thüringen, goose-women from Sonneberg—and August had begun to grow tired when with a mysterious air his father led him into the room of pictures. Pictures in museums looked all the same to August, and he was disappointed and irritable as he looked about at the faded landscapes showing little people here and there, and sometimes dogs, and ships on the horizon. He was relieved when his father did not make him stop in front of the pictures, but led him over to a guard in a dark green uniform, who smiled at August—how he hated that—and then stepped over to a picture which was not hung on the wall but stood upon a cabinet. The picture showed a castle and parks in the background, some gardens closer up, then a road with a wagon on it alongside a river with rowboats, and in the foreground some little people standing by the river with fishing poles in their hands. The thick frame, carved with fruits and flowers, seemed just as interesting, and the guard appeared to agree with him, for he raised his hand to the frame and seemed about to point. But instead he did something with his fingers, and then the strange thing happened: the wagon on the road began to move forward, the horse trotted along, the people in the rowboats began pulling their oars and the boats moved in the river, a fisherman in the foreground cast and slowly drew in his line, a laundress by the riverside began wringing out her clothes—he hardly knew where to look—and beyond the road, in the garden, two men bowed to a lady, who slowly curtsied in return, and far away in the castle park a man swung a croquet mallet and sent a little ball rolling along, while on the other side of the park some dogs chased each other out of sight.

He had guessed the secret of the magic picture at once, which in no way diminished its enchantment, and when the man in the uniform turned the picture around, August recognized the familiar wheels that controlled all the motions. The guard explained how the clock movement drove three endless chains, one for the river, one for the road, and one for the dogs. Two chains turned in one direction, the third in the other. All the other figures were moved by a system of levers worked by pins placed on the different wheels. August asked no questions, which seemed to disappoint his father, and the next day, in his room above the watchmaker's shop, when the twelve-year-old boy began to construct a moving picture of his own, it all seemed so clear to him that he marveled at not having invented such a splendid device himself. He worked obsessively on moving pictures for more than a year, inventing increasingly complex motions—his best picture showed a train moving through a forest, its wheels turning clearly while smoke poured from the stack, and the conductor waved his hat, and in the nick of time a sleepy cow stood up and left the track—but even as he passed from one success to the next he felt an inner impatience, a disappointment, an unappeased hunger, and one day he simply lost interest in moving pictures. He never returned to them.

It sometimes happens that way: Fate blunders into a blind alley, and to everyone's embarrassment must pick itself up and try again. History too was always blundering: the startling illusions of motion produced by Daguerre in his Diorama were in no way related to the history of the cinema, which was directly related to a simple toy illustrating the optical phenomenon known as persistence of vision. Yet perhaps they are not blunders at all, these false turnings, perhaps they are necessary developments in a pattern too complex to be grasped all at once. Or perhaps the truth was that there is no Fate, no pattern, nothing at all except a tired man looking back and forgetting everything but this and that detail which the very act of memory composes into a fate. Eschenburg, remembering his childhood, wondered whether Fate was merely a form of forgetfulness.

Indeed, trying to explain the particular shape of a life, one left out all sorts of things: the earthy smell of wet cobblestones, the glass-covered picture of the tall-masted ships in the harbor at Hamburg, the dull old schoolmaster in a chalky coat who, unlike all the others, turned out to be marvelously animated when it came to the one subject that really interested him: the multiplicity of leaf shapes, the miracle of diversity arranged by Nature in a single square kilometer of any forest.

Yet one had to admit that sometimes a moment came, after which nothing would ever be the same. On August's fourteenth birthday his father took him to the fair in the great meadow beyond the river. He had been to these fairs many times before, and each time they had filled him with wild excitement mixed with faint disappointment, as if a desire had been aroused without being satisfied. Now, at fourteen, with his voice already breaking, and shadows on both sides of his upper lip, he took it all in with a certain reserve: the booths where screaming hawkers displayed their hunting knives, their blood sausages, their green parrots, their jointed marionettes, their steins of foaming beer; the roped platform where a blubber-lipped Negro sat with a silver collar round his neck; the striped tents into which you were invited to step and see Elmo the Fire-Swallower, Heinrich the Learned Horse, the Hairy Lady of Borneo, Professor Schubart the Mesmerist, the Speaking Bust, the Automaton Chess-Player, Bill Swift the American Sharp-Shooter, Wanda the Ossified Girl, Count Cagliostro's Chamber of Horrors, Kristina the Captured Mermaid (A Lovely Natural Wonder), the Two-Headed Calf, Professor Corelli the Venetian Physiognomist. A woman with a red scarf tied round her head turned the handle of a hurdy-gurdy, a blind fiddler played beside a monkey on a rope, there was a smell of sausages and a sweet, hot odor as of boiling caramel. August felt restless and irritable. He envied the rougher boys his age who were allowed to prowl in groups without fathers, and he felt ashamed at being with his father and ashamed at feeling that way. A man with beer foam above his upper lip bent toward a fat-rumped woman in a feathered hat who threw back her head and laughed. August stopped at a booth offering knives and scissors for sale: there were long-bladed hunting knives whose carved handles emerged from fur-lined leather sheaths, bone-handled jackknives with the long blade out and the short blade at right angles, bread knives and butcher knives, knives for paring apples, mysterious knives with wriggly blades, thick knives with blades that sprang out at a secret touch—he could afford none of them. They wandered on, in the narrow lanes with booths on both sides. Hawkers shouted as if in rage; he felt spittle on his cheek. A dark green tent appeared, with a red streamer on top; above the open flap were the words KONRAD THE MAGICIAN. A tired woman in a turban sat on a stool, fanning herself with a folded newspaper. August had always been amused by magic tricks; his father paid the turbaned lady and they stepped inside.

It was dark and horribly hot. On a roped-off platform Konrad the Magician stood behind a table. On each side of him an oil lamp glowed. August saw at once that he had made a mistake: the magician was perspiring, the air was unbreathable, the crowd was composed mostly of children and mothers. Konrad was drawing from his fist a long stream of colorful silk scarves all knotted together; August had seen it a dozen times. If he was a magician, why didn't he make the air cool? Why didn't he turn the scarves into a mountain of gold, and take a steamship to America and live in a white house with pillars and a thousand slaves? Konrad came to the end of the scarves, crumpled them all up in his hand, shook his closed fist, and opened his hand to reveal a dead mouse, which he held up by the tail. The children laughed; August smiled wearily. Konrad wiped his sweating forehead with a black handkerchief. He next reached into his ear and removed a white billiard ball. He looked at it in surprise. Opening his mouth, he struggled to place the ball inside; slowly he closed his lips over it. He swallowed loudly and opened his mouth: the ball was gone. He leaned forward, showing his open mouth. Konrad closed his mouth, placed both hands on his stomach and pushed. Opening his mouth, he removed a red billiard ball. There was delighted laughter and applause. August, removing a watch from his pants pocket to glance at the time, discovered that he had not yet replaced the hour hand. The minute hand pointed to four. The time was twenty past nothing. Konrad removed the white billiard ball from his other ear, turned it into a pigeon, and picked up a curtained box which he placed on the table in front of him. He announced that he was going to shrink himself and appear in the box. August had never seen this trick and wondered faintly how he would manage it. Konrad took out his black handkerchief and mopped his brow. He shook the handkerchief, which became a white sheet. He held up the white sheet before him; a moment later the sheet fell lazily down, revealing empty air.

All eyes were now turned to the box on the table. The curtains slowly parted, revealing a dark stage, in the center of which stood a small table bearing an empty glass bowl. The table and bowl were brilliantly illuminated by three beams of light falling at angles from the ceiling. A music-box melody began to play. From the right wing emerged a shadowy man about the size of a nutcracker. He walked briskly to stage center directly behind the table and stood facing the crowd. He wore tails and a top hat and carried in one hand a black wand. His face was pale and his eyes were restless, dark, and bright. He stood motionless for a few moments and then rapped the glass bowl twice with the top of his wand, as if signaling for attention. He next held up the wand by one end and with his empty hand he pressed against the other end of the wand, slowly collapsing it until it was crushed between his small clasped palms. When he opened his hands there spilled out a bright white tablecloth, which he held up for inspection, turning it first one way and then the other. He laid the tablecloth carefully over the glass bowl, stepped back, and held up his hands for inspection. When he stepped forward and removed the tablecloth, the glass bowl was filled with water, and a little goldfish was swimming about. He bowed to the left and bowed to the right. Again he laid the cloth over the table, covering the bowl. When he lifted the cloth, the bowl was no longer there. He held up the tablecloth, turning it first one way and then the other. He bowed to the left and bowed to the right. He placed the tablecloth over the table. He removed his top hat and held it out for inspection. He shook it vigorously; he turned it topside up and topside down. He placed the black hat brim-down on the white tablecloth. When he suddenly lifted it, he revealed the bowl of water in which the little goldfish was swimming. He bowed to the left and bowed to the right. He put the top hat on his head. He picked up the bowl and he picked up the tablecloth. He set down the bowl and placed the tablecloth over it. When he lifted the tablecloth, the bowl was empty. He bowed to the left and bowed to the right. He held up the tablecloth for inspection, turning it first one way and then the other. He folded the tablecloth in half, and in half again, and in half again, until it was the size of a little handkerchief. He closed his hands over the folded bit of cloth and slowly drew forth the black wand. He bowed to the left and bowed to the right. Then turning on his heel he walked from the stage, exiting on the left. The lights dimmed and went out. Slowly the curtain fell. The whirring stopped.

Now the rumpled sheet lying on the stage began to flutter mysteriously, slowly it rose up ghostlike before the watchers, and from behind it stepped Konrad the Magician. He collapsed the sheet into a black handkerchief, mopped his brow, and placed the handkerchief in his pocket. Gracefully he bowed. The performance was over.

Never had August seen such an extraordinary toy. The tricks of the little magician had amused him, but far more fascinating was the little automaton itself. Although it was evident that he could perform only a fixed number of motions, the number was large and various enough not to fall into an ascertainable pattern, and the motions themselves were entirely without the fatal jerkiness of the tedious clockwork toys he had seen. True, there was a slight stiffness about the little clockwork magician, but that entirely suited his formal manner. Yet even more striking than the smooth and lifelike motions was the uncanny expressiveness of the magician's mobile face. He had moved his mouth and eyes, as well as his head, and August had seemed to catch a glimpse of cheek-muscle tightening. Indeed his face seemed so able to express the several emotions required of him that it was as if he were controlled not by an inner mechanism of wheels and levers but by a thinking mind; and it was above all this illusion of an inner spirit that was so remarkable in the performance of the clockwork magician.

To those few minutes in a drab green tent, August ever after traced his devotion to clockwork art. Even then he disdained the phrase "clockwork toy," for it was precisely those well-loved toys which had failed to strike a responsive chord in him. The clockwork magician was so far superior to the butter-churning maid that it seemed part of another world entirely, and it was that world and only that world which August longed for. Old Joseph encouraged the boy's new hobby, little suspecting he would never outgrow it. Together they made trips to toy shops in Mühlenberg, and in the winter evenings, after the last watch had been repaired for the day, August and his father took apart and reassembled automaton toys. The mechanisms were startlingly easy for him to grasp, but at first the automaton motions proved difficult to foresee, for he was used to transforming the intricate system of wheels and springs into the simple circular motions of clock hands. Even the mechanical pictures worked only in two dimensions, and now he had to think in three. Often he was angry at himself, as if he had wasted his life. But the toys were far simpler in structure than his beloved clocks and watches, and after a month of odd, irritating clumsiness everything seemed suddenly clear. He even began to introduce little improvements of various kinds: a wooden bear who walked on all fours, turning his head from side to side, was made by August to stand up after ten steps, turn around, and walk on all fours in the other direction. But August knew that he would never make any real progress until he constructed the figures himself. Night after night, alone in his room, he practiced anew his old passion for woodcarving, angry that he had not known what his life was going to be, that no one had ever told him.

The clockwork toys, however clever internally, were externally crude in comparison with the carved figures and above all the dolls for which the town of Mühlenberg was well known, and August began to visit the toy shops and the dollmakers' shops with an appraising eye. Dolls at this period were enjoying a burst of popularity, and the Mühlenberg dollmakers were not behindhand in the realistic elaboration which was the order of the day. The older dolls with wooden heads, whose hair was painted directly onto the wood, had for a generation been replaced by china-headed dolls, whose hair was of flax, or of mohair, or even of real human hair. But the china heads were themselves giving way to elegant Parisian heads of tinted bisque, with luminous glass eyes. Even the bisque heads were rivaled in lifelike effect by wax heads, which in England were being made with real eyebrows, real eyelashes, and real hair, each hair being carefully inserted in the wax by means of a hot needle. Meanwhile the doll dressmakers of Paris had been startling the world with their exquisitely detailed costumes. German dollmakers could not ignore the latest foreign methods, and August listened attentively to the dollmakers' talk, taking from it what he needed. He began to purchase arms, legs, and hands from Johannes Molner, an old dollmaker who took an interest in the serious youth. The old man sometimes invited August to stay after the shop closed, and lighting up his meerschaum he would listen with amusement as the boy argued that ball joints should be added to the fingers of dolls, that the movable neck was still in a primitive state and might easily be improved, that movable eyes were only a first step toward total facial mobility. Herr Molner had a strong sense of proper limits, and no understanding of clockwork, but the boy's fire warmed him and he taught August what he knew about the art of dollmaking. He showed August how the porcelain head was hollowed out on top and bottom; inside, the eyes were fastened with wax and plaster to the two holes in the face. A wig of mohair was carefully glued to the top of the head. The body, of white kid, was lined with linen; between the linen and the kid, the edge of the porcelain bust was held in place. The arms were attached next, fastened by iron wire fitting into iron hooks, and last of all the legs. August, curious about the substances of doll bodies, was instructed in the properties of kid, of gutta-percha, of papier-mâché dipped in wax. One day August brought Herr Molner a small gutta-percha hand, attached to an arm; the fingers were jointed, and a clockwork mechanism caused each finger to lift and lower in turn, after which the hand formed itself into a fist and slowly unclenched. Herr Molner stared for a long time at the little clockwork hand, and raising his troubled eyes declared that the proper end of a work of art was to arouse in the beholder a state of quiet reflection and not of astonishment, that the laudable realism of the nineteenth century, when carried too far, became a form of indiscretion, and that the hand in itself was extremely clever but not commercially practical. August, who had hoped for advice concerning the thumb, at first could not understand what Herr Molner was talking about; at the end he lowered his eyes, embarrassed for the kindly old dollmaker.

That spring, August gave his father a gift. Joseph removed the top of the shoe box, unwrapped the loosely folded brown paper, and discovered a mannequin not much longer than his hand. The plump little fellow was impeccably dressed in the manner of a fashionable burgher, in a tailcoat and vest; he had sidewhiskers and bushy eyebrows and wore a pair of bifocals low on his nose. A gold watch-chain hung in a graceful festoon from vest pocket to vest button. Joseph nodded his head slowly in admiration, and August strove to conceal his excitement as his father placed the little man on a table. A small lever was hidden beneath one sleeve. Joseph touched the lever and quickly removed his hand. The little burgher took three steps forward, and stopped. He reached into his vest pocket and removed his watch. He brought the watch close to his face, raised his bushy eyebrows, and returned the watch to his vest pocket. He took six steps forward, and stopped. He reached into his vest pocket and removed his watch. He brought the watch close to his face, raised his bushy eyebrows, lifted his other hand and slapped himself on the forehead. Shaking his head, he replaced his watch. He took three steps forward, and repeated the first set of motions. He took six steps forward, and repeated the second set of motions. It lasted three minutes.

Joseph Eschenburg was delighted with the little man, whose miniature watch kept precise time, and he showed his pleasure in a way that moved August deeply: he replaced the mainspring with a much stronger one, and set up the little man in the window of his shop. There the clockwork burgher marched back and forth for a full sixteen minutes, taking out his watch and raising his eyebrows in surprise, while passersby stopped to look and point. The clockwork burgher brought forth smiles and laughter, and for a while business picked up noticeably. This gave August a wonderful idea: he would make automatons for his father's shopwindow. In this way he could justify his obsession while indulging it to the utmost.

The burgher was soon seen in the company of a little clockwork Frau in a feathered hat, who carried under one arm a Swiss clock from which, every five steps, a cuckoo suddenly emerged—whereupon the lady's mouth opened, her eyebrows lifted, her eyes rolled around. The clockwork burgher and the clockwork Frau, walking back and forth in states of continual alarm, proved highly amusing to all who passed by, and August began to add other figures in rapid succession: a little black schnauzer who ran alongside the Frau, stopping to bark silently each time the cuckoo leaped out; a young man of fashion who sat down on a bench under a linden tree, lazily took out his watch, and suddenly sprang up and hurried away, after which he returned to the bench and repeated the same motions; an old man bent over so that his dirty white beard trailed on the ground, as he carried on his back an elegantly reproduced grandfather clock. Already people spoke admiringly of the sixteen-year-old boy's shrewd business sense, a form of praise that pleased old Joseph but made August secretly uneasy. He felt that the business part of things was a mysterious and amusing accident that had nothing to do with clockwork at all, that some dangerous mistake had been made, that someday he would be exposed as a dreamer, a ne'er-do-well, a seedy magician in a drab green tent.

One day about a year later a well-dressed gentleman came into the shop, carrying an ebony walking stick whose ivory top was shaped like the head of a roaring lion. After a cursory examination of an ormolu clock, which he praised without interest, the man removed a business card and handed it to Joseph Eschenburg. Herr Preisendanz was the owner of one of the big department stores that were springing up everywhere in the new Germany, and he offered to purchase three of the clockwork figures for a startling sum. When Joseph replied that they were not for sale, Herr Preisendanz smiled, tripled the sum, and offered to purchase the entire stock of figures at comparable prices, even though not all were suitable for his purposes. When Joseph explained that his son had made them, and that they were not for sale, Herr Preisendanz narrowed his eyes, considered doubling the last sum named, but after a rapid examination of the old man's face—Herr Preisendanz had had dealings with these small-town shop owners before, some of them could be extremely stubborn—he decided to try another tack instead. He stated that he wished to bring Joseph Eschenburg's son back with him to Berlin, where he would be extremely well paid to make automated displays for the block-long shopwindow of the Preisendanz Emporium. He well understood that the prospect of parting would be a jolt to the old man, but he declared himself certain that the father would not stand in his son's way. Moreover, he would personally see to it that the young man was comfortably lodged.

Joseph listened gravely to all that was said and then called in his son. August was amused by the coarse-featured, red-faced man in his elegant clothes, not least because he so strikingly resembled a recent clockwork figure that had proved quite popular. But the offer frightened him; again he felt that somehow he was deceiving people, that they ought to realize . . . he wasn't sure what. Besides, he didn't in the least care for Herr Preisendanz and wanted to remain forever with his father, who understood him as no one else ever could. And Berlin was Prussia, he detested the very idea of Prussia. Without hesitation he turned down the offer, and was startled when his father said that every question had many sides. With grave graciousness the old watchmaker asked Herr Preisendanz to return the next day for a final decision. Herr Preisendanz, who had business to attend to, bowed slightly and took his leave.

Joseph Eschenburg knew perfectly well that the stranger from Berlin did not have his son's true interests at heart, and that the glib words about not standing in August's way had been uttered merely to win his compliance. But he was far too intelligent not to see that the offer was a very good one. The rich store-owner had mentioned a salary far greater than August could ever hope to earn in the watchmaker's shop, despite the recent increase in business; and Mühlenberg, though noted for its dolls, and even for its silverware factory, had little to offer in comparison with the Prussian capital. August ought to be given his chance; if things worked out badly, the boy could always come home. That very spring he would conclude his Gymnasium courses; a university was out of the question, for August showed little interest in formal study and had proved a restless and mediocre student. He seemed to look forward to nothing except working in the watchmaker's shop by day and constructing clockwork figures by night. And August had a gift, there was no denying it. The boy ought to be given his chance. It might never come again.

THE PREISENDANZ EMPORIUM

And so that summer, shortly after his eighteenth birthday, and rather against his own inclination, August Eschenburg parted from his father and traveled by coach and rail to the capital of the new Reich. Later he could recall nothing of this journey, and Berlin itself remained oddly shadowy in his memory, as if his attention had been elsewhere—although his memory of a particular stretch of shady side-street was so precise that he could still see the brilliant green reflection of heart-shaped linden leaves in a certain plate-glass window as well as in the individual dark wine bottles behind the glass. It was along this street that he walked each day on his way from his two comfortable rooms on the fourth floor of a quiet boarding house to the hot, bright avenue where the Preisendanz Emporium was situated between a fashionable tobacconist's and a jewelry shop. August could no more tell you the name of that avenue than he could tell you how many Frenchmen had surrendered at Sedan, but he still saw clearly every gleaming item in the tobacconist's window, from the long, ebon-stemmed and silver-lidded meerschaum displayed in a case lined with blue velvet, as if the pipe were a violin, to the little bronze tobacco-grinder shaped like a shepherdess. The Emporium, which extended from the tobacconist's on one corner to the jeweler's on the other, was furnished with four large plate-glass windows in which were displayed, respectively: six female dummies wearing the latest Parisian fashions; a group of glittering optical instruments such as telescopes, ivory-handled magnifying glasses, binoculars, stereoscopes, and cameras; a handsome array of toys, from varnished rocking horses to onyx chess sets; and a nice set of mahogany bedsteads, mattresses, and elegant sheets and spreads. It was August's job to create miniature clockwork figures for three of these windows. For the fourth, Preisendanz had borrowed a splendid idea from one of the big New York department stores: on two mattresses displayed side by side, a wax figure and a live actor, both wearing striped pajamas, lay as if asleep, and spectators were invited to guess which was the real man.

August had to admit to himself that he found his new work unexpectedly pleasant. Much to his surprise he took an instant liking to the Preisendanz Emporium, whose insistent and even strident modernity was supposed to be a sign of the new Germany but revealed delightful contradictions. Thus the new plate-glass windows were inserted in a façade modeled on a Renaissance palazzo, and the new steam-powered elevators imported from America, which floated you up through all five floors, detracted not at all from the grand stairway of the ground floor, with its marble pillars and its air of Old World elegance. August saw at once that all these effects had been carefully planned by Preisendanz to attract a public easily stirred by two contradictory impulses: love of a vague, mythical, heroic past, and love of a vague, thrilling future representing something entirely new. Both loves betrayed a secret hatred of the present which August felt was the unspoken truth of the new order. But quite aside from these stimulating reflections he enjoyed the look and feel of the place: the thick rugs, the elevator boys in their red uniforms, the glass display cases that reminded him of a museum, the ground-floor drinking fountain that was said to be the first of its kind in Germany. The goods themselves were of high quality; Preisendanz, for all his vulgarity, had surprisingly good taste. But above all August enjoyed his work. He was given a workroom all to himself, on the fifth floor, and was supplied promptly with whatever he required. Never had his clockwork needs been so lavishly, so painstakingly, satisfied; it seemed as if his thought could instantly be turned into matter before his eyes. Preisendanz proved to be a keen and intelligent judge of clockwork figures, and was himself surprised at August's lack of historical knowledge of his craft; August did not even seem to know that the great age of automatons was past, that it was already a quaint art-form whose true place was in museums and in the cabinets of private collectors, although it continued a last, desperate, and degraded life in fair booths and traveling museums. Preisendanz had been in London when the great Robert-Houdin had arrived from Paris with his Soirées Fantastiques and had displayed his famous pastry-maker, who emerged from his shop bearing whatever confections the audience had called for. It was all extremely clever, but Preisendanz had been somewhat disappointed; the automaton lacked the elegance of the best late-eighteenth-century examples. It could in no way compare, for instance, with the miniature automatons of John Joseph Merlin, a Belgian mechanist who had displayed his figures in London in the sixties of the last century, and whose fifteen-inch clockwork women were said to have imitated human motions with unusual precision, including motions of the neck, the fingers, and even the eyelids. He had seen one of these remarkable figures, badly damaged, in the collection of a viscount. Preisendanz had followed closely the vogue of life-sized automatons, for he felt those old mainstays of the exhibitions had unheralded commercial possibilities; and he himself owned a life-sized automaton writer, clearly based on the famous Jacquet-Droz figure, though no longer in working condition. To all this, August listened with a curious mixture of keen interest and indifference.

Preisendanz was pleased with August's first creation, a six-inch boy in short pants who played in turn with five exquisitely rendered miniature toys, the gigantic originals of which were displayed nearby: a Hampelmann or jumping jack, a little pull-along poodle on red wheels, a jack-in-the-box woodcutter with a little ax over his shoulder, a shiny rocking horse that was actually a rocking zebra, and a little easel on which with a piece of charcoal the clockwork boy drew, very neatly and clearly, a smiling clown.

At first August enjoyed the walk to and from his rooms on the leafy side-street, with its delightful collection of shops: a shop with great wheels of cheese in every shade of orange and yellow, a bakery that sold thick black pumpernickel hot from the oven, a private doorway above a high brick stairway, a window displaying a collection of riding crops and shiny leather boots, a shop where gleaming pearly fish with glassy eyes and gaping mouths lay beside slices of brilliant yellow lemon, two private doorways above flights of stone steps, a window displaying a fine collection of hearing trumpets and wooden legs and glass eyes, a window with dark bottles of wine showing bright green linden leaves, and the corner tobacconist's. His boarding house stood between the cheese shop and a glover's. But more and more he found himself lingering in the workshop on the fifth floor of the Emporium, and when Preisendanz gave him permission to remain overnight, and even supplied him with a Preisendanz mattress, August moved in permanently, though without giving up his unoccupied rooms on the side-street. He never quite understood why he wanted those rooms, which he never visited; perhaps they represented a possibility of independence from the Emporium, an independence which he liked to have at his command even though he never made use of it. Preisendanz locked the Emporium every night at six, and was not displeased to have a light burning late on the fifth floor to discourage burglars. During the afternoon August would buy bread and cheese and fruit, which he brought to the workshop, and sometimes at night, during a difficult stretch of work, he would leave the workshop and wander through the dark rooms of the department store with their rows of mysterious and night-enchanted merchandise, lit by gleams from the gaslights outside.

Sometimes August was disturbed by the strangeness of his new life, as if it were all a dream from which he must wake up at any moment, but these very thoughts only made him throw himself more ardently into his work. Besides, he was engaged in an exciting new project.

One day Preisendanz had had the damaged, life-sized automaton writer delivered to the workshop, and August had carefully taken it apart in an effort to penetrate the secret of its construction. The external figure, a boy with curly locks, was stiff and crude in comparison with the delicate clockwork miniatures that August was constructing, but the internal clockwork was far more complex than any he had yet encountered. The boy sat before a small desk and held in one hand a quill pen. Before him on the desk was a piece of writing paper, and at the edge of the desk sat a small inkwell. Preisendanz, who had seen one like it in Paris, explained that the automaton was supposed to dip his pen into the inkstand, shake off a few drops of ink, and slowly and carefully copy onto the sheet of paper the words already written there. The automaton had left the proper spaces between words and, at the end of each word requiring it, had gone back to dot the *i*'s and cross the *t*'s. He could remember no other details. The piece of paper on the desk before the automaton boy bore the message, in English: "In the second century of the Christian era, the Empire of Rome comprehended the fairest part of the earth, and the most civilized portion of mankind."

August, while constructing miniatures for Preisendanz, labored over the life-sized boy writer for six months before discovering its secret: someone had removed three different sets of wheels, evidently with the intention of preventing anyone else from operating the automaton. After much experimentation August filled in the gaps, and called in Preisendanz to see the demonstration. Preisendanz was delighted, and wondered aloud whether they should start producing life-sized automatons. August, looking up in surprise, was shocked at this revelation of vulgarity. And once again he had the sensation that everything was uncertain, that things were bound to end badly.

He had learned a great deal from his reconstruction of the boy writer, especially about the internal structure of the hand, and at once applied his knowledge in a set of new miniature figures that surpassed all his others in grace and complexity. He improved the boy at the easel, who instead of drawing a simple clown now wrote in neat German script: "Ladies and gentlemen, welcome to the Priesendanz Emporium," after which he stepped back, examined his message, stepped forward, crossed out the "ie" and wrote "ei" above it, turned around, and bowed. At this point spectators on the sidewalk often burst into applause. August next improved his two other displays. For the window of optical instruments he had originally created a little man with binoculars around his neck, who strolled about, lifting his miniature binoculars to his eyes and examining various items about him, and finally turning to the spectators themselves. He had proved quite a popular little figure. August now added a second figure, who sat at a desk and made four different sketches of objects on display: a telescope on a tripod, a microscope, a stereoscope with a handle, and the miniature man with the binoculars. The little draftsman looked up from time to time at the object he was sketching, and bent over his work with a frown of concentration—never had anyone seen a figure so lifelike. For the window of life-sized mannequins he had originally created two fashionable clockwork women strolling along from dummy to dummy, glancing up and exchanging droll looks. He now added a miniature couturier, who at the bidding of the women took up a pair of little scissors, cut material from a bolt of cloth, and proceeded to make before their eyes a dress worn by one of the life-sized figures. The boy writer, the draftsman, and the couturier drew so many spectators that lines had to be formed before each window, and people were urged to walk slowly past and give others a chance to see. Business increased markedly, word began to spread; and all over the city people were heard to speak of the Preisendanz automatons.

It was inevitable that other large department stores should imitate the new Preisendanz attraction, and long before August had solved the mystery of the automaton writer, small moving figures had begun to appear in rival windows. Preisendanz followed these developments carefully, taking August with him whenever a new display appeared, but the rival figures were so awkward and elementary that they posed no real danger and indeed enhanced the reputation of the Preisendanz windows. Preisendanz feared, however, that the spread of his idea in even a crude and mediocre form would harm him by weakening the sense of novelty by which he had captured public attention, and in order to keep that sense alive he believed it was important to add new figures as often as possible. More than once he suggested to August that the production of new figures might be speeded up by certain simplifications, and more than once they had come close to quarreling, for August knew that his figures were still far too crude and was shocked at the suggestion that he ignore the direction in which his art was moving: the precise imitation of all human motions. Preisendanz had always backed down from an outright quarrel, for he was worried about losing the valuable service of his increasingly temperamental automatist, and in any case he as yet had no real rivals in the realm of window automatons. The three new figures had captured wider crowds than ever before, and he only hoped that August would complete his next figures while he had the public in the palm of his hand. But then a development took place that changed everything.

An older department store, four stories high, had for a long time stood on the same avenue, one block over and on the other side of the street. Indeed, Preisendanz had chosen the location for his Emporium partly with the idea of taking over the first store's business, and this he had largely succeeded in doing. The older store held a clearance sale, the building was sold, and for a time the plate-glass windows stood empty, except for a forgotten tape measure in a pile of wood shavings. But then the new owners arrived, and changes began taking place. The display space was enlarged, the old plate glass was replaced with new and larger sheets of glass, hydraulic elevators were installed, an elaborate doorway with an awning sprang up, boxes of new merchandise began to arrive—and the opening day of the new store, called Die Brüder Grimm, was fast approaching. Preisendanz had been annoyed by the catchy new name, with its shameless appeal to the German hearth, and was surprised to learn that the new owners were in fact called Heinrich and Johann Grimm. The brothers came from Hamburg, were brisk young men in their twenties who both wore their hair *en brosse,* and appeared to know exactly what they were doing. All this was disturbing enough, but the blow came on opening day: the gleaming new windows were unveiled to reveal artful displays of first-rate merchandise, which served as background to a remarkable set of automatons.

Preisendanz saw at once that the eight-inch figures could not compare with his in complexity of performance, fluidity of motion, and precision of detail. Their fingers moved only at one joint, their movements were stiff and inelegant, they performed the most elementary motions. And yet they possessed a striking and unmistakable quality, one might say an originality, that lifted them far above other automatons of their degree of complexity, and challenged even his own. For these new figures were somehow—and it was difficult to find the precise word—somehow sensual. They were by no means openly and shamelessly erotic, for the respectable crowds on the fashionable avenue would have been shocked and disgusted by too direct an appeal to their animal natures, but the skill of these automatons, one was tempted to say their brilliance, lay precisely in the degree to which they were able to appear decorous while conveying an unmistakable flavor of lasciviousness. In the window of women's fashions, for example, two female automatons strolled up and down before the spectators and did not even look at the clothes on display. One was a woman and one a girl of perhaps sixteen. Both had bright blue eyes and blond braids. They were dressed impeccably in the latest French fashion, and yet their anatomy had been distorted slightly to produce a definite effect: their rumps had been exaggerated in a manner approaching that of certain picture postcards, and had been given a faint but distinct motion under the closely clinging fabric of their boudoir gowns, and their breasts were of a kind rarely or perhaps never seen in natural females, suggesting rather the protuberant dream-roundness of adolescent fantasy. The Frau and Mädchen seemed thrust out before and behind, and brilliantly approached indecency without stepping over the line of the respectable. At each end of their walk, they sat down on a couch and crossed their legs, revealing for a moment a fetching glimpse of tight silken stockings—a glimpse, moreover, that changed slightly each time. Even the window of toys was a triumph of lubricity: in a circus ring a little horse went round and round—the movements were awkward and elementary, though the horse was painted a lovely shiny black—and on top of him stood a bareback rider with her arms spread and one leg lifted behind her. She was half the size of the other automatons, as if to express her toylike nature, and she was capable of so few motions that in reality she was little more than a doll. But she had been dressed in flesh-colored tights, an allusion no doubt to the famous English bareback rider, and although one could not quite accuse the toy of impropriety, still her legs and little buttocks had been carefully molded to be as suggestive as possible, an effect heightened by the black-mustached ringmaster in his shiny leather boots who from time to time gave a rather awkward crack with his whip. Preisendanz could not swear to it, but each time the horse carried the bareback rider around a certain turn he had the fleeting sense that he could see a disturbing darkness between her legs.

These effects he meticulously pointed out to August later that morning, but August's contempt for the workmanship was insurmountable. Preisendanz urged him to ignore the workmanship for the sake of the effects, but August replied that the ludicrous effects were a result of the inept craft, and that personally he saw nothing desirable about a fat behind. The automatons, although worthless as clockwork, did in his opinion betray one technical skill: the flesh had been rendered remarkably well, so well that one might almost call the result brilliant, though it seemed a shame such talent should be wasted on trash. Preisendanz saw at once that it was so: the flesh of those women was terribly desirable. Once again he tried to impress upon his stubborn automatist the hidden virtues of the rival automatons, but August, who at first had laughed gaily, became abruptly sullen.

Preisendanz knew that the world of modern commerce obeyed one all-embracing principle: novelty. This principle was divisible into two laws: novelty is necessary, and novelty never lasts. The second law might also be phrased: today's novelty is tomorrow's ennui. The Grimm brothers had introduced a novelty, and had thus dealt the Preisendanz Emporium a blow, but it remained to be seen how quickly the public grew tired of those sensual toys. An opening-day crowd was deceptive, for people were of course curious and out for bargains. Preisendanz was prepared to be patient, before approaching young Eschenburg again.

By the end of the second week the crowd of window-shoppers before Die Brüder Grimm had nearly doubled, and with a shock Preisendanz saw why: all the automatons had been replaced by new ones, in the same sensual style. The audience was therefore provided with the same piquant effects, yet at the same time given the stimulating sense of something entirely new. One of the new figures, in a daring climax, lifted her dress all the way to mid-thigh in order to display her peacock-blue Parisian stockings. Preisendanz hurried back to his Emporium and in the workroom on the fifth floor asked August how soon his next figure would be ready. August wasn't certain: two months, perhaps three . . . he was working on a new motion. To August's amazement, Preisendanz suddenly lost his temper, but at once regained it. Pacing up and down with one hand held behind his back and one hand lifted in emphatic gesture, he explained to August that he could no longer afford to wait so long; the volume of business for the past week had already fallen off, though not too sharply, but it was a sign of worse to come unless the crowds were drawn in. August's automatons, as automatons, were of course far superior to the Grimm automatons, but as crowd-drawing devices they frankly left a great deal to be desired. People wanted to see automatons of the risqué variety, and they wanted to see as many as possible, and for that they were willing to do without a perfection of craft which in itself was admirable but which perhaps smacked too much of a bygone age. August replied that if Preisendanz was correct, then the people did not want to see automatons at all but simply plump behinds and fat thighs, in which case—but here Preisendanz begged leave to point out that motion was part of the piquant effect. He was certain that August could capture it and indeed, with his greater mastery of motion, surpass it readily. August was about to reply that surely there was a contradiction somewhere, since Preisendanz had just been urging him to do away with craft, when suddenly he lost interest and fell into gloomy silence.

When Preisendanz left, August knew that something serious had happened, and that his pleasant way of life was being dangerously threatened, but he felt certain that Preisendanz would come round to the correct view of things when he saw August's newest automaton. If he reduced his sleep to four hours a night, and worked with supreme concentration, perhaps the new figure could be completed in as short a time as one month. He had already lavished untold hours upon her, and she promised to be his finest creation. She was a young woman, a year or two younger than August, and even he realized that he was half in love with her. He felt like another Pygmalion, but a Pygmalion who knew the secret of bringing his statue to life. He had labored lovingly over the neck and face until she far surpassed his earlier figures in her capacity to reproduce human motions and emotions: her nostrils could dilate, and even her lips possessed an admirable mobility that greatly enhanced her range of expressiveness. She was constructed to walk across the window space and try on a fur coat that a comical, pot-bellied salesman would hold out for her; she would then look at herself in a three-way mirror, experience indecision, and at last, in a burst of joy, decide to purchase it. After paying the correct amount in beautifully reproduced little bills and coins, she would walk along in her new fur coat, crossing the entire display area until she disappeared behind a curtain. The little drama called for a high degree of facial expressiveness, and August was still dissatisfied with the mirror episode, which did not quite reveal her inner struggle. But far more important was the final walk, when every motion of her body must express her delight. There was no doubt: he had fallen in love with her, and felt that he was giving her the glorious gift of life.

Business declined slightly during the next week. Preisendanz was anxious, but not yet alarmed: there was still no sharp falling off, and he felt he could afford to wait until August was ready with the new figure, about which the boy had been unusually secretive. Meanwhile Preisendanz fired the sleeping actor, removed the wax figure, and placed in the window of beds and mattresses a pretty twelve-year-old girl, the blue-eyed daughter of a woman friend who was a painter's model. The girl wore a short, frilly nightdress and was instructed to make the beds with different kinds of sheets, plump up the pillows, flop about on the mattresses, and in general keep moving about as much as possible. Preisendanz had selected her with great care: she had an angelic face and no breasts, so that she could appear in his window without scandal, but her legs were coming along nicely, and the movements of her little rump were really very appealing.

A week later there appeared in the mattress window of Die Brüder Grimm two new automatons. They were blue-eyed girls in frilly nightdresses, and the way they wriggled about was simply—well, indecent. The crowds enjoyed it immensely, for it seemed to be a great joke—a joke unmistakably directed at the Preisendanz Emporium. Preisendanz was frantic, and was only partially soothed when August, looking pale and drawn, assured him that the new figure would be ready by the end of the week. Preisendanz wondered whether in the meantime he might try a new idea: the girl in the nightdress might be placed in a tub of water, from which she could emerge shivering to take refuge in a warm, soft Preisendanz bed. The wet nightdress clinging to her ripening curves might be extremely effective. He was still turning this idea over in his mind when August announced that his figure was ready. That night, behind the closed curtain of the display window, Preisendanz watched the young woman walk across the floor, try on her fur coat, and walk back, while August stood by, pale and grim. As August watched the shy maiden he forgot his exhaustion, for he knew without arrogance that he had created a work of supreme beauty. When it was over he turned to Preisendanz, who appeared strangely meditative. Preisendanz muttered a few words, praised the wrong thing (the putting on of the coat was in fact a little awkward, the shoulders needed a bit more work), and left for dinner. August, elated by his triumph, and puzzled by Preisendanz's curious behavior, returned to his studio to work on the shoulder: the left one in particular was unsatisfactory. When he opened his eyes he realized he had fallen asleep at his workbench. Before him lay his Fräulein, a few hands, an envelope. There was still a half hour until opening time.

He washed quickly and hurried down to the display window, where parting the back curtain he stopped in amazement.

There in the window, before a small crowd only some of whose eyes lifted to the parted curtain where he stood, two hideous automatons were marching back and forth. Their gestures were jerky; they had plump calves, fat behinds, and grotesquely protuberant bosoms. Their eyes rolled, their shiny red mouths appeared to smirk. He recognized them at once as the work of his crude rival. Wind from a concealed bellows was being blown at them through a tube, so that their dresses were pressed against their bodies and sometimes fluttered up.

August, feeling dazed, hurried away to find Preisendanz. He found the owner in the toy window, over which the front curtain had been drawn. Preisendanz was pacing back and forth excitedly while a handsome young man with thick, wavy yellow hair was setting up a pair of ugly child-automatons, one of whom was dressed in nothing but a pair of white drawers with pink bows. Preisendanz, who kept looking at his watch, seemed irritated at seeing August, and, while keeping his attention upon the child-automatons, asked whether August had not received the note which had been sent up to him. August, who suddenly realized what was happening, became strangely calm and returned to his workshop, where opening the envelope he read that financial considerations of the most urgent kind had regrettably forced Herr Preisendanz to terminate their association. A generous sum of money was enclosed. August removed a single small bill—enough to cover the cost of the train and coach home—gathered his few belongings and his Fräulein, and was about to leave when he noticed the life-sized boy writer in a corner. Stepping over to it, he prepared to remove the three gear trains he had added, thought better of it, left the room, and took the first train back to Mühlenberg.

THE MAGIC THEATER

August had not seen his father for nearly two years. Their meeting was tearful, as their parting had not been, and once again August took up his work in the watchmaker's shop. Joseph seemed remarkably unchanged, as if time did indeed obey different laws in the shop of clocks, but

August sensed a slight difference that at first he could not account for. He soon realized what it was: his father moved a little more slowly. It was as if Joseph's body had aged while his face had remained unchanged by time. For that matter, August had seen in his father's face how he himself had changed, and his reflection in that mirror startled him and made him seem strange to himself, even though he knew perfectly well that he had grown at least a foot over the last two years and now sported a thick, soft mustache. But the change that most troubled him was in the repairing of watches. Although he enjoyed his old trade, and worked for his father as a virtual partner, he found himself impatient at the loss of hours from his true work. Preisendanz had spoiled him—he had forgotten what it meant not to labor day and night on the increasingly complex and beautiful processes of automaton clockwork—and he had to struggle against an inner restlessness that seemed to him almost a betrayal of his love for his father. Joseph knew where his son's heart lay, and urged him to reduce the hours he spent in the shop, but the very fact of his secret restlessness made August unwilling to accede to it. Meanwhile he had his nights, and his precious Sundays. He converted his old room into a workshop, and with the money he had saved as well as the money he now earned he ordered materials from Paris, London, and Berlin. During his Berlin years he had become slowly adept in the highly complex matter of ordering supplies, and although he could never hope to duplicate the superb conditions of his work-life in the Emporium, when the need for a tool, or a rare kind of cloth, or a chemical dye was quickly satisfied by the expert knowledge of Preisendanz, and although he now had far less money at his command, nevertheless he was soon able to work well enough under the new conditions. And he was free of Preisendanz. He no longer had to care about store windows, and customers, and the imitation of clothes and goods, but could devote his energy to the only thing that mattered: the creation of living motion by the art of clockwork. Never again would he permit his creatures to be used in windows, never again would he sell them into slavery. The crude old automatons in his father's window were permitted to remain, for he thought of them as toys, but he never added a new one.

One morning about two years after his return to Mühlenberg, a stranger walked into the shop. He was a handsome, slender young man of about August's age, dressed in a beautifully tailored dark blue suit that he wore with a careless ease and that, August noticed with amusement, precisely matched the color of his eyes. He held under one arm an elegant walking stick with a top shaped like the head of a grimacing troll—it was really a clever piece of work, and August for some reason imagined it coming to life and biting a finger—and he carried in one hand a parcel wrapped in brown paper. He asked in a Berlin accent if he might speak to August Eschenburg. August was alone in the shop that morning and at once presented himself to the elegant stranger, who proceeded to study him with a cool, amused frankness that might have been insolent had it not seemed so good-natured. A dim memory stirred, but August could not quite place him. "I've a package for you," the stranger then said, and handed him the parcel, adding the single word: "Hausenstein." August, amused and not at all irritated by the deliberate air of mystery, opened the package. It contained his miniature boy writer. He looked up in surprise, and recognized the blond-haired youth whom he had fleetingly seen in the window with Preisendanz.

"I thought you might want it as a keepsake. A pleasant little souvenir of the dear old days. Ah, the days of our fled youth—pity they didn't flee a little quicker. It's quite clever, Eschenburg—brilliant, as a matter of fact. They're forgotten now—the fools are more fickle than even I supposed. You're still at it, I trust?" He glanced around keenly. "Incidentally, I'm the fellow whose trash drove you out. Do you have a few minutes? Odd question to put in a clock shop."

Preisendanz had hired him out from under the noses of the Grimm brothers, who within a year had sold their premises to an insurance agency and returned to Hamburg. Hausenstein—he never gave his first name, and August never asked—had been paid a small fortune to supply his new master with an uninterrupted stream of automatons cleverly combining the genteel and the lascivious, and although for a time he had found the work stimulating, it had soon begun to pall. He could not look forward with excessive ardor to spending the rest of his life in the production of rubbish for the likes of Preisendanz and the beloved German *populus*. Oh, he knew it was rubbish, and he was superb at his job precisely because he knew exactly what was required—and now that he had a bit of money he wanted to strike out on his own. He had recognized at once the astonishing quality of the Eschenburg automatons, for he himself possessed a small talent in that line, and he had recognized at the same time that those automatons were fated to be driven out by the sort of cheap approximation that was the true symbol of the new age. Since this fate was inevitable, he had decided to be its instrument. It amused him to calculate to the finest hair's-breadth the precise level of vulgarity to which one must sink in order to gain the hearts of the modern masses—the German masses in particular. But really the entire century was rushing toward a mediocrity that a youthful cynic could only find delightful, justifying as it did his low opinion of mankind in its present form. Nietzsche, bless his romantic soul, had invented the Übermensch, but Hausenstein had countered with a far better word: the Untermensch. By "Untermensch" he certainly did not wish to suggest the rabble—they were far too poor and hungry to concern themselves with anything at all except scraping out a miserable living in a wretched world. No, the Untermensch was a strictly spiritual term, and by it he meant the kind of soul that, in the presence of anything great, or noble, or beautiful, or original, instinctively longed to pull it down and reduce it to a common level. The Untermensch did this always in the name of some resounding principle: patriotism, for example, or the spirit of mankind, or social progress, or morality, or truth. The Untermensch had always existed in the world, but until the second half of the nineteenth century he had remained a relatively modest force, only occasionally rising up to tear down something he could not understand—a statue, say, or a book, or a liberator. But in the present half-century the spirit of the Untermensch had spread until it had taken over the Western world—it ruled in America, in France, in Britain, and above all in that newest nation, that quintessentially modern nation which had patched itself together in the latter days of history, Germany herself, the immortal Vaterland. In Germany the spirit was far more pervasive than elsewhere, and far more dangerous, for there the mediocre and modern joined hands with darker and more ancient forces; the union was perfectly expressed in the Prussian army, which combined the modern idea of efficiency with ancient bloodlust. But he was digressing; he meant only to suggest that he was a student of the modern age, and as a student he had seen clearly that the automatons of Eschenburg must give way before the automatons of Hausenstein, that cheerful apostle of the Untermensch.

Well, it had been amusing for a time, and he had made quite a pile; but even he had to confess that a prolonged submersion in the rank swamplands of the modern mass soul was not the most pleasant way in which to spend one's bit of time on the merry way to extinction. Besides, it was clear that even the most tedious cynic such as himself could not be a cynic except in relation to an ideal, and it therefore followed that even he, and perhaps he especially, had a sense of what was being dragged down. His dabbling in the clockwork line had enabled him to recognize that August's figures were brilliant, and entirely out of place in the windows of the Preisendanz Emporium. He, Hausenstein, confessed to a weakness for brilliance, on the rare occasions when he came across the real thing; and his wealth now permitted him to indulge a whim. In short, he was proposing to finance August Eschenburg in the little matter of an automaton theater. He had the place selected already, in Berlin; he himself would manage the theater but would exercise no control whatever over August. He did not pretend to be disinterested: he had reason to believe that he would rake in a nice profit, and in addition he was curious to see the direction Eschenburg's talent would take, once left to its own devices.

August listened to all this with amusement, with interest, and with growing irritation. He felt irritated because he felt tempted; somehow or other, this debonair and embittered visitor had given voice to one of his deepest longings. Even during the Preisendanz years, when from the sidewalk he had watched his early automatons going through their motions, the idea of a theater had scattered its seeds across his mind; and since his return to Mühlenberg, the idea had taken secret root and begun to grow. And now, at the touch of Hausenstein's words, it had burst into dangerous flower. August could not make sense of Hausenstein: he distrusted him, and yet there was a disarming frankness about him that left August puzzled and uneasy. Why had he come? Hausenstein was obviously bored, bored deep in his spirit, in the manner of someone whose intelligence is far greater than his talent; but ennui had distractions far more amusing than the automatons of a watchmaker in Mühlenberg. Was he—this mocker of men and self-declared apostle of the Untermensch—was he perhaps secretly afraid that he too was one of the mediocre? Did he need to bathe himself in the fluid of another's creativity, in the hope that he would be washed clean of all that was common in him?

August, uncertain, asked Hausenstein to return in the evening and visit him in his workshop. That evening he showed Hausenstein the figures he had created in the last two years, and only when the demonstration was over did he realize that he had been testing Hausenstein: one false note of praise, one inaccuracy of judgment or coarseness of perception, and August would have sent him off with his tedious boredom and his mocking mouth. But Hausenstein, no less than Preisendanz before him, knew what he was talking about. Without becoming falsely earnest, without altering his manner of worldiness, amusement, and contempt, Hausenstein spoke with authority and precision about what he called the Eschenburg automatons. He said he liked women with more blood in them, and told August to visit brothels for the sake of his art; he pointed out a very minor flaw in one figure that only an expert could possibly have detected. His praise was also precise; and he compared the Eschenburg figures in detail with the greatest automatons of the last hundred and fifty years. Technically, August had carried the art beyond any point it had reached before; it was clear that he would never rest until he had created a figure capable of all the motions of the human musculature. In this striving, there was madness; but no doubt it was as good a way as another to pass the time.

Hausenstein spoke a great deal that night, and not only about the art of automatons. Not all of what he said made sense to August, for Hausenstein, despite his gift of exact criticism, was given to the spinning of elaborate theories, but one idea did make a strong impression on him. Hausenstein maintained that the nineteenth century was, above all, the century of motion. By this he did not mean simply, or even primarily, that the age was obsessed with speed: frankly, trains bored him, though this did not prevent him from seeing their spiritual significance, and incidentally there was a rather nice description of a moving landscape watched from a train in a little poem by Verlaine in *La Bonne Chanson* which was probably the first description in French verse of this very modern phenomenon. Someday he would perhaps write a little paper comparing such descriptions with earlier ones of landscapes glimpsed from coaches. But trains were only a crude expression of the century's love of motion, which was far more strikingly expressed in its arts and entertainments. The new painters in France, for instance, might speak as much as they liked about sunlight and chromatic values; what struck an observer above all in the curious products of *l'impressionisme* was the sense of leaves stirring, of reflections rippling, of air trembling—it was an art consisting entirely of shimmer and vibration, of solid things broken into trembling points: sunlight as motion, the universe as nothing but motion. But such effects were capable of only a moderate development and would inevitably be replaced by the far more compelling illusions of motion that the century was already developing in its popular entertainments. Photography, that characteristic invention of the age, was considered by many learned gentlemen to have driven painting into the excesses of the modern school, but these same gentlemen would do better to realize that *l'impressionisme* was merely one expression of a much wider tendency. More than a decade before Daguerre displayed his first light-picture in 1839, a far more important discovery had been made in the realm of optics. It was discovered that an image cast onto the retina remains there for a fraction of a second after the object is removed. This profoundly significant phenomenon—surely August had heard of persistence of vision?—had been demonstrated by means of an ingenious toy. It was called the thaumatrope, and was no more than a small paper disk with a different image on each side: a bald man on one side and a toupee on the other, a parrot on one side and a cage on the other. Strings were attached to the opposite ends of the disk to permit twirling. When the disk whirled about, the two different images merged into one: the bald man wore his toupee, the parrot sat in the cage. But the thaumatrope, while demonstrating the principle of persistence of vision, did not present the illusion of motion. It was in 1832 that Monsieur Plateau invented his phenakistoscope, lovely name, that slotted disk attached to a handle and spun before a mirror. On one side of the disk a number of drawings were arranged in phase, and when the disk was rotated before the mirror, the reflected image viewed through the whirling slots became a single continuous motion: the little girl skipped rope. Thus was born the moving image, which already in this crude and childish form surpassed the effects of the clockwork pictures of the previous century. There had followed a stream of charming and ingenious toys, each improving the illusion of motion and each bearing a splendid name—but he would not bore August to death with descriptions of the zoetrope, the praxinoscope, and other such toys of genius. He would mention only that as early as mid-century the magic lantern had been combined with one of these devices to project moving images on a screen. And at this very moment, in Paris, the brilliant Émile Reynaud, using his own praxinoscope, was projecting colored moving pictures onto a background cast by a second projector. These pictures were all of course painted by hand, but it was only a matter of time before the photograph itself—that authoritative illusion—would be used in place of the hand-painted picture. Indeed, serial photographs had already been invented across the ocean, in dear old America; it remained only for some sublime tinkerer to discover a practical way to produce and project them. Then a new art would be born, and the century's striving for the illusion of motion would at last be satisfied. It was amusing that Daguerre, the inventor of light-pictures, had also invented that hoary popular entertainment the Diorama, which had drawn large crowds early in the century with its quite different illusions of motion, produced by ingenious lighting effects, and doomed to extinction. *L'impressionisme,* the Diorama, pictures that move—these were the inventions that he found far more revealing than the railroad and the dynamo, for in these arts the century's love of motion had invaded a medium that by its very nature was motionless.

And that brought him round to August; he apologized if he had talked too much already, he hated bores. For August too was part of the century's great tendency. True, he had chosen an eighteenth-century form, one might say an obsolete form, but he had developed it so much further than the old automatists had done that in his hands it became almost new. He had simply carried their experiments to an extreme—and what more modern than this lack of a sense of bounds, this need to take something as far as it would go? The art of the automaton was a dead art—he hoped August did not deceive himself into thinking otherwise—but in August's hands it had taken on a last, brilliant life, it had achieved a realism surpassing the old art of waxwork, for his fanatically imitative figures seemed to live and breathe. And because the age desired the illusion of motion, and because the devices that made pictures move were still in a crude state, and because the photograph had not yet been adapted to its final purpose—because of all this, the time was right for an automaton theater. He did not want August to think that he hadn't considered the matter rather carefully.

August scarcely knew what to make of this speech, which he had not been able to follow in all its turnings—he himself was accustomed to thinking mostly with his fingers—but one thing struck him forcibly: he did not like to be told that he was out of step with his time, or in step with his time. He felt that his work had nothing whatever to do with such questions, which obscurely threatened him by ignoring everything that mattered most. What mattered was that one day in a drab green tent something had lit up in him and had never gone out. The art of clockwork was his fate, but clockwork was also a sort of accident; what he cared about was something else, which had no name and had only an accidental relation to time and place. He did not say any of this to Hausenstein, but he was grateful to Hausenstein for having made him have those thoughts. The long speech had another curious effect: somehow, and he could not quite say why, he felt sorry for Hausenstein, and knew that he must never reveal this to him. The evening exhausted August, but before it was over he had decided to go to Berlin. He would need six months in Mühlenberg to solve three clockwork problems. Hausenstein said that he himself planned to knock about for a few months before getting down to business. When he rose to leave, he drew on his gloves, picked up his walking stick, and remarked, "Amusing, isn't it?" Suddenly the grimacing troll snapped its jaws shut. August was uncertain whether Hausenstein's words had referred to the clever troll, to the automaton theater, or to life itself.

A few weeks later August received a postcard from Genoa, which Hausenstein said was hot and boring, and three days after that a postcard from Vienna, containing the single word "Ciao," and then nothing at all for five and a half months, when he received a card from Berlin, telling him what train to take and where to get off. Somewhat to August's surprise, Hausenstein was there at the station to meet him, looking entirely the same, and behaving as if they had last spoken a few hours ago. It was ten at night and August had been traveling since early morning. Hausenstein hailed a cabriolet, and soon August found himself clattering through a district of narrow streets and bright-flaring gas jets that lit with a smoky green-yellow glow the masklike faces of Damen and Herren on the sidewalks. There were shouts of laughter, a light piano tune burst from a passing doorway, through a dimly lit window came a clash of steins. A lady in a great wide-brimmed hat and a feather boa walked arm in arm with a little pale bald man who had a large, beautiful, shiny-black mustache. The cab turned into a darker but still lively side-street and stopped. August hoped the hotel room would not be facing the street. Hausenstein, carrying one of August's traveling bags, led him to a narrow doorway half-illuminated by a nearby light. He drew out a great iron key, opened the door, and lighting a match led August along a narrow, dark corridor at the end of which was a curtain. August followed him through the curtain; the match went out. Hausenstein fumbled about in the blackness and at last lit a gas lamp. August saw that he was standing at the back of a high small room with rows of seats and a stage. "Like it?"

said Hausenstein, and still for another second or two August could not understand where he was.

Hausenstein had chosen a location at the edge of the café and theater district, and after a week or two at a nearby hotel August simply moved into his theater, sleeping on a cot in the small room behind the stage. It was not so much a theater as a small hall that, before Hausenstein had rented it for August's use, had seen a wide variety of arts and talents: a lecture on the science of phrenology, an exhibition of anatomical waxworks, a showing of *images animées*, a demonstration of the wonders of electricity, a stereoscopic slide show devoted to modern Egypt, a concert on the Mechanical Orchestra, an evening of songs and recitations by a troupe of child actors, and a program of nature-whistling in which Professor Ekelund of Uppsala imitated the calls of more than two hundred birds and beasts. Hausenstein, reciting this history gleefully to August, compared the stage with its red curtain to a redheaded whore welcoming all comers. "You will be her aristocrat," he added, trying to make August smile, but August was engrossed in practical problems. The small theater had scarcely more than a hundred seats, but even so the stage was far too large for his purposes, and he set about constructing a small portable theater, about the height of a man, that could be placed in the center of the stage and illuminated from within. The structure of the little plays or pieces proved far more difficult, and here Hausenstein revealed himself to be full of helpful and technically expert advice. At the same time, Hausenstein was overseeing a host of matters down to the smallest detail: the painting and restructuring of the hall, the design of scenery for the portable theater, the advertisements. The new name of the theater was to be painted on a red awning hung over the door, but he decided not to make the name public until three weeks before opening day. Meanwhile, August labored day and night over the construction of automaton actors. The performance would consist of three pieces, each about fifteen minutes long, with two interludes upon which he worked no less fiercely.

Four weeks before opening day, yellow handbills began to appear on streetlamps and in shopwindows, announcing in handsome black-letter the opening date of what was called the Automaton Theater. Advertisements were placed in the leading newspapers. One week later, a red awning was unfurled over the doorway, bearing the words: DAS ZAUBERTHEATER.

Hausenstein had not doubted for a moment that he could fill the small theater on opening night; the test was whether it could be filled night after night. The first show was therefore of vital importance. August had worked down to the last minute, making infinitesimal changes that suddenly became a matter of life and death; he continually rearranged the one hundred twenty-one seats, sitting in each one and worrying whether the view was good. Tickets were sold out in advance; Hausenstein wished to admit standees, but August refused so vehemently that there was no arguing with him. And so, on opening night, the people came and took their seats, it was really quite simple. August had planned to sit in the audience, in the back row, but suddenly he abandoned his seat and spent the performance restlessly pacing the room backstage. As a result there was a single empty seat on opening night. Hausenstein made a brief introductory speech in front of the closed, large curtain, then stepped into one of the wings, where he remained throughout the entire performance.

The curtain opened to reveal August's theater, itself provided with a curtain, as well as with an elaborately carved proscenium arch flanked by fluted Corinthian columns. The automaton theater was illuminated from the large stage by gaslights which went out as the curtain slowly opened upon a moonlit scene in a forest glade. It was Hausenstein who had persuaded August to begin with *Pierrot,* the piece that of the three permitted the most striking scenic effects and that, because of its association with the pantomime, was best suited to accustoming the crowd to automaton silence. This was the romantic Pierrot of recent imagination, the artist-lover hiding behind his comic mask, but in August's handling of the pale, white-gowned figure with his long sleeves and his row of big buttons, who with blood-red roses and a lute pursues without success his charming Columbine, the melancholy and despair of the spurned lover slowly deepened and darkened until, in the final scene, it seemed to become entwined with the moonlight itself, and under the brilliant, dissolving power of the mysterious moon was transformed into a frantic gaiety: the piece ended in a wild and silent dance, in which Pierrot with his dark eyes and broken lute seemed to soar above his despair and to dissolve in the beauty of the moonlit night. The piece lasted twelve minutes and forty seconds. Hausenstein, watching from the wings, saw that the audience was held.

The first interlude followed immediately. The curtain of the automaton theater opened to reveal a little grand piano, held in a spotlight. From one wing a little man in black evening dress strode forward. At the piano bench he threw out his tails, sat down, and played three of Schumann's *Kinderscenen.* The audience, who had remained respectfully silent after *Pierrot,* burst into applause after each piece, most vigorously after *Träumerei.* At the end the little pianist stood up and bowed gracefully. Someone called "Encore!" and the cry was taken up, but the stern little pianist strode off the stage. Hausenstein saw that an encore would have brought down the house.

The second piece, which lasted fourteen minutes, was heavily applauded: it was entitled *Undine,* an adaptation by August of the story of the water sprite and the knight, based on the novella by Fouqué. Hausenstein had been concerned lest this well-worn darling of the romantic age should prove an embarrassment, but the enchanted landscape was extremely effective, and the Undine automaton had an expressivity of gesture that was unsurpassed. The second interlude was a pas de deux from *Swan Lake,* danced to piano accompaniment; Hausenstein wondered whether the reappearance of the pianist—actually a second pianist exactly resembling the first—was not a mistake. But he was far more concerned about the success of the third piece, which August had created himself. Entitled *Fantasiestück,* though bearing no relation to Schumann, it opened with a display of toys in a toy-store window. The audience was looking at the display from the inside, for the plate glass was toward the back of the little stage, and behind it passed several recognizable Berlin types, who stopped to look before passing on. Slowly it grew dark—Hausenstein noted that the lighting effects were simply splendid—and in the dim light of the gas jets the dolls began to wake. Slowly they rose, waking to fuller and fuller life but never losing a certain clumsy, jerky motion, until with a burst of energy they joined hands and danced round and round, the wooden soldier and the English duchess and the engineer on the Nürnberg train and Madame de Pompadour—and as the first light of dawn began to break, their motions grew heavier and heavier until at last, yawning jerkily, they resumed their rigid positions in the light of another morning. The curtain closed. August, lying on his cot and smoking a French cigarette, heard dim applause. All at once the door opened and Hausenstein was seizing him by the arm and drawing him out onto the stage. Hausenstein led the applause; the audience rose to its feet. August, looking with alarm at all the standing people, kept brushing cigarette ash from his sleeve, and suddenly left the stage in confusion.

It had been a superb success; the question was whether it would hold. Hausenstein was disappointed when the next morning only a single review appeared, and not in a major paper. The review, which asked whether such a production, for all its ingenuity, could properly be called artistic in the truest sense, was nevertheless favorable, and Hausenstein trusted that other notices would follow in due course. Indeed, the very next day a brilliant review appeared, taking issue with the first, and expounding the principles of automaton art with clarity and precision. The long article was signed "Ingeniosus." "Now there's a fellow who knows what he's talking about," said Hausenstein, who had circled several paragraphs admiringly, and who in fact had written the review himself; but other reviewers soon took up the cause. Meanwhile the one hundred twenty-one seats of the Zaubertheater continued to be filled night after night, and August worked on another piece with which to vary the program; eventually Hausenstein hoped to have a different set of pieces every week. Together they made innumerable minor improvements in lighting and scenery, and one day toward the end of the fourth week, when cries of "Encore!" followed the performance of the *Kinderscenen,* the little pianist returned to his bench and brought down the house with a Chopin mazurka. While still working feverishly on his larger piece, August substituted for the pas de deux, which had never quite satisfied him, a passionate violinist with long black hair, who along with the surprisingly well-liked pianist gave a spirited performance of the first movement of the Kreutzer Sonata. One day a long review appeared, not written by Hausenstein, wherein August Eschenburg was called a master. The house continued to fill each night, and Hausenstein noted with satisfaction that some of the faces were the same.

Within three months two rival automaton theaters opened. Hausenstein had anticipated and indeed hoped for this development, since not only did it show that automatons had taken hold of the public imagination, but also it provided the critics with a chance to compare the masterful figures of the Zaubertheater with the blundering mechanisms that had sprung up in its shadow. More disturbing to him was the notable increase in other forms of automaton art. Some showman had constructed two life-sized automatons based on the old Jacquet-Droz figures, and his exhibitions were drawing large crowds; another exhibitor opened a hall of waxworks whose grisly effects were enhanced by clockwork mechanisms that caused arms to lift, eyes to move back and forth, and heads to turn. These rather tedious effects, insofar as they were a sign of automaton fever, were all to the good, but nevertheless they threatened to detract from the Zaubertheater by making clockwork gestures overly familiar and therefore unmysterious. A certain nostalgia seemed to be taking hold; imitations of eighteenth-century toys began to appear in expensive shops, a puppet theater opened, and a professor of philology at Heidelberg took time out from his scrupulous investigations of Sanskrit to write a thoroughly idiotic article in which he defended Maelzel's chess player against the American denigrator Edgar Allen [sic] Poe, despite the fact that Poe had practically stolen his account from Sir David Brewster's *Letters on Natural Magic*. The famous, fraudulent chess-playing automaton, invented not by Maelzel as the misinformed professor supposed, but by Wolfgang von Kempelen, had long ago been destroyed by fire, an event which the professor suggested had been contrived by enemies of the Second Reich. It was all the most pitiful patriotic trash, and was yet another sign of the startling interest in early automatons, an interest that Hausenstein feared for a second reason as well: those in sympathy with new forms of art might be led to associate Eschenburg with outmoded forms. And it happened: an article in a radical journal of the arts contained a paragraph attacking the Zaubertheater as a force for conservatism against which all lovers of artistic freedom must fight to the death. The blundering writer was under the impression that Eschenburg was an exhibitor of chess-playing automatons, and the journal was reputed to be read only by its contributors, but still it was a sign. Yet Hausenstein's disturbance over the increase of rival forms of automaton art, and his fear that the Zaubertheater might be misunderstood in certain influential quarters, were slight in comparison with a more general uneasiness: he feared automaton fever itself. An apparent sign of triumph, such sudden and intense ardor, such flaming interest, could not conceal from him the terrible fate of all bright flames. And well he knew the restlessness, the secret boredom, of the last quarter of the nineteenth century, which sometimes seemed to be rushing headlong toward some unimaginable doom.

And indeed, before another six months had passed, automaton fever seemed to be dying out. Exhibitors of life-sized automatons could no longer fill their halls, which now were devoted to spirit-rapping and demonstrations of the wonders of chemical science. One of the rival theaters had already closed and reopened as a cabaret, and the other had begun to alternate evenings of the automaton theater with evenings devoted to much improved magic-lantern shows and scientific lectures. Attendance at the Zaubertheater was still good but had fallen off after the first triumphant months; some evenings only half the seats were filled, although weekend performances continued to draw full houses. August had created a small group of fanatically devoted admirers, but the circle had not widened; there were so many other distractions, so many other entertainments. By the end of the first year August had created nine different pieces, which he presented in varying combinations of three, but it was becoming clear that attendance had dropped sharply: some nights, only a handful of the faithful were present. It was about this time that a new theater sprang up, and threatened the very life of the Zaubertheater.

Hausenstein had repeatedly urged August to enliven his repertoire in certain ways. He had suggested that Undine's girlish breasts, concealed by her long hair, be teasingly exposed, significantly enlarged, and piquantly provided with stylish French nipples pointing slightly upward. He had also suggested that Columbine, whose charming buttocks might well be plumper, should fall down during her dance and, throwing up her handsome legs—real works of genius, those legs—expose herself briefly to good effect. And he had urged replacing the rather stodgy interludes with lighter entertainments—for instance, a cabaret singer kicking her legs. But to all such suggestions August opposed a contemptuous silence. His later pieces had moments of dark, disturbing beauty to which Hausenstein was by no means insensitive, yet even as he experienced them he could not help wondering whether the audience was quite up to it. August was more and more clearly using automaton art to express spiritual states, and such lofty experiments were bound to seem rather confusing to all but the most stubborn adherents of the Zaubertheater. And now, four blocks away, the new theater had appeared.

It was called Zum Schwarzen Stiefel—At the Sign of the Black Boot—and August first learned of it through Hausenstein, who insisted on bringing him there one night. From an iron post above the door hung a long, tight-laced, shiny black boot, from which emerged a pink calf, a pink knee, and part of a pink thigh, all seen through the meshes of a black net stocking. The lifelike leg had been executed in three dimensions and was illuminated by two lanterns, one red and one green. Inside, in a narrow corridor, August's eyes smarted with cigar smoke. A tight-corseted woman with half-bared, very round breasts, between which sprouted an artificial rose, took their tickets. The rose disturbed August; he wondered whether it had artificial thorns. The theater itself was somewhat larger than the Zaubertheater—Hausenstein estimated a seating capacity of one hundred eighty—and not only were all the seats filled but people stood along the walls, waving at their perspiring faces with gloves or magazines. Most of the audience were men, but a number of well-dressed women were also present.

The curtain of the large stage opened to reveal a smaller theater, obviously modeled on August's automaton theater, but nearly twice the size. As the curtain lifted, a rollicking cabaret tune was struck up on a real piano at the side of the large stage; the music continued during the entire performance. There were three pieces, without interlude. In the first piece, six cabaret dancers, about a foot high, came strutting onto the stage. They wore long, full skirts beneath which one glimpsed petticoats and frilly drawers; their glossy black boots were laced very tight, and their large breasts were partly exposed. They kicked their plump legs high, strutted about with a great rolling of rumps, and sat down from time to time with parted knees. Though the clockwork was elementary, care and attention had been lavished on their black silk stockings, their petticoats, their drawers, above all on their wriggling buttocks and bouncy breasts. At the end, each buxom Mädchen placed her hands on the plump shoulders of the girl before her, and they all tripped off prettily with a great shaking of skirts. In the second piece the same six girls returned and performed precisely the same motions, but this time they wore only glossy black boots, black silk stockings encircled above the knee by brilliant red garters adorned with black rosettes, and loose-clinging drawers trimmed with ruffles and ribbons and reaching scarcely to mid-thigh. The illusion of naked, trembling flesh was aided by the reddish light that dimly illuminated the bodies and to some extent concealed gross errors of construction. Their big breasts were impossibly round and firm, and their nipples bright rosy red, but their elaborately clad buttocks were parodic masterpieces of round, rolling plumpness. Though lacking skirts, the automaton maidens reached down as if to lift them slightly for their kicks—a clumsiness that seemed only to delight the audience, who applauded lustily as the six smiling lasses wriggled into the wings. August left in the middle of the third piece. The curtain lifted on a drably lit stage showing a crooked fence across a moonlit field. From one wing entered an automaton lady dressed charmingly for a country outing. On her head was a wide-brimmed straw hat heaped with grapes and cherries, and she wore a peasant dress with long full skirts and a trimmed white bodice with short puffed sleeves and a square neckline prettily revealing the tops of her breasts. She wore glossy black boots and long white gloves. Walking somewhat clumsily to the fence, she leaned her elbows on the top rail with her back to the audience and looked out across the moonlit field. There now entered from the other wing a male automaton wearing a black top hat and a handsome cutaway coat and matching trousers and carrying a gold-handled cane. When he came up to the girl, who did not seem to notice him, he stood gazing at her without expression. Reaching forward with his cane, he slowly lifted her full skirt and flouncy petticoats to reveal a charming pair of legs in black silk stockings, encircled above the knee by bright red garters adorned with black rosettes. The girl, paying not the slightest attention to him, continued to gaze out over the moonlit field. Rather clumsily the male automaton continued to lift her garments until he had exposed two very round and pink and plump buttocks nicely set off by the glistening black of the stockings. When the skirt and petticoats lay over the back and head of the girl, the man proceeded to undo his trousers—he touched a lever in his side to release his belt—and stood sideways for a few moments contemplating his long red erection, which resembled a bloody limb. Turning to the girl, he appeared to be having some trouble as August rose and left. On the street Hausenstein spoke of a certain *je ne sais quoi* of aesthetic mastery which distinguished one artist's work from another, of the unknown artist's sure and penetrating grasp of the national soul. August was not amused. "These same burghers demand first-rate lenses for their cameras and they'd be enraged if they received a cheap substitute—yet when it comes to clockwork they can admire the cheapest, most technically mediocre work. So long as it's accompanied by lots of fat behinds."

"It's what I've been saying, my friend: your good blue-eyed German likes plenty of beef on his plate and plenty of beef on his women. It's good middle-class training from first to last: Podsnappery, as the English Raabe calls it. The heavier the better, in art as in gravy. You won't listen to me—well, listen to the applause at the Black Boot. You've got to throw the dogs a little meat, and while they're licking their chops you'll have time enough to go to work on their souls—though frankly the blessed German soul is much overrated in these latter days of her most glorious century and reminds me of nothing so much as Maelzel's or rather Kempelen's chess player: a hollow sham with a humbug inside. Did you know, by the way, that Maelzel also constructed an ear trumpet for Beethoven? Yes, there you have the German soul in all its dialectical splendor: the maestro listening to the universe through the ear trumpet of a successful fraud. This same Maelzel, charming fellow, built a mechanical orchestra of forty-two life-sized musicians, which had quite a vogue at one time. He also swindled the public into believing that he'd invented the metronome—not bad for one lifetime. But to return to the admirable precision of German cameras: those estimable lenses you spoke of are responsible for some highly detailed and extremely instructive photographs which one can see in certain private collections. I think the real trouble with Germany is that she's too close to Paris: visions of *le beau monde* torment her dark, uneasy sleep. Of course *le beau monde* for your blue-eyed German means fashionable women in expensive underwear. Fifteen hundred years ago, Rome tormented her in the same way—your blue-eyed Visigoth must have dreamed of dark-eyed Roman ladies lying back in elegant tunics, eating grapes, and revealing from time to time a fetching glimpse of the latest in Latin under-tunics and leather breastbands. In any case, I merely wish to suggest that capitalism and history are both against you, if you persist in serving up visions of high beauty to an upright citizen of Kaiser Wilhelm's Reich. He won't stand for it for very long; give him his roast beef and French underwear."

August was less tolerant than usual of his friend's facile manner, which seemed to attack the very idea of seriousness while continually inviting a serious response. He returned to his theater workshop in a bad humor. He recognized no law requiring the world to pay the slightest attention to him or his work, but by the same token he saw no reason to bend himself out of spiritual shape in the hope of pleasing a corrupt public. He would do what he had to do, in obedience to the only law he knew, and if they did not like it—well, so much the worse for him, and perhaps for them too. His ambition was to insert his dreams into the world, and if they were the wrong dreams, then he would dream them in solitude. August now threw himself feverishly into a single long piece that, even as he worked on it, he knew would surpass his finest achievements in automaton art. The eyes and especially the lips of his creatures were capable of a new expressivity so subtle and striking that his automatons seemed indeed to live and think and suffer and breathe. But while they represented yet another advance in the direction of precise imitation, another stage in the mastery of realism, at the same time they seemed to reach a height far above the merely material, as if realism itself were being pressed into the service of a higher law. So, at least, Hausenstein expressed it, when the new composition was completed, although he added with a weary sigh that he supposed it would lose them half of the remaining faithful. And yet, one never knew; the dark-eyed suffering automaton girl, whom August called simply Marie, had a brilliancy of flesh, a radiance, that was quite remarkable, and in her walk there was a new suggestion of ripeness, of sexual wakening, of sensual knowledge too innocent to be entirely conscious of itself yet disturbedly aware of the dark secret of menstruation: it was a sense of girlhood blossoming into womanhood, a sense of womanhood about to wake from the long sleep of girlhood and needing only the kiss of the prince to make life stir in the sleep-enchanted palace that was her heart. August, barely listening to Hausenstein, knew that he had created her with tenderness, with something akin to love-anguish, and he stood before his creature now as if in awe of his own work. "Yes yes," he said, when Hausenstein was done, "but you see—she's alive."

Hausenstein proved correct: Marie captivated her audience, but only after that audience had dwindled to twenty or thirty a night. At such a rate the Zaubertheater could not long survive, and August noticed that Hausenstein spent less and less time in the largely empty theater, as if avoiding an unhappiness. He no longer urged August to appeal to a wider public, but seemed content to let him go his own way—a change that would have pleased August had it not so clearly been the result of giving up. And far, far back in his mind there was something that disturbed August, something he could not quite bring to awareness. At times he felt that it was all very familiar, that his life was repeating a pattern whose outcome he did not quite want to remember.

One night when the performance was over and the audience of fifteen had slowly begun to put on their coats, August, who had silently come out to take a seat and watch the last few minutes, heard a young woman say to another woman: "It's remarkable, but I think I could watch her night after night and never have enough. But I wonder how they manage. The man who runs this place is a martyr." "Oh, but you know what they say," her friend replied. "It seems this Hausenstein has a finger in more than one pie. I've heard he runs the Black Boot—and, my dear, I can assure you it is not a *maison de souliers.*"

August had a sensation that the wind had just been knocked out of him. At the same time, his heart was beating violently, blood was rushing through him. The figures were not the same, but he knew there had been something familiar about them: the extremely well-rendered flesh. Feeling a little dizzy, and with a strange tremor in his stomach, he set off in search of Hausenstein. The ticket woman at the Black Boot, who remembered August, seemed to evade his eyes; no, she hadn't seen Herr Hausenstein recently. August was relieved to see that the artificial rose had been replaced by a bunch of real violets, rather drooped and faded in the warm, oppressive air. He bought a ticket and entered the smoky hall. Every seat was taken, people stood against the walls. Nothing had changed: the six automaton girls in their boots and stockings lumbered about the red-lit stage. Pushing his way past people standing in the aisle, who strained around him to see, August made his way to a little stairway at the left of the stage that led through a curtain to the door of a dressing room. The door was locked, but when he rapped it was opened quickly by a thin, flour-pale man in suspenders and shirtsleeves who was holding by the ankle a naked leg in a black boot. "I'm looking for Hausenstein," said August, who saw that the room was empty. "Who the devil are you?" said the man, but August had already left. Perhaps he was crazy, after all it was only a rumor. . . . Out on the street he breathed deep, wiped the back of his hand slowly across his closed eyes, then set off for the Zaubertheater. He had not even locked the outer door: it could have been vandalized. In the dark empty theater, lit only by dim gas jets, he stumbled over the leg of a chair. "So there you are," said Hausenstein, emerging from a wing onto the stage. "I've been trying to get hold of you. Rather careless of you to leave the—" "You make them," said August, and sat down exhausted in the front row. Up on the stage Hausenstein appeared to freeze; August had the impression that he would move off jerkily, with a faint whirring sound. But Hausenstein was a far more convincing figure: his motions were superbly smooth, though with a telltale sense of brilliant contrivance. "I was wondering how long it would take you to congratulate me," he remarked, stepping forward and sitting down on the edge of the stage so that his legs dangled a few feet before and above August. "Besides, I don't precisely make them: I oversee. But you should have recognized my work—I'd know yours anywhere."

"Why did you do it?" His own voice sounded weary to him; he must sleep.

"Sheer love of the art, of course, and then there's the little matter of"—he rubbed two fingers briskly against the thumb—"filthy lucre. Our Zaubertheater has fallen on evil days. When you refused to do homage to the noble buttock—" He shrugged. "After all, I know them better than you do. But don't look so downcast. The proceeds are what keep you afloat."

"Not anymore. I'm through."

"I was afraid you might take it badly. That's why, when you failed to recognize my work—and I did bring you there myself, pray remember—I hesitated to insist. Listen, don't be a fool. Tainted money, eh? A bit too literary: Pip and Magwitch. Where else will you get a chance like this? I have news for you, my gifted but oh-so-innocent friend: automatons are dead. A handful care—they're not enough. Oh, who knows, perhaps if we held on for twenty years, for thirty years . . . even so, you are about to become outmoded. *L'image animée* is the wave of the future: I've explained it to you before. My friend, you are a brilliant poet writing a late-nineteenth-century poem in Middle High German: three scholars, one with a hearing difficulty, one with an unfortunate *tic douloureux*, and one requiring a bedpan, compose your audience."

"I express what I have to in a particular medium. What else is art? I don't study fads and trends."

"But I do, and I tell you, my friend: the day of the automaton is over."

"As I conceive it, the day has never even begun. But this is a useless discussion."

"And therefore quite artistic, at least according to one of the century's more charming notions—though I'm afraid the boyfriend of Beatrice might have disagreed. Who cares where the money comes from? Turn the sow's purse into a silk ear."

"It's not that, exactly. You should have told me. You're playing some kind of game. . . ."

"I'm a playful fellow—it's my artistic nature. Look, I know them: they're swine. I supply them with troughs. It amuses me; many things do. I like to see them prating about Liebe and Schönheit—and coming to the trough in the end. Did you notice, my inattentive friend, how many of the faces are familiar? They start out at the Zaubertheater and end up at the Schwarzen Stiefel: yes, it pleases me to make certain experiments, I won't deny it. Let me tell you something. When I was a lad of sixteen I went about with a blue-eyed maiden from a cultured family. Or to be more precise: the father was the owner of a pork butcher shop and the mother read Kleist and Nietzsche and Baudelaire and played Liszt and Wagner on the pianoforte. She took an interest in me, lent me books, and was in every way so superior to her empty-headed daughter that I soon dropped every pretense of caring about the girl and looked forward only to my next dose of spiritual food from the lips of the mother. I wasn't by any means unaware of the more material charms of my maternal Beatrice, but I no more thought of violating that shrine than I thought of attempting to discuss the Übermensch with her daughter. Need I say more? One twilit afternoon, as I turned the pages of a Chopin nocturne while she played, she seemed to grow faint as she neared the end of the piece, and as the last chords died away I was astonished to feel her head against my shoulder. Like a nice young idiot I asked her if she wanted a glass of water. She asked me to lead her to the couch. She was very direct. One detail I remember quite vividly: at the moment all youth dreams of—I had never been with a woman before, and had to be shown how to make her wet—but at that famous moment I saw, not far beyond her tense, flushed face, which appeared to be the strangely distorted mask of the woman whose soul I adored—I saw, lying upon a little mahogany table, a copy of volume two of *Dichtung und Wahrheit*, from which she had earlier read me a passage in order to compare it unfavorably to the nervous prose of Kleist. It was then I realized that art is nothing but a beautiful cool hand placed by a woman, sometimes not very carefully, over her hot pudendum. She spoke to me of beauty and the soul, but she really meant to speak of less rarefied matters. During her orgasms, which she herself compared to the Liebestod, she was fond of sighing out 'Beautiful . . . oh, beautiful . . .'—a chant varied by the frequent interpolation of choice obscenities. Our meetings grew less and less artistic until one day—but that, my friend, is a story I shall save for my memoirs. I still have a dread of pork butchers. And so at the tender age of sixteen I learned an important secret: all words are masks, and the lovelier they are, the more they are meant to conceal. If it pleases me to be an unmasker—why, all to the good, I serve the

Fatherland in my own generous way. They chatter about the soul, I give them what they really want, and in the process I satisfy a sense of world-irony and a love of truth. Yes, I drag them down, the swine—I drag them down."

"But that makes you one of the Unter—"

"Yes?" said Hausenstein sharply, but August had caught himself, though not in time. The half-spoken word seemed to float in the space between them, preventing speech. Hausenstein slapped angrily at a fly on his sleeve. After a while he said, "Well. You'll stay?" August looked up in amazement.

"So you're going, eh? Splendid. And what will you do? Spend the rest of your life tightening springs in a clock shop? With me you could—oh, to hell with it. It's been an instructive evening, I always enjoy talking to a genuine artist, however passé."

August felt a burst of pity for Hausenstein, and hoped he would say no more.

"And let me tell you something, Eschenburg: you aren't that pure. You think you're the purest soul on earth, but you knew the theater was started with the money I made from Preisendanz. Who cares if it continues courtesy of the Black Boot?"

Wearily August answered, "I don't think I'm pure."

"Just too pure for me, is that it? Too pure to dirty your hands with my filthy money? And I'll tell you something else: you're not much of a friend. The minute something happens that doesn't suit your taste, it's good-bye friendship. I can't trust you. There's something cold about you. . . ." He stood up. "You just sit there. . . ." August looked up wearily and saw Hausenstein staring down at him with glowing bitter eyes. Had he hurt him that much? August felt bone-weary, and he seemed to have a headache in the center of each eye. Hausenstein turned suddenly and walked with rapid sharp steps along the stage and down the wooden stairs at the side. He appeared to be leaving brusquely, but suddenly he sat down in the aisle seat, eight seats away from August.

"It's been a long night. You have a difficult temperament, August. I too upon occasion have been known to be less than charming. Look, we've been together a long time. No one knows your work the way I do. No one." He paused. "You look tired. Get a good night's sleep. I'll see you in the morning." There was a pause, and he stood up violently. "Where will you ever find a friend like me?" Turning on his heel, he strode down the aisle. August heard his steps in the corridor and the sound of the outer door closing.

For a long while he sat there, trying to change his mind. He knew Hausenstein cared about him, and he asked himself whether he was being a bad friend. But he felt he could no longer trust Hausenstein. It was as if some boundary had been crossed, after which trust became impossible. Those naked automatons were a parody of everything he believed in. Hausenstein couldn't understand, because he believed in nothing. But that wasn't so: he believed in August. Or did he? Did he want him to fail? Did he take some secret delight in undermining the Zaubertheater? Did he want to drag him down into that trough of his, whose true vice was not its filthiness but its coziness, its air of conspiratorial chumminess, its secret banality masquerading as boldness? These were not the questions you asked of a man you called a friend. And yet, aside from Hausenstein, August had no friend. He was alone. August felt a deep pity for himself, for Hausenstein, for the Zaubertheater, for the universe. Suddenly he remembered that something was bothering him, something Hausenstein had said. What was it? Yes: that he would see him in the morning.

August left that night, taking with him half his creatures and leaving behind enough of them so that Hausenstein might continue operating the Zaubertheater if he wished. After all, it had been paid for with his money. August felt no desire for revenge, only a compelling need to be alone. He never saw Hausenstein again. At this point his recollections became brisk and fragmentary: he wandered with his creatures from town to town, renting small halls where he could, and staging performances in makeshift miniature theaters that were sometimes little more than a large empty box with a single hastily painted backdrop and a crude lamp that threw distorting shadows. The performances were sometimes well attended, but the audiences were generally scanty and a little confused. People seemed to come out of curiosity, as they might come to see a ventriloquist, a Fireproof Female, or a magician, and the automaton theater left them with a feeling of puzzlement, as if they had expected something else, something a little different. Hausenstein was right: automatons were dead. Here and there a face lit up with enchantment and understanding, and once a young woman burst into tears during a performance of *Pierrot,* but far more often there was coughing, a creaking of seats, a fanning of flushed cheeks. Once he heard someone say, "It must be some sort of trick—that box must have a false bottom." Tired, always tired, he moved from town to town; often he thought of the magician in the drab green tent. Yes, the art of the automaton was a magical art, for when all was said and done there was something mysterious and unaccountable about clockwork: you breathed into the nostrils of a creature of dust, and lo! it was alive. And so the art of clockwork was a high and noble art: the universe itself had been constructed by the greatest clockwork master of all, and remained obedient to mysterious laws of motion. And on the moving earth, all was ceaseless motion: wind and tide and fire. One day, coming to still another town, August read everywhere of preparations for a fair. And he was pleased: in the rented tent, not green but yellow-brown, he displayed his automatons before children.

He decided to return to Mühlenberg; perhaps he could take up his old trade. But first he wanted to pay a visit to Berlin. He arrived at night and went with wildly beating heart to the Zaubertheater, but the Zaubertheater was no longer there. A small, flourishing restaurant stood in its place, but so transformed in look that he had to stare very hard to be certain. The doorway had been widened and replaced with glass, a glass window had been built into the outer wall, the corridor wall had been torn down, and the stage itself had vanished into thin air. Only the old florid decorations high up on the ceiling remained to tell their tale. August was not unhappy. He would have liked to order a light dinner with a glass of wine—the hake looked first-rate—but the menu in the window was forbidding. A woman inside looked up at him with a frown; he stepped away from the glass. His coat was shabby, his hair long and unclean. On an impulse he decided to seek out the Black Boot, but that too was gone: in its place was a nightclub of a somewhat shady kind. Hausenstein was right: they were deader than a doornail. He thought of paying a visit to the Preisendanz Emporium but was suddenly afraid it might not be there; he wanted something to remain. He took the last train that night.

The train for Mühlenberg does not go as far as Mühlenberg itself, but stops at Ulmbach before continuing to the southwest. At Ulmbach August learned that the coach would leave in forty-six minutes. It was a sunny afternoon. Leaving his battered traveling bag at the coach house, but carrying his rope-tied suitcase of automatons, August took a walk to the back of the coach house and down to the small and nearly dry river, spanned by a wooden bridge. On the other side of the river was a small wood, beyond which he saw factory smokestacks. He crossed the bridge into the wood, spotted with sunlight. He looked for a shady place where he might sit down and eat the pear in his pocket. The wood was deserted; it appeared to be dying. He found a shady spot under a broad, decaying tree. He recognized it as a linden and thought, Hausenstein would have said something witty about that: Unter den Linden. He kicked away a mulch of old leaves covering its half-exposed roots. Sitting down wearily between two roots and half-closing his eyes, he felt shut away peacefully from the river and the factory. He noticed that his suitcase was half-sunk in the leaves and shifted it slightly. There were many leaves lying about, brown leaves and green leaves, and leaves that were green and brown together. August had a sudden idea. Laying the suitcase on its side, he began covering it with leaves. It was done quickly: the leaves had been lying in a depression, and the suitcase was well buried.

For it often happens that way: Fate blunders into a blind alley, and even an entire life can be a mistake. Perhaps one day a child, playing in the leaves, would discover a funny old suitcase. August leaned back against the linden and tried to understand. Was it really his fault that the world no longer cared about clockwork? He supposed it was: Hausenstein had explained it all to him a dozen times. But was beauty subject to fashion? He did not understand. What was a life? One day his father had opened the back of a watch and shown him the wheels inside. Was that his life? A bird inside a funny paper man, the boats in the picture that suddenly began to move, a perspiring magician in a drab green tent—were these the secret signs of a destiny, as intimate and precise as the watermark on a postage stamp? Or were they merely accidents, chosen by memory among the many accidents that constitute a life? He tried desperately to understand. Had it all been a mistake? His art was outmoded: the world had no need for him. And so it had all come to nothing. He had given his life away to a childish passion. And now it was over. He was terribly tired. Sitting under the warm shade of the linden, August grieved for his lost youth. Slowly his eyes closed, and his head fell forward.

August woke with a start. The sun shone brightly through the leaves of the wood. He had dreamed of his rooms in the boarding house near the Preisendanz Emporium. He took out his watch: he hadn't missed the coach. It was warm in the shade. A thrush landed on a branch of the linden, paused as if looking for something, and flew away. Suddenly August looked about in alarm. Where was his suitcase? Where? Stolen while he slept? Thieves in the wood? How? Where? He remembered.

He replaced the watch in his pocket and leaned back against the linden. His heart was beating quickly, and he noticed that a hand was trembling. It was warm in the shade. Two factory smokestacks showed bright white through the trees. August felt that he needed to rest for a long time. But his little nap had refreshed him.

A short while later, he picked up his suitcase and started back to the coach house.

Snowmen

One sunny morning I woke and pushed aside a corner of the blinds. Above the frosted, sun-dazzled bottom of the glass I saw a brilliant blue sky, divided into luminous rectangles by the orderly white strips of wood in my window. Down below, the backyard had vanished. In its place was a dazzling white sea, whose lifted and immobile waves would surely have toppled if I had not looked at them just then. It had happened secretly, in the night. It had snowed with such abandon, such fervor, such furious delight, that I could not understand how that wildness of snowing had failed to wake me with its white roar. The topmost twigs of the tall backyard hedge poked through the whiteness, but here and there a great drift covered them. The silver chains of the bright yellow swing-frame plunged into snow. Snow rose high above the floor of the old chicken coop at the back of the garage, and snow on the chicken-coop roof swept up to the top of the garage gable. In the corner of the white yard the tilted clothespole rose out of the snow like the mast of a sinking ship. A reckless snow-wave, having dashed against the side of the pole, flung up a line of frozen spray, as if straining to pull it all under. From the flat roof of the chicken coop hung a row of thick icicles, some in sun and some in shade. They reminded me of glossy and matte prints in my father's albums. Under the sunny icicles were dark holes in the snow where the water dripped. Suddenly I remembered a rusty rake-head lying teeth down in the dirt of the vegetable garden. It seemed more completely buried than ships under the sea, or the quartz and flint arrowheads that were said to lie under the dark loam of the garden, too far down for me to ever find them, forever out of reach.

I hurried downstairs, shocked to discover that I was expected to eat breakfast on such a morning. In the sunny yellow kitchen I dreamed of dark tunnels in the snow. There was no exit from the house that day except by way of the front door. A thin, dark, wetly gleaming trail led between high snowbanks to the two cement steps before the buried sidewalk, where it stopped abruptly, as if in sudden discouragement. Jagged hills of snow thrown up by the snowplow rose higher than my head. I climbed over the broken slabs and reached the freedom of the street. Joey Czukowski and Mario Salvio were already there. They seemed struck with wonder. Earmuffs up and cap peaks pulled low, they both held snowballs in their hands, as if they did not know what to do with them. Together we roamed the neighborhood in search of Jimmy Shaw. Here and there great gaps appeared in the snow ranges, revealing a plowed driveway and a vista of snowy yard. At the side of Mario's house a sparkling drift swept up to the windowsill. A patch of bright green grass, in a valley between drifts, startled us as if waves had parted and we were looking at the bottom of the sea. High above, white and black against the summer-blue sky, the telephone wires were heaped with snow. Heavy snow-lumps fell thudding. We found Jimmy Shaw banging a stick against a snow-covered stop sign on Collins Street. Pagliaro's lot disturbed us: in summer we fought there with trash-can covers, sticks, and rusty cans, and now its dips and rises, its ripples and contours, which we knew as intimately as we knew our cellar floors, had been transformed into a mysterious new pattern of humps and hollows, an unknown realm reminding us of the vanished lot only by the distorted swelling of its central hill.

Dizzy with discovery, we spent that morning wandering the newly invented streets of more alien neighborhoods. From a roof gutter hung a glistening four-foot icicle, thick as a leg. Now and then we made snowballs, and feebly threw ourselves into the conventional postures of a snowball fight, but our hearts were not really in it—they had surrendered utterly to the inventions of the snow. There was about our snow a lavishness, an ardor, that made us restless, exhilarated, and a little uneasy, as if we had somehow failed to measure up to that white extravagance.

It was not until the afternoon that the first snowmen appeared. There may have been some in the morning, but I did not see them, or perhaps they were only the usual kind and remained lost among the enchantments of the snow. But that afternoon we began to notice them, in the shallower places of front and back yards. And we accepted them at once, indeed were soothed by them, as if only they could have been the offspring of such snow. They were not commonplace snowmen composed of three big snowballs piled one on top of the other, with carrots for noses and big black buttons or smooth round stones for eyes. No, they were passionately detailed men and women and children of snow, with noses and mouths and chins of snow. They wore hats of snow and coats of snow. Their shoes of snow were tied with snow laces. One snowgirl in a summer dress of snow and a straw hat of snow stood holding a delicate snow parasol over one shoulder.

I imagined that some child in the neighborhood, unsettled by our snow, had fashioned the first of these snow statues, perhaps little more than an ordinary snowman with roughly sculpted features. Once seen, the snowman had been swiftly imitated in one yard after another, always with some improvement—and in that rivalry that passes from yard to yard, new intensities of effort had led to finer and finer figures. But perhaps I was mistaken. Perhaps the truth was that a child of genius, maddened and inspired by our fervent snow, had in a burst of rapture created a new kind of snowman, perfect in every detail, which others later copied with varied success.

Fevered and summoned by those snowmen, we returned to our separate yards. I made my snowman in a hollow between the swing and the crab-apple tree. My first efforts were clumsy and oppressive, but I restrained my impatience and soon felt a passionate discipline come over me. My hands were inspired, it was as if I were coaxing into shape a form that longed to spring forth from the fecund snow. I shaped the eyelids, gave a tenseness to the narrow nostrils, completed the tight yet faintly smiling lips, and stepped back to admire my work. Beyond the chicken coop, in Joey's yard, I saw him admiring his own. He had made an old woman in a babushka, carrying a basket of eggs.

Together we went to Mario's yard, where we found him furiously completing the eyes of a caped and mustached magician who held in one hand a hollow top hat of snow from which he was removing a long-eared rabbit. We applauded him enviously and all three went off to find Jimmy Shaw, who had fashioned two small girls holding hands. I secretly judged his effort sentimental, yet was impressed by his leap into doubleness.

Restless and unappeased, we set out again through the neighborhood, where already a change was evident. The stiffly standing snowmen we had seen earlier in the afternoon were giving way to snowmen that assumed a variety of poses. One, with head bent and a hand pressed to his hat, appeared to be walking into a wind, which blew back the skirt of his long coat. Another, in full stride, had turned with a frown to look over his shoulder, and you could see the creases in his jacket of snow. A third bowed low from the waist, his hat swept out behind him. We returned dissatisfied to our yards. My snowman looked dull, stiff, and vague. I threw myself into the fashioning of a more lively snowman, and as the sun sank below a rooftop I stood back to admire my snowy father, sitting in an armchair of snow with one leg hooked over the arm, holding a book in one hand as, with the other, he turned a single curling page of snow.

Yet even then I realized that it was not enough, that already it had been surpassed, that new forms yearned to be born from our restless, impetuous snow.

That night I could scarcely sleep. With throbbing temples and burning eyes I hurried through breakfast and rushed outside. It was just as I had suspected: a change had been wrought. I could feel it everywhere. Perhaps bands of children, tormented by white dreams, had worked secretly through the night.

The snowmen had grown more marvelous. Groups of snowy figures were everywhere. In one backyard I saw three ice-skaters of snow, their heels lifted and their scarves of snow streaming out behind them. In another yard I saw, gripping their instruments deftly, the fiercely playing members of a string quartet. Individual figures had grown more audacious. On a backyard clothesline I saw a snowy tightrope walker with a long balancing stick of snow, and in another yard I saw a juggler holding two snowballs in one hand while, suspended in the air, directly above his upward-gazing face. . . . But it was precisely a feature of that second day, when the art of the snowman appeared to reach a fullness, that one could no longer be certain to what extent the act of seeing had itself become infected by these fiery snow-dreams. And just when it seemed that nothing further could be dreamed, the snow animals began to appear. I saw a snow lion, a snow elephant with uplifted trunk, a snow horse rearing, a snow gazelle. But once the idea of "snowman," already fertile with instances, had blossomed to include animals, new and dizzying possibilities presented themselves, for there was suddenly nothing to prevent further sproutings and germinations; and it was then that I began to notice, among the graceful white figures and the daring, exquisite animals, the first maples and willows of snow.

It was on the afternoon of that second day that the passion for replication reached heights none of us could have foreseen. Sick with ecstasy, pained with wonder, I walked the white streets with Joey Czukowski and Mario Salvio and Jimmy Shaw. "Look at that!" one of us would cry, and "Cripes, look at that!" Our own efforts had already been left far behind, but it no longer mattered, for the town itself had been struck with genius. Trees of snow had been composed leaf by leaf, with visible veins, and upon the intricate twigs and branches of snow, among the white foliage, one could see white sparrows, white cardinals, white jays. In one yard we saw a garden of snow tulips, row on row. In another yard we saw a snow fountain with arching water jets of finespun snow. And in one backyard we saw an entire parlor all of snow, with snow lamps and snow tables and, in a snow fireplace, logs and flames of snow. Perhaps it was this display that inspired one of the more remarkable creations of that afternoon—in the field down by the stream, dozens of furiously intense children were completing a great house of snow, with turrets and gables and chimneys of snow, and splendid rooms of snow, with floors of snow and furniture of snow, and stairways of snow and mirrors of snow, and cups and rafters and sugar bowls of snow, and, on a mantelpiece of marble snow, a clock of snow with a moving ice pendulum.

I think it was the very thoroughness of these successes that produced in me the first stirrings of uneasiness, for I sensed in our extravagant triumphs an inner impatience. Already, it seemed to me, our snowmen were showing evidence of a skill so excessive, an elaboration so painfully and exquisitely minute, that it could scarcely conceal a desperate restlessness. Someone had fashioned a leafy hedge of snow in which he had devised an intricate snow spiderweb, whose frail threads shimmered in the late afternoon light. Someone else had fashioned a kaleidoscope of snow, which turned to reveal, in delicate ice mirrors, changing arabesques of snow. And on the far side of town we discovered an entire park of snow, already abandoned by its makers: the pine trees had pinecones of snow and individual snow needles, on the snow picnic tables lay fallen acorns of snow, snow burrs caught on our trouser legs, and under an abandoned swing of snow I found, beside an empty Coke bottle made of snow, a snow nickel with a perfectly rendered buffalo.

Exhausted by these prodigies, I sought to pierce the outward shapes and seize the unquiet essence of the snow, but I saw only whiteness there. That night I spent in anxious dreams, and I woke feverish and unrefreshed to a sunny morning.

The world was still white, but snow was dripping everywhere. Icicles, longer and more lovely, shone forth in a last, desperate brilliance, rainspouts trickled, rills of bright black snow-water rushed along the sides of streets and poured through the sewer grates. I did not notice them at first, the harbingers of the new order. It was Mario who pointed the first one out to me. From the corner of a roof it thrust out over the rainspout. I did not understand it, but I was filled with happiness. I began to see others. They projected from roof corners, high above the yards, their smiles twisted in mockery. These gargoyles of snow had perhaps been shaped as a whim, a joke, a piece of childish exuberance, but as they spread through the town I began to sense their true meaning. They were nothing less than a protest against the solemnity, the rigidity, of our snowmen. What had seemed a blossoming forth of hidden powers, that second afternoon, suddenly seemed a form of intricate constriction. It was as if those bird-filled maples, those lions, those leaping ballerinas and prancing clowns, had been nothing but a failure of imagination.

On that third and last day, when our snowmen, weary with consummation, swerved restlessly away, I sensed a fever in the wintry air, as if everyone knew that such strains and ecstasies were bound to end quickly. Scarcely had the gargoyles sprouted from the roofs when, among the trees and tigers, one began to see trolls and ogres and elves. They squatted in the branches of real elms and snow elms, they peeked out through the crossed slats of porch aprons, they hid behind the skirts of snow women. Fantastical snowbirds appeared, nobly lifting their white, impossible wings. Griffins, unicorns, and sea serpents enjoyed a brief reign before being surpassed by splendid new creatures that disturbed us like half-forgotten dreams. Here and there rose fanciful dwellings, like unearthly castles, like fairy palaces glimpsed at the bottoms of lakes on vanished summer afternoons, with soaring pinnacles, twisting passageways, stairways leading nowhere, snow chambers seen in fever dreams.

Yet even these visions of the morning partook of the very world they longed to supplant, and it was not until the afternoon that our snowmen began to achieve freedoms so dangerous that they threatened to burn out the eyes of beholders. It was then that distorted, elongated, disturbingly supple figures began to replace our punctilious imitations. And yet I sensed that they were not distortions, those ungraspable figures, but direct expressions of shadowy inner realms. To behold them was to be filled with a sharp, troubled joy. As the afternoon advanced, and the too-soon-darkening sky warned us of transitory pleasures, I felt a last, intense straining. My nerves trembled, my ears rang with white music. A new mystery was visible everywhere. It was as if snow were throwing off the accident of accumulated heaviness and returning to its original airiness. Indeed these spiritual forms, disdaining the earth, seemed scarcely to be composed of white substance, as if they were striving to escape from the limits of snow itself. Walking the ringing streets in the last light, my nerves stretched taut, I felt in that last rapture of snow a lofty and criminal striving, and all my senses seemed to dissolve in the dark pleasures of transgression.

Drained by these difficult joys, I was not unhappy when the rain came.

It rained all that night, and far into the morning. In the afternoon the sun came out. Bright green grass shone among thin patches of snow. Joey Czukowski, Mario Salvio, Jimmy Shaw, and I roamed the neighborhood before returning to my cellar for a game of ping-pong. Brilliant black puddles shone in the sunny streets. Here and there on snow-patched lawns we saw remains of snowmen, but so melted and disfigured that they were only great lumps of snow. We did not discuss the events of the last few days, which already seemed as fantastic as vanished icicles, as unseizable as fading dreams. "Look at that!" cried Mario, and pointed up. On a telephone wire black as licorice, stretched against the bright blue sky, a bluejay sat and squawked. Suddenly it flew away. A dark yellow willow burned in the sun. On a wooden porch step I saw a brilliant red bowl. "Let's do something," said Joey, and we tramped back to my house, our boots scraping against the asphalt, our boot buckles jangling.

from

The Barnum Museum

The Barnum Museum

1

The Barnum Museum is located in the heart of our city, two blocks north of the financial district. The Romanesque and Gothic entranceways, the paired sphinxes and griffins, the gilded onion domes, the corbeled turrets and mansarded towers, the octagonal cupolas, the crestings and crenellations, all these compose an elusive design that seems calculated to lead the eye restlessly from point to point without permitting it to take in the whole. In fact the structure is so difficult to grasp that we cannot tell whether the Barnum Museum is a single complex building with numerous wings, annexes, additions, and extensions, or whether it is many buildings artfully connected by roofed walkways, stone bridges, flowering arbors, booth-lined arcades, colonnaded passageways.

2

The Barnum Museum contains a bewildering and incalculable number of rooms, each with at least two and often twelve or even fourteen doorways. Through every doorway can be seen further rooms and doorways. The rooms are of all sizes, from the small chambers housing single exhibits to the immense halls rising to the height of five floors. The rooms are never simple, but contain alcoves, niches, roped-off divisions, and screened corners; many of the larger halls hold colorful tents and pavilions. Even if, theoretically, we could walk through all the rooms of the Barnum Museum in a single day, from the pyramidal roof of the highest tower to the darkest cave of the third subterranean level, in practice it is impossible, for we inevitably come to a closed door, or a blue velvet rope stretching across a stairway, or a sawhorse in an open doorway before which sits a guard in a dark green uniform. This repeated experience of refused admittance, within the generally open expanses of the museum, only increases our sense of unexplored regions. Can it be a deliberately calculated effect on the part of the museum directors? It remains true that new rooms are continually being added, old ones relentlessly eliminated or rebuilt. Sometimes the walls between old rooms are knocked down, sometimes large halls are divided into smaller chambers, sometimes a new extension is built into one of the gardens or courtyards; and so constant is the work of renovation and rearrangement that we perpetually hear, beneath the hum of voices, the shouts of children, the shuffle of footsteps, and the cries of the peanut vendors, the faint undersound of hammers, pickaxes, and crumbling plaster. It is said that if you enter the Barnum Museum by a particular doorway at noon and manage to find your way back by three, the doorway through which you entered will no longer lead to the street, but to a new room, whose doors give glimpses of further rooms and doorways.

3

The Hall of Mermaids is nearly dark, lit only by lanterns at the tops of posts. Most of the hall is taken up by an irregular black lake or pool, which measures some hundred yards across at its widest point and is entirely surrounded by boulders that rise from the water. In the center of the pool stands a shadowy rock-island with many peaks and hollows. The water and its surrounding boulders are themselves surrounded by a low wooden platform to which we ascend by three steps. Along the inner rim of the platform stand many iron posts about six feet apart, joined by velvet ropes; at the top of every third post glows a red or yellow lantern. Standing on the platform, we can see over the lower boulders into the black water with its red and yellow reflections. From time to time we hear a light splash and, if we are lucky, catch a sudden glimpse of glimmering dark fishscales or yellow hair. Between the velvet ropes and the boulders lies a narrow strip of platform where two guards ceaselessly patrol; despite their vigilance, now and then a hand, glowing red in the lantern light, extends across the ropes and throws into the water a peanut, a piece of popcorn, a dime. There are said to be three mermaids in the pool. In the dark hall, in the uncertain light, you can see the faces at the ropes, peering down intently.

4

The enemies of the Barnum Museum say that its exhibits are fraudulent; that its deceptions harm our children, who are turned away from the realm of the natural to a false realm of the monstrous and fantastic; that certain displays are provocative, erotic, and immoral; that this temple of so-called wonders draws us out of the sun, tempts us away from healthy pursuits, and renders us dissatisfied with our daily lives; that the presence of the museum in our city encourages those elements which, like confidence men, sharpers, palmists, and astrologers, prey on the gullible; that the very existence of this grotesque eyesore and its repellent collection of monstrosities disturbs our tranquillity, undermines our strength, and reveals our secret weakness and confusion. Some say that these arguments are supported and indeed invented by the directors of the museum, who understand that controversy increases attendance.

5

In one hall there is a marble platform surrounded by red velvet ropes. In the center of the platform a brown man sits cross-legged. He has glossy black eyebrows and wears a brilliant white turban. Before him lies a rolled-up carpet. Bending forward from the waist, he unrolls the carpet with delicate long fingers. It is about four feet by six feet, dark blue, with an intricate design of arabesques in crimson and green. Each of the two ends bears a short white fringe. The turbaned man stands up, steps to the center of the carpet, turns to face one of the fringed ends, and sits down with his legs crossed. His long brown hands rest on his lap. He utters two syllables, which sound like "ah-lek" or "ahg-leh," and as we watch, the carpet rises and begins to fly slowly about the upper reaches of the hall. Unlike the Hall of Mermaids, this hall is brightly lit, as if to encourage our detailed observation. He flies back and forth some thirty feet above our heads, moving in and out among the great chandeliers, sometimes swooping down to skim the crowd, sometimes rising to the wide ledge of a high window, where he lands for a moment before continuing his flight. The carpet does not lie stiffly beneath him, but appears to have a slight undulation; the weight of his seated body shows as a faint depression in the carpet's underside. Sometimes he remains aloft for an entire afternoon, pausing only on the shadowy ledges of the upper windows, and because it is difficult to strain the neck in a continual act of attention, it is easy to lose sight of him there, high up in the great spaces of the hall.

6

In the rooms and halls of the Barnum Museum there is often an atmosphere of carnival, of adventure. Wandering jugglers toss their brightly colored balls in the air, clowns jump and tumble, the peanut vendors in their red-white-and-blue caps shout for attention; here and there, in roped-off corners, an artist standing at an easel paints a picture of a bird that suddenly flies from the painting and perches on a window ledge, a magician shakes from his long black hat a plot of grass, an oak tree hung with colored lanterns, and white chairs and tables disposed beneath the branches. In such a hall it is difficult to know where to turn our eyes, and it is entirely possible that we will give only a casual glance to the blue-and-yellow circus cage in the corner where, tired of trailing his great wings in the straw, the griffin bows his weary head.

7

One school of thought maintains that the wonders of the Barnum Museum deliberately invite mechanical explanations that appear satisfactory without quite satisfying, thereby increasing our curiosity and wonder. Thus some claim that the flying carpet is guided by invisible wires, others argue that it must conceal a small motor, still others insist that it is controlled electronically from within the marble platform. One branch of this school asserts that if in fact the explanation is mechanical, then the mechanism is more marvelous than magic itself. The mermaids are readily explained as real women with false fish-tails covering their bottom halves, but it must be reported that no one has ever been able to expose the imposture, even though photographs are permitted on Sundays from three o'clock to five. The lower halves, which all of us have seen, give every appearance of thickness and substance, and behave in every way like fish bodies; no trace of concealed legs is visible; the photographs reveal a flawless jointure of flesh and scale. Many of us who visit the Hall of Mermaids with a desire to glimpse naked breasts soon find our attention straying to the lower halves, gleaming mysteriously for a moment before vanishing into the black pool.

8

There are three subterranean levels of the Barnum Museum. The first resembles any of the upper levels, with the exception that there are no windows and that no sunlight dilutes the glow of the fluorescent ceiling lights. The second level is darker and rougher; old-fashioned gas lamps hiss in the air, and winding corridors lead in and out of a maze of chambers. Crumbling stone stairways lead down to the third level. Here the earthen paths are littered with stones, torches crackle on the damp stone walls, bands of swarthy dwarfs appear suddenly and scamper into the dark. Moldering signs, of which only a few letters are legible, stand before the dark caves. Few venture more than a step or two into the black openings, which are said to contain disturbing creatures dangerous to behold. Some believe that the passageways of the third level extend beyond the bounds of the upper museum, burrowing their way to the very edges of the city. Now and then along the dark paths an opening appears, with black stairs going down. Some say the stairways of the third level lead to a fourth level, which is pitch black and perilous; to descend is to go mad. Others say that the stairways lead nowhere, continuing down and dizzyingly down, beyond the endurance of the boldest venturer, beyond the bounds of imagination itself.

9

It may be thought that the Barnum Museum is a children's museum, and it is certainly true that our children enjoy the flying carpet, the griffin in his cage, the winged horse, the homunculus in his jar, the grelling, the lorax, the giant in his tower, the leprechauns, the Invisibles, the great birds with the faces and breasts of women, the transparent man, the city in the lake, the woman of brass. But quite apart from the fact that adults also enjoy these exhibits, I would argue that the Barnum Museum is not intended solely or even primarily for children. For although there are always children in the halls, there are also elderly couples, teenagers, men in business suits, slim women in blue jeans and sandals, lovers holding hands; in short, adults of all kinds, who return again and again. Even if one argues that certain exhibits appeal most directly to children, it may be argued that other exhibits puzzle or bewilder them; and children are expressly forbidden to descend to the third subterranean level and to enter certain tents and pavilions. But the real flaw in the suggestion that the Barnum Museum is a children's museum lies in the assumption that children are an utterly identical tribe consisting of simple creatures composed of two or three abstract traits, such as innocence and wonder. In fact our children are for the most part shrewd and skeptical, astonished in spite of themselves, suspicious, easily bored, impatient for mechanical explanations. It is not always pleasing to take a child to the Barnum Museum, and many parents prefer to wander the seductive halls alone, in the full freedom of adult yearning, monotony, and bliss.

10

Passing through a doorway, we step into a thick forest and make our way along dark winding paths bordered by velvet ropes. Owls hoot in the nearby branches. The ceiling is painted to resemble a night sky and the forest is illuminated by the light of an artificial moon. We come out onto a moonlit grassy glade. The surrounding wood is encircled by posts joined by velvet ropes; here and there an opening between posts indicates a dark path winding into the trees. It is in the glade that the Invisibles make themselves known. They brush lightly against our arms, bend down the grass blades as they pass, breathe against our cheeks and eyelids, step lightly on our feet. The children shriek in joyful fear, wives cling to their husbands' arms, fathers look about with uncertain smiles. Now and then it happens that a visitor bursts into sobs and is led quickly away by a museum guard. Sometimes the Invisibles do not manifest themselves, and it is only when the visitor, glancing irritably at his watch, begins to make his way toward one of the roped paths, that he may feel, suddenly against his hair, a touch like a caress.

11

It is probable that at some moment between birth and death, every inhabitant of our city will enter the Barnum Museum. It is less probable, but not impossible, that at some moment in the history of the museum our entire citizenry, by a series of overlapping impulses, will find themselves within these halls: mothers pushing their baby carriages, old men bent over canes, au pair girls, policemen, fast-food cooks, Little League captains. For a moment the city will be deserted. Our collective attention, directed at the displays of the Barnum Museum, will cause the halls to swell with increased detail. Outside, the streets and buildings will grow vague; street corners will begin to dissolve; unobserved, a garbage-can cover, blown by the wind, will roll silently toward the edge of the world.

12

The Chamber of False Things contains museum guards made of wax, trompe l'oeil doorways, displays of false mustaches and false beards, false-bottomed trunks, artificial roses, forged paintings, spurious texts, quack medicines, faked fossils, cinema snow, joke-shop ink spills, spirit messages, Martian super-bees, ectoplasmic projections, the footprints of extraterrestrials, Professor Ricardo and Bobo the Talking Horse, false noses, glass eyes, wax grapes, pubic wigs, hollow novels containing flasks of whiskey, and, in one corner, objects from false places: porphyry figurines from Atlantis, golden cups from El Dorado, a crystalline vial of water from the Fountain of Youth. The meaning of the exhibit is obscure. Is it possible that the directors of the museum wish to enhance the reality of the other displays by distinguishing them from this one? Or is it rather that the directors here wittily or brazenly allude to the nature of the entire museum? Another interpretation presents itself: that the directors intend no meaning, but merely wish to pique our interest, to stimulate our curiosity, to lure us by whatever means deeper and deeper into the museum.

13

As we wander the halls of the Barnum Museum, our attention is struck by all those who cannot, as we can, leave the museum whenever they like. These are the museum workers, of whom the most striking are the guards in their dark green uniforms and polished black shoes. The museum is known to be strict in its hiring practices and to demand of all workers long hours, exemplary performance, and unremitting devotion. Thus the guards are expected to be attentive to the questions of visitors, as well as unfailingly courteous, alert, and cheerful. The guards are offered inexpensive lodgings for themselves and their families on the top floor of one wing; few are wealthy enough to resist such enticements, and so it comes about that the guards spend their lives within the walls of the museum. In addition to the guards, whom we see in every room, there are the janitors in their loose gray uniforms, the peanut vendors, the gift-shop salesgirls, the ticket sellers, the coat-check women, the guides in their maroon uniforms, the keepers of the caged griffin, of the unicorn in the wooded hill, of the grelling in his lair, the wandering clowns and jugglers, the balloon men, the lamplighters and torchlighters of the second and third subterranean levels, as well as the carpenters, plasterers, and electricians, who appear to work throughout the museum's long day, from nine to nine. These are the workers we see, but there are others we have heard about: the administrators in small rooms in remote corridors on the upper floors, the researchers and historians, the archivists, the typists, the messengers, the accountants and legal advisers. What is striking is not that there are so many workers, but that they spend so much of their lives inside the museum—as if, absorbed by this realm of enchantments, they are gradually becoming a different race, who enter our world uneasily, in the manner of revenants or elves.

14

Hannah Goodwin was in her junior year of high school. She was a plain, quiet girl with lank pale-brown hair parted in the middle and a pale complexion marred by always erupting whiteheads that she covered with a flesh-colored ointment. She wore plain, neat shirts and drab corduroys. She walked the halls alone, with lowered eyes; she never initiated a conversation, and if asked a question would raise her startled eyes and answer quickly, shifting her gaze to one side. She worked hard, never went out with boys, and had one girlfriend, who moved away in the middle of the year. Hannah seemed somewhat depressed at the loss of her friend, and for several weeks was more reserved than usual. It was about this time that she began to visit the Barnum Museum every day after school. Her visits grew longer, and she soon began returning at night. And a change came over her: although she continued to walk the halls alone, and to say nothing in class, there was about her an inner animation, an intensity, that expressed itself in her gray eyes, in her partly open lips, in the very fall of her hair on her shoulders. Even her walk was subtly altered, as if some stiffness or constraint had left her. One afternoon at the lockers a boy asked her to go to the movies; she refused with a look of surprised irritation, as if he were interrupting a conversation. Although her schoolwork did not suffer, for discipline was an old habit, she was visibly impatient with the dull routines of the day; and as her step grew firmer and her gaze surer, and her bright gray eyes, burning with anticipation, swept up to the big round clock above the green blackboard, it was clear that she had been released from some inner impediment, and like a woman in love had abandoned herself utterly to the beckoning halls, the high towers and winding tunnels, the always alluring doorways of the Barnum Museum.

15

The bridges of the Barnum Museum are external and internal. The external bridges span the courtyards, the statued gardens, the outdoor cafés with their striped umbrellas, so that visitors on the upper floors of one wing can pass directly across the sky to a nearby wing simply by stepping through a window; while down below, the balloon man walks with his red and green balloons shaped like griffins and unicorns, the hurdy-gurdy man turns his crank, a boy in brown shorts looks up from his lemon ice and shades his eyes, a young woman with long yellow hair sits down in the grass in a laughing statue's shade. The internal bridges span the upper reaches of the larger halls. At any moment, on an upper floor, we may step through an arched doorway and find ourselves not on the floor of an adjacent room, but on a bridge high above a hall that plunges down through five stories. Some of these bridges are plain wooden arches with sturdy rails, permitting us to see not only the floor below but pieces of rooms through open doorways with ironwork balconies. Other bridges are broad stone spans lined on both sides with penny-toss booths, puppet theaters, and shops selling jack-in-the-boxes, chocolate circus animals, and transparent glass marbles containing miniature mermaids, winged horses, and moonlit forests; between the low roofs, between the narrow alleys separating the shops, we catch glimpses of the tops of juggled balls, the pointed top of a tent, the arched doorway of a distant room.

16

There are times when we do not enjoy the Barnum Museum. The exhibits cease to enchant us; the many doorways, leading to further halls, fill us with a sense of boredom and nausea; beneath the griffin's delicate eyelids we see the dreary, stupefied eyes. In hatred we rage through the gaudy halls, longing for the entire museum to burst into flame. It is best, at such moments, not to turn away, but to abandon oneself to desolation. Gaze in despair at the dubious halls, the shabby illusions, the fatuous faces; drink down disillusion; for the museum, in its patience, will survive our heresies, which only bind us to it in yet another way.

17

Among the festive rooms and halls of the Barnum Museum, with their flying carpets, their magic lamps, their mermaids and grellings, we come now and then to a different kind of room. In it we may find old paint cans and oilcans, a green-stained gardening glove in a battered pail, a rusty bicycle against one wall; or perhaps old games of Monopoly, Sorry, and Risk, stacks of dusty 78 records with a dog and Victrola pictured on the center labels, a thick oak table-base dividing into four claw feet. These rooms appear to be errors or oversights, perhaps proper rooms awaiting renovation and slowly filling with the discarded possessions of museum personnel, but in time we come to see in them a deeper meaning. The Barnum Museum is a realm of wonders, but do we not need a rest from wonder? The plain rooms scattered through the museum release us from the oppression of astonishment. Such is the common explanation of these rooms, but it is possible to find in them a deeper meaning still. These everyday images, when we come upon them suddenly among the marvels of the Barnum Museum, startle us with their strangeness before settling to rest. In this sense the plain rooms do not interrupt the halls of wonder; they themselves are those halls.

18

It must be admitted that among the many qualities of the Barnum Museum there is a certain coarseness, which expresses itself in the stridency of its architecture, the sensual appeal of certain displays, and the brash abundance of its halls, as well as in smaller matters that attract attention from time to time. Among the latter are the numerous air ducts concealed in the floors of many halls and passageways. Erratically throughout the day, jets of air are released upward, lifting occasional skirts and dresses. This crude echo of the fun house has been criticized sharply by enemies of the museum, and it is certainly no defense to point out that the ducts were installed in an earlier era, when women of all ages wore elaborate dresses to the Barnum Museum—a fact advertised by framed photographs that show well-dressed women in broad-brimmed hats attempting to hold down their skirts and petticoats, which blow up above the knees as gallants in straw hats look on in amusement. For despite the apparent absurdity of air ducts in a world of pants, it remains true that we continue to see a fair number of checked gingham dresses, pleated white skirts, trim charcoal suits, belted poplin shirtwaists, jungle-print shifts, flowery wraparounds, polka-dot dirndls, ruffled jumpers, all of which are continually blowing up in the air to reveal sudden glimpses of green or pink panty hose, lace-trimmed white slips, gartered nylon stockings, and striped bikini underpants amidst laughter and shrill whistles. Our women can of course defeat the ducts by refusing to wear anything but pants to the Barnum Museum, but in fact the ducts appear to have encouraged certain women, in a spirit either of rebellion or capitulation, to dress up in long skirts and decorative underwear, a fad especially popular among girls in junior high school. These girls of twelve and thirteen, who often visit the museum in small bands, make themselves up in bright red or bright green lipstick and false eyelashes, carry shiny leather pocketbooks, and wear flowing ankle-length skirts over glossy plastic boots. The skirts rise easily in the jets of air and reveal a rich array of gaudy underwear: preposterous bloomers with pink bows, candy-colored underpants with rosettes and streamers, black net stockings attached to black lacy garter belts over red lace underwear, old-fashioned white girdles with grotesque pictures of winking eyes and stuck-out tongues printed on the back. Whatever we may think of such displays, the presence of fun-house air ducts in the Barnum Museum is impossible to ignore. To defend them is not to assert their irrelevance; rather, it is to insist that they lend to the museum an air of the frivolous, the childish, the provocative, the irresponsible. For is it not this irresponsibility, this freedom from solemnity, that permits the museum to elude the mundane, and to achieve the beauty and exaltation of its most daring displays?

19

The museum researchers work behind closed doors in small rooms in remote sections of the uppermost floors. The general public is not admitted to the rooms, but some visitors, wandering among the upper exhibits, have claimed to catch glimpses of narrow corridors and perhaps a suddenly opened door. The rooms are said to be filled with piles of dusty books, reaching from floor to ceiling. Although the existence of the researchers is uncertain, we do not doubt its likelihood; although the nature of their task is unknown, we do not doubt its necessity. It is in these remote rooms that the museum becomes conscious of itself, reflects upon itself, and speaks about itself in words that no one reads. The results of research are said to be published rarely, in heavy volumes that are part of immense multivolume collections stored in upper rooms of the museum and consulted only by other researchers. Sometimes, in a narrow corridor on an upper floor, a door opens and a chalk-pale man appears. The figure vanishes so swiftly behind the door that we can never be certain whether we have actually seen one of the legendary researchers, elusive as elves, or whether, unable to endure the stillness, the empty corridors, and the closed doors, we have summoned him into existence through minuscule tremors of our eye muscles, photochemical reactions in our rods and cones, the firing of cells in the visual cortex.

20

In the gift shops of the Barnum Museum we may buy old sepia postcards of mermaids and sea dragons, little flip-books that show flying carpets rising into the air, peep-show pens with miniature colored scenes from the halls of the Barnum Museum, mysterious rubber balls from Arabia that bounce once and remain suspended in the air, jars of dark blue liquid from which you can blow bubbles shaped like tigers, elephants, lions, polar bears, and giraffes, Chinese kaleidoscopes showing ceaselessly changing forms of dragons, enchanting pleniscopes and phantatropes, boxes of animate paint for drawing pictures that move, lacquered wooden balls from the Black Forest that, once set rolling, never come to a stop, bottles of colorless jellylike stuff that will assume the shape and color of any object it is set before, shiny red boxes that vanish in direct sunlight, Japanese paper airplanes that glide through houses and over gardens and rooftops, storybooks from Finland with tissue-paper-covered illustrations that change each time the paper is lifted, tin sets of specially treated watercolors for painting pictures on air. The toys and trinkets of the Barnum Museum amuse us and delight our children, but in our apartments and hallways, in air thick with the smells of boiling potatoes and furniture polish, the gifts quickly lose their charm, and soon lie neglected in dark corners of closets beside the eyeless Raggedy Ann doll and the dusty Cherokee headdress. Those who disapprove of the Barnum Museum do not spare the gift shops, which they say are dangerous. For they say it is here that the museum, which by its nature is contemptuous of our world, connects to that world by the act of buying and selling, and indeed insinuates itself into our lives by means of apparently innocent knickknacks carried off in the pockets of children.

21

The museum eremites must be carefully distinguished from the drifters and beggars who occasionally attempt to take up residence in the museum, lurking in dark alcoves, disturbing visitors, and sleeping in the lower passageways. The guards are continually on the lookout for such intruders, whom they usher out firmly but discreetly. The eremites, in contrast, are a small and rigorously disciplined sect who are permitted to dwell permanently in the museum. Their hair is short, their dark robes simple and neat, their vows of silence inviolable. They drink water, eat leftover rolls from the outdoor cafés, and sleep on bare floors in roped-off corners of certain halls. They are said to believe that the world outside the museum is a delusion and that only within its walls is a true life possible. These beliefs are attributed to them without their assent or dissent; they themselves remain silent. The eremites tend to be young men and women in their twenties or early thirties; they are not a foreign sect, but were born in our city and its suburbs; they are our children. They sit cross-legged with their backs straight against the wall and their hands resting lightly on their knees; they stare before them without appearing to take notice of anything. We are of two minds about the eremites. Although on the one hand we admire their dedication to the museum, and acknowledge that there is something praiseworthy in their extreme way of life, on the other hand we reproach them for abandoning the world outside the museum, and feel a certain contempt for the exaggeration and distortion we sense in their lives. In general they make us uneasy, perhaps because they seem to call into question our relation to the museum, and to demand of us an explanation that we are unprepared to make. For the most part we pass them with tense lips and averted eyes.

22

Among the myriad halls and chambers of the Barnum Museum we come to a crowded room that looks much like the others, but when we place a hand on the blue velvet rope our palm falls through empty air. In this room we pass with ease through the painted screens, the glass display cases, the stands and pedestals, the dark oak chairs and benches against the walls, and as we do so we stare intently, moving our hands about and wriggling our fingers. The images remain undisturbed by our penetration. Sometimes, passing a man or woman in the crowd, we see our arms move through the edges of arms. Here and there we notice people who rest their hands on the ropes or the glass cases; a handsome young woman, smiling and fanning herself with a glossy postcard, sits down gratefully on a chair; and it is only because they behave in this manner that we are able to tell they are not of our kind.

23

It has been said, by those who do not understand us well, that our museum is a form of escape. In a superficial sense, this is certainly true. When we enter the Barnum Museum we are physically free of all that binds us to the outer world, to the realm of sunlight and death; and sometimes we seek relief from suffering and sorrow in the halls of the Barnum Museum. But it is a mistake to imagine that we flee into our museum in order to forget the hardships of life outside. After all, we are not children, we carry our burdens with us wherever we go. But quite apart from the impossibility of such forgetfulness, we do not enter the museum only when we are unhappy or discontent, but far more often in a spirit of peacefulness or inner exuberance. In the branching halls of the Barnum Museum we are never forgetful of the ordinary world, for it is precisely our awareness of that world which permits us to enjoy the wonders of the halls. Indeed I would argue that we are most sharply aware of our town when we leave it to enter the Barnum Museum; without our museum, we would pass through life as in a daze or dream.

24

For some, the moment of highest pleasure is the entrance into the museum: the sudden plunge into a world of delights, the call of the far doorways. For others, it is the gradual losing of the way: the sense, as we wander from hall to hall, that we can no longer find our way back. This, to be sure, is a carefully contrived pleasure, for although the museum is constructed so as to help us lose our way, we know perfectly well that at any moment we may ask a guard to lead us to an exit. For still others, what pierces the heart is the stepping forth: the sudden opening of the door, the brilliant sunlight, the dazzling shop windows, the momentary confusion on the upper stair.

25

We who are not eremites, we who are not enemies, return and return again to the Barnum Museum. We know nothing except that we must. We walk the familiar and always changing halls now in amusement, now in skepticism, now seeing little but cleverness in the whole questionable enterprise, now struck with enchantment. If the Barnum Museum were to disappear, we would continue to live our lives much as before, but we know we would experience a terrible sense of diminishment. We cannot explain it. Is it that the endless halls and doorways of our museum seem to tease us with a mystery, to promise perpetually a revelation that never comes? If so, then it is a revelation we are pleased to be spared. For in that moment the museum would no longer be necessary, it would become transparent and invisible. No, far better to enter those dubious and enchanting halls whenever we like. If the Barnum Museum is a little suspect, if something of the sly and gimcrack clings to it always, that is simply part of its nature, a fact among other facts. We may doubt the museum, but we do not doubt our need to return. For we are restless, already we are impatient to move through the beckoning doorways, which lead to rooms with other doorways that give dark glimpses of distant rooms, distant doorways, unimaginable discoveries. And is it possible that the secret of the museum lies precisely here, in its knowledge that we can never be satisfied? And still the hurdy-gurdy plays, the jugglers' bright balls turn in the air, somewhere the griffin stirs in his sleep. Welcome to the Barnum Museum! For us it's enough, for us it is almost enough.

The Eighth Voyage of Sinbad

For Mark Lehman

Late afternoon, the slant sun bright and the sky blue fire, Sinbad the merchant sits in the warm shade of an orange tree, in the northeast corner of his courtyard garden. Through half-closed eyes he sees spots of sun in leafshade, the white column of the marble sundial, the flash of light on a far white fountain's rim. The voyages flicker and tremble like sunlight on fountain water, and Sinbad cannot remember on which of the seven voyages he arrives at a shore where the trees have ripe yellow fruit and the streams flow crystal clear, he cannot remember, he cannot remember whether the old man clinging to his back comes before or after the hairy apelike creatures who swarm upon the ship, gnawing the ropes and cables with their sharp teeth.

The first European translation of *The Arabian Nights* was made by the French orientalist Antoine Galland, in twelve volumes published between 1704 and 1717. Galland's *Les Mille et Une Nuit* [*sic*], *Contes Arabes*, contains only twenty-one stories, including the *Histoire de Sindbad le Marin*. It is interesting to consider that neither Shakespeare, nor Milton, nor Dante, nor Rabelais, nor Cervantes knew the story of Sinbad the Sailor, or indeed of *The Arabian Nights*, which did not exist in the imagination of Europe until the eighteenth century.

I abode awhile in Baghdad-city savoring my prosperity and happiness and forgetting all I had endured of perils and hardships and sufferings, till I was again seized with a longing to travel and see strange sights, whereupon I bought costly merchandise meet for trade, and binding it into bales, repaired to Bassorah. There I found a tall and noble ship ready to sail, with a full crew and a company of merchants. I took passage with them and set forth in all cheer with a fair wind, sailing from island to island and sea to sea, till one day a great darkness came over the sun, whereat the captain cried out, "Alas! Alas!" and cast his turban to the deck. Then the merchants and the sailors crowded around him and asked in great fear, "O master, what is the matter?" Whereupon he answered, "Know, O my brethren (may Allah preserve you!), that we have come to the sea of whirling waters. There is no might save in Allah the Most High, who alone can deliver us from destruction." Hardly had he made an end of speaking when the ship struck a great swirling and tumbling of waters, which carried it round and round. Some of the merchants were thrown from the ship and drowned, and others made shift to shelter themselves; I seized a rope and lashed myself to the mast, from which post I saw our ship plunge down in the turning water-funnel till the walls of ocean reached high overhead. Then as I fell to weeping and trembling, and besought the succor of Allah the Almighty, behold, a great force smote the ship and broke it into planks, throwing me into the sea, where I seized a piece of mast and continued to be carried down by the turning water; and I was as a dead man for weariness and anguish of heart.

From the pillowed divan in the northeast corner of the courtyard garden, under the shady orange tree, Sinbad can see, through leafshade and sunshine, the white column of the marble sundial that stands in a hexagon of red sand in the center of the courtyard. He cannot see the black shadow on top of the sundial, cast by the triangle of bronze, but he can see the slightly rippling shadow of the column on the red sand. The shadow is twice the length of the column and extends nearly to the edge of the hexagon. Sometimes he remembers only what he has spoken of, say the tall white dome soaring above him and how he walked all around it, finding no door. But sometimes he remembers what he has never spoken of: the stepping from sun to shadow and shadow to sun as he circled the white dome of the roc's egg, the grass, crushed by his footsteps, rising slowly behind him, the sudden trickle of perspiration on his cheek, the itching of his left palm scraped on a branch of the tree he had climbed shortly before, his head among the leaves, and there, beyond the great white thing in the distance, a greenish-blue hill shaped like a slightly crushed turban, a slash of yellow shore, the indigo sea.

There are two different versions of the Sinbad story, each of which exists in several Arabic texts, which themselves differ from one another. The A version is "bald and swift, even sketchy" (Gerhardt, *The Art of Story-Telling: A Literary Study of the Thousand and One Nights*, 1963); the B version is "much more circumstantial." The B redaction may be an embellished version of A, as Gerhardt thinks likely, or else A and B may both derive from an earlier version now lost. The matter of embellishment deserves further attention. B does not simply supply an additional adjective here and there, but regularly provides details entirely lacking in A. In the first voyage, for example, when Sinbad is shipwrecked and reaches an island by floating on a washtub, he reports in the B version that "I found my legs cramped and numbed and my feet bore traces of the nibbling of fish upon their soles" and that, waking the next morning, "I found my feet swollen, so made shift to move by shuffling on my breech and crawling on my knees" (Burton)—details not present in A. In this sense, B is a series of different voyages, experienced by a different voyager.

So clinging to my piece of broken mast and turning in the sea I bemoaned myself and fell to weeping and wailing, blaming myself for having left Baghdad and ventured once again upon the perils of voyages; and as I thus lamented, lo! I was flung forth from the whirling waters, and felt land beneath my side. And marveling at this I lifted my head and saw the sides of the sea rising far above me and at the top a circle of sky. At this my fear and wonder redoubled and looking about me I saw many broken ships lying on the ocean floor, and in the mud of the floor I saw red and green and yellow and blue stones. And taking up a red stone I saw it was a ruby, and taking up a green stone I saw it was an emerald; and the yellow stones and blue stones were topazes and sapphires; for these were jewels that had spilled from the treasure chests of the ships. Then I went about filling my pockets with treasure until I could scarcely walk from the heaviness of the jewels I had gathered. And looking up at the water-walls all about me I berated myself bitterly, for I knew not how I could leave the bottom of the sea; and I felt a rush of wind and heard a roar of waters from the ocean turning in a great whirlpool about me. And seeing that the walls of the sea were coming together, my heart misgave me, and I looked where I might run and hide, but there was no escape from drowning. Then I repented of bringing destruction on myself by leaving my home and my friends and relations to seek adventures in strange lands; and as I looked about, presently I caught sight of a ring of iron lying in the mud and seaweed of the ocean floor. And lifting the ring, which was attached to a heavy stone, I saw a stairway going down, whereat I marveled exceedingly.

Odor of oleander and roses. From a window beyond the garden a dark sound of flutes, soft slap of the black feet of slave girls against tiles. The shout of a muleteer in the street. Although he can no longer reconstruct the history of each voyage, although he is no longer certain of the order of voyages, or of the order of adventures within each voyage, Sinbad can summon to mind, with sharp precision, entire adventures or parts of adventures, as well as isolated images that suddenly spring to enchanted life behind his eyelids, there in the warm shade of the orange tree, and so it comes about that within the seven voyages new voyages arise, which gradually replace the earlier voyages as the face of an old man replaces the face of a child.

According to Gerhardt (*The Art of Story-Telling*), the story of Sinbad was probably composed at the end of the ninth or beginning of the tenth century. According to Joseph Campbell (*The Portable Arabian Nights*, 1952), the story probably dates from the early fifteenth century. According to P. Casanova (*Notes sur les Voyages de Sindbâd le Marin*, 1922), the story dates from the reign of Haroun al Raschid (786–809). According to the translator Enno Littmann (*Die Erzählungen aus den Tausendundein Nächten*, 1954), the story probably dates from the eleventh or twelfth century.

Now when I had descended four of the stairs I replaced the stone over my head, for fear the waters of the sea would rush down on me; after which I continued down the stairway, till the steps of stone grew wet and I came to a dark stream, into which the steps passed. Presently I saw floating on that stream a raft whereon sat an old man of reverend aspect who wore black robes and a black turban, and I cried out to him, but he spake not a word; and stopping at the steps he waited till I sat down behind him. Then we two set forth along the dark stream, which flowed between walls of black marble. Though I accosted him, he turned not his head toward me, nor uttered a word; so in silence we passed along that stream for two days and two nights, till waking on the third day I saw that our way was along the banks of a broad river in sunlight, past date groves and palm groves and stately gardens that came down to the river. Then I saw white minarets and the gilded domes of mosques, and I cried out in astonishment and wonder, for it was Baghdad-city. So I called out to people passing over a bridge, but no one took notice of me; and seizing the pole from the old man, who made no motion to resist, I pushed to shore. Then I passed along the riverbank till I came to the bridge-gate that led into the market street, where I saw people passing; and though I cried out to them, none answered me, nor looked at me; nor did I hear any sound of voices or of passing feet, but all was still as stone. And a great fear coming over me, I wept over myself, saying, "Would Heaven I had died at the bottom of the sea."

Above the rows of orange trees that border the south and west sides of the courtyard, Sinbad sees the tops of pink marble pillars. The deep, pillared corridor runs along all four sides of the courtyard and is surmounted by a gallery upon which all the rooms of the upper story open. Beyond the south wall is a second courtyard with a corridor of pillars, and beyond that a garden, and beyond the garden wall a grove of date palms and orange trees, leading down to the Tigris. The seven voyages have enriched him. In the warm shade and stillness of the garden, it seems to Sinbad that the dreamlike roc's egg, the legendary Old Man of the Sea, the fantastic giant, the city of apes, the cavern of corpses, all the shimmering and insubstantial voyages of his youth, have been pressed together to form the hard marble of those pillars, the weight of that orange bending a branch, that sharp-edged shadow. Then at times it is quite different: the pillars, the gallery, the slave girls and concubines, the gold-woven carpets, the silk-covered divans, the carved fruits and flowers on the ceilings, the wine-filled flagons shimmer, tremble, become diaphanous, and dissolve to reveal the unwound turban binding his waist to the leg of the roc, the giant's sharp eyeteeth the size of boar's tusks, the leg bone of the corpse with which he smashes the skulls of wives and husbands buried alive in the cavern, the shadow of the roc darkening the sun, the jewels torn from the necks of corpses, the legs of the clinging old man black and rough as a buffalo hide.

The three major English translations of *The Arabian Nights* are by Edward William Lane (three volumes, 1839–41), John Payne (nine volumes, 1882–84), and Richard Burton (ten volumes, 1885; six supplemental volumes, 1886–88). The translation by Lane contains roughly two-fifths of the original material; the tales he does include are heavily bowdlerized. In the story of Sinbad, for example, the episode of the mating horses in the first voyage is omitted. The translation by John Payne is the first complete and unexpurgated version in English. Burton's translation is likewise complete and unexpurgated; it relies so heavily on Payne, borrowing entire sentences and even paragraphs, that Burton cannot escape the charge of plagiarism. "Burton's translation," Gerhardt states, "really is Payne's with a certain amount of stylistic changes." Burton, in his "Terminal Essay" (vol. X), defines the difference between Payne's translation and his own thus: "Mr. Payne's admirable version appeals to the Orientalist and the 'stylist,' not to the many-headed; and mine to the anthropologist and student of Eastern manners and customs." He is here calling attention to his voluminous footnotes. Burton, who never fails to praise Payne's style, is less kind to Lane, referring to his "curious harsh and latinized English, at once turgid and emasculated." Gerhardt finds Lane's style "plodding but honest"; he says of Payne's translation that it is written in "a tortured and impossible prose, laboriously constructed out of archaic and rare words and turns." Campbell finds Payne's translation "superb" and calls it the "most readable" version in English, which "omits, moreover, not a syllable of the vigorous erotica." Gerhardt judges Burton's translation to be generally reliable but adds: "The English prose in which it is written, however, is doubtless still worse than Payne's."

So as I walked about the streets of the city I came to the gate of a great house, with a stone bench beside the door, and within the gate I saw a flower garden. Now at this sight my wit became dazed, and a trembling came over me; and I passed within the gate and through the garden. Then I entered the house and passed from room to room, wherein I saw pages and slave girls and servants and attendants, but none took notice of me, till coming to a wide door I stepped forth from the house into the inner courtyard. There I saw orange trees and date trees, and an abundance of sweet-smelling flowers, and marble fountains, and a sundial in red sand; and beneath an orange tree sat a man whose eyes were closed and whose beardsides were streaked with white. Then I was confounded, and I fell to trembling, and knew not what to do; and all was silent in that place. So after a time I cried out "Sinbad!" but he stirred not. Then I fled from that garden, and passing through many rooms I came to an orchard of date trees, which led down to the river. And finding a boat at the riverbank I seized the oars and rowed along the water, till my arms ached and my hands were sore; and as my course continued, the channel grew straiter and the air darker, and I saw banks of stone rising high on both sides. Then a voice called out to me from the bank, and I saw an opening in the stone, where an old man squatted on a rock; and he said, "Who art thou and whence farest thou? How camest thou into this river?" Then I answered him, "I am the merchant Sinbad, whose ship went down to the bottom of the sea, and there I found a stairway leading to this place. What city is that behind me, which I have seen?" Quoth he, "Unhappiest of mortals, that is a demon-city. Better it is, never to have seen that city, than to find a ship filled with pearls." Then seeing my unhappiness, and seeing that I was weak from thirst and hunger, he offered to lead me to his city, that I might rest and refresh me, whereat I thanked him; after which he hopped from the rock into my boat beside me, which was great wonder to see, for his legs were as the legs of frogs; and squatting beside me he bade me enter the opening in the cliff.

In the warm shade of the orange tree, leaning back against the silk pillows of the divan, Sinbad half dreams of the telling of the voyages. At first the telling had made the voyages so vivid to him that it was as if the words had given them life, it was as if, without the words, the voyages had been slowly darkening or disappearing. Thus the voyages took shape about the words, or perhaps took shape within the words. But a change had been wrought, by the telling. For once the voyages had been summoned by the words, a separation had seemed to take place, as if, just to one side of the words, half-hidden by their shadows, the voyages lay dreaming in the grass. In the shade of the orange tree Sinbad tries to remember. Are there then two septads of voyages, the seven that are told and the seven that elude the telling? Before the telling, what were the voyages? Unspoken, did they exist at all? Are there perhaps three septads: the seven voyages, the memory of the seven voyages, and the telling of the seven voyages? Sinbad shifts in his seat. From a bough a blackbird shrills.

The seven voyages of Sinbad are cast as first-person narratives, told by the protagonist (Sinbad). But it is important to remember that Sinbad himself is a character in a story narrated "in time long gone before" (Burton) by Scheherazade to King Shahriyar of Persia. Scheherazade in turn is a character in *The Arabian Nights*. The unnamed omniscient narrator of *The Arabian Nights* recounts the story of Scheherazade, the well-read daughter of the King's vizier, who over the course of one thousand and one nights tells nearly two hundred stories to the King to prevent him from killing her; during the course of the thousand and one nights, she bears him three children. In what sense therefore may we say that Sinbad narrates his voyages? Scheherazade, who reports his words, has a strong motive for her storytelling, which has nothing whatever to do with Sinbad and his storytelling. Perhaps she inserts words in his mouth that serve her own purposes. Each night of storytelling begins with the words: "She said, It hath reached me, O auspicious King, that . . ." —a formula that invites speculation. We may wonder whether Sinbad's words are his own or Scheherazade's, we may wonder whether Scheherazade has omitted details for the sake of shaping her tale effectively, we may wonder whether there are episodes from the seven voyages, or even entire voyages, that did not reach her.

Then we passed along the stream and came to a town built on one side of the water, and on the other side was a great marsh; and I was received courteously by the folk of that town, and ate and drank till my strength returned. Now the inhabitants of that place lived there by day, but by night they swam across the water to the marsh, for they were frog folk with sinewy and slick legs like the legs of marsh frogs; and they moved by hopping from one place to another. Yet by day they lived in fine houses and drank wine from cups and listened to the music of flutes and had servants and slaves and were in all ways courteous and kind. These folk fed on fish, which they hunted in strange wise. They concealed themselves in hollow dwellings at the bottom of the river, for they were amphibious folk that could breathe under water, and they swam out through a cunning door hidden in the side of the dwelling and thrust sharp sticks at fish that swam there. And though they were exceeding kind, yet when I enquired how I might return to Baghdad, they knew naught of it, nor how I might return there. I abode with the frog folk for many days and nights, remaining alone in the town when they swam across the river to the marsh, till one night, when I could not sleep for sorrow, I rose from the floor and walked for solace into the meadow behind the town. There I sat down and bemoaned myself, saying, "Would Heaven I had been drowned in the sea! That were better than to live among frog folk to the end of my days. But what the Lord willeth must come to pass, for there is no Majesty and there is no Might save in Allah the Glorious." Scarcely had I spoken when I heard a fluttering in that field and saw not far distant a flock of low-flying birds. Then I rose and went over to those birds, to see what sort they were, and behold, they were no birds, but strange creatures such as I knew not, for they had no wings, nor tails, nor feathers, nor faces, yet they flew in the air. So as I drew near I saw some settling in the grass, and I approached them warily, for fear they might attack me and put out my eyes.

Through half-closed eyes heavy with heat and shadow, Sinbad watches the brilliant column of the sundial in its hexagon of red sand. Dim cries sound from the river beyond the date grove. Murmur of insects, sweet smell of rotting orange blossoms. Dark blue shadows of leaves on the white rim of the fountain. Slowly a great bird descends. It settles on the sundial and folds its dark blue wings. Its long tail touches the sand. Sinbad has never seen such a bird before and rising from the divan he steps over to touch its shimmering, warm side. The bird lifts a wing, sweeping Sinbad onto its back, and at once rises into the air. Sinbad clutches the thick oily feathers as the bird flies over the city. Far below he can see the brown river with its boats and barges, the shadow of the bridges on the water, the palm trees the size of date stones, the slender white towers, the gilded onion domes like scattered gold dinars, the little green gardens, the little dromedaries in the little streets. Slowly the bird descends, the garden rises, Sinbad slides from the back of the bird and watches as it lifts its wings and soars into the fierce blue sky. In the warm shade of the orange tree he watches the brilliant column of the sundial in its hexagon of red sand. The mysterious, the magical, the unexpected do not happen in his garden, and after deep thought he concludes that the bird was a dream or illusion, summoned by the heat, the flicker of leaf-shade, an old man's weariness.

The frontispiece of Burton's Volume VI (Illustrated Benares Edition) shows an engraving of two rocs attacking a ship. These are not the rocs of the second voyage, who nest above the Valley of Diamonds, but the two rocs of the fifth voyage, who drop great boulders on Sinbad's ship. The female roc is shown grasping a boulder in her claws. One of her wings is as long as the two-masted ship below, and the boulder is as thick as the height of the men cowering on deck. The roc resembles a great eagle, but with a long neck; at the top of the hooked beak, between the eyes, is a disturbing hump. The male roc, at the top of the engraving, is closer to the viewer and is visible only as a pair of immense talons and some half-dozen feathers. The talons resemble the feet of roosters and have sharp, curved nails on each long toe. They have just released their boulder, as indicated by a splash beside the ship's bow in the lower left-hand corner of the engraving. We know from the story that the second boulder will strike the ship. One little man holds up his arms as if to ward off a blow; another lies face down on the deck; a third is diving over the side. The water about the ship is mostly white, with several curving lines indicating agitation; in the background the water is darker, drawn with many lines, and appears thick.

Now when I drew close to those creatures in the grass, suddenly they rose up and flew a little distance away, whereat I followed; and in this manner I drew farther and farther from the town, till looking about me I saw I had lost my way. I was among steep hills, which rose up on all sides; and I was as a dead man for weariness, and knew not what to do. So looking about, I saw those creatures rise from the grass, and I followed them into a nearby valley, where I beheld a marvelous sight. The valley was filled with flying creatures, which made a noise as of many winds. Then I saw that one lay in the grass not far from where I stood, and when I descended a small way to see what it was, all unknowing I stumbled on one hidden in the grass, and fell upon it fearfully, and lo! it rose in the air bearing me on its back. And I saw that it was a carpet, that flew like a bird; and I was in a valley of flying carpets, that flew to and fro. So lying on my stomach and quaking in great fear, for I knew not whether I would plunge to destruction, I gripped the sides of my carpet and flew down into the valley. And the valley was so thick with those flying creatures that I felt them brush against my cheeks and fingers; and I held tight with one hand, and covered my face with the other. At the bottom of the valley there was an opening in the hillside, and thither my carpet carried me; and I entered a great dark cavern. Now at the bottom of the cavern sat three men with beards who worked at three looms. And one, seeing me, cried out as if in anger; and that old man picked up a stone and threw it at me, striking the underside of the carpet, so that I felt a blow in my ribs. Then another called up to me coaxingly, saying, "Come down, and we will reward you"; but I trusted them not.

Old man's hour: heat and shade of late afternoon. Green hands, blue shadows, a slight oppression in the chest. Behind the eyelids rings of light, red-yellow, dancing. Bone-weariness and a dull drumming in the ears. The voyages are rings of red light dancing. There are no voyages, only the worm-thick veins on the back of the hand. Only the heavy body, the laboring heart, blossoms rotting under the sun. Dead hour: his hands green corpses. The stench of corpses, the groans of the dying in the cavern under the mountain. His dead wife beside him, rotting in her jewels. A pitcher of water and seven cakes of bread. He swings the leg bone and crushes the skull. He lifts the stone and crushes the skull of the old man with buffalo-hide legs. A shrill cry cuts him like a blade. Bright blue sky, the cry of the blackbird. Heat, shade: old man's hour.

Sinbad addresses his tales to a double audience: a company of lords and nobles, who are his friends, and a poor porter, also named Sinbad, who is a stranger and whose melancholy verses recited outside the gate have incited Sinbad the merchant to narrate his seven voyages. Sinbad's immediate purpose is to persuade the poor porter that he became wealthy only after hardship and misfortune, as represented by the voyages; that is, to persuade the poor man that the merchant's immense wealth is deserved. To put it another way, Sinbad is attempting to justify his life. His purpose in narrating the voyages to the lords and nobles is less clear. We know that Sinbad has been struck by the identity of his name and that of the poor porter, because he asserts it for all to hear; a moment later he greets the porter as "brother." Perhaps, then, in the presence of the poor man Sinbad feels a need to set himself apart from his wealthy friends, to insist on his difference. It is evident that he has never spoken to them of his voyages before; they are his secret. In this sense the narration of the voyages to the lords and nobles is a form of confession. It is difficult to state precisely the nature of this confession, but surely it has to do with Sinbad's restlessness, his craving for violent adventure, his inner wildness and boredom—everything, in short, that separates him from the sober and respectable, everything that secretly undermines his shrewd merchant's nature. In any case, Sinbad requires for the recital of his story the presence of both the wealthy company and the poor porter; each morning the porter arrives early at Sinbad's house and is made to wait for the rest of the company before the story of the next voyage begins. We may imagine Sinbad now directing a sharp glance at Sinbad the porter as he relates the details of a shipwreck or a fit of despair, now lowering his eyes modestly as he describes a cunning stratagem, now casting a broad gaze over the company of lordly friends as he recounts the story of his marriage to a beautiful and wealthy woman of noble lineage, the ruby cup, the audience with the caliph.

Now though I trusted them not, I cried down to them, "How may I come down to you? For I know not how to manage this steed, and would come among you as a friend." With that I took forth from a fold in my robe one of the jewels I had gathered from the sea bottom, and let it fall among them as earnest of my good will; whereupon the men at the looms called up to me in friendly voices, and urged me to come down to them, which I might do by turning down the corner of my carpet beside my right hand. Now when I heard those words I was loath to come down, but grasping the corner of my carpet I pulled it upward, and behold, I rose high above them. Then the old men began shouting at me in anger, but I flew all about them, making my carpet go higher and lower as I desired, till seeing another opening at the base of the cavern I directed my way thither and entered in. There I found myself in a long passageway with doors of brass and silver on both sides. One of the brazen doors being open, I directed my way within, where I discovered a stately garden with trees bearing red and yellow fruits, and a great mountain beyond the garden; and being hungry I flew low to pluck a piece of fruit, but the red fruit were rubies, and the yellow fruit topazes, whereat I rejoiced and seized as many as I could from the thick-fruited branches. On the far side of the garden I came to the base of the great mountain, where I saw a fissure in the rock, and flying into the fissure I found myself in a vast and darksome cavern, wherein was no light save a faint glimmer high above.

There is peace in Sinbad's garden. Sunlight falls on the date trees and orange trees; in sun and shade, the waters of marble fountains fall. A hidden fountain stands in a walnut grove; a pomegranate tree burns in the sun. Sinbad can distinguish the songs of blackbirds, ringdoves, and nightingales. He listens for turtledoves and mockingbirds. He has even purchased twelve parrots, which reveal themselves from time to time among the dark leaves as vivid flashes of orange and yellow. At this moment, in the warm shade of the orange tree, the voyages are bereft of enchantment. The flight through the air, the giant's eyeteeth like boar's tusks, the old man clinging to his back, the serpents the size of palm trees in the Valley of Diamonds, all are banal and boring images, of no more interest than someone else's dream or the fantasies of young children, and tainted by suspicious resemblances to the commonplace reports of all voyagers. They cannot compare with the cry of the blackbird, the sunstruck dome of a mosque, the creak of rigging in the harbor ships, the miraculous structure of a pomegranate or a camel, the shouts of the sellers of dried fruits, the beating out of copper basins in the market of the coppersmiths, the trembling blue shadow cast by falling water on a marble fountain's rim, the immense collection of precise details that compose the city of Baghdad at this moment.

The story of Sinbad is set during the reign of the Caliph Haroun al Raschid, who himself is the hero of a cycle of stories in *The Arabian*

Nights. In the third chapter of *Ulysses*, Stephen Dedalus walks along the beach at Sandymount and thinks:

> After he woke me up last night same dream or was it? Wait. Open hallway. Street of harlots. Remember. Haroun al Raschid.

Leopold Bloom, falling asleep beside his wife, thinks of Sinbad and the roc's egg. Earlier we learn that Bloom once attempted to write a song called *If Brian Boru could but come back and see old Dublin now,* to be "introduced into the sixth scene, the valley of diamonds, of the second edition (30 January 1893) of the grand annual Christmas pantomime *Sinbad the Sailor.*" If Bloom is Ulysses, he is also Sinbad, setting forth on a voyage through the perilous seas of Dublin. During a single day in June 1904, both Bloom and Stephen think of characters in *The Arabian Nights;* it is another of the spiritual habits that secretly unite them. Molly Bloom, toward the end of her immortal monologue, remembers her girlhood in Gibraltar: the handsome Moors with turbans, the sailors playing "All Birds Fly," the Arabs, the Moorish wall. These memories, which seem to carry her away from the husband sleeping beside her, secretly unite her with Bloom-Sinbad, the returned voyager, the sailor home from the sea.

Then I directed my carpet upward toward the gleam, but though I flew higher and higher I could not reach that height. And I could have cried out for weariness and heart-sorrow, when suddenly I drew near the light, which was an opening in the rock; and I flew out through a cave into blue sky above the salt sea. Then I rejoiced that I had escaped from the land beneath the sea, and gave thanks to Allah Almighty for my deliverance. Yet was I sore dismayed to see the empty ocean reaching away, and to feel my precarious mount under me; whereupon I directed my carpet down to the shore of the sea, there to rest me and take counsel with myself. But so eager was I to set my feet on earth, that I took no care to secure the carpet, which rose into the air without me and returned into the opening in the cliff. So I blamed myself for my folly, yet could do naught but abide there till it should please Almighty Allah to send me relief by means of some passing ship. Thus I abode for many days and nights, feeding on wild berries that grew on bushes at the base of the cliff, till one day I caught sight of a ship; and removing my turban and placing it on the end of a branch I waved it to and fro till they espied me, and sent a boat to fetch me to them.

Beyond the warm shade of the orange tree, the late afternoon sun burns on the garden grass. The shadow of the sundial extends to the rim of the hexagon of red sand. With half-closed eyes Sinbad broods over his half-remembered voyages. If all the voyages taken together are defined as a single vast collection of sensations, is it necessary to order them chronologically? Are not other arrangements possible? Sinbad imagines the telling of other tales: a tale of shipwrecks, a tale of odors, a tale of monsters, a tale of clouds, a tale of breakfasts, a tale of murders, a tale of jewels, a tale of wives, a tale of despairs, a tale of Mondays, a tale of fauna and flora, a tale of eyes (eyes of the roc, eyes of wives, eyes of the giant, merchants' eyes).

Sinbad recites each of his voyages from start to finish in an unbroken monologue during a single day. It is not clear at what time Sinbad the porter enters his house on the first day, but starting with the second day he arrives early in the morning and sits with Sinbad the merchant until the company of friends arrives. All are served breakfast, and the entire gathering listens to the recital of a complete voyage, after which they eat dinner and depart. Sinbad's recital of the voyages therefore takes seven full days, from breakfast to dinner. But there is a second narrative movement that intersects this one. The story of Sinbad, who recites his story by day, is told by Scheherazade, who recites her story at night. There is something deeply pleasing about this scheme, which seems to permit the voyages to take place simultaneously during the day and night. But Scheherazade's recital takes much longer than Sinbad's: she begins the story at the very end of Night 536 and completes it toward the end of Night 566. It therefore takes Scheherazade thirty nights, from evening to dawn, to recite the seven voyages of Sinbad, who himself requires only seven days, from breakfast to dinner. This curious asymmetry provokes conjecture. Are we to imagine a number of unreported interruptions in Scheherazade's story—for example, bouts of lovemaking—that account for the much greater time required for her story than for Sinbad's identical one? Are we to imagine that Scheherazade speaks much more slowly than Sinbad, whose voice she adopts? Does Scheherazade perhaps begin very late at night, so that the total number of hours spent reciting the story of Sinbad is not more than the number of hours he himself requires? Are we to imagine that Scheherazade recites a much longer version of the voyages, which only the King is permitted to hear, and that we have been allowed to overhear only selected portions of those longer tales? However we account for the discrepancy, it remains true that the seven voyages narrated by Scheherazade are interrupted thirty times by the words: "And Shahrazad perceived the dawn of day and ceased saying her permitted say" (Burton). The break never comes at the end of a voyage. In the second voyage, for example, the first break comes in the middle of the opening sentence; in the third voyage, the first break comes several pages into the narrative, after the description of the frightful giant. There are thus two distinct narrative movements: that of the seven voyages, each of which forms a single narrative unit and takes a single day for Sinbad to recite, and that of Scheherazade's recital, which breaks the voyages into thirty units that never coincide with the beginning or end of a voyage. There is also a third movement to be considered. The reader may complete the entire story of Sinbad at a sitting, or he may divide his reading into smaller units, which will not necessarily coincide with the narratives of Sinbad or Scheherazade, and which will change from one reading to another.

The captain of the ship was a merchant, who heard my tale with wonder and amazement and promised me passage to the Isle of Kullah, from whence I might take ship to Baghdad-city. So we pursued our voyage from island to island and sea to sea, till one day a great serpent rose from the waves and struck at our ship, cracking the mainmast in twain and turning the sails to tatters and staving in the ship sides. We were thrown into the sea, where some drowned and others were devoured by the serpent; but by permission of the Most High I seized a plank of the ship, whereon I climbed, bestriding it as I would a horse and paddling with my feet. I clung thus two days and two nights, helped on by a wind, and on the third day shortly after sunrise the waves cast me upon dry land, where I crawled onto high ground and lay as one dead. When I woke I fed on some herbs that grew on the shore, and at once fell into a deep sleep that lasted for a day and a night; and my strength returning little by little, I soon set out to explore the place whither Destiny had directed me. I came to a wood of high trees, of which many stood without tops, or lay fallen with their roots raised high, whereat I wondered greatly, till climbing a hill I saw below me a city on the shore of the sea. But a great calamity had befallen the city, for the houses stood without roofs to cover them, great ships lay half-sunk in the harbor, and carts lay overturned in the streets; and everywhere came a sound of lamenting from the inhabitants of that town.

The trunks of the date palms in the southwest corner of the garden are enclosed from root to top in carved teakwood, encircled with gilt copper rings. Sunlight flashes on the rings of the palm trees, on the white rim of the fountain, on the hexagon's red sand. In the warm shade of the orange tree, in the northeast corner of the courtyard, it occurs to Sinbad that his voyages are nothing but illusions. He is attracted by the idea, which has come to him before. The fantastic creatures, such as the roc, the black giant, the serpents the size of palm trees, the Old Man of the Sea, are clearly the stuff of dream or legend, and dissolve into mist when set beside the sharp realities of a merchant's life in Baghdad. True, travelers have often reported strange sights, but it is well known that such accounts tend toward exaggeration and invention. As if the implausible creatures themselves were not proof enough, there is the repeated pattern of shipwreck and rescue, of hairbreadth escapes, of relentless and improbable good fortune. And then there is the suspect number of voyages: seven, that mysterious and magical number, which belongs to the planets, the metals, the colors, the precious stones, the parts of the body, the days of the week. No, the evidence points clearly to illusion, and the explanation is not far to seek: the tedium of a merchant's life, the long hours in the countinghouse, the breeding images of release. Impossible to say whether he imagined the voyages in his youth, and now remembers them as if they had actually taken place, or whether he imagined them in his old age and placed them back, far back, in a youth barely remembered. Does it matter? Sinbad is weary. On the rings of the palm trees, sunlight flashing.

There is one major difference between the A and B versions of "Sinbad the Sailor": the seventh voyage. In the seventh voyage of A, Sinbad is captured by pirates and sold to a master for whom he hunts elephants. In the seventh voyage of B, Sinbad is shipwrecked and comes to an island where he finds, under a mountain, a city whose inhabitants grow wings once a month and fly. In A, Sinbad returns alone to Baghdad; in B, he returns with a wife, and learns that he has been away for twenty-seven years. Burton, stating in a note that "All respecting Sinbad the Seaman has an especial interest," offers the reader translations of each of the seventh voyages, first B and then A. His readers have the curious privilege of reading a brief report of Sinbad's death and, immediately after it, Sinbad's account of another voyage—the voyage beyond the final voyage.

So I descended into the ruined city and asked one whom I found there what had befallen that place. Answered he, "Know, stranger, that our King hath incurred the wrath of a great Rukh, who once a year lays waste our city. Now I desire that thou tell me who thou art; for none comes hither willingly." Thereupon I acquainted him with my story, and he taking pity on me brought me food and drink from the ruins of his home; and when I was refreshed and satisfied he offered to lead me to his King, that I might acquaint him with my case; for it was a custom of that island, that strangers be brought before the King. Then I set forth with him and fared on without ceasing till we came to a great palace all in ruins, so that pillars of white marble lay scattered about the gardens, and many rooms and apartments stood without walls, and were exposed to view. We came to a garden where a great boulder lay beside a shattered fountain, and in the shadow of the boulder sat the King, who gave me a cordial welcome and bade me tell my tale. So I related to him all that I had seen and all that had befallen me from first to last, whereupon he wondered with great wonder at my adventures, and bade me sit beside him; and he called for food and drink, and I ate with him and drank with him and returned thanks to Allah Almighty, glorifying his name. Then when we had done eating I asked whether I might take ship from that port, but he sighed a sigh of deep sorrow, saying that all his ships lay sunk in the harbor; and he said no ship dared approach his isle for fear of the Rukh that was his enemy. Then the King fell into grievous silence. And I seeing the case he was in, and fearing to live out my days far from my native place, took counsel with myself, saying in my mind, "Peradventure this King will deal kindly with me, and reward me, if by permission of Allah the Glorious I rid him of his enemy the Rukh."

In the warm shade of the orange tree, Sinbad imagines another Sinbad from across the sea. He is a Sinbad who lives in a land of rocs, giants, ape-folk, immense serpents, streams strewn with pearls and rubies, valleys of diamonds. One day, intending to do business on a neighboring island, Sinbad mounts the back of a roc and sets forth through the sky. A sudden storm blows the roc off course; in the wind and rain Sinbad loses his grip and falls through the air. He splashes into a river, swims to shore, and finds himself in Baghdad. The palm trees astonish him; he has never seen a silk pillow or a camel; he is enchanted by the miraculous birds no bigger than a man's hand. He walks in wonder, entranced by a porter bent under a bundle, frightened by a ship with sails gliding magically along the river, amazed by a stone bench, a sticky date, a turban. One day he takes passage on a ship and arrives back in the land of rocs and giants. He tells his tale of wonders to a group of friends who listen in attitudes of astonishment, while beyond the open doorway rocs glide in the blue sky, serpents the size of palm trees glisten in the sun, somewhere a giant lies down and shuts his weary eyes.

Sinbad inhabits two Baghdads. The first Baghdad is a place of "ease and comfort and repose," where he lives in a great house among servants, slaves, musicians, concubines, and a rather vague "family," and where he continually entertains many friends, all of whom are lords and noblemen. It is the familiar and well-loved place, the place to which he longs to return in the midst of his perilous voyages. The second Baghdad is never described but is no less present. It is the hellish place of all that is known, the place of boredom and despair, the place that banishes surprise. In the second Baghdad he is continually assaulted by a longing to travel, a longing so fierce, irrational, and destructive that more than once he refers to it as an evil desire: "the carnal man was once more seized with longing for travel and diversion and adventure" (Burton, third voyage). The voyages, in relation to the first Baghdad, are dangerous temptations, succumbed to in moments of weakness; in relation to the second Baghdad, they are release and deliverance. Or perhaps it is more accurate to say that hellish Baghdad creates the voyages, which in turn create heavenly Baghdad. In this sense the two Baghdads may be seen as spiritual states between which Sinbad continually oscillates. The restlessness of Sinbad, as he alternately seeks rupture and repose, is so much the secret rhythm of the story that it is difficult for us to believe in a Sinbad who chooses one Baghdad over the other, difficult for us to believe in a contented Sinbad who settles down peacefully with paunch and pantofles among his friends and concubines, a Sinbad who severs himself from the unknown, a Sinbad who does not set forth on an eighth voyage.

Then when I had taken counsel with myself I said to the King, "Know, O my lord, that I have a plan whereby to catch the Rukh; which if it succeed, I ask only passage from your port." Now when the King heard this, he said that if I spake true, he would have me a great ship builded, and filled with pieces of gold; but if I lied, then he would command that I be buried alive. Then did my flesh quake, but I solaced myself, saying within, "Better it is to be buried alive than to live out my days in a strange land, far from my native place." Then I bethought me of the frog folk that live under the ocean and conceal themselves in hollow dwellings when they would catch fish. And I instructed that a great egg be fashioned of marble, fifty paces in circumference, and left hollow within, and set in the meadowlands without the town. So the King gathered about him his engineers, his miners of marble, his sculptors and his palace architect, and devised how they should bring the stone to the field and fashion the egg therefrom. And when the work was accomplished, the people of the city gathered round it in wonder. Then I instructed that twenty great boulders be brought to the field and laid about the egg, and thick ropes fashioned by the ropemakers. Then the ropes were fastened about the boulders and the ends left in the grass. And a cunning door was in the egg, so that when the door was shut the egg was smooth. Then forty of the King's chosen soldiers entered the egg, and the door was shut behind them.

The white column of the marble sundial shimmers in the sun. It stands in the center of the garden, far beyond the leaves that shade Sinbad and allow only small spaces of light to fall on his hands and lap. The sun beats down on the white sundial and the warm shade presses against Sinbad's eyelids. In the intense light the sundial in its hexagon of red sand seems to tremble. It shimmers, it trembles, slowly it becomes a white roc's egg in the sand. The egg begins to turn slowly and unwind. It is a white turban, unwinding. Sinbad grasps an end of the turban and ties himself to the leg of a roc. He feels himself lifted high in the air and sees that he has tied himself to a serpent. He undoes the turban and falls into a dark cavern where a giant with eyeteeth like boar's tusks seizes the captain and thrusts a long spit up his backside, bringing it forth with a gush of blood at the crown of his head. Sinbad plunges the red-hot iron into the giant's eye and sees his wife lying dead at his feet. He lies down beside her and touches her cheek with his hand. Her eyes open. Tears flow from her eyes and become red and green jewels. Sinbad gathers the jewels faster and faster and runs through the cavern of corpses with jewels in his arms. He stops to drink at the side of a stream and when he lifts his head an old man asks him to carry him across on his back. Sinbad feels oppressed. The old man begins to shimmer and tremble.

In Lane, "khaleefah"; in Payne, "khalif"; in Burton, "caliph." In Lane, "Haroon Er-Rasheed"; in Payne, "Haroun er Reshid"; in Burton, "Harun al-Rashid." In Lane, "wezeer"; in Payne, "vizier"; in Burton, "wazir." In Lane, "The Story of Es-Sindibád of the Sea and Es-Sindibád of the Land"; in Payne, "Sindbad the Seaman and Sindbad the Porter"; in Burton, "Sindbad the Seaman and Sindbad the Landsman." In Lane, *The Thousand and One Nights: Commonly Called, in England, The Arabian Nights' Entertainments.* In Payne, *The Book of the Thousand Nights and One Night.* In Burton, *A Plain and Literal Translation of the Arabian Nights' Entertainments, Now Entituled The Book of the Thousand Nights and a Night.*

And behold, the sun was suddenly hid from me and the air became dark. And looking up into the sky, I saw the Rukh, which was greater and more terrible than any I had seen, and I quaked for fear of the bird. Then the Rukh espied the white egg in the meadow and alighted on the dome, brooding over it with its wings covering the egg and its legs stretching out behind on the ground. In this posture it fell asleep, whereupon I rose from out my hiding place in the side of the hill and went down to the bird, which was greater than two ships full-sailed; and my gall bladder was like to burst, for the violence of my fear. So I walked in the shadow of the Rukh, each of whose feathers was longer than a man, till I came to the door in the egg, and there I released a pin. Presently the door drew open and the King's forty soldiers came forth. And two going to one rope in the grass, and two to another, till all twenty ropes were in readiness, at a signal they rushed at the Rukh: and they placed four ropes about one leg where it lay on the grass, and four ropes about the other leg, and secured them with sliding knots; and they laid four great ropes across the tail where it rested on the grass, and they carried those ropes through the space under the tail, and secured them with sliding knots; and in like manner they carried four ropes about each wing, and secured them. Then when the work was accomplished we began to flee, but the great bird awoke. And when it made to lift its wings, lo! they were held down by great blocks of marble larger than elephants. So in its wrath the Rukh stretched down its head and seized one of the fleeing soldiers in its bill, whereat I heard his cries and saw his arms over the sides of the beak; and throwing him to the ground the Rukh thrust his bill through the man's back, so that I heard the crack of bones. Yet did I and the others escape without harm, nor could the Rukh break free of his fetters, though he thrashed and cried out in mighty cries.

Sinbad, opening his heavy-lidded eyes, sees that he is in green water at the bottom of the sea. He is able to breathe in the water, a fact that does not surprise him. He moves his hand in the water and the water becomes a green garden. Sinbad sees that he is in a garden, sitting in the shade of an orange tree. The brilliant column of the sundial glows in its hexagon of red sand. He hears the plash of fountains, the cries of blackbirds and ringdoves. It occurs to him that perhaps the garden itself is his dream, perhaps he is fast asleep on a desolate shore dreaming of the warm shade of the orange tree and the bright column of the sundial, but for the moment, at least, he chooses not to think so. Sunlight and shadow tremble on his hands: is it a breath of air stirring the leaves? He looks forward to the evening meal, flute music, the laughter of friends. He will eat chicken breasts flavored with cumin and rosewater. Sinbad is in his garden. Peace, shade, and the cry of the blackbird. Perhaps in the evening he will walk past the needle makers' wharf to the market of the cloth makers and look at bright-colored cloth from India, China, Persia.

Every reading of a text is limited and contingent: no two readings are alike. In this sense there are as many voyages as there are readers, as many voyages as there are readings. From an infinite number of possible readings, let us imagine one. It is a hot summer afternoon in southern Connecticut. Under the tall pines on the bank of the Housatonic, the shady picnic tables look down at the brown-green water. Bright white barrels mark the swimming area and bob up and down in low waves made by a passing speedboat. In the shade of the far bank stand little wharves and white houses at the base of wooded hills. The sky is rich blue, with a few thin, translucent sweeps of cloud. Between two pines, Grandma sits in the orange-and-white aluminum lawn chair reading a library book with a black mask and a knife on the cover. The boy is lying on his stomach on a blanket next to her, not too close, reading a book. The sun is shining on the backs of his legs, but his shoulders and neck are in shadow. He is deep in the second voyage of Sinbad and has come to the part where Sinbad, walking in a valley surrounded by tall mountains, discovers that the floor of the valley is strewn with diamonds, some of which are of astonishing size. They are probably the size of the fat pinecone lying on the blanket near his elbow. Beyond the picnic table his father is turning the hot dogs on the grill; drippings hiss on the charcoal. His mother is laying out the paper plates, opening the box of red, yellow, and blue paper cups, taking out the salt and mustard and relish and potato salad and cucumber slices and carrot sticks. His sister is trying to find a way to make her doll sit at the picnic table without falling over. She is trying to lean the doll against the thermos jug of pink lemonade. Suddenly he discovers great serpents in the valley, serpents the size of palm trees. The smallest of them can swallow an elephant in one gulp. Fortunately they emerge from their hiding places only at night. When dusk comes, Sinbad enters a small cave and closes the entrance with a stone. In the blackness of the cave Sinbad hears the hiss of serpents outside, and for a moment the boy experiences, with intense lucidity, a double world: he is in the black cave, in the Valley of Diamonds, and at the same time he feels his arm pressing against the fuzzy blue blanket and smells the smoking hot dogs and the river. The great mountains soar, waves from the speedboat lap the sand, diamonds glisten, the sun burns down on the backs of his legs, the serpents hiss outside the cave, a pinecone the size of a valley diamond lies on the blanket beside his mother's straw beach bag and her white rubber bathing cap. He would like to prolong this moment, when the two worlds are held in harmony, he would like this moment to last forever.

And when the Rukh was thus caught, the King ordered that a great cage be built on the meadow, to keep the bird captive; for he said, it was the most wondrous bird that ever lived. Then the King ordered that the ships be raised from the harbor and made seaworthy; and when my ship was ready, he had it filled with pieces of gold. So I gave thanks to the King, and set sail with the blessing of Allah (whose name be extolled!) with some merchants of that city. We pursued our voyage and sailed from island to island and sea to sea, ceasing not to buy and sell; and whenever we stopped, I purchased goods with my gold pieces and traded with them at the next port. In this manner Allah the Most High requited me more than I erst had. In the Island of Al-Kamar I took in a great store of teakwood and an abundance of ginger and cinnamon; and there in the waves I saw fishes with wings that lay their eggs in the branches of trees that hang down in the water. In this island is a beast like a lion but covered with long black hair; this beast feedeth upon horses and hath a great tooth that it thrusts into the horses' bellies. So we fared forth from island to island and sea to sea, committing ourselves to the care of Allah, till we arrived safely at Bassorah. Here I abode a few days packing up my bales and then went on to Baghdad-city. I repaired to my quarter and entered my home, where I foregathered with my friends and relations, who rejoiced at my happy return; and I laid up my goods and valuables in my storehouses. Then I distributed alms and largesse and clothed the widow and the orphan, and fell to feasting and making merry with my companions, and soon forgot the perils and hardships I had suffered; and I applied myself to all manner of joys and pleasures and delights.

Eisenheim the Illusionist

In the last years of the nineteenth century, when the Empire of the Hapsburgs was nearing the end of its long dissolution, the art of magic flourished as never before. In obscure villages of Moravia and Galicia, from the Istrian peninsula to the mists of Bukovina, bearded and black-caped magicians in market squares astonished townspeople by drawing streams of dazzling silk handkerchiefs from empty paper cones, removing billiard balls from children's ears, and throwing into the air decks of cards that assumed the shapes of fountains, snakes, and angels before returning to the hand. In cities and larger towns, from Zagreb to Lvov, from Budapest to Vienna, on the stages of opera houses, town halls, and magic theaters, traveling conjurers equipped with the latest apparatus enchanted sophisticated audiences with elaborate stage illusions. It was the age of levitations and decapitations, of ghostly apparitions and sudden vanishings, as if the tottering Empire were revealing through the medium of its magicians its secret desire for annihilation. Among the remarkable conjurers of that time, none achieved the heights of illusion attained by Eisenheim, whose enigmatic final performance was viewed by some as a triumph of the magician's art, by others as a fateful sign.

Eisenheim, né Eduard Abramowitz, was born in Bratislava in 1859 or 1860. Little is known of his early years, or indeed of his entire life outside the realm of illusion. For the scant facts we are obliged to rely on the dubious memoirs of magicians, on comments in contemporary newspaper stories and trade periodicals, on promotional material and brochures for magic acts; here and there the diary entry of a countess or ambassador records attendance at a performance in Paris, Krakow, Vienna. Eisenheim's father was a highly respected cabinetmaker, whose ornamental gilt cupboards and skillfully carved lowboys with lion-paw feet and brass handles shaped like snarling lions graced the halls of the gentry of Bratislava. The boy was the eldest of four children; like many Bratislavan Jews, the family spoke German and called their city Pressburg, although they understood as much Slovak and Magyar as was necessary for the proper conduct of business. Eduard went to work early in his father's shop. For the rest of his life he would retain a fondness for smooth pieces of wood joined seamlessly by mortise and tenon. By the age of seventeen he was himself a skilled cabinetmaker, a fact noted more than once by fellow magicians who admired Eisenheim's skill in constructing trick cabinets of breathtaking ingenuity. The young craftsman was already a passionate amateur magician, who is said to have entertained family and friends with card sleights and a disappearing-ring trick that required a small beechwood box of his own construction. He would place a borrowed ring inside, fasten the box tightly with twine, and quietly remove the ring as he handed the box to a spectator. The beechwood box, with its secret panel, was able to withstand the most minute examination.

A chance encounter with a traveling magician is said to have been the cause of Eisenheim's lifelong passion for magic. The story goes that one day, returning from school, the boy saw a man in black sitting under a plane tree. The man called him over and lazily, indifferently, removed from the boy's ear first one coin and then another, and then a third, coin after coin, a whole handful of coins, which suddenly turned into a bunch of red roses. From the roses the man in black drew out a white billiard ball, which turned into a wooden flute that suddenly vanished. One version of the story adds that the man himself then vanished, along with the plane tree. Stories, like conjuring tricks, are invented because history is inadequate to our dreams, but in this case it is reasonable to suppose that the future master had been profoundly affected by some early experience of conjuring. Eduard had once seen a magic shop, without much interest; he now returned with passion. On dark winter mornings on the way to school he would remove his gloves to practice manipulating balls and coins with chilled fingers in the pockets of his coat. He enchanted his three sisters with intricate shadowgraphs representing Rumpelstiltskin and Rapunzel, American buffalos and Indians, the golem of Prague. Later a local conjurer called Ignacz Molnar taught him juggling for the sake of coordinating movements of the eye and hand. Once, on a dare, the thirteen-year-old boy carried an egg on a soda straw all the way to

Bratislava Castle and back. Much later, when all this was far behind him, the Master would be sitting gloomily in the corner of a Viennese apartment where a party was being held in his honor, and reaching up wearily he would startle his hostess by producing from the air five billiard balls that he proceeded to juggle flawlessly.

But who can unravel the mystery of the passion that infects an entire life, bending it away from its former course in one irrevocable swerve? Abramowitz seems to have accepted his fate slowly. It was as if he kept trying to evade the disturbing knowledge of his difference. At the age of twenty-four he was still an expert cabinetmaker who did occasional parlor tricks.

As if suddenly, Eisenheim appeared at a theater in Vienna and began his exhilarating and fatal career. The brilliant newcomer was twenty-eight years old. In fact, contemporary records show that the cabinetmaker from Bratislava had appeared in private performances for at least a year before moving to the Austrian capital. Although the years preceding the first private performances remain mysterious, it is clear that Abramowitz gradually shifted his attention more and more fully to magic, by way of the trick chests and cabinets that he had begun to supply to local magicians. Eisenheim's nature was like that: he proceeded slowly and cautiously, step by step, and then, as if he had earned the right to be daring, he would take a sudden leap.

The first public performances were noted less for their daring than for their subtle mastery of the stage illusions of the day, although even then there were artful twists and variations. One of Eisenheim's early successes was the Mysterious Orange Tree, a feat made famous by Robert-Houdin. A borrowed handkerchief was placed in a small box and handed to a member of the audience. An assistant strode onto the stage, bearing in his arms a small green orange tree in a box. He placed the box on the magician's table and stepped away. At a word from Eisenheim, accompanied by a pass of his wand, blossoms began to appear on the tree. A moment later, oranges began to emerge; Eisenheim plucked several and handed them to members of the audience. Suddenly two butterflies rose from the leaves, carrying a handkerchief. The spectator, opening his box, discovered that his handkerchief had disappeared; somehow the butterflies had found it in the tree. The illusion depended on two separate deceptions: the mechanical tree itself, which produced real flowers, real fruit, and mechanical butterflies by means of concealed mechanisms;

and the removal of the handkerchief from the trick box as it was handed to the spectator. Eisenheim quickly developed a variation that proved popular: the tree grew larger each time he covered it with a red silk cloth, the branches produced oranges, apples, pears, and plums, at the end a whole flock of colorful, real butterflies rose up and fluttered over the audience, where children screamed with delight as they reached up to snatch the delicate silken shapes, and at last, under a black velvet cloth that was suddenly lifted, the tree was transformed into a birdcage containing the missing handkerchief.

At this period, Eisenheim wore the traditional silk hat, frock coat, and cape and performed with an ebony wand tipped with ivory. The one distinctive note was his pair of black gloves. He began each performance by stepping swiftly through the closed curtains onto the stage apron, removing the gloves, and tossing them into the air, where they turned into a pair of sleek ravens.

Early critics were quick to note the young magician's interest in uncanny effects, as in his popular Phantom Portrait. On a darkened stage, a large blank canvas was illuminated by limelight. As Eisenheim made passes with his right hand, the white canvas gradually and mysteriously gave birth to a brighter and brighter painting. Now, it is well known among magicians and mediums that a canvas of unbleached muslin may be painted with chemical solutions that appear invisible when dry; if sulfate of iron is used for blue, nitrate of bismuth for yellow, and copper sulfate for brown, the picture will appear if sprayed with a weak solution of prussiate of potash. An atomizer, concealed in the conjurer's sleeve, gradually brings out the invisible portrait. Eisenheim increased the mysterious effect by producing full-length portraits that began to exhibit lifelike movements of the eyes and lips. The fiendish portrait of an archduke, or a devil, or Eisenheim himself would then read the contents of sealed envelopes, before vanishing at a pass of the magician's wand.

However skillful, a conjurer cannot earn and sustain a major reputation without producing original feats of his own devising. It was clear that the restless young magician would not be content with producing clever variations of familiar tricks, and by 1890 his performances regularly concluded with an illusion of striking originality. A large mirror in a carved frame stood on the stage, facing the audience. A spectator was invited onto the stage, where he was asked to walk around the mirror and examine it to his satisfaction. Eisenheim then asked the spectator to don a hooded red robe and positioned him some ten feet from the mirror, where the vivid red reflection was clearly visible to the audience; the theater was darkened, except for a brightening light that came from within the mirror itself. As the spectator waved his robed arms about, and bowed to his bowing reflection, and leaned from side to side, his reflection began to show signs of disobedience—it crossed its arms over its chest instead of waving them about, it refused to bow. Suddenly the reflection grimaced, removed a knife, and stabbed itself in the chest. The reflection collapsed onto the reflected floor. Now a ghostlike white form rose from the dead reflection and hovered in the mirror; all at once the ghost emerged from the glass, floated toward the startled and sometimes terrified spectator, and at the bidding of Eisenheim rose into the dark and vanished. This masterful illusion mystified even professional magicians, who agreed only that the mirror was a trick cabinet with black-lined doors at the rear and a hidden assistant. The lights were probably concealed in the frame between the glass and the lightly silvered back; as the lights grew brighter the mirror became transparent and a red-robed assistant showed himself in the glass. The ghost was more difficult to explain, despite a long tradition of stage ghosts; it was said that concealed magic lanterns produced the phantom, but no other magician was able to imitate the effect. Even in these early years, before Eisenheim achieved disturbing effects unheard of in the history of stage magic, there was a touch of the uncanny about his illusions; and some said even then that Eisenheim was not a showman at all, but a wizard who had sold his soul to the devil in return for unholy powers.

Eisenheim was a man of medium height, with broad shoulders and large, long-fingered hands. His most striking feature was his powerful head: the black intense eyes in the austerely pale face, the broad black beard, the thrusting forehead with its receding hairline, all lent an appearance of unusual mental force. The newspaper accounts mention a minor trait that must have been highly effective: when he leaned his head forward, in intense concentration, there appeared over his right eyebrow a large vein shaped like an inverted *Y*.

As the last decade of the old century wore on, Eisenheim gradually came to be acknowledged as the foremost magician of his day. These were the years of the great European tours, which brought him to Egyptian Hall in London and the Théâtre Robert-Houdin in Paris, to royal courts and ducal palaces, to halls in Berlin and Milan, Zurich and

Salamanca. Although his repertoire continued to include perfected variations of popular illusions like the Vanishing Lady, the Blue Room, the Flying Watch, the Spirit Cabinet (or Specters of the Inner Sanctum), the Enchanted House, the Magic Kettle, and the Arabian Sack Mystery, he appeared to grow increasingly impatient with known effects and began rapidly replacing them with striking inventions of his own. Among the most notable illusions of those years were the Tower of Babel, in which a small black cone mysteriously grew until it filled the entire stage; the Satanic Crystal Ball, in which a ghostly form summoned from hell smashed through the glass globe and rushed out onto the stage with unearthly cries; and the Book of Demons, in which black smoke rose from an ancient book, which suddenly burst into flames that released hideous dwarfs in hairy jerkins who ran howling across the stage. In 1898 he opened his own theater in Vienna, called simply Eisenheimhaus, or the House of Eisenheim, as if that were his real home and all other dwellings illusory. It was here that he presented the Pied Piper of Hamelin. Holding his wand like a flute, Eisenheim led children from the audience into a misty hill with a cavelike opening and then, with a pass of his wand, caused the entire hill to vanish into thin air. Moments later a black chest materialized, from which the children emerged and looked around in bewilderment before running back to their parents. The children told their parents they had been in a wondrous mountain, with golden tables and chairs and white angels flying in the air; they had no idea how they had gotten into the box, or what had happened to them. A few complaints were made; and when, in another performance, a frightened child told his mother that he had been in hell and seen the devil, who was green and breathed fire, the chief of the Viennese police, one Walther Uhl, paid Eisenheim a visit. The Pied Piper of Hamelin never appeared again, but two results had emerged: a certain disturbing quality in Eisenheim's art was now officially acknowledged, and it was rumored that the stern master was being closely watched by Franz Josef's secret police. This last was unlikely, for the Emperor, unlike his notorious grandfather, took little interest in police espionage; but the rumor surrounded Eisenheim like a mist, blurring his sharp outline, darkening his features, and enhancing his formidable reputation.

Eisenheim was not without rivals, whose challenges he invariably met with a decisiveness, some would say ferocity, that left no doubt of his self-esteem. Two incidents of the last years of the century left a deep impression among contemporaries. In Vienna in 1898 a magician called Benedetti had appeared. Benedetti, whose real name was Paul Henri Cortot, of Lyon, was a master illusionist of extraordinary smoothness and skill; his mistake was to challenge Eisenheim by presenting imitations of original Eisenheim illusions, with clever variations, much as Eisenheim had once alluded to his predecessors in order to outdo them. Eisenheim learned of his rival's presumption and let it be known through the speaking portrait of a devil that ruin awaits the proud. The very next night, on Benedetti's stage, a speaking portrait of Eisenheim intoned in comic accents that ruin awaits the proud. Eisenheim, a proud and brooding man, did not allude to the insult during his Sunday night performance. On Monday night, Benedetti's act went awry: the wand leaped from his fingers and rolled across the stage; two fishbowls with watertight lids came crashing to the floor from beneath Benedetti's cloak; the speaking portrait remained mute; the levitating lady was seen to be resting on black wires. The excitable Benedetti, vowing revenge, accused Eisenheim of criminal tampering; two nights later, before a packed house, Benedetti stepped into a black cabinet, drew a curtain, and was never seen again. The investigation by Herr Uhl failed to produce a trace of foul play. Some said the unfortunate Benedetti had simply chosen the most convenient way of escaping to another city, under a new name, far from the scene of his notorious debacle; others were convinced that Eisenheim had somehow spirited him off, perhaps to hell. Viennese society was enchanted by the scandal, which made the round of the cafés; and Herr Uhl was seen more than once in a stall of the theater, nodding his head appreciatively at some particularly striking effect.

If Benedetti proved too easy a rival, a far more formidable challenge was posed by the mysterious Passauer. Ernst Passauer was said to be Bavarian; his first Viennese performance was watched closely by the Austrians, who were forced to admit that the German was a master of striking originality. Passauer took the city by storm; and for the first time there was talk that Eisenheim had met his match, perhaps even—was it possible?—his master. Unlike the impetuous and foolhardy Benedetti, Passauer made no allusion to the Viennese wizard; some saw in this less a sign of professional decorum than an assertion of arrogant indifference, as if the German refused to acknowledge the possibility of a rival. But the pattern of their performances, that autumn, was the very rhythm of rivalry: Eisenheim played on Sunday, Wednesday, and Friday nights, and Passauer on Tuesday, Thursday, and Saturday nights. It was noted that as his rival presented illusions of bold originality, Eisenheim's own illusions became more daring and dangerous; it was as if the two of them had outsoared the confines of the magician's art and existed in some new realm of dexterous wonder, of sinister beauty. In this high but by no means innocent realm, the two masters vied for supremacy before audiences that were increasingly the same. Some said that Eisenheim appeared to be struggling or straining against the relentless pressure of his brilliant rival; others argued that Eisenheim had never displayed such mastery; and as the heavy century lumbered to its close, all awaited the decisive event that would release them from the tension of an unresolved battle.

And it came: one night in mid-December, after a particularly daring illusion, in which Passauer caused first his right arm to vanish, then his left arm, then his feet, until nothing was left of him but his disembodied head floating before a black velvet curtain, the head permitted itself to wonder whether Herr "Eisenzeit," or Iron Age, had ever seen a trick of that kind. The mocking allusion caused the audience to gasp. The limelight went out; when it came on, the stage contained nothing but a heap of black cloth, which began to flutter and billow until it gradually assumed the shape of Passauer, who bowed coolly to tumultuous applause; but the ring of a quiet challenge was not lost in the general uproar. The following night Eisenheim played to a packed, expectant house. He ignored the challenge while performing a series of new illusions that in no way resembled Passauer's act. As he took his final bow, he remarked casually that Passauer's hour had passed. The fate of the unfortunate Benedetti had not been forgotten, and it was said that if the demand for Passauer's next performance had been met, the entire city of Vienna would have become a magic theater.

Passauer's final performance was one of frightening brilliance; it was well attended by professional magicians, who agreed later that as a single performance it outshone the greatest of Eisenheim's evenings. Passauer began by flinging into the air a handful of coins that assumed the shape of a bird and flew out over the heads of the audience, flapping its jingling wings of coins; from a silver thimble held in the flat of his hand he removed a tablecloth, a small mahogany table, and a silver salver on which sat a steaming roast duck. At the climax of the evening, he caused the properties of the stage to vanish one by one: the magician's table, the beautiful assistant, the far wall, the curtain. Standing alone in a vanished world, he looked at the audience with an expression that grew more and more fierce. Suddenly he burst into a demonic laugh, and reaching up to his face he tore off a rubber mask and revealed himself to be Eisenheim. The collective gasp sounded like a great furnace igniting; someone burst into hysterical sobs. The audience, understanding at last, rose to its feet and cheered the great master of illusion, who himself had been his own greatest rival and had at the end unmasked himself. In his box, Herr Uhl rose to his feet and joined in the applause. He had enjoyed the performance immensely.

Perhaps it was the strain of that sustained deception, perhaps it was the sense of being alone, utterly alone, in any case Eisenheim did not give another performance in the last weeks of the fading century. As the new century came in with a fireworks display in the Prater and a hundred-gun salute from the grounds of the Imperial Palace, Eisenheim remained in his Vienna apartment, with its distant view of the same river that flowed through his childhood city. The unexplained period of rest continued, developing into a temporary withdrawal from performance, some said a retirement; Eisenheim himself said nothing. In late January he returned to Bratislava to attend to details of his father's business; a week later he was in Linz; within a month he had purchased a three-story villa in the famous wooded hills on the outskirts of Vienna. He was forty or forty-one, an age when a man takes a hard look at his life. He had never married, although romantic rumors occasionally united him with one or another of his assistants; he was handsome in a stern way, wealthy, and said to be so strong that he could do thirty knee-bends on a single leg. Not long after his move to the Wienerwald he began to court Sophie Ritter, the twenty-six-year-old daughter of a local landowner who disapproved of Eisenheim's profession and was a staunch supporter of Lueger's anti-Semitic Christian Social Party; the girl appears to have been in love with Eisenheim, but at the last moment something went wrong, she withdrew abruptly, and a month later married a grain merchant from Graz. For a year Eisenheim lived like a reclusive country squire. He took riding lessons in the mornings, in the afternoons practiced with pistols at his private shooting range, planted a spring garden, stocked his ponds, designed a new orchard. In a meadow at the back of his house he supervised the building of a long low shedlike structure that became known as the Teufelsfabrik, or Devil's Factory, for it housed his collection of trick cabinets, deceptive mirrors, haunted portraits, and magic caskets. The walls were lined with cupboards that had sliding glass doors and held Eisenheim's formidable collection of magical apparatus: vanishing birdcages, inexhaustible punch bowls, devil's targets, Schiller's bells, watch-spring flowers, trick bouquets, and an array of secret devices used in sleight-of-hand feats: ball shells, coin droppers, elastic handkerchief-pulls for making handkerchiefs vanish, dummy cigars, color-changing tubes for handkerchief tricks, hollow thumb-tips, miniature spirit lamps for the magical lighting of candles, false fingers, black silk ball-tubes. In the basement of the factory was a large room in which he conducted chemical and electrical experiments, and a curtained darkroom; Eisenheim was a close student of photography and the new art of cinematography. Often he was seen working late at night, and some said that ghostly forms appeared in the dim-lit windows.

On the first of January 1901, Eisenheim suddenly returned to his city apartment with its view of the Danube and the Vienna hills. Three days later he reappeared onstage. A local wit remarked that the master of illusion had simply omitted the year 1900, which with its two zeros no doubt struck him as illusory. The yearlong absence of the Master had sharpened expectations, and the standing-room-only crowd was tensely quiet as the curtains parted on a stage strikingly bare except for a plain wooden chair before a small glass table. For some in that audience, the table already signaled a revolution; others were puzzled or disappointed. From the right wing Eisenheim strode onto the stage. A flurry of whispers was quickly hushed. The Master wore a plain dark suit and had shaved off his beard. Without a word he sat down on the wooden chair behind the table and faced the audience. He placed his hands lightly on the tabletop, where they remained during the entire performance. He stared directly before him, leaning forward slightly and appearing to concentrate with terrific force.

In the middle of the eighteenth century the magician's table was a large table draped to the floor; beneath the cloth an assistant reached through a hole in the tabletop to remove objects concealed by a large cone. The modern table of Eisenheim's day had a short cloth that exposed the table legs, but the disappearance of the hidden assistant and the general simplification of design in no sense changed the nature of the table, which remained an ingenious machine equipped with innumerable contrivances to aid the magician in the art of deception: hidden receptacles or *servantes* into which disappearing objects secretly dropped, invisible wells and traps, concealed pistons, built-in spring-pulls for effecting the disappearance of silk handkerchiefs. Eisenheim's transparent glass table announced the end of the magician's table as it had been known throughout the history of stage magic. This radical simplification was not only aesthetic: it meant the refusal of certain kinds of mechanical aid, the elimination of certain effects.

And the audience grew restless: nothing much appeared to be happening. A balding man in a business suit sat at a table, frowning. After fifteen minutes a slight disturbance or darkening in the air was noticeable near the surface of the table. Eisenheim concentrated fiercely; over his right eyebrow the famous vein, shaped like an inverted *Y*, pressed through the skin of his forehead. The air seemed to tremble and thicken—and before him, on the glass table, a dark shape slowly formed. It appeared to be a small box, about the size of a jewel box. For a while its edges quivered slightly, as if it were made of black smoke. Suddenly Eisenheim raised his eyes, which one witness described as black mirrors that reflected nothing; he looked drained and weary. A moment later he pushed back his chair, stood up, and bowed. The applause was uncertain; people did not know what they had seen.

Eisenheim next invited spectators to come onto the stage and examine the box on the table. One woman, reaching for the box and feeling nothing, nothing at all, stepped back and raised a hand to her throat. A girl of sixteen, sweeping her hand through the black box, cried out as if in pain.

The rest of the performance consisted of two more "materializations": a sphere and a wand. After members of the audience had satisfied themselves of the immaterial nature of the objects, Eisenheim picked up the wand and waved it over the box. He next lifted the lid of the box, placed the sphere inside, and closed the lid. When he invited spectators onto the stage, their hands passed through empty air. Eisenheim opened the box, removed the sphere, and laid it on the table between the box and the wand. He bowed, and the curtain closed.

Despite a hesitant, perplexed, and somewhat disappointed response from that first audience, the reviews were enthusiastic; one critic called it a major event in the history of stage illusions. He connected Eisenheim's phantom objects with the larger tradition of stage ghosts, which he traced back to Robertson's Phantasmagoria at the end of the eighteenth century. From concealed magic lanterns Robertson had projected images onto smoke rising from braziers to create eerie effects. By the middle of the nineteenth century, magicians were terrifying spectators with a far more striking technique: a hidden assistant, dressed like a ghost and standing in a pit between the stage and the auditorium, was reflected onto the stage through a tilted sheet of glass invisible to the audience. Modern ghosts were based on the technique of the black velvet backdrop: overhead lights were directed toward the front of the stage, and black-covered white objects appeared to materialize when the covers were pulled away by invisible black-hooded assistants dressed in black. But Eisenheim's phantoms, those immaterial materializations, made use of no machinery at all—they appeared to emerge from the mind of the magician. The effect was startling, the unknown device ingenious. The writer considered and rejected the possibility of hidden magic lanterns and mirrors; discussed the properties of the cinematograph recently developed by the Lumière brothers and used by contemporary magicians to produce unusual effects of a different kind; and speculated on possible scientific techniques whereby Eisenheim might have caused the air literally to thicken and darken. Was it possible that one of the Lumière machines, directed onto slightly misted air above the table, might have produced the phantom objects? But no one had detected any mist, no one had seen the necessary beam of light. However Eisenheim had accomplished the illusion, the effect was incomparable; it appeared that he was summoning objects into existence by the sheer effort of his mind. In this the master illusionist was rejecting the modern conjurer's increasing reliance on machinery and returning the spectator to the troubled heart of magic, which yearned beyond the constricting world of ingenuity and artifice toward the dark realm of transgression.

The long review, heavy with *fin de siècle* portentousness and shot through with a secret restlessness or longing, was the first of several that placed Eisenheim beyond the world of conjuring and saw in him an expression of spiritual striving, as if his art could no longer be talked about in the old way.

During the next performance Eisenheim sat for thirty-five minutes at his glass table in front of a respectful but increasingly restless audience before the darkening was observed. When he sat back, evidently spent from his exertions, there stood on the table the head and shoulders of a young woman. The details of witnesses differ, but all reports agree that the head was of a young woman of perhaps eighteen or twenty with short dark hair and heavy-lidded eyes. She faced the audience calmly, a little dreamily, as if she had just wakened from sleep, and spoke her name: Greta. Fräulein Greta answered questions from the audience. She said she came from Brünn; she was seventeen years old; her father was a lens grinder; she did not know how she had come here. Behind her, Eisenheim sat slumped in his seat, his broad face pale as marble, his eyes staring as if sightlessly. After a while Fräulein Greta appeared to grow tired. Eisenheim gathered himself up and fixed her with his stare; gradually she wavered and grew dim, and slowly vanished.

With Fräulein Greta, Eisenheim triumphed over the doubters. As word of the new illusion spread, and audiences waited with a kind of fearful patience for the darkening of the air above the glass table, it became clear that Eisenheim had touched a nerve. Greta-fever was in the air. It was said that Fräulein Greta was really Marie Vetsera, who had died with Crown Prince Rudolf in the bedroom of his hunting lodge at Mayerling; it was said that Fräulein Greta, with her dark, sad eyes, was the girlhood spirit of the Empress Elizabeth, who at the age of sixty had been stabbed to death in Geneva by an Italian anarchist. It was said that Fräulein Greta knew things, all sorts of things, and could tell secrets about the other world. For a while Eisenheim was taken up by the spiritualists, who claimed him for one of their own: here at last was absolute proof of the materialization of spirit forms. A society of disaffected Blavatskyites called the Daughters of Dawn elected Eisenheim to an honorary membership, and three bearded members of a Salzburg Institute for Psychic Research began attending performances with black notebooks in hand. Magicians heaped scorn on the mediumistic confraternity but could not explain or duplicate the illusion; a shrewd group of mediums, realizing they could not reproduce the Eisenheim phenomena, accused him of fraud while defending themselves against the magicians' charges. Eisenheim's rigorous silence was taken by all sides as a sign of approval. The "manifestations," as they began to be called, soon included the head of a dark-haired man of about thirty, who called himself Frankel and demonstrated conventional tricks of mind reading and telepathy before fading away. What puzzled the professionals was not the mind reading but the production of Frankel himself. The possibility of exerting a physical influence on air was repeatedly argued; it was suggested in some quarters that Eisenheim had prepared the air in advance with a thickening agent and treated it with invisible chemical solutions, but this allusion to the timeworn trick of the muslin canvas convinced no one.

In late March Eisenheim left Vienna on an Imperial tour that included bookings in Ljubljana, Prague, Teplitz, Budapest, Kolozsvar, Czernowitz, Tarnopol, Uzghorod. In Vienna, the return of the Master was awaited with an impatience bordering on frenzy. A much publicized case was that of Anna Scherer, the dark-eyed sixteen-year-old daughter of a Vienna banker, who declared that she felt a deep spiritual bond with Greta and could not bear life without her. The troubled girl ran away from home and was discovered by the police two days later wandering disheveled in the wooded hills northeast of the city; when she returned home she shut herself in her room and wept violently and uncontrollably for six hours a day. An eighteen-year-old youth was arrested at night on the grounds of Eisenheim's villa and later confessed that he had planned to break into the Devil's Factory and learn the secret of raising the dead. Devotees of Greta and Frankel met in small groups to discuss the Master, and it was rumored that in a remote village in Carinthia he had demonstrated magical powers of a still more thrilling and disturbing kind.

And the Master returned, and the curtains opened, and fingers tightened on the blue-velvet chair arms. On a bare stage stood nothing but a simple chair. Eisenheim, looking pale and tired, with shadowy hollows in his temples, walked to the chair and sat down with his large, long hands resting on his knees. He fixed his stare at the air and sat rigidly for forty minutes, while rivulets of sweat trickled along his high-boned cheeks and a thick vein pressed through the skin of his forehead. Gradually a darkening of the air was discernible and a shape slowly emerged. At first it seemed a wavering and indistinct form, like shimmers above a radiator on a wintry day, but soon there was a thickening, and before the slumped form of Eisenheim stood a beautiful boy. His large brown eyes, fringed with dark lashes, looked out trustingly, if a little dreamily; he had a profusion of thick hay-colored curls and wore a school uniform with dark green shorts and high gray socks. He seemed surprised and shy, uncomfortable before the audience, but as he began to walk about he became more animated and told his name: Elis. Many commented on the striking contrast between the angelic boy and the dark, brooding magician.

The sweetness of the creature cast a spell over the audience, broken only when a woman was invited onto the stage. As she bent over to run her fingers through Elis's hair, her hand passed through empty air. She gave a cry that sounded like a moan and hurried from the stage in confusion. Later she said that the air had felt cold, very cold.

Greta and Frankel were forgotten in an outbreak of Elis-fever. The immaterial boy was said to be the most enchanting illusion ever created by a magician; the spiritualist camp maintained that Elis was the spirit of a boy who had died in Helgoland in 1787. Elis-fever grew to such a pitch that often sobs and screams would erupt from tense, constricted throats as the air before Eisenheim slowly began to darken and the beautiful boy took shape. Elis did not engage in the conventions of magic, but simply walked about on the stage, answering questions put to him by the audience or asking questions of his own. He said that his parents were dead; he seemed uncertain of many things, and grew confused when asked how he had come to be there. Sometimes he left the stage and walked slowly along the aisle, while hands reached out and grasped empty air. After half an hour Eisenheim would cause him to waver and grow dim, and Elis would vanish away. Screams often accompanied the disappearance of the beautiful boy; and after a particularly troubling episode, in which a young woman leaped onto the stage and began clawing the vanishing form, Herr Uhl was once again seen in attendance at the theater, watching with an expression of keen interest.

He was in attendance when Eisenheim stunned the house by producing a companion for Elis, a girl who called herself Rosa. She had long dark hair and black, dreamy eyes and Slavic cheekbones; she spoke slowly and seriously, often pausing to think of the exact word. Elis seemed shy of her and at first refused to speak in her presence. Rosa said she was twelve years old; she said she knew the secrets of the past and future, and offered to predict the death of anyone present. A young man with thin cheeks, evidently a student, raised his hand. Rosa stepped to the edge of the stage and stared at him for a long while with her earnest eyes; when she turned away she said that he would cough up blood in November and would die of tuberculosis before the end of the following summer. Pale, visibly shaken, the young man began to protest angrily, then sat down suddenly and covered his face with his hands.

Rosa and Elis were soon fast friends. It was touching to observe Elis's gradual overcoming of shyness and the growth of his intense attachment to her. Immediately after his appearance he would begin to look around sweetly, with his large, anxious eyes, as if searching for his Rosa. As Eisenheim stared with rigid intensity, Elis would play by himself but steal secret glances at the air in front of the magician. The boy would grow more and more agitated as the air began to darken; and a look of almost painful rapture would glow on his face as Rosa appeared with her high cheekbones and her black, dreamy eyes. Often the children would play by themselves onstage, as if oblivious of an audience. They would hold hands and walk along imaginary paths, swinging their arms back and forth, or they would water invisible flowers with an invisible watering can; and the exquisite charm of their gestures was noted by more than one witness. During these games Rosa would sing songs of haunting, melancholy beauty in an unfamiliar Low German dialect.

It remains unclear precisely when the rumor arose that Eisenheim would be arrested and his theater closed. Some said that Uhl had intended it from the beginning and had simply been waiting for the opportune moment; others pointed to particular incidents. One such incident occurred in late summer, when a disturbance took place in the audience not long after the appearance of Elis and Rosa. At first there were sharp whispers, and angry shushes, and suddenly a woman began to rise and then leaned violently away as a child rose from the aisle seat beside her. The child, a boy of about six, walked down the aisle and climbed the stairs to the stage, where he stood smiling at the audience, who immediately recognized that he was of the race of Elis and Rosa. Although the mysterious child never appeared again, spectators now began to look nervously at their neighbors; and it was in this charged atmosphere that the rumor of impending arrest sprang up and would not go away. The mere sight of Herr Uhl in his box each night caused tense whispers. It began to seem as if the policeman and the magician were engaged in a secret battle: it was said that Herr Uhl was planning a dramatic arrest, and Eisenheim a brilliant escape. Eisenheim for his part ignored the whispers and did nothing to modify the disturbing effects that Elis and Rosa had on his audience; and as if to defy the forces gathering against him, one evening he brought forth another figure, an ugly old woman in a black dress who frightened Elis and Rosa and caused fearful cries from the audience before she melted away.

The official reason given for the arrest of the Master, and the seizure of his theater, was the disturbance of public order; the police reports, in preparation for more than a year, listed more than one hundred incidents. But Herr Uhl's private papers reveal a deeper cause. The chief of police was an intelligent and well-read man who was himself an amateur conjurer, and he was not unduly troubled by the occasional extreme public responses to Eisenheim's illusions, although he recorded each instance scrupulously and asked himself whether such effects were consonant with public safety and decorum. No, what disturbed Herr Uhl was something else, something for which he had difficulty finding a name. The phrase "crossing of boundaries" occurs pejoratively more than once in his notebooks; by it he appears to mean that certain distinctions must be strictly maintained. Art and life constituted one such distinction; illusion and reality, another. Eisenheim deliberately crossed boundaries and therefore disturbed the essence of things. In effect, Herr Uhl was accusing Eisenheim of shaking the foundations of the universe, of undermining reality, and in consequence of doing something far worse: subverting the Empire. For where would the Empire be, once the idea of boundaries became blurred and uncertain?

On the night of February 14, 1902—a cold, clear night, when horseshoes rang sharply on the avenues, and fashionable women in chin-high black boas plunged their forearms into heavy, furry muffs—twelve uniformed policemen took their seats in the audience of Eisenheimhaus. The decision to arrest the Master during a performance was later disputed; the public arrest was apparently intended to send a warning to devotees of Eisenheim, and perhaps to other magicians as well. Immediately after the appearance of Rosa, Herr Uhl left his box. Moments later he strode through a side door onto the stage and announced the arrest of Eisenheim in the name of His Imperial Majesty and the city of Vienna. Twelve officers stepped into the aisles and stood at attention. Eisenheim turned his head wearily toward the intruding figure and did not move. Elis and Rosa, who had been standing at the edge of the stage, began to look about fearfully: the lovely boy shook his head and murmured "No" in his angelic voice, while Rosa hugged herself tightly and began to hum a low melody that sounded like a drawn-out moan or keen. Herr Uhl, who had paused some ten feet from Eisenheim in order to permit the grave Master to rise unaided, saw at once that things were getting out of hand—someone in the audience began murmuring "No," the chant was taken up. Swiftly Uhl strode to the seated magician and placed a hand on his shoulder. That was when it happened: his hand fell through Eisenheim's shoulder, he appeared to stumble, and in a fury he began striking at the magician, who remained seated calmly through the paroxysm of meaningless blows. At last the officer drew his sword and sliced through Eisenheim, who at this point rose with great dignity and turned to Elis and Rosa. They looked at him imploringly as they wavered and grew dim. The Master then turned to the audience; and slowly, gravely, he bowed. The applause began in scattered sections and grew louder and wilder until the curtains were seen to tremble. Six officers leaped onto the stage and attempted to seize Eisenheim, who looked at them with an expression of such melancholy that one policeman felt a shadow pass over his heart. And now a nervousness rippled through the crowd as the Master seemed to gather himself for some final effort: his face became rigid with concentration, the famous vein pressed through his forehead, the unseeing eyes were dark autumn nights when the wind picks up and branches creak. A shudder was seen to pass along his arms. It spread to his legs, and from the crowd rose the sound of a great inrush of breath as Eisenheim began his unthinkable final act: bending the black flame of his gaze inward, locked in savage concentration, he began to unknit the threads of his being. Wavering, slowly fading, he stood dark and unmoving there. In the Master's face some claimed to see, as he dissolved before their eyes, a look of fearful exaltation. Others said that at the end he raised his face and uttered a cry of icy desolation. When it was over the audience rose to its feet. Herr Uhl promptly arrested a young man in the front row, and a precarious order was maintained. On a drab stage, empty except for a single wooden chair, policemen in uniform looked tensely about.

Later that night the police ransacked the apartment with a distant view of the Danube, but Eisenheim was not there. The failed arrest was in one respect highly successful: the Master was never seen again. In the Devil's Factory trick mirrors were found, exquisite cabinets with secret panels, ingenious chests and boxes representing high instances of the art of deception, but not a clue about the famous illusions, not one, nothing. Some said that Eisenheim had created an illusory Eisenheim from the first day of the new century; others said that the Master had gradually grown illusory from trafficking with illusions. Someone suggested that Herr Uhl was himself an illusion, a carefully staged part of the final performance. Arguments arose over whether it was all done with lenses and mirrors, or whether the Jew from Bratislava had sold his soul to the devil for the dark gift of magic. All agreed that it was a sign of the times; and as precise memories faded, and the everyday world of coffee cups, doctors' visits, and war rumors returned, a secret relief penetrated the souls of the faithful, who knew that the Master had passed safely out of the crumbling order of history into the indestructible realm of mystery and dream.

from

The Knife Thrower

The Knife Thrower

When we learned that Hensch, the knife thrower, was stopping at our town for a single performance at eight o'clock on Saturday night, we hesitated, wondering what we felt. Hensch, the knife thrower! Did we feel like clapping our hands for joy, like leaping to our feet and bursting into smiles of anticipation? Or did we, after all, want to tighten our lips and look away in stern disapproval? That was Hensch for you. For if Hensch was an acknowledged master of his art, that difficult and faintly unsavory art about which we knew very little, it was also true that he bore with him certain disturbing rumors, which we reproached ourselves for having failed to heed sufficiently when they appeared from time to time in the arts section of the Sunday paper.

Hensch, the knife thrower! Of course we knew his name. Everyone knew his name, as one knows the name of a famous chess player or magician. What we couldn't be sure of was what he actually did. Dimly we recalled that the skill of his throwing had brought him early attention, but that it wasn't until he had changed the rules entirely that he was taken up in a serious way. He had stepped boldly, some said recklessly, over the line never before crossed by knife throwers, and had managed to make a reputation out of a disreputable thing. Some of us seemed to recall reading that in his early carnival days he had wounded an assistant badly; after a six-month retirement he had returned with his new act. It was here that he had introduced into the chaste discipline of knife throwing the idea of the artful wound, the mark of blood that was the mark of the master. We had even heard that among his followers there were many, young women especially, who longed to be wounded by the master and to bear his scar proudly. If rumors of this kind were disturbing to us, if they prevented us from celebrating Hensch's arrival with innocent delight, we nevertheless acknowledged that without such dubious enticements we'd have been unlikely to attend the performance at all, since the art of knife throwing, for all its apparent danger, is really a tame art, an outmoded art—little more than a quaint old-fashioned amusement in these times of ours. The only knife throwers any of us had ever seen were in the circus sideshow or the carnival ten-in-one, along with the fat lady and the human skeleton. It must, we imagined, have galled Hensch to feel himself a freak among freaks; he must have needed a way out. For wasn't he an artist, in his fashion? And so we admired his daring, even as we deplored his method and despised him as a vulgar showman; we questioned the rumors, tried to recall what we knew of him, interrogated ourselves relentlessly. Some of us dreamed of him: a monkey of a man in checked pants and a red hat, a stern officer in glistening boots. The promotional mailings showed only a knife held by a gloved hand. Is it surprising we didn't know what to feel?

At eight o'clock precisely, Hensch walked onto the stage: a brisk unsmiling man in black tails. His entrance surprised us. For although most of us had been seated since half past seven, others were still arriving, moving down the aisles, pushing past half-turned knees into squeaking seats. In fact we were so accustomed to delays for latecomers that an 8:00 performance was understood to mean one that began at 8:10 or even 8:15. As Hensch strode across the stage, a busy no-nonsense man, black-haired and top-bald, we didn't know whether we admired him for his supreme indifference to our noises of settling in, or disliked him for his refusal to countenance the slightest delay. He walked quickly across the stage to a waist-high table on which rested a mahogany box. He wore no gloves. At the opposite corner of the stage, in the rear, a black wooden partition bisected the stage walls. Hensch stepped behind his box and opened it to reveal a glitter of knives. At this moment a woman in a loose-flowing white gown stepped in front of the dark partition. Her pale hair was pulled tightly back and she carried a silver bowl.

While the latecomers among us whispered their way past knees and coats, and slipped guiltily into their seats, the woman faced us and reached into her bowl. From it she removed a white hoop about the size of a dinner plate. She held it up and turned it from side to side, as if for our inspection, while Hensch lifted from his box half a dozen knives. Then he stepped to the side of the table. He held the six knives fanwise in his left hand, with the blades pointing up. The knives were about a foot long, the blades shaped like elongated diamonds, and as he stood there at the side of the stage, a man with no expression on his face, a man with nothing to do, Hensch had the vacant and slightly bored look of an overgrown boy holding in one hand an awkward present, waiting patiently for someone to open a door.

With a gentle motion the woman in the white gown tossed the hoop lightly in the air in front of the black wooden partition. Suddenly a knife sank deep into the soft wood, catching the hoop, which hung swinging on the handle. Before we could decide whether or not to applaud, the woman tossed another white hoop. Hensch lifted and threw in a single swift smooth motion, and the second hoop hung swinging from the second knife. After the third hoop rose in the air and hung suddenly on a knife handle, the woman reached into her bowl and held up for our inspection a smaller hoop, the size of a saucer. Hensch raised a knife and caught the flying hoop cleanly against the wood. She next tossed two small hoops one after the other, which Hensch caught in two swift motions: the first at the top of its trajectory, the second near the middle of the partition.

We watched Hensch as he picked up three more knives and spread them fanwise in his left hand. He stood staring at his assistant with fierce attention, his back straight, his thick hand resting by his side. When she tossed three small hoops, one after the other, we saw his body tighten, we waited for the *thunk-thunk-thunk* of knives in wood, but he stood immobile, sternly gazing. The hoops struck the floor, bounced slightly, and began rolling like big dropped coins across the stage. Hadn't he liked the throw? We felt like looking away, like pretending we hadn't noticed. Nimbly the assistant gathered the rolling hoops, then assumed her position by the black wall. She seemed to take a deep breath before she tossed again. This time Hensch flung his three knives with extraordinary speed, and suddenly we saw all three hoops swinging on the partition, the last mere inches from the floor. She motioned grandly toward Hensch, who did not bow; we burst into vigorous applause.

Again the woman in the white gown reached into her bowl, and this time she held up something between her thumb and forefinger that even those of us in the first rows could not immediately make out. She stepped forward, and many of us recognized, between her fingers, an orange and black butterfly. She returned to the partition and looked at Hensch, who had already chosen his knife. With a gentle tossing gesture she released the butterfly. We burst into applause as the knife drove the butterfly against the wood, where those in the front rows could see the wings helplessly beating.

That was something we hadn't seen before, or even imagined we might see, something worth remembering; and as we applauded we tried to recall the knife throwers of our childhood, the smell of sawdust and cotton candy, the glittering woman on the turning wheel.

Now the woman in white removed the knives from the black partition and carried them across the stage to Hensch, who examined each one closely and wiped it with a cloth before returning it to his box.

Abruptly, Hensch strode to the center of the stage and turned to face us. His assistant pushed the table with its box of knives to his side. She left the stage and returned pushing a second table, which she placed at his other side. She stepped away, into half-darkness, while the lights shone directly on Hensch and his tables. We saw him place his left hand palm up on the empty tabletop. With his right hand he removed a knife from the box on the first table. Suddenly, without looking, he tossed the knife straight up into the air. We saw it rise to its rest and come hurtling down. Someone cried out as it struck his palm, but Hensch raised his hand from the table and held it up for us to see, turning it first one way and then the other: the knife had struck between the fingers. Hensch lowered his hand over the knife so that the blade stuck up between his second and third fingers. He tossed three more knives into the air, one after the other: *rat-tat-tat* they struck the table. From the shadows the woman in white stepped forward and tipped the table toward us, so that we could see the four knives sticking between his fingers.

Oh, we admired Hensch, we were taken with the man's fine daring; and yet, as we pounded out our applause, we felt a little restless, a little dissatisfied, as if some unspoken promise had failed to be kept. For hadn't we been a trifle ashamed of ourselves for attending the performance, hadn't we deplored in advance his unsavory antics, his questionable crossing of the line?

As if in answer to our secret impatience, Hensch strode decisively to his corner of the stage. Quickly the pale-haired assistant followed, pushing the table after him. She next shifted the second table to the back of the stage and returned to the black partition. She stood with her back against it, gazing across the stage at Hensch, her loose white gown hanging from thin shoulder straps that had slipped down to her upper arms.

At that moment we felt in our arms and along our backs a first faint flutter of anxious excitement, for there they stood before us, the dark master and the pale maiden, like figures in a dream from which we were trying to awake.

Hensch chose a knife and raised it beside his head with deliberation; we realized that he had worked very quickly before. With a swift sharp drop of his forearm, as if he were chopping a piece of wood, he released the knife. At first we thought he had struck her upper arm, but we saw that the blade had sunk into the wood and lay touching her skin. A second knife struck beside her other upper arm. She began to wriggle both shoulders, as if to free herself from the tickling knives, and only as her loose gown came rippling down did we realize that the knives had cut the shoulder straps. Hensch had us now, he had us. Long-legged and smiling, she stepped from the fallen gown and stood before the black partition in a spangled silver leotard. We thought of tightrope walkers, bareback riders, hot circus tents on blue summer days. The pale yellow hair, the spangled cloth, the pale skin touched here and there with shadow, all this gave her the remote, enclosed look of a work of art, while at the same time it lent her a kind of cool voluptuousness, for the metallic glitter of her costume seemed to draw attention to the bareness of her skin, disturbingly unhidden, dangerously white and cool and soft.

Quickly the glittering assistant stepped to the second table at the back of the stage and removed something from the drawer. She returned to the center of the wooden partition and placed on her head a red apple. The apple was so red and shiny that it looked as if it had been painted with nail polish. We looked at Hensch, who stared at her and held himself very still. In a single motion Hensch lifted and threw. She stepped out from under the red apple stuck in the wood.

From the table she removed a second apple and clenched the stem with her teeth. At the black partition she bent slowly backward until the bright red apple was above her upturned lips. We could see the column of her trachea pressing against the skin of her throat and the knobs of her hips pushing up against the silver spangles. Hensch took careful aim and flung the knife through the heart of the apple.

Next from the table she removed a pair of long white gloves, which she pulled on slowly, turning her wrists, tugging. She held up each tight-gloved hand in turn and wriggled the fingers. At the partition she stood with her arms out and her fingers spread. Hensch looked at her, then raised a knife and threw; it stuck into her fingertip, the middle fingertip of her right hand, pinning her to the black wall. The woman stared straight ahead. Hensch picked up a clutch of knives and held them fan-wise in his left hand. Swiftly he flung nine knives, one after the other, and as they struck her fingertips, one after the other, bottom to top, right-left right-left, we stirred uncomfortably in our seats. In the sudden silence she stood there with her arms outspread and her fingers full of knives, her silver spangles flashing, her white gloves whiter than her pale arms, looking as if at any moment her head would drop forward—looking for all the world like a martyr on a cross. Then slowly, gently, she pulled each hand from its glove, leaving the gloves hanging on the wall.

Now Hensch gave a sharp wave of his fingers, as if to dismiss everything that had gone before, and to our surprise the woman stepped forward to the edge of the stage, and addressed us for the first time.

"I must ask you," she said gently, "to be very quiet, because this next act is very dangerous. The master will mark me. Please do not make a sound. We thank you."

She returned to the black partition and simply stood there, her shoulders back, her arms down but pressed against the wood. She gazed steadily at Hensch, who seemed to be studying her; some of us said later that at this moment she gave the impression of a child who was about to be struck in the face, though others felt she looked calm, quite calm.

Hensch chose a knife from his box, held it for a moment, then raised his arm and threw. The knife struck beside her neck. He had missed—had he missed?—and we felt a sharp tug of disappointment, which changed at once to shame, deep shame, for we hadn't come out for blood, only for—well, something else; and as we asked ourselves what we had come for, we were surprised to see her reach up with one hand and pull out the knife. Then we saw, on her neck, the thin red trickle, which ran down to her shoulder; and we understood that her whiteness had been arranged for this moment. Long and loud we applauded, as she bowed and held aloft the glittering knife, assuring us, in that way, that she was wounded but well, or well-wounded; and we didn't know whether we were applauding her wellness or her wound, or the touch of the master, who had crossed the line, who had carried us, safely, it appeared, into the realm of forbidden things.

Even as we applauded she turned and left the stage, returning a few moments later in a long black dress with long sleeves and a high collar, which concealed her wound. We imagined the white bandage under the black collar; we imagined other bandages, other wounds, on her hips, her waist, the edges of her breasts. Black against black they stood there, she and he, bound now it seemed in a dark pact, as if she were his twin sister, or as if both were on the same side in a game we were all playing, a game we no longer understood; and indeed she looked older in her black dress, sterner, a schoolmarm or maiden aunt. We were not surprised when she stepped forward to address us again.

"If any of you, in the audience, wish to be marked by the master, to receive the mark of the master, now is the time. Is there anyone?"

We all looked around. A single hand rose hesitantly and was instantly lowered. Another hand went up; then there were other hands, young bodies straining forward, eager; and from the stage the woman in black descended and walked slowly along an aisle, looking closely, considering, until she stopped and pointed: "You." And we knew her, Susan Parker, a high school girl, who might have been our daughter, sitting there with her face turned questioningly toward the woman, her eyebrows slightly raised, as she pointed to herself; then the faint flush of realization; and as she climbed the steps of the stage we watched her closely, wondering what the dark woman had seen in her, to make her be the one, wondering too what she was thinking, Susan Parker, as she followed the dark woman to the wooden partition. She was wearing loose jeans and a tight black short-sleeved sweater; her reddish-brown and faintly shiny hair was cut short. Was it for her white skin she had been chosen? or some air of self-possession? We wanted to cry out, Sit down! you don't have to do this! but we remained silent, respectful. Hensch stood at his table, watching without expression. It occurred to us that we trusted him at this moment; we clung to him; he was all we had; for if we weren't absolutely sure of him, then who were we, what on earth were we, who had allowed things to come to such a pass?

The woman in black led Susan Parker to the wooden partition and arranged her there: back to the wood, shoulders straight. We saw her run her hand gently, as if tenderly, over the girl's short hair, which lifted and fell back in place. Then taking Susan Parker's right hand in hers, she stepped to the girl's right, so that the entire arm was extended against the black partition. She stood holding Susan Parker's raised hand, gazing at the girl's face—comforting her, it seemed; and we observed that Susan Parker's arm looked very white between the black sweater and the black dress, against the black wood of the partition. As the women gazed at each other, Hensch lifted a knife and threw. We heard the muffled bang of the blade, heard Susan Parker's sharp little gasp, saw her other hand clench into a fist. Quickly the dark woman stepped in front of her and pulled out the knife; and turning to us she lifted Susan Parker's arm, and displayed for us a streak of red on the pale forearm. Then she reached into a pocket of her black dress and removed a small tin box. From the box came a ball of cotton, a patch of gauze, and a roll of white surgical tape, with which she swiftly bound the wound. "There, dear," we heard her say. "You were very brave." We watched Susan Parker walk with lowered eyes across the stage, holding her bandaged arm a little away from her body; and as we began to clap, because she was still there, because she had come through, we saw her raise her eyes and give a quick shy smile, before lowering her lashes and descending the steps.

Now arms rose, seats creaked, there was a great rustling and whispering among us, for others were eager to be chosen, to be marked by the master, and once again the woman in black stepped forward to speak.

"Thank you, dear. You were very brave, and now you will bear the mark of the master. You will treasure it all your days. But it is a light mark, do you know, a very light mark. The master can mark more deeply, far more deeply. But for that you must show yourself worthy. Some of you may already be worthy, but I will ask you now to lower your hands, please, for I have with me someone who is ready to be marked. And please, all of you, I ask for your silence."

From the right of the stage stepped forth a young man who might have been fifteen or sixteen. He was dressed in black pants and a black shirt and wore rimless glasses that caught the light. He carried himself with ease, and we saw that he had a kind of lanky and slightly awkward beauty, the beauty, we thought, of a waterbird, a heron. The woman led him to the wooden partition and indicated that he should stand with his back against it. She walked to the table at the rear of the stage and removed an object, which she carried back to the partition. Raising the boy's left arm, so that it was extended straight out against the wall at the level of his shoulder, she lifted the object to his wrist and began fastening it into the wood. It appeared to be a clamp, which held his arm in place at the wrist. She then arranged his hand: palm facing us, fingers together. Stepping away, she looked at him thoughtfully. Then she stepped over to his free side, took his other hand, and held it gently.

The stage lights went dark, then a reddish spotlight shone on Hensch at his box of knives. A second light, white as moonlight, shone on the boy and his extended arm. The other side of the boy remained in darkness.

Even as the performance seemed to taunt us with the promise of danger, of a disturbing turn that should not be permitted, or even imagined, we reminded ourselves that the master had so far done nothing but scratch a bit of skin, that his act was after all public and well traveled, that the boy appeared calm; and though we disapproved of the exaggerated effect of the lighting, the crude melodrama of it all, we secretly admired the skill with which the performance played on our fears. What it was we feared, exactly, we didn't know, couldn't say. But there was the knife thrower bathed in blood-light, there was the pale victim manacled to a wall; in the shadows the dark woman; and in the glare of the lighting, in the silence, in the very rhythm of the evening, the promise of entering a dark dream.

And Hensch took up a knife and threw; some heard the sharp gasp of the boy, others a thin cry. In the whiteness of the light we saw the knife handle at the center of his bloody palm. Some said that at the moment the knife struck, the boy's shocked face shone with an intense, almost painful joy. The white light suddenly illuminated the woman in black, who raised his free arm high, as if in triumph; then she quickly set to work pulling out the blade, wrapping the palm in strips of gauze, wiping the boy's drained and sweating face with a cloth, and leading him off the stage with an arm firmly around his waist. No one made a sound. We looked at Hensch, who was gazing after his assistant.

When she came back, alone, she stepped forward to address us, while the stage lights returned to normal.

"You are a brave boy, Thomas. You will not soon forget this day. And now I must say that we have time for only one more event, this evening. Many of you here, I know, would like to receive the palm mark, as Thomas did. But I am asking something different now. Is there anyone in this audience tonight who would like to make"—and here she paused, not hesitantly, but as if in emphasis—"the ultimate sacrifice? This is the final mark, the mark that can be received only once. Please think it over carefully, before raising your hand."

We wanted her to say more, to explain clearly what it was she meant by those riddling words, which came to us as though whispered in our ears, in the dark, words that seemed to mock us even as they eluded us—

and we looked about tensely, almost eagerly, as if by the sheer effort of our looking we were asserting our vigilance. We saw no hands, and maybe it was true that at the very center of our relief there was a touch of disappointment, but it was relief nonetheless; and if the entire performance had seemed to be leading toward some overwhelming moment that was no longer to take place, still we had been entertained by our knife thrower, had we not, we had been carried a long way, so that even as we questioned his cruel art we were ready to offer our applause.

"If there are no hands," she said, looking at us sharply, as if to see what it was we were secretly thinking, while we, as if to avoid her gaze, looked rapidly all about. "Oh: yes?" We saw it too, the partly raised hand, which perhaps had always been there, unseen in the half-darkened seats, and we saw the stranger rise, and begin to make her way slowly past drawn-in knees and pulled-back coats and half-risen forms. We watched her climb the steps of the stage, a tall mournful-looking girl in jeans and a dark blouse, with lank long hair and slouched shoulders. "And what is your name?" the woman in black said gently, and we could not hear the answer. "Well then, Laura. And so you are prepared to receive the final mark? Then you must be very brave." And turning to us she said, "I must ask you, please, to remain absolutely silent."

She led the girl to the black wooden partition and arranged her there, unconfined: chin up, hands hanging awkwardly at her sides. The dark woman stepped back and appeared to assess her arrangement, after which she crossed to the back of the stage. At this point some of us had confused thoughts of calling out, of demanding an explanation, but we didn't know what it was we might be protesting, and in any case the thought of distracting Hensch's throw, of perhaps causing an injury, was repellent to us, for we saw that already he had selected a knife. It was a new kind of knife, or so we thought, a longer and thinner knife. And it seemed to us that things were happening too quickly, up there on the stage, for where was the spotlight, where was the drama of a sudden darkening, but Hensch, even as we wondered, did what he always did—he threw his knife. Some of us heard the girl cry out, others were struck by her silence, but what stayed with all of us was the absence of the sound of the knife striking wood. Instead there was a softer sound, a more disturbing sound, a sound almost like silence, and some said the girl looked down, as if in surprise. Others claimed to see in her face, in the expression of her eyes, a look of rapture. As she fell to the floor the dark woman stepped forward and swept her arm toward the knife thrower, who for the first time turned to acknowledge us. And now he bowed: a deep, slow, graceful bow, the bow of a master, down to his knees. Slowly the dark red curtain began to fall. Overhead the lights came on.

As we left the theater we agreed that it had been a skillful performance, though we couldn't help feeling that the knife thrower had gone too far. He had justified his reputation, of that there could be no question; without ever trying to ingratiate himself with us, he had continually seized our deepest attention. But for all that, we couldn't help feeling that he ought to have found some other way. Of course the final act had probably been a setup, the girl had probably leaped smiling to her feet as soon as the curtain closed, though some of us recalled unpleasant rumors of one kind or another, run-ins with the police, charges and countercharges, a murky business. In any case we reminded ourselves that she hadn't been coerced in any way, none of them had been coerced in any way. And it was certainly true that a man in Hensch's position had every right to improve his art, to dream up new acts with which to pique curiosity, indeed such advances were absolutely necessary, for without them a knife thrower could never hope to keep himself in the public eye. Like the rest of us, he had to earn his living, which admittedly wasn't easy in times like these. But when all was said and done, when the pros and cons were weighed, and every issue carefully considered, we couldn't help feeling that the knife thrower had really gone too far. After all, if such performances were encouraged, if they were even tolerated, what might we expect in the future? Would any of us be safe? The more we thought about it, the more uneasy we became, and in the nights that followed, when we woke from troubling dreams, we remembered the traveling knife thrower with agitation and dismay.

A Visit

Although I had not heard from my friend in nine years, I wasn't surprised, not really, to receive a short letter from him dashed off in pencil, announcing that he had "taken a wife," and summoning me to visit him in some remote upstate town I had never heard of. "Come see me on the 16th and 17th" was what he had actually written. "Be here for lunch." The offhand peremptory tone was Albert all over. He had scribbled a map, with a little black circle marked VILLAGE and a little white square marked MY HOUSE. A wavy line connected the two. Under the line were the words 3½ MILES, MORE OR LESS. Over the line were the words COUNTY ROAD 39. I knew those desolate little upstate villages, consisting of one Baptist church, three bars, and a gas station with a single pump, and I imagined Albert living at an ironic distance, with his books and his manias. What I couldn't imagine was his wife. Albert had never struck me as the marrying kind, though women had always liked him. I had plans for the weekend, but I canceled them and headed north.

I still considered Albert my friend, in a way my best friend, even though I hadn't heard from him in nine years. He had once been my best friend and it was hard to think of him in any other way. Even in the flourishing time of our friendship, in the last two years of college and the year after, when we saw each other daily, he had been a difficult and exacting friend, scornful of convention though quiet in his own habits, subject to sudden flare-ups and silences, earnest but with an edge of mockery, intolerant of mediocrity, and cursed with an unfailing scent for the faintly fraudulent in a gesture or a phrase or a face. He was handsome in a sharp-featured New England way—his family, as he put it, had lived in Connecticut since the fall of the Roman Empire—but despite the inviting smiles of girls in his classes he confined himself to brisk affairs with leather-jacketed town girls with whom he had nothing in common. After graduating, we roomed together for a year in a little college town full of cafés and bookstores, sharing the rent and drifting from one part-time job to another, as I put off the inevitable suit-and-tie life that awaited me while he mocked my conventional fear of becoming conventional, defended business as America's only source of originality, and read his Plato and his *Modern Chess Openings* and tootled his flute. One day he left, just like that, to start what he called a new life. In the next year I received postcards from small towns all over America, showing pictures of Main Streets and quaint village railroad stations. They bore messages such as "Still looking" or "Have you seen my razor? I think I left it on the bathtub." Then there was nothing for six months, and then a sudden postcard from Eugene, Oregon, on which he described in minute detail a small unknown wooden object that he had found in the top drawer of the bureau in his rented bedroom, and then nine years of silence. During that time I had settled into a job and almost married an old girlfriend. I had bought a house on a pleasant street lined with porches and maples, thought quite a bit about my old friend Albert, and wondered whether this was what I had looked forward to, this life I was now leading, in the old days, the days when I still looked forward to things.

The town was even worse than I had imagined. Slowly I passed its crumbling brick paper mill with boarded-up windows, its rows of faded and flaking two-family houses with sagging front porches where guys in black T-shirts sat drinking beer, its tattoo parlor and its sluggish stream. County Road 39 wound between fields of Queen Anne's lace and yellow ragweed, with now and then a melancholy house or a patch of sun-scorched corn. Once I passed a rotting barn with a caved-in roof. At 3.2 miles on the odometer I came to a weathered house near the edge of the road. A bicycle lay in the high grass of the front yard and an open garage was entirely filled with old furniture. Uncertainly I turned onto the unpaved drive, parked with the motor running, and walked up to the front door. There was no bell. I knocked on the wooden screen door, which banged loudly against the frame, and a tall, barefoot, and very pale woman with sleepy eyes came to the door, wearing a long rumpled black skirt and a lumberjack shirt over a T-shirt. When I asked for Albert she looked at me suspiciously, shook her head quickly twice, and slammed the inner door. As I walked back to the car I saw her pale face looking out at me past a pushed-aside pink curtain. It occurred to me that perhaps Albert had married this woman and that she was insane. It further occurred to me, as I backed out of the drive, that I really ought to turn back now, right now, away from this misguided adventure in the wilderness. After all, I hadn't seen him for nine long years, things were bound to be different. At 4.1 miles on the odometer I rounded a bend of rising road and saw a shadowy house set back in a cluster of dusty-looking trees. I turned into the unknown dirt drive, deep-rutted and sprouting weeds, and as I stepped on the brake with a sharp sense of desolation and betrayal, for here I was, in the godforsaken middle of nauseating nowhere, prowling around like a fool and a criminal, the front door opened and Albert came out, one hand in his pocket and one hand waving.

He looked the same, nearly the same, though browner and leatherier than I remembered, as if he had lived all those years in the sun, his face a little longer and leaner—a handsome man in jeans and a dark shirt. "I wondered if you'd show up," he said when he reached the car, and suddenly seemed to study me. "You look just the way you ought to," he then said.

I let the words settle in me. "It depends what I ought to look like," I answered, glancing at him sharply, but he only laughed.

"Isn't this a great place?" he said, throwing out one arm as he began carrying my traveling bag toward the house. "Ten acres and they're practically giving it away. First day after I bought the place I go walking around and bingo! what do you think I found? Grapes. Billions of grapes. An old fallen-down grape arbor, grapes growing all over the ground. Italy in New York. Wait till you see the pond."

We stepped into the shade of the high trees, a little thicket of pines and maples, that grew close to the house. Big bushes climbed halfway up the windows. It struck me that the house was well protected from view, a private place, a shadowy isle in a sea of fields. "And yet," I said, looking around for his wife, "somehow I never thought of you as getting married, somehow."

"Not back then," he said. "Watch that rail."

We had climbed onto the steps of the long, deep-shaded front porch, and I had grasped a wobbly iron handrail that needed to be screwed into the wood. A coil of old garden hose hung over the porch rail. A few hornets buzzed about the ceiling light. On the porch stood a sunken chaise longue, an old three-speed bicycle, a metal garbage can containing a rusty snow shovel, and a porch swing on which sat an empty flowerpot.

He opened the wooden screen door and with a little flourish urged me in. "Humble," he said, "but mine own." He looked at me with a kind of excitement, an excitement I couldn't entirely account for, but which reminded me of the old excitement, and I wondered, as I entered the house, whether that was what I had been looking for, back then. The house was cool and almost dark, the dark of deep shade lightened by streaks of sun. Under the half-drawn window shades I saw bush branches growing against the glass. We had entered the living room, where I noticed a rocking chair that leaned too far back and a couch with one pillow. Ancient wallpaper showed faded scenes of some kind repeating themselves all over the room. Albert, who seemed more and more excited, led me up the creaking worn-edged stairs to my room—a bed with a frilly pink spread, a lamp table on which lay a screwdriver with a transparent yellow handle—and quickly back down.

"You must be starving," he said, with that odd quiver of excitement, as he led me through an open doorway into a dining room that was almost dark. At a big round table there were three place settings, which glowed whitely in the gloom. One of the round-backed chairs appeared to be occupied. Only as I drew closer through the afternoon darkness did I see that the occupant was a large frog, perhaps two feet high, which sat with its throat resting on the table edge. "My wife," Albert said, looking at me fiercely, as if he were about to spring at my face. I felt I was being tested in some fiendish way. "Pleased to meet you," I said harshly, and sat down across from her. The table lay between us like a lake. I had thought she might be something else, maybe a stuffed toy of some sort, but even in the dark daylight I could see the large moist eyes looking here and there, I could see her rapid breathing and smell her marshy odor. I thought Albert must be making fun of me in some fashion, trying to trick me into exposing what he took to be my hideous bourgeois soul, but whatever his game I wasn't going to give myself away.

"Help yourself," Albert said, pushing toward me a breadboard with a round loaf and a hunk of cheese on it. A big-bladed knife lay on the table and I began cutting the bread. "And if you'd cut just a little piece of cheese for Alice." I immediately cut a little piece of cheese for Alice. Albert disappeared into the kitchen and in the room's dusk I stared across the round table at Alice before looking away uncomfortably.

Albert returned with a wax carton of orange juice and a small brown bottle of beer, both of which he set before me. "The choice," he said with a little bow, "is yours entirely." He picked up the piece of cheese I had cut for Alice, placed it on her plate, and broke it into smaller pieces. Alice looked at him—it seemed to me that she looked at him—with those moist and heavy-lidded eyes, and flicked up her cheese. Then she placed her throat on the table edge and sat very still.

Albert sat down and cut himself a piece of bread. "After lunch I want to show you the place. Take you down to the pond and so on." He looked at me, tilting his head in a way I suddenly remembered. "And you? It's been a while."

"Oh, still a roving bachelor," I said, and immediately disliked my fatuous tone. I had a sudden urge to talk seriously to Albert, as we'd done in the old days, watching the night turn slowly gray through our tall, arched windows. But I felt constrained, it had been too long a time, and though he had summoned me after all these years, though he had shown me his wife, it was all askew somehow, as if he hadn't shown me anything, as if he'd kept himself hidden away. And I remembered that even then, in the time of our friendship, he had seemed intimate and secretive at the same time, as if even his revelations were forms of concealment. "Not that I have any fixed plan," I continued. "I see women, but they're not the right one. You know, I was always sure I'd be the one to get married, not you."

"It wasn't something I planned. But when the moment comes, you'll know." He looked at Alice with tenderness and suddenly leaned over and touched the side of her head lightly with his fingertips.

"How did you," I began, and stopped. I felt like bursting into screams of wild laughter, or of outrage, pure outrage, but I held myself down, I pretended everything was fine. "I mean, how did you meet? You two. If I may ask."

"So formal! If you may ask! Down by the pond—if I may answer. I saw her in the reeds one day. I'd never seen her before, but she was always there, after that. I'll show you the exact place after lunch."

His little mocking rebuke irritated me, and I recalled how he had always irritated me, and made me retreat more deeply into myself, because of some little reproach, some little ironic look, and it seemed strange to me that someone who irritated me and made me retreat into myself was also someone who released me into a freer version of myself, a version superior to the constricted one that had always felt like my own hand on my throat. But who was Albert, after all, that he should have the power to release me or constrict me—this man I no longer knew, with his run-down house and his ludicrous frog-wife. Then I ate for a while in sullen silence, looking only at my food, and when I glanced up I saw him looking at me kindly, almost affectionately.

"It's all right," he said quietly, as if he understood, as if he knew how difficult it was for me, this journey, this wife, this life. And I was grateful, as I had always been, for we had been close, he and I, back then.

After lunch he insisted on showing me his land—his domain, as he called it. I had hoped that Alice might stay behind, so that I could speak with him alone, but it was clear that he wanted her to come with us. So as we made our way out the back door and into his domain she followed along, taking hops about two strides in length, always a little behind us or a little before. At the back of the house a patch of overgrown lawn led to a vegetable garden on both sides of a grassy path. There were vines of green peas and string beans climbing tall sticks, clusters of green peppers, rows of carrots and radishes identified by seed packets on short sticks, fat heads of lettuce and flashes of yellow squash—a rich and well-tended oasis, as if the living center of the house were here, on the outside, hidden in back. At the end of the garden grew a scattering of fruit trees, pear and cherry and plum. An old wire fence with a broken wooden gate separated the garden from the land beyond.

We walked along a vague footpath through fields of high grass, passed into thickets of oak and maple, crossed a stream. Alice kept up the pace. Alice in sunlight, Alice in the open air, no longer seemed a grotesque pet, a monstrous mistake of Nature, a nightmare frog and freakish wife, but rather a companion of sorts, staying alongside us, resting when we rested—Albert's pal. And yet it was more than that. For when she emerged from high grass or tree shade into full sunlight, I saw or sensed for a moment, with a kind of inner start, Alice as she was, Alice in the sheer brightness and fullness of her being, as if the dark malachite sheen of her skin, the pale shimmer of her throat, the moist warmth of her eyes, were as natural and mysterious as the flight of a bird. Then I would tumble back into myself and realize that I was walking with my old friend beside a monstrous lumbering frog who had somehow become his wife, and a howl of inward laughter and rage would erupt in me, calmed almost at once by the rolling meadows, the shady thickets, the black crow rising from a tree with slowly lifted and lowered wings, rising higher and higher into the pale blue sky touched here and there with delicate fernlike clouds.

The pond appeared suddenly, on the far side of a low rise. Reeds and cattails grew in thick clusters at the marshy edge. We sat down on flat-topped boulders and looked out at the green-brown water, where a few brown ducks floated, out past fields to a line of low hills. There was a desolate beauty about the place, as if we had come to the edge of the world. "It was over there I first saw her," Albert said, pointing to a cluster of reeds. Alice sat off to one side, low to the ground, in a clump of grass at the water's edge. She was still as a rock, except for her sides moving in and out as she breathed. I imagined her growing in the depths of the pond, under a mantle of lily pads and mottled scum, down below the rays of green sunlight, far down, at the silent bottom of the world.

Albert leaned back on both elbows, a pose I remembered well, and stared out at the water. For a long while we sat in a silence that struck me as uncomfortable, though he himself seemed at ease. It wasn't so much that I felt awkward in Alice's presence as that I didn't know what I had come all this way to say. Did I really want to speak at all? Then Albert said, "Tell me about your life." And I was grateful to him, for that was exactly what I wanted to talk about, my life. I told him about my almost-marriage, my friendships that lacked excitement, my girlfriends who lacked one thing or another, my good job that somehow wasn't exactly what I had been looking for, back then, my feeling that things were all right but not as all right as they might be, that I was not unhappy but not really happy either, but caught in some intermediate place, looking both ways. And as I spoke it seemed to me that I was looking in one direction toward a happiness that was growing vaguer, and in the other direction toward an unhappiness that was emerging more clearly, without yet revealing itself completely.

"It's hard," Albert then said, in the tone of someone who knew what I was talking about, and though I was soothed by his words, which were spoken gently, I was disappointed that he didn't say more, that he didn't show himself to me.

And I said, "Why did you write to me, after all this time?" which was only another way of saying, why didn't you write to me, in all this time.

"I waited," he said, "until I had something to show you." That was what he said: something to show me. And it seemed to me then that if all he had to show me after nine years was his run-down house and his marshy frog-wife, then I wasn't so badly off, in my own way, not really.

After that we continued walking about his domain, with Alice always at our side. He showed me things, and I looked. He showed me the old grape arbor that he had put back up; unripe green grapes, hard as nuts, hung in bunches from the decaying slats. "Try one," he said, but it was bitter as a tiny lemon. He laughed at my grimace. "We like 'em this way," he said, plucking a few into his palm, then tossing them into his mouth. He pulled off another handful and held them down to Alice, who devoured them swiftly: *flick flick flick.* He showed me a woodpecker's nest, and a slope of wild tiger lilies, and an old toolshed containing a rusty hoe and a rusty rake. Suddenly, from a nearby field, a big bird rose up with a loud beating of wings. "Did you see that!" cried Albert, seizing my arm. "A pheasant! Protecting her young. Over there." In the high grass six fuzzy little ducklike creatures walked in a line, their heads barely visible.

At dinner Alice sat in her chair with her throat resting on the edge of the table while Albert walked briskly in and out of the kitchen. I was pleased to see a fat bottle of red wine, which he poured into two juice glasses. The glasses had pictures of Winnie the Pooh and Eeyore on them. "Guy gave them to me at a gas station," Albert said. He frowned suddenly, pressed his fingertips against his forehead, looked up with a radiant smile. "I've got it. The more it *snows,* tiddely-pom, the more it *goes,* tiddely-pom." He poured a little wine into a cereal bowl and placed it near Alice.

Dinner was a heated-up supermarket chicken, fresh squash from his garden, and big bowls of garden salad. Albert was in high spirits, humming snatches of songs, lighting a stub of candle in a green wine bottle, filling our wineglasses and Alice's bowl again and again, urging me to drink up, crunching lustily into his salad. The cheap wine burned my tongue but I kept drinking, taken by Albert's festive spirit, eager to carry myself into his mood. Even Alice kept finishing the wine he put in her cereal bowl. The candle flame seemed to grow brighter in the darkening air of the room; through bush branches in the window I saw streaks of sunset. A line of wax ran down the bottle and stopped. Albert brought in his breadboard, more salad, another loaf of bread. And as the meal continued I had the sense that Alice, sitting there with her throat resting on the table edge, flicking up her wine, was looking at Albert with those large eyes of hers, moist and dark in the flame-light. She was looking at him and trying to attract his attention. Albert was leaning back in his chair, laughing, throwing his arm about as he talked, but it seemed to me that he was darting glances back at her. Yes, they were exchanging looks, there at the darkening dinner table, looks that struck me as amorous. And as I drank I was filled with a warm, expansive feeling, which took in the room, the meal, the Winnie the Pooh glasses, the large moist eyes, the reflection of the candle flame in the black window, the glances of Albert and his wife; for after all, she was the one he had chosen, up here in the wilderness, and who was I to say what was right, in such matters.

Albert leaped up and returned with a bowl of pears and cherries from his fruit trees, and filled my glass again. I was settling back with my warm, expansive feeling, looking forward to the night of talk stretching lazily before me, when Albert announced that it was getting late, he and Alice would be retiring. I had the run of the house. Just be sure to blow out the candle. Nighty night. Through the roar of wine I was aware of my plunging disappointment. He pulled back her chair and she hopped to the floor. Together they left the dining room and disappeared into the dark living room, where he turned on a lamp so dim that it was like lighting a candle. I heard him creaking up the stairs and thought I heard a dull thumping sound, as I imagined Alice lumbering her way up beside him.

I sat listening to the thumps and creaks of the upper hall, a sudden sharp rush of water in the bathroom sink, a squeak—what was that squeak?—a door shutting. In the abrupt silence, which seemed to spread outward from the table in widening ripples, I felt abandoned, there with the wine and the candle and the glimmering dishes. Yet I saw that it was bound to be this way, and no other way, for I had watched their amorous looks, it was only to be expected. And hadn't he, back then, been in the habit of unexpected departures? Then I began to wonder whether they had ever taken place, those talks stretching into the gray light of dawn, or whether I had only desired them. Then I imagined Alice hopping onto the white sheets. And I tried to imagine frog-love, its possible pleasures, its oozy raptures, but I turned my mind violently away, for in the imagining I felt something petty and cruel, something in the nature of a violation.

I drank down the last of the wine and blew out the candle. From the dark room where I sat I could see a ghostly corner of refrigerator in the kitchen and a dim-lit reddish couch-arm in the living room, like a moonlit dead flower. A car passed on the road. Then I became aware of the crickets, whole fields and meadows of them, the great hum that I had always heard rising from backyards and vacant lots in childhood summers, the long sound of summer's end. And yet it was only the middle of summer, was it not, just last week I had spent a day at the beach. So for a long time I sat at the dark table, in the middle of a decaying house, listening to the sound of summer's end. Then I picked up my empty glass, silently saluted Albert and his wife, and went up to bed.

But I could not sleep. Maybe it was the wine, or the mashed mattress, or the early hour, but I lay there twisting in my sheets, and as I turned restlessly, the day's adventures darkened in my mind and I saw only a crazed friend, a ruined house, an ugly and monstrous frog. And I saw myself, weak and absurd, wrenching my mind into grotesque shapes of sympathy and understanding. At some point I began to slide in and out of dreams, or perhaps it was a single long dream broken by many half-wakings. I was walking down a long hall with a forbidden door at the end. With a sense of mournful excitement I opened the door and saw Albert standing with his arms crossed, looking at me sternly. He began to shout at me, his face became very red, and bending over he bit me on the hand. Tears ran down my face. Behind him someone rose from a chair and came toward us. "Here," said the newcomer, who was somehow Albert, "use this." He held up a handkerchief draped over his fist, and when I pulled off the handkerchief a big frog rose angrily into the air with wild flappings of its wings.

I woke tense and exhausted in a sun-streaked room. Through a dusty window I saw tree branches with big three-lobed leaves and between the leaves pieces of blue sky. It was nearly nine. I had three separate headaches: one behind my left eye, one in my right temple, and one at the back of my head. I washed and dressed quickly and made my way down the darkening stairs, through a dusk that deepened as I drew toward the bottom. On the faded wallpaper I could make out two scenes repeating themselves into the distance: a faded boy in blue lying against a faded yellow haystack with a horn at his side, and a girl in white drawing water from a faded well.

The living room was empty. The whole house appeared to be deserted. On the round table in the twilight of the dining room the dishes still sat from dinner. All I wanted was a cup of coffee before leaving. In the slightly less gloomy kitchen I found an old jar of instant coffee and a chipped blue teapot decorated with a little decal picturing an orange brontosaurus. I heard sharp sounds, and through the leaves and branches in the kitchen window I saw Albert with his back to me, digging in the garden. Outside the house it was a bright, sunny day. Beside him, on the dirt, sat Alice.

I brought my cup of harsh-tasting, stale coffee into the dining room and drank it at the table while I listened to the sounds of Albert's shovel striking the soil. It was peaceful in the darkish room, at the round brown table. A thin slant of sun glittered in the open kitchen. The sun-slant mingled with the whistle of a bird, leaves in the window, the brown dusk, the sound of the shovel striking loam, turning it over. It occurred to me that I could simply pack my things now, and glide away without the awkwardness of a leave-taking.

I finished the dismal coffee and carried the cup into the kitchen, where the inner back door stood slightly open. There I paused, holding the empty cup in my hand. Obeying a sudden impulse, I opened the door a little more and slipped between it and the wooden screen door.

Through the buckled screen I could see Albert some ten feet away. His sleeves were rolled up and his foot was pressing down on the blade of the shovel. He was digging up grassy dirt at the edge of the garden, turning it over, breaking up the soil, tossing away clumps of grass roots. Nearby sat Alice, watching him. From time to time, as he moved along the edge of the garden, he would look over at her. Their looks seemed to catch for a moment, before he returned to his garden. Standing in the warm shade of the half-open door, looking through the rippling screen at the garden quivering with sunlight, I sensed a mysterious rhythm trembling between Albert and his wife, a kind of lightness or buoyancy, a quivering sunlit harmony. It was as if both of them had shed their skins and were mingling in air, or dissolving into light—and as I felt that airy mingling, that tender dissolution, as I sensed that hidden harmony, clear as the ringing of a distant bell, it came over me that what I lacked, in my life, was exactly that harmony. It was as if I were composed of some hard substance that could never dissolve in anything, whereas Albert had discovered the secret of air. But my throat was beginning to hurt, the bright light burned my eyes, and setting down my cup on the counter, which sounded like the blow of a hammer, I pushed open the door and went out.

Albert turned around in the sun. "Sleep well?" he said, running the back of his hand slowly across his dripping forehead.

"Well enough. But you know, I've got to be getting back. A million things to do! You know how it is."

"Sure," Albert said. He rested both hands on the top of the long shovel handle and placed his chin on his hands. "I know how it is." His tone struck me as brilliantly poised between understanding and mockery.

He brought my bag down from my room and loaded it in the car. Alice had hopped through the dining room and living room and had come to rest in the deep shade of the front porch. It struck me that she kept carefully out of sight of the road. Albert bent over the driver's window and crossed his arms on the door. "If you're ever up this way," he said, but who would ever be up that way, "drop in." "I'll do that," I said. Albert stood up and stretched out an elbow, rubbed his shoulder. "Take care," he said, and gave a little wave and stepped away.

As I backed up the dirt driveway and began edging onto County Road 39, I had the sense that the house was withdrawing into its trees and shadows, fading into its island of shade. Albert had already vanished. From the road I could see only a stand of high trees clustered about a dark house. A few moments later, at the bend of the road, I glanced back again. I must have waited a second too long, because the road was already dipping, the house had sunk out of sight, and in the bright sunshine I saw only a scattering of roadside trees, a cloudless sky, fields of Queen Anne's lace stretching away.

Flying Carpets

In the long summers of my childhood, games flared up suddenly, burned to a brightness, and vanished forever. The summers were so long that they gradually grew longer than the whole year, they stretched out slowly beyond the edges of our lives, but at every moment of their vastness they were drawing to an end, for that's what summers mostly did: they taunted us with endings, marched always into the long shadow thrown backward by the end of vacation. And because our summers were always ending, and because they lasted forever, we grew impatient with our games, we sought new and more intense ones; and as the crickets of August grew louder, and a single red leaf appeared on branches green with summer, we threw ourselves as if desperately into new adventures, while the long days, never changing, grew heavy with boredom and longing.

I first saw the carpets in the backyards of other neighborhoods. Glimpses of them came to me from behind garages, flickers of color at the corners of two-family houses where clotheslines on pulleys stretched from upper porches to high gray poles, and old Italian men in straw hats stood hoeing between rows of tomatoes and waist-high corn. I saw one once at the far end of a narrow strip of grass between two stucco houses, skimming lightly over the ground at the level of the garbage cans. Although I took note of them, they were of no more interest to me than games of jump rope I idly watched on the school playground, or dangerous games with jackknives I saw the older boys playing at the back of the candy store. One morning I noticed one in a backyard in my neighborhood; four boys stood tensely watching. I was not surprised a few days later when my father came home from work with a long package under his arm, wrapped in heavy brown paper, tied with straw-colored twine from which little prickly hairs stuck up.

The colors were duller than I had expected, less magical—only maroon and green: dark green curlings and loopings against a maroon that was nearly brown. At each end the fringes were thickish rough strings. I had imagined crimson, emerald, the orange of exotic birds. The underside of the carpet was covered with a coarse, scratchy material like burlap; in one corner I noticed a small black mark, circled in red, shaped like a capital *H* with a slanting middle line. In the backyard I practiced cautiously, close to the ground, following the blurred blue directions printed on a piece of paper so thin I could see my fingertips touching the other side. It was all a matter of artfully shifted weight: seated cross-legged just behind the center of the carpet, you leaned forward slightly to send the carpet forward, left to make it turn left; right, right. The carpet rose when you lifted both sides with fingers cupped beneath, lowered when you pushed lightly down. It slowed to a stop when the bottom felt the pressure of a surface.

At night I kept it rolled up in the narrow space at the foot of my bed, alongside old puzzle boxes at the bottom of my bookcase.

For days I was content to practice gliding back and forth about the yard, passing under the branches of the crab-apple trees, squeezing between the swing and ladder of the yellow swing set, flying into the bottoms of sheets on the clothesline, drifting above the row of zinnias at the edge of the garden to skim along the carrots and radishes and four rows of corn, passing back and forth over the wooden floor of the old chicken coop that was nothing but a roof and posts at the back of the garage, while my mother watched anxiously from the kitchen window. I was no more tempted to rise into the sky than I was tempted to plunge downhill on my bike with my arms crossed over my chest. Sometimes I liked to watch the shadow of my carpet moving on the ground, a little below me and to one side; and now and then, in a nearby yard, I would see an older boy rise on his carpet above a kitchen window, or pass over the sunlit shingles of a garage roof.

Sometimes my friend Joey came skimming over his low picket fence into my yard. Then I followed him around and around the crab-apple trees and through the open chicken coop. He went faster than I did, leaning far forward, tipping sharply left or right. He even swooped over my head, so that for a moment a shadow passed over me. One day he landed on the flat tar-papered roof of the chicken coop, where I soon joined him. Standing with my hands on my hips, the sun burning down on my face, I could see over the tall backyard hedge into the weed-grown lot where in past summers I had hunted for frogs and garden snakes. Beyond the lot I saw houses and telephone wires rising on the hill beside the curving sun-sparkling road; and here and there, in backyards hung with clotheslines, against the white-shingled backs of houses, over porch rails and sloping cellar doors and the water arcs of lawn sprinklers shot through with faint rainbows, I could see the children on their red and green and blue carpets, riding through the sunny air.

One afternoon when my father was at work and my mother lay in her darkened bedroom, breathing damply with asthma, I pulled out the carpet at the foot of the bed, unrolled it, and sat down on it to wait. I wasn't supposed to ride my carpet unless my mother was watching from the kitchen window. Joey was in another town, visiting his cousin Marilyn, who lived near a department store with an escalator. The thought of riding up one escalator and down the next, up one and down the next, while the stairs flattened out or lifted up, filled me with irritation and boredom. Through the window screen I could hear the sharp, clear blows of a hammer, like the ticking of a gigantic clock. I could hear the *clish-clish* of hedge clippers, which made me think of movie swordfights; the uneven hum of a rising and falling bee. I lifted the edges of the carpet and began to float about the room. After a while I passed through the door and down the stairs into the small living room and big yellow kitchen, but I kept bumping into pots and chair-tops; and soon I came skimming up the stairs and landed on my bed and looked out the window into the backyard. The shadow of the swing frame showed sharp and black against the grass. I felt a tingling or tugging in my legs and arms. Dreamily I pushed the window higher and raised the screen.

For a while I glided about the room, then bent low as I approached the open window and began to squeeze the carpet through. The wooden bottom of the raised window scraped along my back, the sides of the frame pressed against me. It was like the dream where I tried to push myself through the small doorway, tried and tried, though my bones hurt, and my skin burned, till suddenly I pulled free. For a moment I seemed to sit suspended in the air beyond my window; below I saw the green hose looped on its hook, the handles and the handle-shadows on the tops of the metal garbage cans, the mountain laurel bush pressed against the cellar window; then I was floating out over the top of the swing and the crab-apple trees; below me I saw the shadow of the carpet rippling over grass; and drifting high over the hedge and out over the vacant lot, I looked down on the sunny tall grass, the milkweed pods and pink thistles, a green Coke bottle gleaming in the sun; beyond the lot the houses rose behind each other on the hill, the red chimneys clear against the blue sky; and all was sunny, all was peaceful and still; the hum of insects; the far sound of a hand mower, like distant scissors; soft shouts of children in the warm, drowsy air; heavily my eyelids began to close; but far below I saw a boy in brown shorts looking up at me, shading his eyes; and seeing him there, I felt suddenly where I was, way up in the dangerous air; and leaning fearfully to one side I steered the carpet back to my yard, dropped past the swing, and landed on the grass near the back steps. As I sat safe in my yard I glanced up at the high, open window; and far above the window the red shingles of the roof glittered in the sun.

I dragged the heavy carpet up to my room, but the next day I rose high above Joey as he passed over the top of the swing. In a distant yard I saw someone skim over the top of a garage roof and sink out of sight. At night I lay awake planning voyages, pressing both hands against my heart to slow its violent beating.

One night I woke to a racket of crickets. Through the window screen I could see the shadow of the swing frame in the moonlit backyard. I could see the streetlamp across from the bakery down by the field and the three streetlamps rising with the road as it curved out of sight at the top of the hill. The night sky was the color of a dark blue marble I liked to hold up to a bulb in the table lamp. I dressed quickly, pulled out my carpet, and slowly, so as not to make scraping noises, pushed up the window and the screen. From the foot of the bed I lifted the rolled rug. It suddenly spilled open, like a dark liquid rushing from a bottle. The wood of the window pressed against my back as I bent my way through.

In the blue night I sailed over the backyard, passing high over the hedge and into the lot, where I saw the shadow of the carpet rippling over moonlit high grass. I turned back to the yard, swooped over the garage roof, and circled the house at the level of the upper windows, watching myself pass in the glittery black glass; and rising a little higher, into the dark and dream-blue air, I looked down to see that I was passing over Joey's yard toward Ciccarelli's lot, where older boys had rock fights in the choked paths twisting among high weeds and thornbushes; and as when, standing up to my waist in water, I suddenly bent my legs and felt the cold wetness covering my shoulders, so now I plunged into the dark blue night, crossing Ciccarelli's lot, passing over a street, sailing over garage roofs, till rising higher I looked down on telephone wires glistening as if wet with moonlight, on moon-greened treetops stuffed with blackness, on the slanting rafters and open spaces of a half-built house crisscrossed with shadows; in the distance I could see a glassy stream going under a road; spots of light showed the shapes of far streets; and passing over a roof close by a chimney, I saw each brick so sharp and clear in the moonlight that I could make out small bumps and holes in the red and ocher surfaces; and sweeping upward with the wind in my hair I flew over moon-flooded rooftops striped with chimney shadows, until I saw below me the steeple of a white church, the top of the firehouse, the big red letters of the five-and-dime, the movie marquee sticking out like a drawer, the shop windows dark-shining in the light of streetlamps, the street with its sheen of red from the traffic light; then out over rows of rooftops on the far side of town, a black factory with lit-up windows and white smoke that glowed like light; a field stretching away; gleaming water; till I felt I'd strayed to the farthest edge of things; and turning back I flew high above the moonlit town, when suddenly I saw the hill with three streetlamps, the bakery, the swing frame, the chicken coop—and landing for a moment on the roof of the garage, sitting with my legs astride the peak, exultant, unafraid, I saw, high in the blue night sky, passing slowly across the white moon, another carpet with its rider.

With a feeling of exhilaration and weariness—a weariness like sadness—I rose slowly toward my window, and bending my way through, I plunged into sleep.

The next morning I woke sluggish and heavy-headed. Outside, Joey was waiting for me on his carpet. He wanted to race around the house. But I had no heart for carpets that day, stubbornly I swung on the old swing, threw a tennis ball onto the garage roof and caught it as it came rushing over the edge, squeezed through the hedge into the vacant lot where I'd once caught a frog in a jar. At night I lay remembering my journey in sharp detail—the moon-glistening telephone wires above their shadow-stripes, the clear bricks in the chimney—while through the window screen I heard the *chik-chik-chik* of crickets. I sat up in bed and shut the window and turned the metal lock on top.

I had heard tales of other voyages, out beyond the ends of the town, high up into the clouds. Joey knew a boy who'd gone up so high you couldn't see him anymore, like a balloon that grows smaller and smaller and vanishes—as if suddenly—into blue regions beyond the reach of sight. There were towns up there, so they said; I didn't know; white cloud-towns, with towers. Up there, in the blue beyond the blue, there were rivers you could go under the way you could walk under a bridge; birds with rainbow-colored tails; ice mountains and cities of snow; flattened shining masses of light like whirling disks; blue gardens; slow-moving creatures with leathery wings; towns inhabited by the dead. My father had taught me not to believe stories about Martians and spaceships, and these tales were like those stories: even as you refused to believe them, you saw them, as if the sheer effort of not believing them made them glow in your mind. Beside such stories, my forbidden night journey over the rooftops seemed tame as a stroll. I could feel dark desires ripening within me; stubbornly I returned to my old games, as carpets moved in backyards, forming bars of red and green across white shingles.

There came a day when my mother let me stay home while she went shopping at the market at the top of the hill. I wanted to call out after her: Stop! Make me go with you! I saw her walking across the lawn toward the open garage. My father had taken the bus to work. In my room I raised the blinds and looked out at the brilliant blue sky. For a long time I looked at the sky before unlocking the window, pushing up the glass and screen.

I set forth high over the backyard and rose smoothly into the blue. I kept my eyes ahead and up, though now and then I let my gaze fall over the carpet's edge. Down below I saw little red and black roofs, the shadows of houses thrown all on one side, a sunny strip of road fringed with sharp-bent tree-shadows, as if they had been blown sideways by a wind—and here and there, on neat squares of lawn, little carpets flying above their moving shadows. The sky was blue, pure blue. When I next glanced down I saw white puffballs hanging motionless over factory smokestacks, oil tanks like white coins by a glittering brown river. Up above, in all that blue, I saw only a small white cloud, with a little rip at the bottom, as if someone had started to tear it in half. The empty sky was so blue, so richly and thickly blue, that it seemed a thing I ought to be able to feel, like lake water or snow. I had read a story once about a boy who walked into a lake and came to a town on the bottom, and now it seemed to me that I was plunging deep into a lake, even though I was climbing. Below me I saw a misty patch of cloud, rectangles of dark green and butterscotch and brown. The blue stretched above like fields of snow, like fire. I imagined myself standing in my yard, looking up at my carpet growing smaller and smaller until it vanished into blue. I felt myself vanishing into blue. He was vanishing into blue. Below my carpet I saw only blue. In this blue beyond blue, all nothing everywhere, was I still I? I had passed out of sight, the string holding me to earth had snapped, and in these realms of blue I saw no rivers and white towns, no fabulous birds, but only shimmering distances of skyblue heavenblue blue. In that blaze of blue I tried to remember whether the boy in the lake had ever come back; and looking down at that ungraspable blue, which plunged away on both sides, I longed for the hardness under green grass, tree bark scraping my back, sidewalks, dark stones. Maybe it was the fear of never coming back, maybe it was the blue passing into me and soaking me through and through, but a dizziness came over me, I closed my eyes—and it seemed to me that I was falling through the sky, that my carpet had blown away, that the rush of my falling had knocked the wind out of me, that I had died, was about to die, as in a dream when I felt myself falling toward the sharp rocks, that I was running, tumbling, crawling, pursued by blue; and opening my eyes I saw that I had come down within sight of housetops, my hands clutching the edges of my carpet like claws. I swooped lower and soon recognized the rooftops of my neighborhood. There was Joey's yard, there was my garden, there was my chicken coop, my swing; and landing in the yard I felt the weight of the earth streaming up through me like a burst of joy.

At dinner I could scarcely keep my eyes open. By bedtime I had a temperature. There were no fits of coughing, no itchy eyes, or raw red lines under runny nostrils—only a steady burning, a heavy weariness, lasting three days. In my bed, under the covers, behind closed blinds, I lay reading a book that kept falling forward onto my chest. On the fourth day I woke feeling alert and cool-skinned. My mother, who for three days had been lowering her hand gently to my forehead and staring at me with grave, searching eyes, now walked briskly about the room, opening blinds with a sharp thin sound, drawing them up with a clatter. In the morning I was allowed to play quietly in the yard. In the afternoon I stood behind my mother on an escalator leading up to boys' pants. School was less than two weeks away; I had outgrown everything; Grandma was coming up for a visit; Joey's uncle had brought real horseshoes with him; there was no time, no time for anything at all; and as I walked to school along hot sidewalks shaded by maples, along the sandy roadside past Ciccarelli's lot, up Franklin Street and along Collins Street, I saw, in the warm and summery September air, like a gigantic birthmark, a brilliant patch of red leaves among the green.

One rainy day when I was in my room looking for a slipper, I found my rolled-up carpet under the bed. Fluffs of dust stuck to it like bees. Irritably I lugged it down into the cellar and laid it on top of an old trunk under the stairs. On a snowy afternoon in January I chased a ping-pong ball into the light-striped darkness under the cellar stairs. Long spiderwebs like delicate rigging had grown in the dark space, stretching from the rims of barrels to the undersides of the steps. My old carpet lay on the crumbly floor between the trunk and a wooden barrel. "I've got it!" I cried, seizing the white ball with its sticky little clump of spiderweb, rubbing it clean with my thumb, bending low as I ducked back into the yellow light of the cellar. The sheen on the dark green table made it look silky. Through a high window I could see the snow slanting down, falling steadily, piling up against the glass.

Clair de Lune

The summer I turned fifteen, I could no longer fall asleep. I would lie motionless on my back, in a perfect imitation of sleep, and imagine myself lying fast asleep with my head turned to one side and a tendon pushed up along the skin of my neck, but even as I watched myself lying there dead to the world I could hear the faint burr of my electric clock, a sharp creak in the attic—like a single footstep—a low rumbling hum that I knew was the sound of trucks rolling along the distant thruway. I could feel the collar of my pajama top touching my jaw. Through my trembling eyelids I sensed that the darkness of the night was not dark enough, and suddenly opening my eyes, as if to catch someone in my room, I'd see the moonlight streaming past the edges of the closed venetian blinds.

I could make out the lampshade and bent neck of the standing lamp, like a great drooping black sunflower. On the floor by a bookcase the white king and part of a black bishop glowed on the moon-striped chessboard. My room was filling up with moonlight. The darkness I longed for, the darkness that had once sheltered me, had been pushed into corners, where it lay in thick, furry lumps. I felt a heaviness in my chest, an oppression—I wanted to hide in the dark. Desperately I closed my eyes, imagining the blackness of a winter night: snow covered the silent streets, on the front porch the ice chopper stood leaning next to the black mailbox glinting with icicles, lines of snow lay along the crosspieces of telephone poles and the tops of metal street signs: and always through my eyelids I could feel the summer moonlight pushing back the dark.

One night I sat up in bed harshly and threw the covers off. My eyes burned from sleeplessness. I could no longer stand this nightly violation of the dark. I dressed quietly, tensely, since my parents' room stood on the other side of my two bookcases, then made my way along the hall and out into the living room. A stripe of moonlight lay across a couch cushion. On the music rack I could see a pattern of black notes on the moon-streaked pages of Debussy's "Second Arabesque," which my mother had left off practicing that evening. In a deep ashtray shaped like a shell, the bowl of my father's pipe gleamed like a piece of obsidian.

At the front door I hesitated a moment, then stepped out into the warm summer night.

The sky surprised me. It was deep blue, the blue of a sorcerer's hat, of night skies in old Technicolor movies, of deep mountain lakes in Swiss countrysides pictured on old puzzle boxes. I remembered my father removing from a leather pouch in his camera bag a circle of silver and handing it to me, and when I held it up I saw through the dark blue glass a dark blue world the color of this night. Suddenly I stepped out of the shadow of the house into the whiteness of the moon. The moon was so bright I could not look at it, as if it were a night sun. The fierce whiteness seemed hot, but for some reason I thought of the glittering thick frost on the inside of the ice-cream freezer in a barely remembered store: the Popsicles and ice-cream cups crusted in ice crystals, the cold air like steam.

I could smell low tide in the air and thought of heading for the beach, but I found myself walking the other way. For already I knew where I was going, knew and did not know where I was going, in the sorcerer-blue night where all things were changed, and as I passed the neighboring ranch houses I took in the chimney-shadows black and sharp across the roofs, the television antennas standing clean and hard against the blue night sky.

Soon the ranch houses gave way to small two-story houses, the smell of the tide was gone. The shadows of telephone wires showed clearly on the moon-washed streets. The wire-shadows looked like curved musical staves. On a brilliant white garage door the slanting, intricate shadow of a basketball net reminded me of the rigging on the wooden ship model I had built with my father, one childhood summer. I could not understand why no one was out on a night like this. Was I the only one who'd been drawn out of hiding and heaviness by the summer moon? In an open, empty garage I saw cans of moonlit paint on a shelf, an aluminum ladder hanging on hooks, folded lawn chairs. Under the big-leafed maples moonlight rippled across my hands.

Oh, I knew where I was going, didn't want to know where I was going, in the warm blue air with little flutters of coolness in it, little bursts of grass-smell and leaf-smell, of lilac and fresh tar.

At the center of town I cut through the back of the parking lot behind the bank, crossed Main Street, and continued on my way.

When the thruway underpass came into view, I saw the top halves of trucks rolling high up against the dark blue sky, and below them, framed by concrete walls and the slab of upper road, a darker and greener world: a beckoning world of winding roads and shuttered houses, a green blackness glimmering with yellow spots of streetlamps, white spots of moonlight.

As I passed under the high, trembling roadbed on my way to the older part of town, the dark walls, spattered with chalked letters, made me think of hulking creatures risen from the underworld, bearing on their shoulders the lanes of a celestial bowling alley.

On the other side of the underpass I glanced up at the nearly full moon. It was a little blurred on one side, but so hard and sharp on the other that it looked as if I could cut my finger on it.

When I next looked up, the moon was partly blocked by black-green oak leaves. I was walking under high trees beside neck-high hedges. A mailbox on a post looked like a loaf of bread. Shafts of moonlight slanted down like boards.

I turned onto a darker street, and after a while I stopped in front of a large house set back from the road.

And my idea, bred by the bold moon and the blue summer night, was suddenly clear to me: I would make my way around the house into the backyard, like a criminal. Maybe there would be a rope swing. Maybe she'd see me from an upper window. I had never visited her before, never walked home with her. What I felt was too hidden for that, too lost in dark, twisting tunnels. We were school friends, but our friendship had never stretched beyond the edges of school. Maybe I could leave some sign for her, something to show her that I'd come through the summer night, into her backyard.

I passed under one of the big tulip trees in the front yard and began walking along the side of the house. In a black windowpane I saw my sudden face. Somewhere I seemed to hear voices, and when I stepped around the back of the house into the full radiance of the moon, I saw four girls playing ball.

They were playing Wiffle ball in the brilliant moonlight, as though it were a summer's day. Sonja was batting. I knew the three other girls, all of them in my classes: Marcia, pitching; Jeanie, taking a lead off first; Bernice, in the outfield, a few steps away from me. In the moonlight they were wearing clothes I'd never seen before, dungarees and shorts and sweatshirts and boys' shirts, as if they were dressed up in a play about boys. Bernice had on a baseball cap and wore a jacket tied around her waist. In school they wore knee-length skirts and neatly ironed blouses, light summer dresses with leather belts. The girl-boys excited and disturbed me, as if I'd stumbled into some secret rite. Sonja, seeing me, burst out laughing. "Well look who's here," she said, in the slightly mocking tone that kept me wary and always joking. "Who is that tall stranger?" She stood holding the yellow Wiffle-ball bat on her shoulder, refusing to be surprised. "Come on, don't just stand there, you can catch." She was wearing dungarees rolled halfway up her calves, a floppy sweatshirt with the sleeves pushed up above the elbows, low white sneakers without socks. Her hair startled me: it was pulled back to show her ears. I remembered the hair falling brown-blond along one side of her face.

They all turned to me now, smiled and waved me toward them, and with a sharp little laugh I sauntered in, pushing back my hair with my fingers, thrusting my hands deep into my dungaree pockets.

Then I was standing behind home plate, catching, calling balls and strikes. The girls took their game seriously, Sonja and Jeanie against Marcia and Bernice. Marcia had a sharp-breaking curveball that kept catching the corner of the upside-down pie tin. "Strike?" yelled Sonja. "My foot. It missed by a mile. Kill the umpire!" The flattened-back tops of her ears irritated me. Jeanie stood glaring at me, fists on hips. She wore an oversized boy's shirt longer than her shorts, so that she looked naked, as if she'd thrown a shirt over a pair of underpants—her tan legs gleamed in the moonlight, her blond ponytail bounced furiously with her slightest motion, and in the folds of her loose shirt her jumpy breasts, appearing and disappearing, made me think of balls of yarn. The girls swung hard, slid into paper-plate bases, threw like boys. They shouted "Hey hey!" and "Way to go!" After a while they let me play, each taking a turn at being umpire. As we played, it seemed to me that the girls were becoming unraveled: Marcia's lumberjack shirt was only partly tucked into her faded dungarees, wriggles of hair fell down along Jeanie's damp cheeks, Bernice, her braces glinting, flung off the jacket tied around her waist, one of Sonja's cuffs kept falling down. Marcia scooped up a grounder, whirled, and threw to me at second, Sonja was racing from first, suddenly she slid—and sitting there on the grass below me, leaning back on her elbows, her legs stretched out on both sides of my feet, a copper rivet gleaming on the pocket of her dungarees, a bit of zipper showing, a hank of hair hanging over one eyebrow, she glared up at me, cried "Safe by a mile!" and broke into wild laughter. Then Jeanie began to laugh, Marcia and Bernice burst out laughing, I felt something give way in my chest and I erupted in loud, releasing laughter, the laughter of childhood, until my ribs hurt and tears burned in my eyes—and again whoops and bursts of laughter, under the blue sky of the summer night.

Sonja stood up, pushed a fallen sleeve of her sweatshirt above her elbow, and said, "How about a Coke? I've about had it." She wiped her tan forearm across her damp forehead. We all followed her up the back steps into the moonlit kitchen. "Keep it down, guys," she whispered, raising her eyes to the ceiling, as she filled glasses with ice cubes, poured hissing, clinking sodas. The other girls went back outside with their glasses, where I could hear them talking through the open kitchen window. Sonja pushed herself up onto the counter next to the dish rack and I stood across from her, leaning back against the refrigerator.

I wanted to ask her whether they always played ball at night, or whether it was something that had happened only on this night, this dream-blue night, night of adventures and revelations—night of the impossible visit she hadn't asked me about. I wanted to hear her say that the blue night was the color of old puzzle boxes, that the world was a blue mystery, that lying awake in bed she'd imagined me coming through the night to her backyard, but she only sat on the counter, swinging her legs, drinking her soda, saying nothing.

A broken bar of moonlight lay across the dish rack, fell sharply along a door below the counter, bent halfway along the linoleum before stopping in shadow.

She sat across from me with her hands on the silver strip at the edge of the counter, swinging her legs in and out of moonlight. Her knees were pressed together, but her calves were parted, and one foot was half-turned toward the other. I could see her anklebones. Her dungarees were rolled into thick cuffs halfway up the calf, one slightly higher than the other. As her calves swung back against the counter, they became wider for a moment, before they swung out. The gentle swinging, the widening and narrowing calves, the rolled-up cuffs, the rubbery ribs of the dish rack, the glimmer of window above the mesh of the screen, all this seemed to me as mysterious as the summer moonlight, which had driven me through the night to this kitchen, where it glittered on knives and forks sticking out of the silverware box at the end of the dish rack and on her calves, swinging back and forth.

Now and then Sonja picked up her glass and, leaning back her head, took a rattling drink of soda. I could see the column of her throat moving as she swallowed, and it seemed to me that although she was only sitting there, she was moving all over: her legs swung back and forth, her throat moved, her hands moved from the counter to the glass and back, and something seemed to come quivering up out of her, as if she'd swallowed a piece of burning-cool moonlight and were releasing it through her legs and fingertips.

Through the window screen I could see the moonlit grass of the backyard, the yellow plastic bat on the grass, a corner of shingled garage and a piece of purplish-blue night, and I could hear Marcia talking quietly, the faint rumble of trucks rolling through the sky, a sharp, clicking insect.

I felt bound in the dark blue spell of the kitchen, of the calves swinging back and forth, the glittering silverware, moonlight on linoleum, silence that seemed to be filling up with something like a stretching skin, somewhere a quivering, and I standing still, in the spell of it all, watchful. Her hands gripped the edge of the counter. Her calves moved back and forth under pressed-together knees. She was leaning forward at the waist, her eyes shone like black moonlight, there was a tension in her arms that I could feel in my own arms, a tension that rippled up into her throat, and suddenly she burst out laughing.

"What are you laughing at?" I said, startled, disappointed.

"Oh, nothing," she said, slipping down from the counter. "Everything. You, for example." She walked over to the screen door. "Let's call it a night, gang," she said, opening the door. The three girls were sitting on the steps.

Marcia, taking a deep breath, slowly stretched out her arms and arched her back; and as her lumberjack shirt flattened against her, she seemed to be lifting her breasts toward the blue night sky, the summer moon.

Then there were quick good nights and all three were walking across the lawn, turning out of sight behind the garage.

"This way, my good man," Sonja said. Frowning, and putting a finger over her lips, she led me from the kitchen through the shadowy living room, where I caught bronze and glass gleams—the edge of the fire shovel, a lamp base, the black glass of the television screen. At the front door flanked by thin strips of glass she turned the knob and opened the wooden door, held open the screen door. Behind her a flight of carpeted stairs rose into darkness. "Fair Knight," she said, with a little mock curtsey, "farewell," and pushed me out the door. I saw her arm rise and felt her fingers touch my face. With a laugh she shut the door.

It had happened so quickly that I wasn't sure what it was that had happened. Somewhere between "farewell" and laughter a different thing had happened, an event from a higher, more hidden realm, something connected with the dark blue kitchen, the glittering silverware and swinging legs, the mystery of the blue summer night. It was as if, under the drifting-down light of the moon, under the white-blue light that kept soaking into things, dissolving the day-world, a new shape had been released.

I stood for a while in front of the darkened front door, as if waiting for it to turn into something else—a forest path, a fluttering curtain. Then I walked away from the house along red-black slabs of slate, looked back once over my shoulder at the dark windows, and turned onto the sidewalk under high oaks and elms.

I felt a new lightness in my chest, as if an impediment to breathing had been removed. It was a night of revelations, but I now saw that each particle of the night was equal to the others. The moonlit path of black notes on the page of the music book, the yellow bat lying on just those blades of grass, the precise tilt of each knife in the dish rack, Sonja's calves swinging in and out of moonlight, Marcia's slowly arching back, the hand rising toward my face, all this was as unique and unrepeatable as the history of an ancient kingdom. For I had wanted to take a little walk before going to bed, but I had stepped from my room into the first summer night, the only summer night.

Under the high trees the moonlight fell steadily. I could see it sifting down through the leaves. All night long it had fallen into backyards, on chimneys and stop signs, on the crosspieces of telephone poles and on sidewalks buckled by tree roots. Down through the leaves it was slowly sifting, sticking to the warm air, forming clumps in the leaf-shadows. I could feel the moonlight lying on my hands. A weariness came over me, a weariness trembling with exhilaration. I had the sensation that I was expanding, growing lighter. Under the branches the air was becoming denser with moonlight, I could scarcely push my way through. My feet seemed to be pressing down on thick, spongy air. I felt an odd buoyancy, and when I looked down I saw that I was walking a little above the sidewalk. I raised my foot and stepped higher. Then I began to climb the thick tangle of moonlight and shadow, slipping now and then, sinking a little, pulling myself up with the aid of branches, and soon I came out over the top of a tree into the clearness of the moon. Dark fields of blue air stretched away in every direction. I looked down at the moonlit leaves below, at the top of a streetlamp, at shafts of moonlight slanting like white ladders under the leaves. I walked carefully forward above the trees, taking light steps that sank deep, then climbed a little higher, till catching a breeze I felt myself borne away into the blue countries of the night.

from

Dangerous Laughter

Cat 'n' Mouse

The cat is chasing the mouse through the kitchen: between the blue chair legs, over the tabletop with its red-and-white-checkered tablecloth that is already sliding in great waves, past the sugar bowl falling to the left and the cream jug falling to the right, over the blue chair back, down the chair legs, across the waxed and butter-yellow floor. The cat and the mouse lean backward and try to stop on the slippery wax, which shows their flawless reflections. Sparks shoot from their heels, but it's much too late: the big door looms. The mouse crashes through, leaving a mouse-shaped hole. The cat crashes through, replacing the mouse-shaped hole with a larger, cat-shaped hole. In the living room they race over the back of the couch, across the piano keys (delicate mouse tune, crash of cat chords), along the blue rug. The fleeing mouse snatches a glance over his shoulder, and when he looks forward again he sees the floor lamp coming closer and closer. Impossible to stop—at the last moment he splits in half and rejoins himself on the other side. Behind him the rushing cat fails to split in half and crashes into the lamp: his head and body push the brass pole into the shape of a trombone. For a moment the cat hangs sideways there, his stiff legs shaking like the clapper of a bell. Then he pulls free and rushes after the mouse, who turns and darts into a mousehole in the baseboard. The cat crashes into the wall and folds up like an accordion. Slowly he unfolds, emitting accordion music. He lies on the floor with his chin on his upraised paw, one eyebrow lifted high in disgust, the claws of his other forepaw tapping the floorboards. A small piece of plaster drops on his head. He raises an outraged eye. A framed painting falls heavily on his head, which plunges out of sight between his shoulders. The painting shows a green tree with bright red apples. The cat's head struggles to rise, then pops up with the sound of a yanked cork, lifting the picture. Apples fall from the tree and land with a thump on the grass. The cat shudders, winces. A final apple falls. Slowly it rolls toward the frame, drops over the edge, and lands on the cat's head. In the cat's eyes, cash registers ring up NO SALE.

The mouse, dressed in a bathrobe and slippers, is sitting in his plump armchair, reading a book. He is tall and slim. His feet rest on a hassock, and a pair of spectacles rest on the end of his long, whiskered nose. Yellow light from a table lamp pours onto the book and dimly illuminates the cozy brown room. On the wall hang a tilted sampler bearing the words HOME SWEET HOME, an oval photograph of the mouse's mother with her gray hair in a bun, and a reproduction of Seurat's *Sunday Afternoon* in which all the figures are mice. Near the armchair is a bookcase filled with books, with several titles visible: *Martin Cheddarwit,* Gouda's *Faust, The Memoirs of Anthony Edam, A History of the Medicheese, The Sonnets of Shakespaw.* As the mouse reads his book, he reaches without looking toward a dish on the table. The dish is empty: his fingers tap about inside it. The mouse rises and goes over to the cupboard, which is empty except for a tin box with the word CHEESE on it. He opens the box and turns it upside down. Into his palm drops a single toothpick. He gives it a melancholy look. Shaking his head, he returns to his chair and takes up his book. In a bubble above his head a picture appears: he is seated at a long table covered with a white tablecloth. He is holding a fork upright in one fist and a knife upright in the other. A mouse butler dressed in tails sets before him a piece of cheese the size of a wedding cake.

From the mousehole emerges a red telescope. The lens looks to the left, then to the right. A hand issues from the end of the telescope and beckons the mouse forward. The mouse steps from the mousehole, collapses the telescope, and thrusts it into his bathrobe pocket. In the moonlit room he tiptoes carefully, lifting his legs very high, over to the base of the armchair. He dives under the chair and peeks out through the fringe. He emerges from beneath the armchair, slinks over to the couch, and dives under. He peeks out through the fringe. He emerges from beneath the couch and approaches the slightly open kitchen door. He stands flat against the doorjamb, facing the living room, his eyes darting left and right. One leg tiptoes delicately around the jamb. His stretched body snaps after it like a rubber band. In the kitchen he creeps to a moonlit chair, stands pressed against a chair leg, begins to climb. His nose rises over the tabletop: he sees a cream pitcher, a gleaming knife, a looming pepper mill. On a breadboard sits a wedge of cheese. The mouse, hunching his shoulders, tiptoes up to the cheese. From a pocket of his robe he removes a white handkerchief that he ties around his neck. He bends over the cheese, half closing his eyes, as if he were sniffing a flower. With a crashing sound the cat springs onto the table. As he chases the mouse, the tablecloth bunches in waves, the sugar bowl topples, and waterfalls of sugar spill to the floor. An olive from a fallen cocktail glass rolls across the table, knocking into a cup, a saltshaker, a trivet: the objects light up and cause bells to ring, as in a pinball machine. On the floor a brigade of ants is gathering the sugar: one ant catches the falling grains in a bucket, which he dumps into the bucket of a second ant, who dumps the sugar into the bucket of a third ant, all the way across the room, until the last ant dumps it into a waiting truck. The cat chases the mouse over the blue chair back, down the chair legs, across the waxed floor. Both lean backward and try to stop as the big door comes closer and closer.

The mouse is sitting in his armchair with his chin in his hand, looking off into the distance with a melancholy expression. He is thoughtful by temperament, and he is distressed at the necessity of interrupting his meditations for the daily search for food. The search is wearying and absurd in itself, but is made unbearable by the presence of the brutish cat. The mouse's disdain for the cat is precise and abundant: he loathes the soft, heavy paws with their hidden hooks, the glinting teeth, the hot, fish-stinking breath. At the same time, he confesses to himself a secret admiration for the cat's coarse energy and simplicity. It appears that the cat has no other aim in life than to catch the mouse. Although the faculty of astonishment is not highly developed in the mouse, he is constantly astonished by the cat's unremitting enmity. This makes the cat dangerous, despite his stupidity, for the mouse recognizes that he himself has long periods when the cat fades entirely from his mind. Moreover, despite the fundamental simplicity of the cat's nature, it remains true that the cat is cunning: he plots tirelessly against the mouse, and his ludicrous wiles require in the mouse an alert attention that he would prefer not to give. The mouse is aware of the temptation of indifference; he must continually exert himself to be wary. He feels that he is exhausting his nerves and harming his spirit by attending to the cat; at the same time, he realizes that his attention is at best imperfect, and that the cat is thinking uninterruptedly, with boundless energy, of him. If only the mouse could stay in his hole, he would be happy, but he cannot stay in his hole, because of the need to find cheese. It is not a situation calculated to produce the peace of mind conducive to contemplation.

The cat is standing in front of the mousehole with a hammer in one hand and a saw in the other. Beside him rests a pile of yellow boards and a big bag of nails. He begins furiously hammering and sawing, moving across the room in a cloud of dust that conceals him. Suddenly the dust clears and the cat beholds his work: a long, twisting pathway that begins at the mousehole and passes under the couch, over the back of the armchair, across the piano, through the kitchen door, and onto the kitchen table. On the tablecloth, at the end of the pathway, is a large mousetrap on which sits a lump of cheese. The cat tiptoes over to the refrigerator, vanishes behind it, and slyly thrusts out his head: his eyes dart left and right. There is the sound of a bicycle bell: *ring ring.* A moment later the mouse appears, pedaling fiercely. He speeds from the end of the pathway onto the table. As he screeches to a stop, the round wheels stretch out of shape and then become round again. The mouse is wearing riding goggles, a riding cap, and gloves. He leans his bicycle against the sugar bowl, steps over to the mousetrap, and looks at it with interest. He steps onto the mousetrap, sits down on the brass bar, and puts on a white bib. From a pocket of his leather jacket he removes a knife and fork. He eats the cheese swiftly. After his meal, he replaces the knife and fork in his pocket and begins to play on the mousetrap. He swings on a high bar, hangs upside down by his legs, walks the parallel bars, performs gymnastic stunts. Then he climbs onto his bicycle and disappears along the pathway, ringing his bell. The cat emerges from behind the refrigerator and springs onto the table beside the mousetrap. He frowns down at the trap. From the top of his head he plucks a single hair: it comes loose with the sound of a snapping violin string. Slowly he lowers the hair toward the mousetrap. The hair touches the spring. The mousetrap remains motionless. He presses the spring with a spoon. The mousetrap remains motionless. He bangs the spring with a sledgehammer. The mousetrap remains motionless. He looks at the trap with rage. Cautiously he reaches out a single toe. The mousetrap springs shut with the sound of a slammed iron door. The cat hops about the table holding his trapped foot as the toe swells to the size of a lightbulb, bright red.

The cat enters on the left, disguised as a mouse. He is wearing a blond wig, a nose mask, and a tight black dress slit to the thigh. He has high and very round breasts, a tiny waist, and round, rolling hips. His lips are bright red, and his black lashes are so tightly curled that when he blinks his eyes the lashes roll out and snap back like window shades. He walks slowly and seductively, resting one hand on a hip and one hand on his blond hair. The mouse is standing in the mousehole, leaning against one side with his hands in his pockets. His eyes protrude from their sockets in the shape of telescopes. In the lens of each telescope is a thumping heart. Slowly, as if mesmerized, the mouse sleepwalks into the room. The cat places a needle on a record, and rumba music begins to play. The cat dances with his hands clasped behind his neck, thrusting out each hip, fluttering his long lashes, turning to face the other way: in the tight black dress, his twitching backside is shaped like the ace of spades. The mouse faces the cat and begins to dance. They stride back and forth across the room, wriggling and kicking in step. As they dance, the cat's wig comes loose, revealing one cat ear. The cat dances over to a bearskin rug and lies down on his side. He closes his long-lashed eyes and purses his red, red lips. The mouse steps up to the cat. He reaches into his pocket, removes a cigar, and places it between the big red lips. The cat's eyes open. They look down at the cigar, look up, and look down again. The cat removes the cigar and stares at it. The cigar explodes. When the smoke clears, the cat's face is black. He gives a strained, very white smile. Many small lines appear in his teeth. The teeth crack into little pieces and fall out.

The cat is lying on his back in his basket in the kitchen. His hands are clasped behind his head, his left knee is raised, and his right ankle rests sideways on the raised knee. He is filled with rage at the thought of the mouse, who he knows despises him. He would like to tear the mouse to pieces, to roast him over a fire, to plunge him into a pan of burning butter. He understands that his rage is not the rage of hunger and he wonders whether the mouse himself is responsible for evoking this savagery, which burns in his chest like indigestion. He despises the mouse's physical delicacy, his weak arms thin as the teeth of combs, his frail, crushable skull, his fondness for books and solitude. At the same time, he is irritably aware that he admires the mouse's elegance, his air of culture and languor, his easy self-assurance. Why is he always reading? In a sense, the mouse intimidates the cat: in his presence, the cat feels clumsy and foolish. He thinks obsessively about the mouse and suspects with rage that the mouse frequently does not think about him at all, there in his brown room. If the mouse were less indifferent, would he burn with such hatred? Might they learn to live peacefully together in the same house? Would he be released from this pain of outrage in his heart?

The mouse is standing at his workbench, curling the eyelashes of a mechanical cat. Her long black hair is shiny as licorice; her lips look like licked candy. She is wearing a tight red dress, black fishnet stockings, and red high heels. The mouse stands the mechanical cat on her feet, unzips the back of her dress, and winds a big key. He zips up the dress and aims her toward the mousehole. In the living room, the mechanical cat struts slowly back and forth; her pointy breasts stick out like party hats. The cat's head rises over the back of the armchair. In his eyes appear hearts pierced by arrows. He slithers over the chair and slides along the floor like honey. When he reaches the strutting cat, he glides to an upright position and stands mooning at her. His heart is thumping so hard that it pushes out the skin of his chest with each beat. The cat reaches into a pocket and removes a straw boater, which he places on his head at a rakish angle. He fastens at his throat a large polka-dot bow tie. He becomes aware of a ticking sound. He removes from his pocket a round yellow watch, places it against his ear, frowns, and returns it to his pocket. He bends close to the face of the cat and sees in each of her eyes a shiny round black bomb with a burning fuse. The cat turns to the audience and then back to the dangerous eyes. The mechanical cat blows up. When the smoke clears, the cat's fur hangs from him in tatters, revealing his pink flesh and a pair of polka-dot boxer shorts.

Outside the mousehole, the cat is winding up a mouse that exactly resembles the real mouse. The mechanical mouse is wearing a bathrobe and slippers, stands with hands in pockets, and has a pair of eyeglasses perched at the end of its nose. The cat lifts open the top of the mouse's head, which is attached in the manner of a hinged lid. He inserts a sizzling red stick of dynamite and closes the lid. He sets the mouse in front of the hole and watches as it vanishes through the arched opening. Inside, the mouse is sitting in his chair, reading a book. He does not raise his eyes to the visitor, who glides over with its hands in its pockets. Still reading, the mouse reaches out and lifts open the head of his double. He removes the sizzling dynamite, thrusts it into a cake, and inserts the cake into the mouse's head. He turns the mechanical mouse around and continues reading as it walks out through the arch. The cat is squatting beside the hole with his eyes shut and his fingers pressed in his ears. He opens his eyes and sees the mouse. His eyebrows rise. He snatches up the mouse, opens its head, and lifts out a thickly frosted cake that says HAPPY BIRTHDAY. In the center of the cake is a sizzling red stick of dynamite. The cat's fur leaps up. He takes a tremendous breath and blows out the fuse with such force that for a moment the cake is slanted. Now the cat grins, licks his teeth, and opens his jaws. He hears a sound. The cake is ticking loudly: *tock tock, tock tock.* Puzzled, the cat holds it up to one ear. He listens closely. A terrible knowledge dawns in his eyes.

The cat rides into the living room in a bright yellow crane. From the boom hangs a shiny black wrecking ball. He drives up to the mousehole and stops. He pushes and pulls a pair of levers, which cause the wrecking ball to be inserted into a gigantic rubber band attached to a gigantic slingshot. The rubber band stretches back and back. Suddenly it releases the shiny black ball, which smashes into the wall. The entire house collapses, leaving only a tall red chimney standing amid the ruins. On top of the chimney is a stork's nest, in which a stork sits with a fishing pole. He is wearing a blue baseball cap. Below, in the rubble, a stirring is visible. The cat rises unsteadily, leaning on a crutch. His head is covered with a white bandage that conceals an eye; one leg is in a cast and one arm in a sling. With the tip of his crutch, he moves away a pile of rubble and exposes a fragment of baseboard. In the baseboard we see the unharmed mousehole. Inside the mousehole, the mouse sits in his chair, reading a book.

The mouse understands that the clownishly inept cat has the freedom to fail over and over again, during the long course of an inglorious lifetime, while he himself is denied the liberty of a single mistake. It is highly unlikely, of course, that he will ever be guilty of an error, since he is much cleverer than the cat and immediately sees through every one of his risible stratagems. Still, might not the very knowledge of his superiority lead to a relaxation of vigilance that will prove fatal, in the end? After all, he is not invulnerable; he is invulnerable only insofar as he is vigilant. The mouse is bored, deeply bored, by the ease with which he outwits the cat; there are times when he longs for a more worthy enemy, someone more like himself. He understands that his boredom is a dangerous weakness against which he must perpetually be on his guard. Sometimes he thinks, If only I could stop watching over myself, if only I could let myself go! The thought alarms him and causes him to look over his shoulder at the mousehole, across which the shadow of the cat has already fallen.

The cat enters from the left, carrying a sack over one shoulder. He sets the sack down beside the mousehole. He unties a rope from the neck of the sack, plunges both hands in, and carefully lifts out a gray cloud. He places the cloud in the air above the mousehole. Rain begins to fall from the cloud, splashing down in great drops. The cat reaches into the sack and removes some old clothes. He swiftly disguises himself as a peddler and rings the mouse's bell. The mouse appears in the arched doorway, leaning against the side with his arms folded across his stomach and his ankles crossed as he stares out at the rain. The cat removes from the sack an array of mouse-size umbrellas, which he opens in turn: red, yellow, green, blue. The mouse shakes his head. The cat removes from the sack a yellow slicker, a pair of hip boots, a fishing rod and tackle box. The mouse shakes his head. The cat removes a red rubber sea horse, a compressed-air tank, a diving bell, a rowboat, a yacht. The mouse shakes his head, steps into his house, and slams the door. He opens the door, hangs a sign on the knob, and slams the door again. The sign reads NOT HOME. The rain falls harder. The cat steps out from under the cloud, which rises above his head and begins to follow him about the room. The storm grows worse: he is pelted with hailstones the size of golf balls. In the cloud appear many golfers, driving golf balls into the room. Forked lightning flashes; thunder roars. The cat rushes around the room trying to escape the cloud and dives under the couch. His tail sticks out. Lightning strikes the tail, which crackles like an electric wire. The couch rises for an instant, exposing the luminous, electrified cat rigid with shock; inside the cat's body, with its rim of spiked fur, his blue-white skeleton is visible. Now snow begins to fall from the cloud, and whistling winds begin to blow. Snow lies in drifts on the rug, rises swiftly up the sides of the armchair, sweeps up to the mantelpiece, where the clock looks down in terror and covers its eyes with its hands. The cat struggles slowly through the blizzard but is soon encased in snow. Icicles hang from his chin. He stands motionless, shaped like a cat struggling forward with bent head. The door of the mousehole opens and the mouse emerges, wearing earmuffs, scarf, and gloves. The sun is shining. He begins shoveling a path. When he comes to the snow-cat, he climbs to the top of his shovel and sticks a carrot in the center of the snowy face. Then he climbs down, steps back, and begins throwing snowballs. The cat's head falls off.

The cat is pacing angrily in the kitchen, his hands behind his back and his eyebrows drawn down in a V. In a bubble above his head a wish appears: he is operating a circular saw that moves slowly, with high whining sounds, along a yellow board. At the end of the board is the mouse, lying on his back, tied down with ropes. The image vanishes and is replaced by another: the cat, wearing an engineer's hat, is driving a great train along a track. The mouse is stretched across the middle of the track, his wrists fastened to one rail and his ankles to the other. Sweat bursts in big drops from the mouse's face as the image vanishes and is replaced by another: the cat is turning a winch that slowly lowers an anvil toward the mouse, who is tied to a little chair. The mouse looks up in terror. Suddenly the cat lets go of the crank and the anvil rushes down with a whistling sound as the winch spins wildly. At the last moment, the mouse tumbles away. The anvil falls through the bubble onto the cat's head.

The cat understands that the mouse will always outwit him, but this tormenting knowledge serves only to inflame his desire to catch the mouse. He will never give up. His life, in relation to the mouse, is one long failure, a monotonous succession of unspeakable humiliations; his unhappiness is relieved only by moments of delusional hope, during which he believes, despite doubts supported by a lifetime of bitter experience, that at last he will succeed. Although he knows that he will never catch the mouse, who will forever escape into his mousehole a half inch ahead of the reaching claw, he also knows that only if he catches the mouse will his wretched life be justified. He will be transformed. Is it therefore his own life that he seeks, when he lies awake plotting against the mouse? Is it, when all is said and done, himself that he is chasing? The cat frowns and scratches his nose.

The cat stands before the mousehole holding in one hand a piece of white chalk. On the blue wall he draws the outline of a large door. The mousehole is at the bottom of the door. He draws the circle of a doorknob and opens the door. He steps into a black room. At the end of the room stands the mouse with a piece of chalk. The mouse draws a white mousehole on the wall and steps through. The cat kneels down and peers into the mousehole. He stands up and draws another door. He opens the door and steps into another black room. At the end of the room stands the mouse, who draws another mousehole and steps through. The cat draws another door, the mouse draws another mousehole. Faster and faster they draw: door, hole, door, hole, door. At the end of the last room, the mouse draws on the wall a white stick of dynamite. He draws a white match, which he takes in his hand and strikes against the wall. He lights the dynamite and hands it to the cat. The cat looks at the white outline of the dynamite. He offers it to the mouse. The mouse shakes his head. The cat points to himself and raises his eyebrows. The mouse nods. The stick of dynamite explodes.

The cat enters on the left, wearing a yellow hard hat and pushing a red wheelbarrow. The wheelbarrow is piled high with boards. In front of the mousehole, the cat puts down the handles of the barrow, pulls a hammer and saw from the pile of boards, and thrusts a fistful of black nails between his teeth. He begins sawing and hammering rapidly, moving from one end of the room to the other as a cloud of dust conceals his work. Suddenly the dust clears and the cat beholds his creation: he has constructed a tall guillotine, connected to the mousehole by a stairway. The blue-black glistening blade hangs between posts high above the opening for the head. Directly below the opening, on the other side, stands a basket. On the rim of the basket the cat places a wedge of cheese. The cat loops a piece of string onto a lever in the side of the guillotine and fastens the other end of the string to the wedge of cheese. Then he tiptoes away with hunched shoulders and vanishes behind a fire shovel. A moment later, the mouse climbs the stairs onto the platform of the guillotine. He stands with his hands in the pockets of his robe and contemplates the blade, the opening for the head, and the piece of cheese. He removes from one pocket a yellow package with a red bow. He leans over the edge of the platform and slips the loop from the lever. He thrusts his head through the head hole, removes the piece of cheese from the rim of the basket, and sets the package in its place. He ties the string to the package, slides his head back through the hole, and fits the loop of the string back over the lever. From his pocket he removes a large pair of scissors, which he lays on the platform. He next removes a length of rope, which he fastens to the lever so that the rope hangs nearly to the floor. On the floor he stands cross-ankled against the wheel of the barrow, eating his cheese. A moment later, the cat leaps onto the platform. He looks up in surprise at the unfallen blade. He crouches down, peers through the head hole, and sees the yellow package. He frowns. He looks up at the blade. He looks at the yellow package. Gingerly he reaches a paw through the opening and snatches it back. He frowns at the string. A cunning look comes into his eyes. He notices the pair of scissors, picks them up, and cuts the string. He waits, but nothing happens. Eagerly he thrusts his head through the opening and reaches for the package. The mouse, eating his cheese with one hand, lazily tugs at the rope with the other. The blade rushes down with the sound of a roaring train; a forlorn whistle blows. The cat tries to pull his head out of the hole. The blade slices off the top half of his head, which drops into the basket and rolls noisily around like a coin. The cat pulls himself out of the hole and stumbles about until he falls over the edge of the platform into the basket. He seizes the top of his head and puts it on like a hat. It is backward. He straightens it with a half turn. In his hand he sees with surprise the yellow package with the red bow. Frowning, he unties it. Inside is a bright red stick of dynamite with a sizzling fuse. The cat looks at the dynamite and turns his head to the audience. He blinks once. The dynamite explodes. When the smoke clears, the cat's face is black. In each eye a ship cracks in half and slowly sinks in the water.

The mouse is sitting in his chair with his feet on the hassock and his open book facedown on his lap. A mood of melancholy has invaded him, as if the brown tones of his room had seeped into his brain. He feels stale and out of sorts: he moves within the narrow compass of his mind, utterly devoid of fresh ideas. Is he perhaps too much alone? He thinks of the cat and wonders whether there is some dim and distant possibility of a connection, perhaps a companionship. Is it possible that they might become friends? Perhaps he could teach the cat to appreciate the things of the mind, and learn from the cat to enjoy life's simpler pleasures. Perhaps the cat, too, feels an occasional sting of loneliness. Haven't they much in common, after all? Both are bachelors, indoor sorts, who enjoy the comforts of a cozy domesticity; both are secretive; both take pleasure in plots and schemes. The more the mouse pursues this line of thought, the more it seems to him that the cat is a large, soft mouse. He imagines the cat with mouse ears and gentle mouse paws, wearing a white bib, sitting across from him at the kitchen table, lifting to his mouth a fork at the end of which is a piece of cheese.

The cat enters from the right with a chalkboard eraser in one hand. He goes over to the mousehole, bends down, and erases it. He stands up and erases the wall, revealing the mouse's home. The mouse is sitting in his chair with his feet on the hassock and his open book facedown on his lap. The cat bends over and erases the book. The mouse looks up in irritation. The cat erases the mouse's chair. He erases the hassock. He erases the entire room. He tosses the eraser over his shoulder. Now there is nothing left in the world except the cat and the mouse. The cat snatches him up in a fist. The cat's red tongue slides over glistening teeth sharp as ice picks. Here and there, over a tooth, a bright star expands and contracts. The cat opens his jaws wider, closes his eyes, and hesitates. The death of the mouse is desirable in every way, but will life without him really be pleasurable? Will the mouse's absence satisfy him entirely? Is it conceivable that he may miss the mouse, from time to time? Is it possible that he needs the mouse, in some disturbing way?

As the cat hesitates, the mouse reaches into a pocket of his robe and removes a red handkerchief. With swift circular strokes he wipes out the cat's teeth while the cat's eyes watch in surprise. He wipes out the cat's eyes. He wipes out the cat's whiskers. He wipes out the cat's head. Still held in the cat's fist, he wipes out the entire cat, except for the paw holding him. Then, very carefully, he wipes out the paw. He drops lightly down and slaps his palms together. He looks about. He is alone with his red handkerchief in a blank white world. After a pause, he begins to wipe himself out, moving rapidly from head to toe. Now there is nothing left but the red handkerchief. The handkerchief flutters, grows larger, and suddenly splits in half. The halves become red theater curtains, which begin to close. Across the closing curtains, words write themselves in black script: THE END.

The Disappearance of Elaine Coleman

The news of the disappearance disturbed and excited us. For weeks afterward, the blurred and grainy photograph of a young woman no one seemed to know, though some of us vaguely remembered her, appeared on yellow posters displayed on the glass doors of the post office, on telephone poles, on windows of the CVS and the renovated supermarket. The small photo showed a serious face turned partly away, above a fur collar; the picture seemed to be an enlargement of a casual snapshot, perhaps originally showing a full-length view—the sort of picture, we imagined, taken carelessly by a bored relative to commemorate an occasion. For a time women were warned not to go out alone at night, while the investigation pursued its futile course. Gradually the posters became rain-wrinkled and streaked with grime, the blurred photos seemed to be fading away, and then one day they were gone, leaving behind a faint uneasiness that itself dissolved slowly in the smoke-scented autumn air.

According to the newspaper reports, the last person to see Elaine Coleman alive was a neighbor, Mrs. Mary Blessington, who greeted her on the final evening as Elaine stepped out of her car and began to walk along the path of red slates leading to the side entrance of the house on Willow Street where she rented two rooms on the second floor. Mary Blessington was raking leaves. She leaned on her rake, waved to Elaine Coleman, and remarked on the weather. She noticed nothing unusual about the quiet young woman walking at dusk toward the side door, carrying in one arm a small paper bag (probably containing the quart of milk found unopened in her refrigerator) and holding her keys in the other hand. When questioned further about Elaine Coleman's appearance as she walked toward the house, Mary Blessington admitted that it was almost dark and that she couldn't make her out "all that well." The landlady, Mrs. Waters, who lived on the first floor and rented upstairs rooms to two boarders, described Elaine Coleman as a quiet person, steady, very polite. She went to bed early, never had visitors, and paid her rent unfailingly on the first of the month. She liked to stay by herself, the landlady added. On the last evening Mrs. Waters heard Elaine's footsteps climbing the stairs as usual to her apartment on the second floor in back. The landlady did not actually see her, on that occasion. The next morning she noticed the car still parked in front, even though it was a Wednesday and Miss Coleman never missed a day of work. In the afternoon, when the mail came, Mrs. Waters decided to carry a letter upstairs to her boarder, who she assumed was sick. The door was locked. She knocked gently, then louder and louder, before opening the door with a duplicate key. She hesitated a long time before calling the police.

For days we spoke of nothing else. We read the newspapers ardently, the local *Messenger* and the papers from neighboring towns; we studied the posters, we memorized the facts, we interpreted the evidence, we imagined the worst.

The photograph, bad and blurry though it was, left its own sharp impression: a woman caught in the act of looking away, a woman evading scrutiny. Her blurred eyes were half closed, the turned-up collar of her jacket concealed the line of her jaw, and a crinkled strand of hair came straggling down over her cheek. She looked, though it was difficult to tell, as if she had hunched her shoulders against the cold. But what struck some of us about the photograph was what it seemed to conceal. It was as if beneath that grainy cheek, that blurred and narrow nose with the skin pulled tight across the bridge, lay some other, younger, more familiar image. Some of us recalled dimly an Elaine, an Elaine Coleman, in our high school, a young Elaine of fourteen or fifteen years ago who had been in our classes, though none of us could remember her clearly or say where she sat or what she did. I myself seemed to recall an Elaine Coleman in English class, sophomore or junior year, a quiet girl, someone I hadn't paid much attention to. In my old yearbook I found her, Elaine Coleman. I did not recognize her face. At the same time it didn't seem the face of a stranger. It appeared to be the missing woman on the poster, though in another key, so that you didn't make the connection immediately. The photograph was slightly overexposed, making her seem a little washed out, a little flat—there was a bright indistinctness about her. She was neither pretty nor unpretty. Her face was half turned away, her expression serious; her hair, done up in the style of the time, showed the shine of a careful combing. She had joined no clubs, played no sports, belonged to nothing.

The only other photograph of her was a group picture of our homeroom class. She stood in the third row from the front, her body turned awkwardly to one side, her eyes lowered, her features difficult to distinguish.

In the early days of her disappearance I kept trying to remember her, the dim girl in my English class who had grown up into a blurred and grainy stranger. I seemed to see her sitting at her maplewood desk beside the radiator, looking down at a book, her arms thin and pale, her brown hair falling partly behind her shoulder and partly before, a quiet girl in a long skirt and white socks, but I could never be certain I wasn't making her up. One night I dreamed her: a girl with black hair who looked at me gravely. I woke up oddly stirred and relieved, but as I opened my eyes I realized that the girl in my dream was Miriam Blumenthal, a witty and laughing girl with blazing black hair, who in dream-disguise had presented herself to me as the missing Elaine.

One detail that troubled us was that Elaine Coleman's keys were discovered on the kitchen table, beside an open newspaper and a saucer. The key ring with its six keys and its silver kitten, the brown leather pocketbook containing her wallet, the fleece-lined coat on the back of a chair, all this suggested a sudden and disturbing departure, but it was the keys that attracted our particular attention, for they included the key to her apartment. We learned that the door could be locked in two ways: from the inside, by turning a knob that slid a bolt, and from the outside, with a key. If the door was locked and the key inside, then Elaine Coleman cannot have left by the door—unless there was another key. It was possible, though no one believed it, that someone with a second key had entered and left through her door, or that Elaine herself, using a second key, had left by the door and locked it from the outside. But a thorough police investigation discovered no record of a duplicate. It seemed far more likely that she had left by one of the four windows. Two were in the kitchen–living room facing the back, and two in the bedroom facing the back and side. In the bathroom there was a small fifth window, no more than twelve inches in height and width, through which it would have been impossible to enter or exit. Directly below the four main windows grew a row of hydrangea and rhododendron bushes. All four windows were closed, though not locked, and the outer storm windows were in place. It seemed necessary to imagine that Elaine Coleman had deliberately escaped through a second-floor window, fifteen feet up in the air, when she might far more easily have left by the door, or that an intruder had entered through a window and carried her off, taking care to pull both panes back into place. But the bushes, grass, and leaves below the four windows showed no trace of disturbance, nor was there any evidence in the rooms to suggest a break-in.

The second boarder, Mrs. Helen Ziolkowski, a seventy-year-old widow who had lived in the front apartment for twenty years, described Elaine Coleman as a nice young woman, quiet, very pale, the sort who kept to herself. It was the first we had heard of her pallor, which lent her a certain allure. On the last evening Mrs. Ziolkowski heard the door close and the bolt turn in the lock. She heard the refrigerator door open and close, light footsteps moving about, a dish rattling, a teapot whistling. It was a quiet house and you could hear a lot. She had heard no unusual sounds, no screams, no voices, nothing at any time that might have suggested a struggle. In fact it had been absolutely quiet in Elaine Coleman's apartment from about seven o'clock on; she had been surprised not to hear the usual sounds of dinner being prepared in the kitchen. She herself had gone to bed at eleven o'clock. She was a light sleeper and was up often at night.

I wasn't the only one who kept trying to remember Elaine Coleman. Others who had gone to high school with me, and who now lived in our town with families of their own, remained puzzled or uncertain about who she was, though no one doubted she had actually been there. One of us thought he recalled her in biology, sophomore year, bent over a frog fastened to the black wax of a dissecting pan. Another recalled her in English class, senior year, not by the radiator but at the back of the room—a girl who didn't say much, a girl with uninteresting hair. But though he remembered her clearly, or said he did, there at the back of the room, he could not remember anything more about her, he couldn't summon up any details.

One night, about three weeks after the disappearance, I woke from a troubling dream that had nothing to do with Elaine Coleman—I was in a room without windows, there was a greenish light, some frightening force was gathering behind the closed door—and sat up in bed. The dream itself no longer upset me, but it seemed to me that I was on the verge of recalling something. In startling detail I remembered a party I had gone to, when I was fifteen or sixteen. I saw the basement playroom very clearly: the piano with sheet music open on the rack, the shine of the piano lamp on the white pages and on the stockings of a girl sitting in a nearby armchair, the striped couch, some guys in the corner playing a child's game with blocks, the cigarette smoke, the bowl of pretzel sticks—and there on a hassock near the window, leaning forward a little, wearing a white blouse and a long dark skirt, her hands in her lap, Elaine Coleman. Her face was sketchy—dark hair some shade of brown, grainy skin—and not entirely to be trusted, since it showed signs of having been infected by the photograph of the missing Elaine, but I had no doubt that I had remembered her.

I tried to bring her into sharper focus, but it was as if I hadn't looked at her directly. The more I tried to recapture that evening, the more sharply I was able to see details of the basement playroom (my hands on the chipped white piano keys, the green and red and yellow blocks forming a higher and higher tower, someone on the swim team moving his arms out from his chest as he demonstrated the butterfly, the dazzling knees of Lorraine Palermo in sheer stockings), but I could not summon Elaine Coleman's face.

According to the landlady, the bedroom showed no signs of disturbance. The pillow had been removed from under the bedclothes and placed against the headboard. On the nightstand a cup half filled with tea rested on a postcard announcing the opening of a new hardware store. The bedspread was slightly rumpled; on it lay a white flannel nightgown printed with tiny pale-blue flowers, and a fat paperback resting open against the spread. The lamp on the nightstand was still on.

We tried to imagine the landlady in the bedroom doorway, her first steps into the quiet room, the afternoon sunlight streaming in past the closed venetian blinds, the pale, hot bulb in the sun-streaked lamp.

The newspapers reported that Elaine Coleman had gone on from high school to attend a small college in Vermont, where she majored in business and wrote one drama review for the school paper. After graduation she lived for a year in the same college town, waitressing at a seafood restaurant; then she returned to our town, where she lived for a few years in a one-room apartment before moving to the two-room apartment on Willow Street. During her college years her parents had moved to California, from where the father, an electrician, moved alone to Oregon. "She didn't have a mean bone in her body," her mother was quoted as saying. Elaine worked for a year on the town paper, waited on tables, worked in the post office and a coffee shop, before getting a job in a business supply store in a neighboring town. People remembered her as a quiet woman, polite, a good worker. She seemed to have no close friends.

I now recalled catching glimpses of a half-familiar face during summers home from college, and later, when I returned to town and settled down. I had long ago forgotten her name. She would be standing at the far end of a supermarket aisle, or on line in a drugstore, or disappearing into a store on Main Street. I noticed her without looking at her, as one might notice a friend's aunt. If our paths crossed, I would nod and pass by, thinking of other things. After all, we had never been friends, she and I—we had never been anything. She was someone I'd gone to high school with, that was all, someone I scarcely knew, though it was also true that I had nothing against her. Was it really the missing Elaine? Only after her disappearance did those fleeting encounters seem pierced by a poignance I knew to be false, though I couldn't help feeling it anyway, for it was as if I should have stopped and talked to her, warned her, saved her, done something.

My second vivid memory of Elaine Coleman came to me three days after my memory of the party. It was sometime in high school, and I was out walking with my friend Roger on one of those sunny autumn afternoons when the sky is so blue and clear that it ought to be summer, but the sugar maples have turned red and yellow, and smoke from leaf fires stings your eyes. We had gone for a long walk into an unfamiliar neighborhood on the other side of town. Here the houses were small, with detached garages; on the lawns you saw an occasional plastic yellow sunflower or fake deer. Roger was talking about a girl he was crazy about, who played tennis and lived in a fancy house on Gideon Hill, and I was advising him to disguise himself as a caretaker and apply for a job trimming her rosebushes. "The yard move," I said. "It gets 'em every time." "She would never respect me," Roger answered seriously. We were passing a garage where a girl in jeans and a dark parka was tossing a basketball into a hoop without a net. The garage door was open and you could see old furniture inside, couches with lamps lying on them and tables holding upside-down chairs. The basketball hit the rim and came bouncing down the drive toward us. I caught it and tossed it back to the girl, who had started after it but had stopped upon seeing us. I recognized Elaine Coleman. "Thanks," she said, holding the basketball in two hands and hesitating a moment before she lowered her eyes and turned away.

What struck me, as I remembered that afternoon, was the moment of hesitation. It might have meant a number of things, such as "Do you and Roger want to shoot a few?" or "I'd like to invite you to shoot a basket but I don't want to ask you if you don't really want to" or maybe something else entirely, but in that moment, which seemed a moment of uncertainty, Roger glanced sharply at me and mouthed a silent "No." What troubled my memory was the sense that Elaine had seen that look, that judgment; she must have been skilled at reading dismissive signs. We walked away into the blue afternoon of high autumn, talking about the girl on Gideon Hill, and in the clear air I could hear the sharp, repeated sound of the basketball striking the driveway as Elaine Coleman walked back toward the garage.

Is it true that whatever has once been seen is in the mind forever? After my second memory I expected an eruption of images, as if they had only been waiting for the chance to reveal themselves. In senior year of high school I must have seen her every day in English class and homeroom, must have passed her in the halls and seen her in the cafeteria, to say nothing of the inevitable chance meetings in the streets and stores of a small town, but aside from the party and the garage I could summon no further image, not one. Nor could I see her face. It was as if she had no face, no features. Even the three photographs appeared to be of three different people, or perhaps they were three versions of a single person no one had ever seen. And so I returned to my two memories, as if they contained a secret that only intense scrutiny could bring to light. But though I saw, always more clearly, the chipped yellowish-white keys of the piano, the glittering stockings, the blue autumn sky, the sun glinting into the shadowy garage with its chairs and tables and boxes, though I saw, or seemed to see, the scuffed black loafer and white ribbed sock of a foot near the piano and the sparkling black shingles on the garage roof, I could not see more of Elaine Coleman than I had already remembered: the hands in the lap, at the party; the moment of hesitation, in the driveway.

During the first few weeks, when the story still seemed important, the newspapers located someone named Richard Baxter, who worked in a chemical plant in a nearby town. He had last seen Elaine Coleman three years ago. "We went out a few times," he was quoted as saying. "She was a nice girl, quiet. She didn't really have all that much to say." He didn't remember too much about her, he said.

The bafflement of the police, the lack of clues, the locked door, the closed windows, led me to wonder whether we were formulating the problem properly, whether we were failing to take into account some crucial element. In all discussions of the disappearance only two possibilities, in all their variations, were ever considered: abduction and escape. The first possibility, although it could never be entirely discounted, had been decisively called into question by the police investigation, which found in the rooms and the yard no evidence whatever of an intruder. It therefore seemed more reasonable to imagine that Elaine Coleman had left of her own volition. Indeed it was tempting to believe that by an act of will she had broken from her lonely routine and set forth secretly to start a new life. Alone, friendless, restless, unhappy, and nearing her thirtieth birthday, she had at last overcome some inner constriction and surrendered herself to the lure of adventure. This theory was able to make clever use of the abandoned keys, wallet, coat, and car, which became the very proof of the radical nature of her break from everything familiar in her life. Skeptics pointed out that she wasn't likely to get very far without her credit card, her driver's license, and the twenty-seven dollars and thirty-four cents found in her wallet. But what finally rendered the theory suspect was the conventional and hopelessly romantic nature of the imagined escape, which not only required her to triumph over the quiet habits of a lifetime, but was so much what we might have wished for her that it seemed penetrated by desires not her own. Thus I wondered whether there might not be some other way to account for the disappearance, some bolder way that called for a different, more elusive, more dangerous logic.

The police searched the north woods with dogs, dragged the pond behind the lumberyard. For a while there were rumors that she'd been kidnapped in the parking lot where she worked, but two employees had seen her drive off, Mary Blessington had waved to her in the evening, and Mrs. Ziolkowski had heard her closing the refrigerator door, rattling a dish, moving around.

If there was no abduction and no escape, then Elaine Coleman must have climbed the stairs, entered her apartment, locked her door, put the milk in the refrigerator, hung her coat over the back of a chair, and—

disappeared. Period. End of discussion. Or to put it another way: the disappearance must have taken place *within the apartment itself.* If one ruled out abduction and escape, then Elaine Coleman ought to have been found somewhere in her rooms—perhaps dead in a closet. But the police investigation had been thorough. She appeared to have vanished from her rooms as completely as she had vanished from my mind, leaving behind only a scattering of clues to suggest she had ever been there.

As the investigation slowly unraveled, as the posters faded and at length disappeared, I tried desperately to remember more of Elaine Coleman, as if I owed her at least the courtesy of recollection. What bothered me wasn't so much the disappearance itself, since I had scarcely known her, or even the possible ugliness of that disappearance, but my own failure of memory. Others recalled her still more dimly. It was as if none of us had ever looked at her, or had looked at her while thinking of something more interesting. I felt that we were guilty of some obscure crime. For it seemed to me that we who had seen her now and then out of the corner of our eyes, we who had seen her without seeing her, who without malice had failed to give her our full attention, were already preparing her for the fate that overtook her, were already, in a sense not yet clear to me, pushing her in the direction of disappearance.

It was during this time of failed recollection that I had what can only be called a pseudo-memory of Elaine Coleman, which haunted me precisely to the extent that I did not know how much of her it contained. The time was two or three years before the disappearance. I remembered that I was at a movie theater with a friend, my friend's wife, and a woman I was seeing then. It was a foreign movie, black and white, with subtitles; I remembered my friend's wife laughing wildly at the childish translation of a curse while the actor on the screen smashed his fist against a door. I recalled a big tub of popcorn that the four of us passed back and forth. I recalled the chill of the air-conditioning, which made me long for the heat of the summer night. Slowly the lights came on, the credits continued to roll, and as the four of us began making our way up the crowded aisle I noticed a woman in dark clothes rising from a seat near the far aisle. I caught only a glimpse of her before looking irritably away. She reminded me of someone I half knew, maybe the girl from my high school whom I sometimes saw and whose name I had forgotten, and I didn't want to catch her eye, didn't want to be forced to exchange meaningless, awkward words with her, whoever she was. In the bright, jammed lobby I braced myself for the worthless meeting. But for some reason she never emerged from the theater, and as I stepped with relief into the heat of the summer night, which already was beginning to seem oppressive, I wondered whether she'd hung back on purpose because she had seen me turning irritably away. Then I felt a moment of remorse for my harshness toward the half-seen woman in the theater, the pseudo-Elaine, for after all I had nothing against her, the girl who had once been in my English class.

Like a detective, like a lover, I returned relentlessly to the few images I had of her: the dim girl at the party, the girl with the basketball who lowered her eyes, the turned-away face in the yearbook picture, the blurred police photo, the vague person, older now, whom I nodded to occasionally in town, the woman in the theater. I felt as if I'd wronged her in some way, as if I had something to atone for. The paltry images seemed to taunt me, as if they held the secret of her disappearance. The hazy girl, the blurred photo . . . Sometimes I felt an inner shaking or trembling, as if I were on the verge of an overwhelming revelation.

One night I dreamed that I was playing basketball with Elaine Coleman. The driveway was also the beach, the ball kept splashing in shallow water, but Elaine Coleman was laughing, her face was radiant though somehow hidden, and when I woke I felt that the great failure in my life was never to have evoked that laughter.

As the weather grew colder, I began to notice that people no longer wanted to talk about Elaine Coleman. She had simply disappeared, that was all, and one day she'd be found, or forgotten, and that would be that. Life would go on. Sometimes I had the impression that people were angry at her, as if by disappearing she had complicated our lives.

One sunny afternoon in January I drove to the house on Willow Street. I knew the street, lined now with bare, twisted maples that threw long shadows across the road and onto the fronts of the houses opposite. A brilliant blue mailbox stood at one corner, beside a telephone pole with a drum-shaped transformer high up under the crossarm. I parked across from the house, but not directly across, and looked at it furtively, as if I were breaking a law. It was a house like many on the block, two-storied and wood-shingled, with side gables and a black roof. The shingles were painted light gray and the shutters black. I saw pale curtains in all the windows, and the path of red slates leading to the door in the side of the house. The door had two small windows near the top, and they too were curtained. I saw a row of bare bushes and a piece of the backyard, where a bird feeder hung from a branch. I tried to imagine her life there, in the quiet house, but I could imagine nothing, nothing at all. It seemed to me that she had never lived there, never gone to my high school—that she was the town's dream, as it lay napping in the cold sun of a January afternoon.

I drove away from that peaceful, mocking street, which seemed to say, "There's nothing wrong here. We're a respectable street. You've had your look, now give it up," but I was farther than ever from letting her go. Helplessly I rummaged through my images, searched for clues, sensed directions that led nowhere. I felt her slipping from me, vanishing, a ghost-girl, a blurred photo, a woman without features, a figure in dark clothes rising from her seat and floating away.

I returned to the newspaper reports, which I kept in a folder on my night table. One detail that struck me was that the landlady had not actually seen Elaine Coleman on the final evening before her disappearance. The neighbor, who had waved to her at dusk, had not been able to make her out all that well.

Two nights later I woke suddenly, startled as if by a dream, though I could recall no dream. A moment later the truth shook me like a blow to the temple.

Elaine Coleman did not disappear suddenly, as the police believed, but gradually, over the course of time. Those years of sitting unnoticed in corners, of not being looked at, must have given her a queasy, unstable sense of herself. Often she must have felt almost invisible. If it's true that we exist by impressing ourselves on other minds, by entering other imaginations, then the quiet, unremarkable girl whom no one noticed must at times have felt herself growing vague, as if she were gradually being erased by the world's inattention. In high school, the process of blurring begun much earlier had probably not yet reached a critical stage; her face, with its characteristically lowered and averted eyes, had grown only a little uncertain. By the time she returned from college, the erasure had become more advanced. The woman glimpsed in town without ever being seen, the unimagined person whom no one could recall clearly, was growing dim, fading away, vanishing, like a room at dusk. She was moving irrevocably toward the realm of dream.

On that last evening, when Mary Blessington waved to her in the dusk without really seeing her, Elaine Coleman was scarcely more than a shadow. She climbed the stairs to her room, locked the door as usual, put the milk in the refrigerator, and hung her coat over the back of a chair. Behind her the secondhand mirror barely reflected her. She heated the kettle and sat at the kitchen table, reading the paper and drinking a cup of tea. Had she been feeling tired lately, or was there a sense of lightness, of anticipation? In the bedroom she set her cup of tea down on a postcard on her nightstand and changed into her heavy white nightgown with its little blue flowers. Later, when she felt rested, she would make dinner. She pulled out the pillow and lay down with a book. Dusk was deepening into early night. In the darkening room she could see a shadowy nightstand, the sleeve of a sweater hanging on a chair, the faint shape of her body on the bed. She turned on the lamp and tried to read. Her eyes, heavy lidded, began to close. I imagined a not-unpleasant tiredness, a feeling of finality, a sensation of dispersion. The next day there was nothing but a nightgown and a paperback on a bed.

It may have been a little different; one evening she may have become aware of what was happening to her, she may, in a profound movement of her being, have embraced her fate and joined forces with the powers of dissolution.

She is not alone. On street corners at dusk, in the corridors of dark movie theaters, behind the windows of cars in parking lots at melancholy shopping centers illuminated by pale orange lamps, you sometimes see them, the Elaine Colemans of this world. They lower their eyes, they turn away, they vanish into shadowy places. Sometimes I seem to see, through their nearly transparent skin, a light or a building behind them. I try to catch their eyes, to penetrate them with my attention, but it's always too late, already they are fading, fixed as they are in the long habit of not being noticed. And perhaps the police, who suspected foul play, were not in the end mistaken. For we are no longer innocent, we who do not see and do not remember, we incurious ones, we conspirators in disappearance. I too murdered Elaine Coleman. Let this account be entered in the record.

History of a Disturbance

You are angry, Elena. You are furious. You are desperately unhappy. Do you know you're becoming bitter?—bitter as those little berries you bit into, remember? in the woods that time. You are frightened. You are resentful. My vow must have seemed to you extremely cruel, or insane. You are suspicious. You are tired. I've never seen you so tired. And of course: you are patient. You're very patient, Elena. I can feel that patience of yours come rolling out at me from every ripple of your unforgiving hair, from your fierce wrists and tense blouse. It's a harsh patience, an aggressive patience. It wants something, as all patience does. What it wants is an explanation, which you feel will free you in some way—if only from the grip of your ferocious waiting. But an explanation is just what's not possible, not now and not ever. What I can give you is only this. Call it an explanation if you like. For me it's a stammer—a shout in the dark.

Do things have beginnings, do you think? Or is a beginning only the first revelation of something that's always been there, waiting to be found? I'm thinking of that little outing we took last summer, the one up to Sandy Point. I'd been working hard, maybe too hard, I had just finished that market-penetration study for Sherwood Merrick Associates, it was the right time to get away. You packed a picnic. You were humming in the kitchen. You were wearing those jeans I like, the ones with the left back pocket torn off, and the top of your bathing suit. I watched as you sliced a sandwich exactly in half. The sun struck your hands. Across your glowing fingers I could see the faint liquidy green cast by the little glass swan on the windowsill. It occurred to me that we rarely took these trips anymore, that we ought to do it more often.

Then we were off, you in that swooping straw hat with its touch of forties glamour, I in that floppy thing that makes me look like a demented explorer. An hour later and there was the country store, with the one red gas pump in front, there was the turn. We passed the summer cottages in the pines. The little parking lot at the end of the road was only half full. Over the stone wall we looked down at the stretch of sand by the lake. We went down the rickety steps, I with the thermos and picnic basket, you with the blanket and towels. Other couples lay in the sun. Some kids were splashing in the water, which rippled from a passing speedboat that made the white barrels rise and fall. The tall lifeguard stand threw a short shadow. Across the lake was a pier, where some boys were fishing. You spread the blanket, took off your hat, shook out your hair. You sat down and began stroking your arm with sunblock. I was sitting next to you, taking it all in, the brown-green water, the wet ropes between the white barrels, the gleam of the lotion on your arm. Everything was bright and clear, and I wondered when the last time was that I'd really looked at anything. Suddenly you stopped what you were doing. You glanced around at the beach, raised your face to the sky, and said, "What a wonderful day!" I turned and looked out at the water.

But I wasn't looking at the water. I was thinking of what you had just said. It was a cry of contentment, a simple expression of delight, the sort of thing anyone might say, on such a day. But I had felt a little sharp burst of irritation. My irritation shocked me. But there it was. I'd been taking in the day, just like you, happy in all my senses. Then you said, "What a wonderful day!" and the day was less wonderful. The day—it's really indecent to speak of these things! But it's as if the day were composed of many separate and diverse presences—that bottle of soda tilted in the sand, that piece of blue-violet sky between the two dark pines, your green hand by the window—which suddenly were blurred together by your words. I felt that something vast and rich had been diminished somehow. I barely knew what you were talking about. I knew of course what you were talking about. But the words annoyed me. I wished you hadn't spoken them. Something uncapturable in the day had been harmed by speech. All at once my irritation passed. The day, which had been banished, came streaming back. Spots of yellow-white sun trembled in brown tree-shadows on the lake-edge. A little girl shouted in the water. I touched your hand.

Was that the beginning? Was it the first sign of a disturbance that had been growing secretly? Two weeks later the Polinzanos had that barbecue. I'd been working hard, harder than usual, putting together a report for Warren and Greene, the one on consumer perception of container shapes for sports beverages. I had all the survey results but I was having trouble writing it up, something was off, I was happy to let it go for an evening. Ralph was in high spirits, flipping over the chicken breasts, pushing down tenderly on the steaks. He waved the spatula about in grand style as he talked real estate. That new three-story monster-house on the block, could you believe two mil, those show-off window arches, and did you get a load of that corny balcony, all of it throwing the neighborhood out of whack, a crazy eyesore, but hey, it was driving property values up, he could live with that. Later, in the near-dark, we sat on the screened porch watching the fireflies. From inside the house came voices, laughter. Someone walked slowly across the dark lawn. You were lying in the chaise. I was sitting in that creaky wicker armchair right next to you. Someone stood up from the glider and went into the kitchen. We were alone on the porch. Voices in the house, the shrill cries of crickets, two glasses of wine on the wicker table, moths bumping against the screens. I was in good spirits, relaxed, barely conscious of that report at the edge of my mind. You turned slowly to me. I remember the lazy roll of your head, your cheek against the vinyl strips, your hair flattened on one side, your eyelids sleepy. You said, "Do you love me?" Your voice was flirtatious, easy—you weren't asking me to put a doubt to rest. I smiled, opened my mouth to answer, and for some reason recalled the afternoon at Sandy Point. And again I felt that burst of irritation, as if words were interposing themselves between me and the summer night. I said nothing. The silence began to swell. I could feel it pressing against both of us, like some big rubbery thing. I saw your eyes, still sleepy, begin to grow alert with confusion. And as if I were waking from a trance, I pushed away the silence, I beat it down with a yes yes yes, of course of course. You put your hand on my arm. All was well.

All was not well. In bed I lay awake, thinking of my irritation, thinking of the silence, which had been, I now thought, not like some big swelling rubbery thing, but like a piece of sharp metal caught in my throat. What was wrong with me? Did I love you? Of course I loved you. But to ask me just then, as I was taking in the night . . . Besides, what did the words mean? Oh, I understood them well enough, those drowsy tender words. They meant, Look, it's a summer night, look, the lawn is dark but there's still a little light left in the sky, they meant you wanted to hear my voice, to hear yourself ask a question that would bring you my voice—it was hardly a question at all, rather a sort of touch, rising out of the night, out of the sounds in the house, the flash of the fireflies. But you said, "Do you love me?," which seemed to require me to understand those words and no others, to think what they might exactly mean. Because they might have meant, Do you still love me as much as you once did even though I know you do, or Isn't it wonderful to sit here and whisper together like teenagers on the dark porch, while people are in the bright living room, talking and laughing, or Do you feel this rush of tender feeling which is rising in me, as I sit here, on this porch, at night, in summer, at the Polinzanos' barbecue, or Do you love everything I am and do, or only some things, and if so, which ones; and it seemed to me that that single word, "love," was trying to compress within itself a multitude of meanings, was trying to take many precise and separate feelings and crush them into a single mushy mass, which I was being asked to hold in my hands like a big sticky ball.

Do you see what was happening? Do you see what I'm trying to say?

Despite these warnings, I hadn't yet understood. I didn't, at this stage, see the connection between the afternoon at Sandy Point, the night at the Polinzanos' barbecue, and the report that was giving me so much trouble. I knew something was wrong, a little wrong, but I thought I'd been working too hard, I needed to relax a little, or maybe—I tried to imagine it—maybe the trouble was with us, with our marriage, a marriage problem. I don't know when I began to suspect it was more dangerous than that.

Not long after the Polinzanos' barbecue I found myself at the supermarket, picking up a few things for the weekend. You know how I love supermarkets. It excites me to walk down those big American avenues piled high with the world's goods, as if the spoils of six continents are being offered to me in the aftermath of a triumphant war. At the same time I enjoy taking note of brand-name readability, shelf positioning, the attention-drawing power of competing package designs. I was in a buoyant mood. My work had gone well that day, pretty well. I wheeled my cart into the checkout line, set out my bags and boxes on the rubber belt, swiped my card. The girl worked her scanner and touchscreen, and I watched with pleasure as the product names appeared sharply on the new LCD monitor facing me above her shoulder. Only two years ago I'd designed a questionnaire on consumer attitudes toward point-of-sale systems in supermarket chains. I signed my slip and handed it to the girl. She smiled at me and said, "Have a good day."

Instantly my mood changed. This time it wasn't irritation that seized me, but a kind of nervousness. What was she trying to say to me? I realized that this thought was absurd. At the same time I stared at the girl, trying to grasp her meaning. Have a good day! What were the words trying to say? At the word "have" her front teeth had pressed into her lip: a big overbite. She looked at me. Have a good day! Good day! Have! "What do you—" I said, and abruptly stopped. Things became very still. I saw two tiny silver rings at the top of her ear, one ring slightly larger than the other. I saw the black plastic edge of the credit-card terminal, a finger with purple nail polish, a long strip of paper with a red stripe running along each border. These elements seemed independent of one another. Somewhere a cash tray slid open, coins clanked. Then the finger joined the girl, the tray banged shut, I was standing by my shopping cart, studying the mesh pattern of the collapsible wire basket, trying to recall what was already slipping away. "You too," I said, as I always do, and fled with my cart.

At dinner that evening I felt uneasy, as if I were concealing a secret. Once or twice I thought you were looking at me strangely. I studied the saltshaker, which looked pretty much the way it had always looked, but with, I thought, some slight change I couldn't account for. In the middle of the night I woke suddenly and thought: Something is happening to me, things will never be the same. Then I felt, across the lower part of my stomach, a first faint ripple of fear.

In the course of the next few days I began listening with close attention to whatever was said to me. I listened to each part of what was said, and I listened to the individual words that composed each part. Words! Had I ever listened to them before? Words like crackles of cellophane, words like sluggish fat flies buzzing on sunny windowsills. The simplest remark began to seem suspect, a riddle—not devoid of meaning, but with a vague haze of meaning that grew hazier as I tried to clutch it. "Not on your life." "You bet!" "I guess so." I would be moving smoothly through my day when suddenly I'd come up against one of them, a word-snag, an obstacle in my path. A group of words would detach themselves from speech and stand at mock attention, sticking out their chests, as if to say: Here we are! Who are you? It was as if some space had opened up, a little rift, between words and whatever they were supposed to be doing. I stumbled in that space, I fell.

At the office I was still having difficulties with my report. The words I had always used had a new sheen of strangeness to them. I found it necessary to interrogate them, to investigate their intentions.

Sometimes they were slippery, like fistfuls of tiny silvery fish. Sometimes they took on a mineral hardness, as if they'd become things in themselves, but strange things, like growths of coral.

I don't mean to exaggerate. I knew what words meant, more or less. A cup was a cup, a window a window. That much was clear. Was that much clear? There began to be moments of hesitation, fractions of a second when the thing I was looking at refused to accept any language. Or rather, between the thing and the word a question had appeared, a slight pause, a rupture.

I recall one evening, it must have been a few weeks later, when I stepped from the darkened dining room into the brightly lit kitchen. I saw a whitish thing on the white kitchen table. In that instant the whitishness on the white table was mysterious, ungraspable. It seemed to spill onto the table like a fluid. I felt a rush of fear. A moment later everything changed. I recognized a cup, a simple white cup. The word pressed it into shape, severed it—as if with the blow of an ax—from everything that surrounded it. There it was: a cup. I wondered what it was I'd seen before the word tightened about it.

I said to myself: You've been working too hard. Your brain is tired. You are not able to concentrate your attention. The words you are using appear to be the same words you have always used, but they've changed in some way, a way you cannot grasp. When this report is done, you are going to take a vacation. That will be good.

I imagined myself in a clean hotel, high up, on the side of a mountain. I imagined myself alone.

I think it was at this period that my own talk began to upset me. The words I uttered seemed like false smiles I was displaying at a party I'd gone to against my will. Sometimes I would overhear myself in the act of speech, like a man who suddenly sees himself in a mirror. Then I grew afraid.

I began to speak less. At the office, where I'd established a long habit of friendliness, I stayed stubbornly at my desk, staring at my screen and limiting myself to the briefest of exchanges, which themselves were not difficult to replace with gestures—a nod, a wave, a smile, a shrug. It's surprising how little you need to say, really. Besides, everyone knew I was killing myself over that report. At home I greeted you silently. I said almost nothing at dinner and immediately shut myself up in my study. You hated my silence. For you it was a knife blade aimed at your neck. You were the victim and I was the murderer. That was the silent understanding we came to, quite early. And of course I didn't murder you just once, I murdered you every day. I understood this. I struggled to be—well, noisier, for your sake. The words I heard emerging from my mouth sounded like imitations of human speech. "Yes, it's hot, but not too hot," I said. "I think that what she probably meant was that she." The fatal fissure was there. On one side, the gush of language. On the other—what? I looked about. The world rushed away on all sides. If only one could be silent! In my study I avoided my irritating desk with its neat binders containing bar charts and statistical tables and sat motionless in the leather chair, looking out the window at the leaves of hydrangea bushes. I felt tremendously tired, but also alert. Not to speak, not to form words, not to think, not to smear the world with sentences—it was like the release of a band of metal tightening around my skull.

I was still able to do some work, during the day, a little work, though I was also staring a lot at the screen. I had command of a precise and specialized vocabulary that I could summon more or less at will. But the doubt had arisen, corroding my belief. Groups of words began to disintegrate under my intense gaze. I was like a man losing his faith, with no priest to turn to.

Always I had the sense that words concealed something, that if only I could abolish them I would discover what was actually there.

One evening I looked for a long time at my hand. Had I ever seen it before? I suppressed the word "hand," rid myself of everything but the act of concentration. It was no longer a hand, not a piece of flesh with nails, wrinkles, bits of reddish-blond hair. There was only a thing, not even that—only the place where my attention fell. Gradually I felt a loosening, a dissolution of the familiar. And I saw: a thickish mass, yellowish and red and blue, a pulsing thing with spaces, a shaded clump. It began to flatten out, to melt into surrounding space, to attach itself to otherness. Then I was staring at my hand again, the fingers slightly parted, the skin of the knuckles like small walnuts, the nails with vertical lines of faint shine. I could feel the words crawling over my hand like ants on a bone. But for a moment I had seen something else.

I am a normal man, wouldn't you say, intelligent and well educated, yes, with an aptitude for a certain kind of high-level work, but fundamentally normal, in temperament and disposition. I understood that what was happening to me was not within the range of the normal, and I felt, in addition to curiosity, an anger that this had come upon me, in the prime of life, like the onset of a fatal disease.

It was during one of those long evenings in my study, while you prowled somewhere in the house, that I recalled an incident from my childhood. For some reason I was in my parents' bedroom, a forbidden place. I heard footsteps approaching. In desperation I stepped over to the closet, with its two sliding doors, then rolled one door open, plunged inside, pushed it shut. The long closet was divided into two parts, my mother's side and my father's side. I knew at once which side I'd entered by the dresses pressing against my cheeks, the tall pairs of high-heeled shoes falling against my ankles as I moved deeper within. Clumsily I crouched down among the fallen shoes, my head and shoulders buried in the bottoms of dresses. And though I liked the sweetish, urine-sharp smell of the leather shoes, the rub of the dresses against my face, the hems heavy on my shoulders, the faint perfume drifting from folds of fabric like dust from a slapped bed, at the same time I felt oppressed by it all, bound tightly in place by the thick leathery smell and the stony fall of cloth, crushed in a black grip. The dresses, the shoes, the pinkish smell of perfume, the scratchy darkness, all pushed against me like the side of a big cat, thrust themselves into my mouth and nose like fur. I could not breathe. I opened my mouth. I felt the dark like fingers closing around my throat. In terror I stumbled up with a harsh scrape of hangers, pulled wildly at the edge of the door, burst outside. Light streamed through the open blinds. Tears of joy burned on my cheeks.

As I sat in my study, recalling my escape from the dresses, it seemed to me that the light streaming through my parents' blinds, in the empty room, was like the silence around me where I sat, and that the heavy dresses, the bittersweet smell of the shoes, the hand on my throat, were the world I had left behind.

I began to sense that there was another place, a place without words, and that if only I could concentrate my attention sufficiently, I might come to that place.

Once, when I was a student and had decided to major in business, I had an argument with a friend. He attacked business as a corrupt discipline, the sole purpose of which was to instill in people a desire to buy. His words upset me, not because I believed that his argument was sound, but because I felt that he was questioning my character. I replied that what attracted me to business was the precision of its vocabulary—a self-enclosed world of carefully defined words that permitted clarity of thought.

At the office I could see people looking at me and also looking away from me. The looks reminded me of the look I had caught in the eyes of the girl with the little rings in her ear, as I tried to understand her words, and the look in your eyes that night at the Polinzanos' barbecue, when I opened my mouth and said nothing.

It was about this time that I began to notice, within me, an intention taking shape. I wondered how long it had been there, waiting for me to notice it. Though my mind was made up, my body hesitated. I was struck by how like me that was: to know, and not to act. Had I always been that way? It would be necessary to arrange a sick leave. There would be questions, difficulties. But aside from all that, finally to go through with it, never to turn back—such acts were not at all in my style.

And if I hesitated, it was also because of you. There you were, in the house. Already we existed in a courteous dark silence trembling with your crushed-down rage. How could I explain to you that words no longer meant what they once had meant, that they no longer meant anything at all? How could I say to you that words interfered with the world? Often I thought of trying to let you know what I knew I would do. But whenever I looked at you, your face was turned partly away.

I tried to remember what it was like to be a very young child, before the time of words. And yet, weren't words always there, filling the air around me? I remember faces bending close, uttering sounds, coaxing me to leave the world of silence, to become one of them. Sometimes, when I moved my face a little, I could almost feel my skin brushing against words, like clusters of tiny, tickling insects.

One night after you'd gone to bed I rose slowly in my study. I observed myself with surprise, though I knew perfectly well what was happening. Without moving my lips I took a vow.

The next morning at breakfast I passed you a slip of paper. You glanced at it with disdain, then crumpled it in your fist. I remember the sound of the paper, which reminded me of fire. Your knuckles stuck up like stones.

When a monk takes a vow of silence, he does so in order to shut out the world and devote himself exclusively to things of the spirit. My vow of silence sought to renew the world, to make it appear before me in all its fullness. I knew that every element in the world—a cup, a tree, a day—was inexhaustible. Only the words that expressed it were vague or limited. Words harmed the world. They took something away from it and put themselves in its place.

When one knows something like that, Elena, one also knows that it isn't possible to go on living in the old way.

I began to wonder whether anything I had ever said was what I had wanted to say. I began to wonder whether anything I had ever written was what I had wanted to write, or whether what I had wanted to write was underneath, trying to push its way through.

After dinner that day, the day of the crumpled paper, I didn't go to my study but sat in the living room. I was hoping to soothe you somehow, to apologize to you with my presence. You stayed in the bedroom. Once you walked from the bedroom to the guest room, where I heard you making up the bed.

One night as I sat in my leather chair, I had the sensation that you were standing at the door. I could feel a hot place at the back of my neck. I imagined you there in the doorway, looking at me with cold fascination, with a sort of tender and despairing iciness. I saw your tired eyes, your strained mouth. Were you trying to understand me? After all, you were my wife, Elena, and we had once been able to understand each other. I turned suddenly, but no one was there.

Do you think it's been easy for me? Do you? Do you think I don't know how grotesque it must seem? A grown man, forty-three years old, in excellent health, happily married, successful enough in his line of work, who suddenly refuses to speak, who flees the sound of others speaking, shuns the sight of the written word, avoids his wife, leaves his job, in order to shut himself up in his room or take long solitary walks—the idea is clownish, disgusting. The man is mad, sick, damaged, in desperate need of a doctor, a lover, a vacation, anything. Stick him in a ward. Inject him with something. But then, think of the other side. Think of it! Think of the terrible life of words, the unstoppable roar of sound that comes rushing out of people's mouths and seems to have no object except the evasion of silence. The talking species! We're nothing but an aberration, an error of Nature. What must the stones think of us? Sometimes I imagine that if we were very still we could hear, rising from the forests and oceans, the quiet laughter of animals, as they listen to us talk.

And then, lovely touch, the invention of an afterlife, a noisy eternity filled with the racket of rejoicing angels. My own heaven would be an immense emptiness—a silence bright and hard as the blade of a sword.

Listen, Elena. Listen to me. I have something to say to you, which can't be said.

As I train myself to cast off words, as I learn to erase word-thoughts, I begin to feel a new world rising up around me. The old world of houses, rooms, trees, and streets shimmers, wavers, and tears away, revealing another universe as startling as fire. We are shut off from the fullness of things. Words hide the world. They blur together elements that exist apart, or they break elements into pieces, bind up the world, contract it into hard little pellets of perception. But the unbound world, the world behind the world—how fluid it is, how lovely and dangerous. At rare moments of clarity, I succeed in breaking through. Then I see. I see a place where nothing is known, because nothing is shaped in advance by words. There, nothing is hidden from me. There, every object presents itself entirely, with all its being. It's as if, looking at a house, you were able to see all four sides and both roof slopes. But then, there's no "house," no "object," no form that stops at a boundary, only a stream of manifold, precise, and nameless sensations, shifting into one another, pullulating, a fullness, a flow. Stripped of words, untamed, the universe pours in on me from every direction. I become what I see. I am earth, I am air. I am all. My eyes are suns. My hair streams among galaxies.

I am often tired. I am sometimes discouraged. I am always sure.

And still you're waiting, Elena—even now. Even now you're waiting for the explanation, the apology, the words that will justify you and set you free. But underneath that waiting is another waiting: you are waiting for me to return to the old way. Isn't it true? Listen, Elena. It's much too late for that. In my silent world, my world of exhausting wonders, there's no place for the old words with which I deceived myself, in my artificial garden. I had thought that words were instruments of precision. Now I know that they devour the world, leaving nothing in its place.

And you? Maybe a moment will come when you'll hesitate, hearing a word. In that instant lies your salvation. Heed the hesitation. Search out the space, the rift. Under this world there is another, waiting to be born. You can remain where you are, in the old world, tasting the bitter berries of disenchantment, or you can overcome yourself, rip yourself free of the word-lie, and enter the world that longs to take you in. To me, on this side, your anger is a failure of perception, your sense of betrayal a sign of the unawakened heart. Shed all these dead modes of feeling and come with me—into the glory of the fire.

Enough. You can't know what these words have cost me, I who no longer have words to speak with. It's like returning to the house of one's childhood: there is the white picket fence, there is the old piano, the Schumann on the music rack, the rose petals beside the vase, and there, look!—above the banister, the turn at the top of the stairs. But all has changed, all's heavy with banishment, for we are no longer who we were. Down with it. You too, Elena: Let it go. Let your patience go, your bitterness, your sorrow—they're nothing but words. Leave them behind, in a box in the attic, the one with all the broken dolls. Then come down the stairs and out into the unborn world. Into the sun. The sun.

The Wizard of West Orange

OCTOBER 14, 1889. But the Wizard's on fire! The Wizard is wild! He sleeps for two hours and works for twelve, sleeps for three hours and works for nineteen. The cot in the library, the cot in Room 12. Hair falling on forehead, vest open, tie askew. He bounds up the stairs, strides from room to room, greeting the experimenters, asking questions, cracking a joke. His boyish smile, his sharp eye. Why that way? Why not this? Notebook open, a furious sketch. Another. On to the next room! Hurls himself into a score of projects, concentrating with fanatical attention on each one before dismissing it to fling himself into next. The automatic adjustment for the recording stylus of the perfected phonograph. The speaking doll. Instantly grasps the essential problem, makes a decisive suggestion. Improved machinery for drawing brass wire. The aurophone, for enhancement of hearing. His trip to Paris has charged him with energy. Out into the courtyard!—the electrical lab, the chemical lab. Dangers of high-voltage alternating current: tests for safety. Improved insulation for electrical conductors. On to the metallurgical lab, to examine the graders and crushers, the belt conveyors, the ore samples. His magnetic ore-separator. "Work like hell, boys!" In Photographic Building, an air of secrecy. Excitement over the new Eastman film, the long strip in which lies the secret of visual motion. The Wizard says kinetoscope will do for the eye what phonograph does for the ear. But not yet, not yet! The men talk. What else? What next? A method of producing electricity directly from coal? A machine for compacting snow to clear city streets? Artificial silk? He hasn't slept at home for a week. They say the Wizard goes down to the Box, the experimental room in basement. Always kept locked. Rumors swirl. Another big invention to rival the phonograph? Surpass the incandescent lamp? The Wizard reads in library in the early mornings. From my desk in alcove I see him turn pages impatiently. Sometimes he thrusts at me a list of books to order. Warburton's *Physiology of Animals*. Greene and Wilson, *Cutaneous Sensation*. Makes a note, slams book shut, strides out. Earnshaw says Wizard spent three hours shut up in the Box last night.

OCTOBER 16. Today a book arrived: Kerner, *Archaeology of the Skin*. Immediately left library and walked upstairs to experimental rooms. Room 12 open, cot empty, the Wizard gone. On table an open notebook, a glass battery, and parts of a dissected phonograph scattered around a boxed motor: three wax cylinders, a recording stylus attached to its diaphragm, a voice horn, a cutting blade for shaving used cylinders. Notebook showed a rough drawing. Identified it at once: design for an automatic adjustment in recording mechanism, whereby stylus would engage cylinder automatically at correct depth. Wizard absolutely determined to crush Bell's graphophone. From window, a view of courtyard and part of chemical lab.

Returned to corridor. Ran into Corbett, an experimental assistant. The Wizard had just left. Someone called out he thought Wizard heading to stockroom. I returned down the stairs. Passed through library, pushed open double door, and crossed corridor to stockroom.

Always exhilarating to enter Earnshaw's domain. Those high walls, lined from floor to ceiling with long drawers—hides, bones, roots, textiles, teeth. Pigeonholes, hundreds of them, crammed with resins, waxes, twines. Is it that, like library itself, stockroom is an orderly and teeming universe—a world of worlds—a finitude with aspirations to allness? Earnshaw hadn't seen him, thought he might be in basement. His hesitation when I held up Kerner and announced my mission. Told him the Wizard had insisted it be brought to him immediately. Earnshaw still hesitant as he took out ring of keys. Is loyal to Wizard, but more loyal to me. Opened door leading to basement storeroom and preceded me down into the maze.

Crates of feathers, sheet metal, pitch, plumbago, cork. Earnshaw hesitated again at locked door of Box. Do not disturb: Wizard's strict orders. But Wizard had left strict orders with me: deliver book immediately. Two unambiguous commands, each contradicting the other. Earnshaw torn. A good man, earnest, but not strong. Unable to resist a sense of moral obligation to me, owing to a number of trifling services rendered to him in the ordinary course of work. In addition, ten years younger. In my presence instinctively assumes an attitude of deference. Rapped lightly on door. No answer. "Open it," I said, not unkindly. He stood outside as I entered.

Analysis of motives. Desire to deliver book (good). Desire to see room (bad). Yielded to base desire. But ask yourself: was it only base? I revere the Wizard and desire his success. He is searching for something, for some piece of crucial knowledge. If I see experiment, may be able to find information he needs. Analyze later.

The small room well-lit by incandescent bulbs. Bare of furnishings except for central table, two armchairs against wall. On table a closed notebook, a copper-oxide battery, and two striking objects. One a long stiff blackish glove, about the length of a forearm, which rests horizontally on two Y-shaped supports about eight inches high. Glove made of some solid dark material, perhaps vulcanized rubber, and covered with a skein of wires emerging from small brass caps. The other: a wooden framework supporting a horizontal cylinder, whose upper surface is in contact with a row of short metal strips suspended from a crossbar. Next to cylinder a small electric motor. Two bundles of wire lead from glove to battery, which in turn is connected to cylinder mechanism by way of motor. On closer inspection I see that interior of glove is lined with black silky material, studded with tiny silver disks like heads of pins. "Sir!" whispers Earnshaw.

I switch off lights and step outside. Footsteps above our heads. I follow Earnshaw back upstairs into stockroom, where an experimental assistant awaits him with request for copper wire. Return to library. Am about to sit down at desk when Wizard enters from other door. Gray gabardine laboratory gown flowing around his legs, tie crooked, hair mussed. "Has that book—?" he says loudly. Deaf in his left ear. "I was just bringing it to you," I shout. Holding out Kerner. Seizes it and throws himself down in an armchair, frowning as if angrily at the flung-open pages.

OCTOBER 17. A quiet day in library. Rain, scudding clouds. Arranged books on third-floor gallery, dusted mineral specimens in their glass-doored cabinets. Restless.

OCTOBER 18. That wired glove. Can it be a self-warming device, to replace a lady's muff? Have heard that in Paris, on cold winter nights, vendors stand before the Opera House, selling hot potatoes for ladies to place in their muffs. But the pinheads? The cylinder? And why then such secrecy? Wizard in locked room again, for two hours, with Kistenmacher.

OCTOBER 20. This morning overheard a few words in courtyard. Immediately set off for stockroom in search of Earnshaw. E.'s passion—his weakness, one might say—is for idea of motion photography. Eager to get hold of any information about the closely guarded experiments in Photographic Building and Room 5. Words overheard were between two machinists, who'd heard an experimental assistant speaking to so-and-so from chemical lab about an experiment in Photographic Building conducted with the new Eastman film. Talk was of perforations along both edges of strip, as in the old telegraph tape. The film to be driven forward on sprockets that engage and release it. This of course the most roundabout hearsay. Nevertheless not first time there has been talk of modifying strip film by means of perforations, which some say the Wizard saw in Paris: studio of Monsieur Marey. Earnshaw thrives on such rumors.

Not in stockroom but down in storeroom, as I knew at once by partially open door. In basement reported my news. Excited him visibly. At that instant—suddenly—I became aware of darker motive underlying my impulse to inform Earnshaw of conversation in courtyard. Paused. Looked about. Asked him to admit me for a moment—only a moment—to the Box.

An expression of alarm invading his features. But Earnshaw particularly well qualified to understand a deep curiosity about experiments conducted in secret. Furthermore: could not refuse to satisfy an indebtedness he felt he'd incurred by listening eagerly to my report. Stationed himself outside door. Guardian of inner sanctum. I quickly entered.

The glove, the battery, the cylinder. I detected a single difference: notebook now open. Showed a hastily executed drawing of glove, surrounded by several smaller sketches of what appeared to be electromagnets, with coils of wire about a core. Under glove a single word: HAPTOGRAPH.

Did not hesitate to insert hand and arm in glove. Operation somewhat impeded by silken lining, evidently intended to prevent skin from directly touching any part of inner structure. When forearm was buried up to elbow, threw switch attached to wires at base of cylinder mechanism.

The excitement returns, even as I write these words. How to explain it? The activated current caused motor to turn cylinder on its shaft beneath the metal rods suspended from crossbar, which in turn caused silver points in lining of glove to move against my hand. Was aware at first of many small gentle pointed pressures. But—behold!—the merely mechanical sensation soon gave way to another, and I felt—distinctly—a sensation as of a hand grasping my own in a firm handshake. External glove had remained stiff and immobile. Switched off current, breathed deep. Repeated experiment. Again the motor turning the cylinder. Sensation unmistakable: I felt my hand gripped in a handshake, my fingers lightly squeezed. At that moment experienced a strange elation, as if standing on a dock listening to water lap against piles as I prepared to embark on a longed-for voyage. Switched off current, withdrew hand. Stood still for a moment before turning suddenly to leave room.

OCTOBER 21. Books borrowed by Kistenmacher, as recorded in library notebook, Oct. 7–Oct. 14: *The Nervous System and the Mind, The Tactile Sphere, Leçons sur la Physiologie du Système Nerveux, Lezioni di Fisiologia Sperimentale, Sensation and Pain.* The glove, the cylinder, the phantom handshake. Clear—is it clear?—that Wizard has turned his attention to sense of touch. To what end, exactly? Yet even as I ask, I seem to grasp principle of haptograph. "The kinetoscope will do for the eye what the phonograph does for the ear." Is he not isolating each of the five senses? Creating for each a machine that records and plays back one sense alone? Voices disembodied, moving images without physical substance, immaterial touches. The phonograph, the kinetoscope, the haptograph. Voices preserved in cylinders of wax, moving bodies in strips of nitrocellulose, touches in pinheads and wires. A gallery of ghosts. Cylinder as it turns must transmit electrical impulses that activate the silver points. Ghosts? Consider: the skin is touched. A firm handshake. Hello, my name is. And yours? Strange thoughts on an October night.

OCTOBER 24. This morning, after Wizard was done looking through mail and had ascended stairs to experimental rooms, Kistenmacher entered library. Headed directly toward me. Have always harbored a certain dislike for Kistenmacher, though he treats me respectfully enough. Dislike the aggressive directness of his walk, arms swinging so far forward that he seems to be pulling himself along by gripping onto chunks of air. Dislike his big hands with neat black hairs growing sideways across fingers, intense stare of eyes that take you in without seeing you, his black stiff hair combed as if violently sideways across head, necktie straight as a plumb line. Kistenmacher one of the most respected of electrical experimenters. Came directly up to my rolltop desk, stopping too close to it, as if the wood were barring his way.

"I wish to report a missing book," he said.

Deeper meaning of Kistenmacher's remark. It happens—infrequently—that a library book is temporarily misplaced. The cause not difficult to wrest from the hidden springs of existence. Any experimenter—or assistant, or indeed any member of staff—is permitted to browse among all three tiers of books, or to remove a volume and read anywhere on premises. Instead of leaving book for me to replace, as everyone is instructed to do, occasionally someone takes it upon self to reshelve. An act well meant but better left undone, since mistakes easy to make. Earnshaw, in particular, guilty of this sort of misplaced kindness. Nevertheless I patrol shelves carefully, several times a day, not only when I replace books returned by staff, or add new books and scientific journals ordered for library, but also on tours of inspection intended to ensure correct arrangement of books on shelves. As a result quite rare for a misplaced volume to escape detection. Kistenmacher's statement therefore not the simple statement of fact it appeared to be, but an implied reproach: You have been negligent in your duties.

"I'm quite certain we can find it without difficulty," I said. Rising immediately. "Sometimes the new assistants—"

"Giesinger," he said. "*Musculo-Cutaneous Feeling.*"

A slight heat in my neck. Wondered whether a flush was visible.

"You see," I said with a smile. "The mystery solved." Lifted from my desk *Musculo-Cutaneous Feeling* by Otto Giesinger and handed it to Kistenmacher. He glanced at spine, to make certain I hadn't made a mistake, then looked at me with interest.

"This is a highly specialized study," said he.

"Yes, a little too specialized for me," I replied.

"But the subject interests you?"

Hesitation. "I try to keep abreast of . . . developments."

"Excellent," he said, and suddenly smiled—a disconcerting smile, of startling charm. "I will be sure to consult with you." Held up book, tightly clasped in one big hand, gave a little wave with it, and took his leave.

The whole incident rich with possibility. My responsibility in library is to keep up with scientific and technical literature, so that I may order books I deem essential. Most of my professional reading confined to scientific journals, technical periodicals, and institutional proceedings, but peruse many books as well, in a broad range of subjects, from psychology of hysteria to structure of the constant-pressure dynamo; my interests are wide. Still, it cannot have failed to strike Kistenmacher that I had removed from shelves a study directly related to his investigations in Box. Kistenmacher perfectly well aware that everyone knows of his secretive experiments, about which many rumors. Is said to enjoy such rumors and even to contribute to them by enigmatic hints of his own. Once told Earnshaw, who reported it to me, that there would soon be no human sensation that could not be replicated mechanically. At time I imagined a machine for production of odors, a machine of tastes. Knows of course that I keep a record of books borrowed by staff, each with name of borrower. Now knows I have been reading Giesinger on musculo-cutaneous feeling.

What else does he know? Can Earnshaw have said something?

OCTOBER 26. A slow day. Reading. From my desk in alcove I can see Wizard's rolltop desk with its scattering of books and papers, the railed galleries of second and third levels, high up a flash of sun on a glass-fronted cabinet holding mineral specimens. The pine-paneled ceiling. Beyond Wizard's desk, the white marble statue brought back from Paris Exposition. Winged youth seated on ruins of a gas streetlamp, holding high in one hand an incandescent lamp. The Genius of Light. In my feet a rumble of dynamos from machine shop beyond stockroom.

OCTOBER 28. In courtyard, gossip about secret experiments in Photographic Building, Room 8, the Box. A machine for extracting nutrients from seaweed? A speaking photograph? Rumors of hidden workrooms, secret assistants. In courtyard one night, an experimental assistant seen with cylinders under each arm, heading in direction of basement.

OCTOBER 29. For the Wizard, there is always a practical consideration. The incandescent lamp, the electric pen, the magnetic ore-separator. The quadruplex telegraph. Origin of moving photographs in study of animal motion: Muybridge's horses, Marey's birds. Even the phonograph: concedes its secondary use as instrument of entertainment, but insists on primary value as business machine for use in dictation. And the haptograph? A possible use in hospitals? A young mother dies. Bereft child comforted by simulated caresses. Old people, lingering out their lives alone, untouched. Shake of a friendly hand. It might work.

NOVEMBER 3. A momentous day. Even now it seems unlikely. And yet, looked at calmly, a day like any other: experimenters in their rooms, visitors walking in courtyard, a group of schoolchildren with their teacher, assistants passing up and down corridors and stairways, men working on grounds. After a long morning decided to take walk in courtyard, as I sometimes do. Warmish day, touch of autumn chill in the shade. Walked length of courtyard, between electrical lab and chemical lab, nodding to several men who stood talking in groups. At end of yard, took a long look at buildings of Phonograph Works. Started back. Nearly halfway to main building when aware of sharp footsteps not far behind me. Drawing closer. Turned and saw Kistenmacher.

"A fine day for a walk," he said. Falling into step beside me.

Hidden significance of Kistenmacher's apparently guileless salutation. His voice addressed to the air—to the universe—but with a ripple of the confidential meant for me. Instantly alert. Common enough of course to meet an experimenter or machinist in courtyard. Courtyard after all serves as informal meeting place, where members of staff freely mingle. Have encountered Kistenmacher himself innumerable times, striding along with great arms swinging. No, what struck me, on this occasion, was one indisputable fact: instead of passing me with habitual brisk nod, Kistenmacher attached himself to me with tremendous decisiveness. So apparent he had something to say to me that I suspected he'd been watching for me from a window.

"My sentiment exactly," I replied.

"I wonder whether you might accompany me to Room 8," he then said.

An invitation meant to startle me. I confess it did. Kistenmacher knows I am curious about experimental rooms on second floor, just up stairs from library. These rooms always kept open—except Room 5, where photographic experiments continue to be conducted secretly, in addition to those in new Photographic Building—but there is general understanding that rooms are domain of experimenters and assistants, and of course of the Wizard himself, who visits each room daily in order to observe progress of every experiment. Kistenmacher's invitation therefore highly unusual. At same time, had about it a deliberate air of mystery, which Kistenmacher clearly enjoying as he took immense energetic strides and pulled himself forward with great swings of his absurd arms.

Room 8: Kistenmacher's room on second floor. On a table: parts of a storage battery and samples of what I supposed to be nickel hydrate. No sign of haptograph. This in itself not remarkable, for experimenters are engaged in many projects. Watched him close door and turn to me.

"Our interests coincide," he said, speaking in manner characteristic of him, at once direct and sly.

I said nothing.

"I invite you to take part in an experiment," he next remarked. An air of suppressed energy. Had sense that he was studying my face for signs of excitement.

His invitation, part entreaty and part command, shocked and thrilled me. Also exasperated me by terrible ease with which he was able to create inner turmoil.

"What kind of experiment?" I asked: sharply, almost rudely.

He laughed—I had not expected Kistenmacher to laugh. A boyish and disarming laugh. Surprised to see a dimple in his left cheek. Kistenmacher's teeth straight and white, though upper-left incisor is missing.

"That," he said, "remains to be seen. Nine o'clock tomorrow night? I will come to the library."

Noticed that, while his body remained politely immobile, his muscles had grown tense in preparation for leaving. Already absolutely sure of my acceptance.

When I returned to library, found Wizard seated at his desk, in stained laboratory gown, gesturing vigorously with both hands as he spoke with a reporter from the *New York World.*

NOVEMBER 5. I will do my utmost to describe objectively the extraordinary event in which I participated on the evening of November 4.

Kistenmacher appeared in library with a punctuality that even in my state of excitement I found faintly ludicrous: over fireplace the big clock-hands showed nine o'clock so precisely that I had momentary grotesque sense they were the false hands of a painted clock. Led me into stockroom, where Earnshaw had been relieved for night shift by young Benson, who was up on a ladder examining contents of a drawer. Looked down at us intently over his shoulder, bending neck and gripping ladder-rails, as if we were very small and very far away. Kistenmacher removed from pocket a circle of keys. Held them up to inform Benson of our purpose. Opened door that led down to basement. I followed him through dim-lit cellar rooms piled high with wooden crates until we reached door of Box. Kistenmacher inserted key, stepped inside to activate electrical switch. Then turned to usher me in with a sweep of his hand and a barely perceptible little bow, all the while watching me closely.

The room had changed. No glove: next to table an object that made me think of a dressmaker's dummy, or top half of a suit of armor, complete with helmet. Supported on stand clamped to table edge. The dark half-figure studded with small brass caps connected by a skein of wires that covered entire surface. Beside it the cylinder machine and the copper-oxide battery. Half a dozen additional cylinders standing upright on table, beside machine. In one corner, an object draped in a sheet.

"Welcome to the haptograph," Kistenmacher said. "Permit me to demonstrate."

He stepped over to figure, disconnected a cable, and unfastened clasps that held head to torso. Lifted off head with both hands. Placed head carefully on table. Next unhooked or unhinged torso so that back opened in two wings. Hollow center lined with the same dark silky material and glittery silver points I had seen in glove.

Thereupon asked me to remove jacket, vest, necktie, shirt. My hesitation. Looked at me harshly. "Modesty is for schoolgirls." Turning around. "I will turn my back. You may leave, if you prefer."

Removed my upper clothing piece by piece and placed each article on back of a chair. Kistenmacher turned to face me. "So! You are still here?" Immediately gestured toward interior of winged torso, into which I inserted my arms. Against my skin felt silken lining. He closed wings and hooked in place. Set helmet over my head, refastened clasps and cable. An opening at mouth enabled me to breathe. At level of my eyes a strip of wire mesh. The arms, though stiff, movable at wrists and shoulders. I stood beside table, awaiting instructions.

"Tell me what you feel," Kistenmacher said. "It helps in the beginning if you close your eyes."

He threw switch at base of machine. The cylinder began to turn.

At first felt a series of very faint pin-pricks in region of scalp. Gradually impression of separate prickings faded away and I became aware of a more familiar sensation.

"It feels," I said, "exactly as if—yes, it's uncanny—but as though I were putting a hat on my head."

"Very good," Kistenmacher said. "And this?" Opened my eyes long enough to watch him slip cylinder from its shaft and replace with new one.

This time felt a series of pin-pricks in region of right shoulder. Quickly resolved into a distinct sensation: a hand resting on shoulder, then giving a little squeeze.

"And this?" Removed cylinder and added another. "Hold out your left hand. Palm up."

Was able to turn my armored hand at wrist. In palm became aware of a sudden sensation: a roundish smooth object—ball? egg?—seemed to be resting there.

In this manner—cylinder by cylinder—Kistenmacher tested three additional sensations. A fly or other small insect walking on right forearm. A ring or rope tightening over left biceps. Sudden burst of uncontrollable laughter: the haptograph had re-created sensation of fingers tickling my ribs.

"And now one more. Please pay close attention. Report exactly what you feel." Slipped a new cylinder onto shaft and switched on current.

After initial pin-pricks, felt a series of pressures that began at waist and rose along chest and face. A clear tactile sensation, rather pleasant, yet one I could not recall having experienced before. Kistenmacher listened intently as I attempted to describe. A kind of upward-flowing ripple, which moved rapidly from waist to top of scalp, encompassing entire portion of body enclosed in haptograph. Like being repeatedly stroked by a soft encircling feather. Or better: repeatedly submerged in some new and soothing substance, like unwet water. As cylinder turned, same sensation—same series of pressures—recurred again and again. Kistenmacher's detailed questions before switching off current and announcing experiment had ended.

At once he removed headpiece and set it on table. Unfastened back of torso and turned away as I extracted myself and quickly began to put on shirt.

"We are still in the very early stages," he said, back still turned to me as I threw my necktie around collar. "We know far less about the tactile properties of the skin than we do about the visual properties of the eye. And yet it might be said that, of all the senses"—here a raised hand, an extended forefinger—"touch is the most important. The good Bishop Berkeley, in his *Theory of Vision*, maintains that the visual sense serves to anticipate the tangible. The same may be said of the other senses as well. Look here."

Turned around, ignoring me as I buttoned my vest. From his pocket removed an object and held it up for my inspection. Surprised to see a common fountain pen.

"If I touch this pen to your hand—hand, please!—what do you feel?"

Extended hand, palm up. He pressed end of pen lightly into skin of my palm.

"I feel a pressure—the pressure of the pen. The pressure of an object."

"Very good. And you would say, would you not, that the skin is adapted to feel things in that way—to identify objects by the sense of touch. But this pen of ours is a rather large, coarse object. Consider a finer object—this, for example."

From another pocket: a single dark bristle. Might have come from a paintbrush.

"Your hand, please. Concentrate your attention. I press here—yes?—and here—yes?—and here—no? No? Precisely. And this is a somewhat coarse bristle. If we took a very fine bristle, you would discover even more clearly that only certain spots on the skin give the sensation of touch. We have mapped out these centers of touch and are now able to replicate several combinations with some success."

He reached over to cylinders and picked one up, looking at it as he continued. "It is a long and difficult process. We are at the very beginning." Turning cylinder slowly in his hand. "The key lies here, in this hollow beechwood tube—the haptogram. You see? The surface is covered with hard wax. Look. You can see the ridges and grooves. They control the flow of current. As the haptogram rotates, the wax pushes against this row of nickel rods: up here. Yes? This is clear? Each rod in turn operates a small rheostat—here—which controls the current. You understand? The current drives the corresponding coil in the glove, thereby moving the pin against the skin. Come here."

He set down cylinder and stepped over to torso. Unfastened back. Carefully pulled away a strip of lining.

"These little devices beneath the brass caps—you see them? Each one is a miniature electromagnet. Look closely. You see the wire coil? There. Inside the coil is a tiny iron cylinder—the core—which is insulated with a sleeve of celluloid. The core moves as the current passes through the coil. To the end of each core is attached a thin rod, which in turn is attached to the lining by a fastener that you can see—here, and here, and all along the lining. Ah, those rods!"

He shook his head. "A headache. They have to be very light, but also stiff. We have tried boar's bristle—a mistake!—zinc, too soft; steel, too heavy. We have tried whalebone and ivory. These are bamboo."

Sighing. "It is all very ingenious—and very unsatisfactory. The haptograms can activate sequences of no more than six seconds. The pattern then repeats. And it is all so very . . . clumsy. What we need is a different approach to the wax cylinder, a more elegant solution to the problem of the overall design."

Pause—glance at sheet-draped object. Seemed to fall into thought. "There is much work to do." Slowly reached into pocket, removed ring of keys. Stared at keys thoughtfully. "We know nothing. Absolutely nothing." Slowly running his thumb along a key. Imagined he was going to press tip of key into my palm—my skin tingling with an expected touch—but as he stepped toward door I understood that our session was over.

NOVEMBER 7. Last night the Wizard shut himself up in Room 12: seven o'clock to three in the morning. Rumor has it he is still refining the automatic adjustment for phonograph cylinder. Hell-bent on defeating the graphophone. Rival machine produces a less clear sound but has great practical advantage of not requiring the wax cylinder to be shaved down and adjusted after each playing. The Wizard throws himself onto cot for two hours, no more. In the day, strides from room to room on second floor, quick, jovial, shrewd-eyed, a little snappish, a sudden edge of mockery. A university man and you don't know how to mix cement? What do they teach you? The quick sketch: fixed gaze, slight tilt of head. Try this. How about that? Acid stains on his fingers. The Phonograph Works, the electrical lab, the Photographic Building. Alone in a back room in chemical lab, quick visit to Box, up to Room 5, over to 12. The improved phonograph, moving photograph, haptograph. Miniature phonograph for speaking doll. Ink for the blind, artificial ivory. A machine for extracting butter directly from milk. In metallurgical lab, Building 5, examines the rock crushers, proposes refinements in electromagnetic separators. A joke in the courtyard: the Wizard is devising a machine to do his sleeping for him.

I think of nothing but the haptograph.

NOVEMBER 12. Not a word. Nothing.

NOVEMBER 14. Haptograph will do for skin what phonograph does for ear, kinetoscope for eye. Understood. But is comparison accurate? Like phonograph, haptograph can imitate sensations in real world: a machine of mimicry. Unlike phonograph, haptograph can create new sensations, never experienced before. The upward-flowing ripple. Any combinations of touch-spots possible. Why does this thought flood my mind with excitement?

NOVEMBER 17. Still nothing. Have they forgotten me?

NOVEMBER 20. Today at a little past two, Earnshaw entered library. Saw him hesitate for a moment and look about quickly—the Wizard long gone, only Grady from chemical lab in room, up on second gallery—before heading over to my desk. Handed me a book he had borrowed some weeks before: a study of the dry gelatin process in making photographic plates. Earnshaw's appetite for the technical minutiae of photography insatiable. And yet: has never owned a camera and unlike most of the men appears to have no desire to take photographs. Have often teased him about this passion of his, evidently entirely mental. He once said in reply that he carries two cameras with him at all times: his eyes.

Touché.

"A lot of excitement out there," I said. Sweeping my hand vaguely in direction of Photographic Building. "I hear they're getting smooth motions at sixteen frames a second."

He laughed—a little uncomfortably, I thought. "Sixteen? Impossible. They've never done it under forty. Besides, I heard just the opposite. Jerky motions. Same old trouble: sprocket a little off. This is for you."

He reached inside jacket and swept his arm toward me. Abrupt, a little awkward. In his hand: a sealed white envelope.

I took envelope while studying his face. "From you?"

"From"—here he lowered his voice—"Kistenmacher." Shrugged. "He asked me to deliver it."

"Do you know what it is?"

"I don't read other people's mail!"

"Of course not. But you might know anyway."

"How should—I know you've been down there."

"You saw me?"

"He told me."

"Told you?"

"That you'd been there too."

"Too!"

Looked at me. "You think you're the only one?"

"I think our friend likes secrets." I reached for brass letter-opener. Slipped it under flap.

"I'll be going," Earnshaw said, nodding sharply and turning away. Halfway to door when I slit open envelope with a sound of tearing cloth.

"Oh there you are, Earnshaw." A voice at the door.

Message read: "Eight o'clock tomorrow night. Kmacher."

It was only young Peters, an experimental assistant, in need of some zinc.

NOVEMBER 20, LATER. Much to think about. Kistenmacher asks Earnshaw to deliver note. Why? Might easily have contrived to deliver it himself, or speak to me in person. By this action therefore wishes to let Earnshaw know that I am assisting in experiment. Very good. But: Kistenmacher has already told Earnshaw about my presence in room. Which means? His intention must be directed not at Earnshaw but at me: must wish me to know that he has spoken to Earnshaw about me. But why? To bind us together in a brotherhood of secrecy? Perhaps a deeper intention: wants me to know that Earnshaw has been in room, that he too assists in experiment.

NOVEMBER 21, 3:00. Waiting. A walk in the courtyard. Sunny but cold: breath-puffs. A figure approaches. Bareheaded, no coat, a pair of fur-lined gloves: one of the experimenters, protecting his fingers.

NOVEMBER 21, 5:00. It is possible that every touch remains present in skin. These buried hapto-memories capable of being reawakened through mechanical stimulation. Forgotten caresses: mother, lover. Feel of a shell on a beach, forty years ago. Memory-cylinders: a history of touches. Why not?

NOVEMBER 21, 10:06 P.M. At two minutes before eight, Earnshaw enters library. I rise without a word and follow him into stockroom. Down stairway, into basement. Unlocks door of experimental room and leaves without once looking at me. His dislike of Box is clear. But what is it exactly that he dislikes?

"Welcome!" Kistenmacher watchful, expectant.

Standing against table: the dark figure of a human being, covered with wires and small brass caps. On table: a wooden frame holding what appears to be a horizontal roll of perforated paper, perhaps a yard wide, partially unwound onto a second reel. Both geared to a chain-drive motor.

A folding screen near one wall.

"In ten years," Kistenmacher remarks, "in twenty years, it may be possible to create tactile sensations by stimulating the corresponding centers of the brain. Until then, we must conquer the skin directly."

A nod toward screen. "Your modesty will be respected. Please remove your clothes behind the screen and put on the cloth."

Behind screen: a high stool on which lies a folded piece of cloth. Quickly remove my clothes and unfold cloth, which proves to be a kind of loincloth with drawstring. Put it on without hesitation. As I emerge from behind screen, have distinct feeling that I am a patient in a hospital, in presence of a powerful physician.

Kistenmacher opens a series of hinged panels in back of figure: head, torso, legs. Hollow form with silken lining, dimpled by miniature electromagnets fastened to silver points. Notice figure is clamped to table. Can now admit a man.

Soon shut up in haptograph. Through wire mesh covering eyeholes, watch Kistenmacher walk over to machine. Briskly turns to face me. With one hand resting on wooden frame, clears throat, stands very still, points suddenly to paper roll.

"You see? An improvement in design. The key lies in the series of perforations punched in the roll. As the motor drives the reel—here—it passes over a nickel-steel roller: here. The roller is set against a row of small metallic brushes, like our earlier rods. The brushes make contact with the nickel-steel roller only through the perforations. This is clear? The current is carried to the coils in the haptograph. Each pin corresponds to a single track—or circular section—of the perforated roll. Tell me exactly what you feel." Throws switch.

Unmistakable sensation of a sock being drawn on over my left foot and halfway up calf. As paper continues to unwind, experience a similar but less exact sensation, mixed with prickles, on right foot and calf. Kistenmacher switches off current and gives source reel a few turns by hand, rewinding perforated paper roll. Switches on current. Repeats sensation of drawn-on socks, making small adjustment that very slightly improves accuracy in right foot and calf.

Next proceeds to test three additional tactile sensations. A rope or belt fastened around my waist. A hand: pressing its spread fingers against my back. Some soft object, perhaps a brush or cloth, moving along upper arm.

Switches off current, seems to grow thoughtful. Asks me to close eyes and pay extremely close attention to next series of haptographic tests, each of which will go beyond simple mimicry of a familiar sensation.

Close my eyes and feel an initial scattering of prickles on both elbows. Then under arms—at hips—at chin. Transformed gradually into multiple sensation of steady upward pushes, as if I've been gripped by a force trying to lift me from ground. Briefly feel that I am hovering in air, some three feet above floor. Open my eyes, see that I haven't moved. Upward-tugging sensation remains, but illusion of suspension has been so weakened that I cannot recapture it while eyes remain open.

Kistenmacher asks me to close eyes again, concentrate my attention. At once the distinct sensation of something pressing down on shoulders and scalp, as well as sideways against rib cage. A feeling as if I were being shut up in a container. Gradually becomes uncomfortable, oppressive. Am about to cry out when suddenly a sensation of release, accompanied by feeling of something pouring down along my body—as though pieces of crockery were breaking up and falling upon me.

"Very good," says Kistenmacher. "And now one more?"

Again a series of prickles, this time applied simultaneously all over body. Prickles gradually resolve themselves into the sensation—pleasurable enough—of being lightly pressed by something large and soft. Like being squeezed by an enormous hand—as if a fraternal handshake were being applied to entire surface of my skin. Enveloped in that gentle pressure, that soft caress, I feel soothed, I feel more than soothed,

I feel exhilarated, I feel an odd and unaccountable joy—a jolt of well-being—a stream of bliss—which fills me to such bursting that tears of pleasure burn in my eyes.

When sensation stops, ask for it to be repeated, but Kistenmacher has learned whatever it was he wanted to know.

Decisively moves toward me. Disappears behind machine. Unlatches panels and pulls them apart.

I emerge backward, in loincloth. Carefully withdraw arms from torso. Across room see Kistenmacher standing with back to me. Yellowish large hands clasped against black suit-jacket.

Behind screen begin changing. Kistenmacher clears his throat.

"The sense of sight is concentrated in a single place—two places, if you like. We know a great deal about the structure of the eye. By contrast, the sense of touch is dispersed over the entire body. The skin is by far the largest organ of sense. And yet we know almost nothing about it."

I step out from behind screen. Surprised to see Kistenmacher still standing with back to me, large hands clasped behind.

"Good night," he says: motionless. Suddenly raises one hand to height of his shoulder. Moves it back and forth at wrist.

"Night," I reply. Walk to door: turn. And raising my own hand, give first to Kistenmacher, and then to haptograph, an absurd wave.

NOVEMBER 22. Mimicry and invention. Splendor of the haptograph. Not just the replication of familiar tactile sensations, but capacity to explore new combinations—pressures, touches, never experienced before. Adventures of feeling. Who can say what new sensations will be awakened, what unknown desires? Unexplored realms of the tangible. The frontiers of touch.

NOVEMBER 23. Conversation with Earnshaw, who fails to share my excitement. His unmistakable dislike of haptograph. Irritable shrug: "Leave well enough alone." A motto that negates with masterful exactitude everything the Wizard represents. And yet: his passion for the slightest advance in motion photography. Instinctive shrinking of an eye-man from the tangible? Safe distance of sight. Noli me tangere. The intimacy, the intrusiveness, of touch.

NOVEMBER 24. Another session in Box. Began with several familiar sensations, very accurate: ball in palm, sock, handshake, the belt. One new one, less satisfactory: sensation of being stroked by a feather on right forearm. Felt at first like bits of sand being sprinkled on my arm; then somewhat like a brush; finally like a piece of smooth wood. Evidently much easier for pins to evoke precise sensations by stimulating touch-spots in limited area than by stimulating them in sequence along a length. Kistenmacher took notes, fiddled with metallic brushes, adjusted a screw. Soon passed on to sensations of uncommon or unknown kind. A miscellaneous assortment of ripples, flutters, obscure thrusts and pushes. Kistenmacher questioned me closely. My struggle to describe. Bizarre sensation of a pressure that seemed to come from inside my skin and press outward, as if I were going to burst apart. At times a sense of disconnection from skin, which seemed to be slipping from my body like clothes removed at night. Once: a variation of constriction and release, accompanied by impression that I was leaving my old body, that I was being reborn. Immediately followed by sensation, lasting no more than a few seconds, that I was flying through the air.

NOVEMBER 26. Walking in courtyard. Clear and cold. Suddenly aware of my overcoat on my shoulders, the grip of shoe leather, clasp of hat about my head. Throughout day, increased awareness of tactile sensations: the edges of pages against my fingers, door handle in palm. Alone in library, a peculiar sharp impression of individual hairs in my scalp, of fingernails set in their places at ends of my fingers. These sensations vivid, though lasting but a short time.

NOVEMBER 27. The Wizard's attention increasingly consumed by his ore-separating machinery and miniature mechanisms of speaking doll. The toy phonograph—concealed within tin torso—repeatedly malfunctions: the little wax cylinders break, stylus becomes detached from diaphragm or slips from its groove. Meanwhile, flying visits to the Box, where he adjusts metallic brushes, studies take-up reel, unhinges back panels, sketches furiously. Leaves abruptly, with necktie bunched up over top of vest. Kistenmacher says Wizard is dissatisfied with design of haptograph and has proposed a different model: a pine cabinet in which subject is enclosed, except for head, which is provided with a separate covering. The Wizard predicts haptograph parlor: a room of cabinet haptographs, operated by nickel-in-slot mechanism. Cabinet haptograph to be controlled by subject himself, by means of a panel of buttons.

NOVEMBER 28. Another encounter with Earnshaw. Distant. Won't talk about machine. So: talked about weather. Cold today. Mm-hmm. But not too cold. Uh-huh. Can't tell what makes him more uncomfortable: that I know he takes part in experiment, or that he knows I do. Talked about frames per second. No heart in it. Relieved to see me go.

NOVEMBER 29. Fourth session in Box. Kistenmacher meticulous, intense. Ran through familiar simulations. Stopped machine, removed roll, inserted new one. Presented theory of oscillations: the new roll perforated in such a way as to cause rapid oscillation of pins. Oscillations should affect kinesthetic sense. At first an unpleasant feeling of many insects attacking skin. Then: sensation of left arm floating away from body. Head floating. Body falling. Once: sensation of flying through air, as in previous session, but much sharper and longer lasting. My whole body tingling. Returned to first roll. Skin as if rubbed new. Heightened receptivity. Seemed to be picking up minuscule touches hidden from old skin. Glorious.

NOVEMBER 29, LATER. Can't sleep for excitement. Confused thoughts, sudden lucidities. Can sense a new world just out of reach. Obscured by old body. What if a stone is not a stone, a tree not a tree? Fire not fire? Face not face? What then? New shapes, new touches: a world concealed. The haptograph pointing the way. Oh, what are you talking about? Shut up. Go to bed.

NOVEMBER 30. Kistenmacher says Earnshaw has asked to be released from experiment—the Wizard refuses. Always the demand for unconditional loyalty. In it together. The boys. "Every man jack of you!"

Saw Earnshaw in courtyard. Avoiding me.

DECEMBER 1. This morning the Wizard filed a caveat with Patents Office, setting forth design of haptograph and enumerating essential features. A familiar stratagem. The caveat protects his invention, while acknowledging its incompleteness. In the afternoon, interviews in library with the *Herald*, the *Sun*, and the *Newark News*. "The haptograph," the Wizard says, "is not yet ready to be placed before the public. I hope to have it in operation within six months." As always, prepares the ground, whets the public appetite. Speaks of future replications: riding a roller coaster, sledding down a hill. Sensations of warmth and cold. The "amusement haptograph": thrilling adventures in complete safety of the machine. The cabinet haptograph, the haptograph parlor. Shifts to speaking doll, the small wax cylinders with their nursery rhymes. In future, a doll that responds to a child's touch. The Wizard's hands cut through the air, his eyes are blue fire.

The reporters write furiously.

Kistenmacher says that if three more men are put on job, and ten times current funds diverted to research, haptograph might be ready for public in three years.

DECEMBER 2. Lively talk in courtyard about haptograph, the machine that records touch. Confusion about exactly what it is, what it does. One man under impression it operates like phonograph: you record a series of touches by pressing a recording mechanism and then play back touches by grasping machine. Someone makes a coarse joke: with a machine like that, who needs a woman? Laughter, some of it anxious. The Wizard can make anything. Why not a woman?

DECEMBER 3. Arrived early this morning. Heard voices coming from library. Entered to find Wizard standing at desk, facing Earnshaw. Wizard leaning forward, knuckles on desk. Nostrils flared. Cheek-ridges brick-red. Earnshaw pale, erect—turns at sound of door.

I, hat in hand: "Morning, gentlemen!"

DECEMBER 5. Fifth session in Box. Kistenmacher at work day and night to improve chain-drive mechanism and smooth turning of reels. New arrangement responsible for miracles of simulation: ball in palm, handshake, the sock, the hat. Haptograph can now mimic perfectly the complex sensation of having a heavy robe placed on shoulders, slipped over each arm in turn, tied at waist. Possible the Wizard's predictions may one day be fulfilled.

But Kistenmacher once again eager to investigate the unknown. Change of paper rolls: the new oscillations. "Please. Pay very close attention." Again I enter exotic realms of the tactile, where words become clumsy, obtuse. A feeling—wondrous—of stretching out to tremendous length. A sensation of passing through walls that crumble before me, of hurtling through space, of shouting with my skin. Once: the impression—how to say it?—of being stroked by the wing of an angel. Awkward approximations, dull stammerings which cannot convey my sense of exhilaration as I seemed to burst impediments, to exceed bounds of the possible, to experience, in the ruins of the human, the birth of something utterly new.

DECEMBER 6. Is it an illusion, a trick played by haptograph? Or is it the revelation of a world that is actually there, a world from which we have been excluded because of the limitations of our bodies?

DECEMBER 6, LATER. Unaccustomed thoughts. For example. Might we be surrounded by immaterial presences that move against us but do not impress themselves upon the touch-spots of our skin? Our vision sharpened by microscopes. Haptograph as the microscope of touch.

DECEMBER 7. Ever since interview, the Wizard not once in Box. His attention taken up by other matters: plans for mining low-grade magnetite, manufacture of speaking dolls in Phonograph Works, testing of a safe alternating current. The rivalry with Westinghouse. Secret experiments in Photographic Building.

DECEMBER 8. My life consumed by waiting. Strong need to talk about haptograph. In this mood, paid visit to stockroom. Earnshaw constrained, uneasy. Hasn't spoken to me in ten days. I pass on some photographic gossip. Won't look me in the eye. Decide to take bull by horns. So! How's the experiment going? Turns to me fiercely. "I hate it in there!" His eyes stern, unforgiving. In the center of each pupil: a bright point of fear.

DECEMBER 9. There are documented cases in which a blind person experiences return of sight. Stunned with vision: sunlight on leaves, the blue air. Now imagine a man who has been wrapped in cotton for forty-five years. One day cotton is removed. Suddenly man feels sensations of which he can have had no inkling. The world pours into his skin. The fingers of objects seize him, shake him. Touch of a stone, push of a leaf. The knife-thrust of things. What is the world? Where is it? Where? We are covered in cotton, we walk through a world hidden away. Blind skin. Let me see!

DECEMBER 10. This afternoon, in courtyard, looked up and saw a hawk in flight. High overhead: wings out, body slowly dipping. The power of its calm. A sign. But of what? Tried to imagine hawkness. Failed.

DECEMBER 11. Long morning, longer afternoon. Picked up six books, read two pages in each. Looked out window four hundred times. Earnshaw's face the other day. Imprint of his ancestors: pale clerics, clean-cheeked, sharp-chinned, a flush of fervor in the white skin. Condemning sinners to everlasting hellfire.

DECEMBER 12. A night of terrors and wonders. Where will it end?

Kistenmacher tense, abrupt, feverish-tired. Proceeded in his meticulous way through familiar mimicries. Repeated each one several times, entered results in notebook. Something perfunctory in his manner. Or was it only me? But no: his excitement evident as he changed rolls. "Please. Tell me exactly." How to describe it? My skin, delicately thrummed by haptograph, gave birth to buried powers. Felt again that blissful expansion of being—that sense of having thrown off old body and assumed a new. I was beyond myself, more than myself, un-me. In old body, could hold out my hand and grasp a pencil, a paperweight. In new body, could hold out my hand and grasp an entire room with all its furniture, an entire town with its chimneys and saltshakers and streets and oak trees. But more than that—more than that. In new skin I was able to touch directly—at every point on my body—any object that presented itself to my mind: a stuffed bear from childhood, wing of a hawk in flight, grass in a remembered field. As though my skin were chock-full of touches, like memories in the brain, waiting for a chance to leap forth.

Opened my eyes and saw Kistenmacher standing at the table. Staring ferociously at unwinding roll of paper. Hum and click of chain-drive motor, faint rustle of metallic brushes. Closed my eyes . . .

. . . and passed at once into wilder regions. Here, the skin becomes so thin and clean that you can feel the touch of air—of light—of dream. Here, the skin shrinks till it's no bigger than the head of a pin, expands till it stretches taut over the frame of the universe. All that is, flowing against you. Drumming against your skin. I shuddered, I rang out like a bell. I was all new, a new creature, glistening, emerging from scaly old. My dull, clumsy skin seemed to break apart into separate points of quivering aliveness, and in this sweet cracking open, this radiant dissolution, I felt my body melting, my nerves bursting, tears streamed along my cheeks, and I cried out in terror and ecstasy.

A knock at the door—two sharp raps. The machine stopped. Kistenmacher over to door.

"I heard a shout," Earnshaw said. "I thought—"

"Fine," Kistenmacher said. "Everything is fine."

DECEMBER 13. A quiet day, cold. Talk of snow. The sky pale, less a color than an absence of color: unblue, ungray: tap water. Through the high arched windows, light traffic on Main. Creak of wagons, knock of hooves. In library fireplace, hiss and crackle of hickory logs. Someone walking in an upper gallery, stopping, removing a book from a shelf. A dray horse snorts in the street.

DECEMBER 14. A sense within me of high anticipation, mixed with anxiousness. Understand the anticipation, but why the other? My skin alert, watchful, as before a storm.

DECEMBER 15. A new life beckons. A shadow-feeling, an on-the-vergeness. Our sensations fixed, rigid, predictable. Must smash through. Into what? The new place. The there. We live off to one side, like paupers beside a railroad track. The center cannot be here, among these constricting sensations. Haptograph as a way out. Over there. Where?

Paradise.

DECEMBER 17. Disaster.

On evening of sixteenth, Kistenmacher came to fetch me at eight o'clock. Said he hadn't been in Box for two days—a last-minute snag in automatic adjustment of phonograph required full attention—and was eager to resume our experiments. Followed him down steps to basement. At locked door of Box he removed his ring of keys. Inserted wrong one. Examined it with expression of irritable puzzlement. Inserted correct one. Opened door, fumbled about. Switched on lights. At this point Kistenmacher emitted an odd sound—a kind of terrible sigh.

Haptograph lay on floor. Wires ripped loose from fastenings. Stuck out like wild hair. Back panels torn off, pins scattered about. On the floor: smashed reels, a chain from the motor, a broken frame. Wires like entrails. Gashed paper, crumpled lumps. In one corner I saw the dark head.

Kistenmacher, who had not moved, strode suddenly forward. Stopped. Looked around fiercely. Lifted his right hand shoulder-high in a fist. Suddenly crouched down over haptograph body and began touching wires with great gentleness.

Awful night. Arrived at library early morning. Earnshaw already dismissed. Story: On night of December 16, about seven o'clock, a machinist from precision room, coming to stockroom to pick up some brass tubing, saw Earnshaw emerging from basement. Seemed distracted, fidgety, quite unlike himself. After discovery of break-in, machinist reports to Wizard. Wizard confronts Earnshaw. E. draws himself up, stiff, defiant, and in sudden passionate outburst resigns, saying he doesn't like goings-on "down there." Wizard shouts, "Get out of here!" Storms away. End of story.

Kistenmacher says it will take three to five weeks to repair haptograph, perforate a new roll. But the Wizard has ordered him to devote himself exclusively to speaking doll. The Wizard sharp-tempered, edgy, not to be questioned. Dolls sell well but are returned in droves. Always same complaint: the doll has stopped speaking, the toy phonograph concealed in its chest has ceased to operate.

DECEMBER 18. No word from Kistenmacher, who shuts himself up in Room 8 with speaking doll.

DECEMBER 19. The Wizard swirling from room to room, his boyish smile, a joke, laughter. Go at it, boys! Glimpse of Kistenmacher: drooping head, a big, punished schoolboy. Can Wizard banish disappointment so easily?

DECEMBER 20. Earnshaw's destructive rage. How to understand it? Haptograph as devil's work. The secret room, naked skin: sin of touch. Those upright ancestors. Burn, witch!

DECEMBER 20, LATER. Saw Kistenmacher walking in courtyard. Forlorn. Didn't see me.

DECEMBER 20, LATER. Or did he?

DECEMBER 20, STILL LATER. Worried about fate of haptograph. Felt we were on the verge. Of what? A tremendous change. A revolution in sensation, ushering in—what, exactly? What? Say it. All right. A new universe. Yes! The hidden world revealed. The haptograph as adventure, as voyage of discovery. In comparison, the phonograph nothing but a clever toy: tunes, voices.

Haptograph: instrument of revelation.

Still no word.

DECEMBER 21. The Wizard at his desk, humming. Sudden thought: is that a disappointed man? The haptograph destroyed, Kistenmacher broken-hearted, the Wizard humming. A happy man, humming a tune. How could I have thought? Of course only a physical and temporary destruction. The machine easily reconstructed. But no work ordered. Takes Kistenmacher off job. Reign of silence. Why this nothing? Why?

Perhaps this. Understands that haptograph is far from complete. Protected by caveat. Sees Kistenmacher's growing obsession. Needs to wrest his best electrical experimenter from a profitless task and redirect his energies more usefully. So: destruction of machine an excuse to put aside experiment. Good. Fine. But surely something more? Relief? Shedding of a tremendous burden? The machine eluding him, betraying him—its drift from the practical, its invitation to heretical pleasures. Haptograph as seductress. Luring him away. A secret desire to be rid of it. No more! Consider: his sudden cheerfulness, his hum. Ergo.

And Earnshaw? His hostility to experiment serves larger design. By striking in rage at Wizard's handiwork, unwittingly fulfills Wizard's secret will. Smash it up, bash it up. Earnshaw as eruption of master's darkness, emissary of his deepest desire. Burn! Die! The Wizard's longing to be rid of haptograph flowing into Earnshaw's hatred of haptograph as wicked machine. Two wills in apparent opposition, working as one. Die! Inescapable conclusion: arm raised in rage against Wizard's work is the Wizard's arm.

Could it be?

It could be.

Kistenmacher entombed with speaking doll. The Wizard flies from room to room, busies himself with a hundred projects, ignores haptograph.

No one enters the Box.

DECEMBER 30. Nothing.

FEBRUARY 16, 1890. Today in courtyard overheard one of the new men speak of haptograph. Seemed embarrassed when I questioned him. Had heard it was shaped like a life-sized woman. Was it true she could speak?

Already passing into legend. Must harden myself. The experiment has been abandoned.

Snow in the streets. Through the high windows, the clear sharp jingle of harness bells.

Perhaps I dreamed it all?

Have become friendly with Watkins, the new stockroom clerk. A vigorous, compact man, former telegraph operator, brisk, efficient, humorous; dark blond side-whiskers. His passion for things electrical. Proposes that, for a fee, the owner of a telephone be permitted to listen to live musical performances: a simple matter of wiring. The electric boot, the electric hat. Electric letter opener. A fortune to be made. One day accompanied him down to storeroom, where he searched for supply of cobalt and magnesium requested by an assistant in electrical lab who was experimenting on new storage battery. Saw with a kind of sad excitement that we were approaching a familiar door. "What's in there?"—couldn't stop myself. "Oh that," said Watkins. Takes out a ring of keys. Inside: piles of wooden crates, up to ceiling. "Horns and antlers," he said. "Look: antelope, roebuck, gazelle. Red deer. Walrus tusks, rhino horns." Laughter. "Not much call for these items. But heck, you never can tell."

A dream, a dream!

No: no dream. Or say, a dream, certainly a dream, nothing but a dream, but only as all inventions are dreams: vivid and impalpable presences that haunt the mind's chambers, escaping now and then into the place where they take on weight and cast shadows. The Wizard's laboratory a dream-garden, presided over by a mage. Why did he abandon haptograph? Because he knew in his bones that it was commercially unfeasible? Because it fell too far short of the perfected phonograph, the elegant promise of kinetoscope? Was it because haptograph had become a terrible temptress, a forbidden delight, luring him away from more practical projects? Or was it—is it possible—did he sense that world was not yet ready for his haptograph, that dangerous machine which refused to limit itself to the familiar feel of things but promised an expansion of the human into new and terrifying realms of being?

Yesterday the Wizard spent ten hours in metallurgical lab. Adjustments in ore-separator. "It's a daisy!" Expects it to revolutionize the industry. Bring in a handsome profit.

The haptograph awaits its time. In a year—ten years—a century—it will return. Then everyone will know what I have come to know: that the world is hidden from us—that our bodies, which seem to bring us the riches of the earth, prevent the world from reaching us. For the eyes of our skin are closed. Brightness streams in on us, and we cannot see. Things flow against us, and we cannot feel. But the light will come. The haptograph will return. Perhaps it will appear as a harmless toy in an amusement parlor, a playful rival of the gustograph and the odoroscope. For a nickel you will be able to feel a ball in the palm of your hand, a hat sitting on your head. Gradually the sensations will grow more complex—more elusive—more daring. You will feel the old body slipping off, a new one emerging. Then your being will open wide and you will receive—like a blow—like a rush of wind—the in-streaming world. The hidden universe will reveal itself like fire. You will leave yourself behind forever. You will become as a god.

I will not return to these notes.

Snow on the streets. Bright blue sky, a cloud white as house paint. Rumble of dynamos from the machine shop. Crackle of hickory logs, a shout from the courtyard. An unremarkable day.

ALSO BY

STEVEN MILLHAUSER

VOICES IN THE NIGHT

Beloved for the lens of the strange he places on small town life, Steven Millhauser further reveals in *Voices in the Night* the darkest parts of our inner selves to brilliant and dazzling effect. Here are stories of wondrously imaginative hyperrealism, stories that pose unforgettably unsettling what-ifs, or that find barely perceivable evils within the safe boundaries of our towns, homes, and even within our bodies. Heightened by magic, the divine, and the uncanny, shot through with sly and winning humor, *Voices in the Night* seamlessly combines the whimsy and surprise of the familiar with intoxicating fantasies that take us beyond our daily lives, all done with the hallmark sleight of hand and astonishing virtuosity of one of our greatest contemporary storytellers.

Fiction/Short Stories

ALSO AVAILABLE

Dangerous Laughter
Edwin Mullhouse
Enchanted Night
The King in the Tree
The Knife Thrower
Little Kingdoms
Martin Dressler